Reckoning

A Novel by Stephanie Baldi

DANCING CROWS
PRESS

Published by Dancing Crows Press
306 Huntington Drive
Temple, GA 30179

ISBN: 978-1-951543-10-5 — Print

ISBN 978-1-951543-11-2 — eBook

Library of Congress Control Number: 2021901059

Edited by Elyse Wheeler, PhD
Cover Design by Mary Rogers
Layout by Colin Wheeler, MFA

Printed in
The United States of America

Dedication

To my Nick, for all your love and encouragement.

Acknowledgments

Dr. Elyse Wheeler, my right hand, I couldn't have done it without you. Thank you for always being there.

To my friends and fans for your love and support.

And as always, the Carrollton Writers Guild, for their continued encouragement.

CHAPTER 1

MIGUEL

Miguel Medina splashed cold water onto his face. A run in the blistering Sedona, Arizona heat had him longing for a cooler climate.

"Miguel, you mustn't exercise outdoors when it is so hot."

Bianca Flores moved through the bathroom doorway. She glided toward him, her sandals tapping on the terracotta-tiled floor. A bright yellow linen sundress highlighted her deep tan. Curly charcoal-colored hair framed her angular face and dipped below her shoulders. Silver hoop earrings dangled from each lobe.

His eyes swept over her. Bianca meant nothing more to him than a poor substitute. Although she cared for him with tremendous passion and understood the black hole lying at the bottom of his soul, she could never replace what he lost.

The woman he loved no longer walked this earth. For a brief time, Carmela Santiago became his reason for living. With each rise and fall of her breath, his love for her grew deeper, up until the moment of her brutal murder.

Miguel pressed Bianca's hand to his lips and kissed her palm. "I must stay fit. My profession requires it." He stripped and stepped into the huge walk-in shower.

"You could just as well use a gym rather than suffer outside."

Water cascaded down his muscular frame. He tilted his head and laughed. "Ah, but it's the suffering which toughens me, not an air-conditioned gym."

"I give up. There is no changing your mind."

When he finished, she handed him a towel. He dried off, then wrapped it around his waist. Bianca's fingertip traced the rough scar running along his left cheek, a reminder of his turbulent past.

His fists clenched at her touch, recalling the night they came for Natalia. Many fell in Tahoe, Diego Silva among them. If only Carmela had survived. Instead, a bullet put an end to her life. It didn't matter who pulled the trigger. Only one man remained responsible for her death. Nicholas D'Angelo destroyed what he treasured more than anything else in the world.

After his confrontation with Nick, he had torn through the woods like a wounded animal until he determined it was safe to return, arriving in time to watch them leave with Natalia and carry Carmela's body away. He'd never forgive himself for not saving her.

With a rag to stem the torrent of blood pouring from the knife wound on his cheek, he'd taken his things, traveling just shy of the Mexican border where he managed to have his face stitched before crossing over into Mexico.

"Three years is a long time, Miguel," Bianca said, sensing his thoughts. "They are living their lives while we hide away here in Arizona."

"I *will* make them pay," he said, brushing a loose tendril back from her forehead. He focused on the flecks of gold in her brown eyes, the same eyes that had seduced him one night in a Mexican Cantina as she set a shot of tequila on the gleaming bar. Later, their lust for each other satisfied in a local hotel, he learned of her premature widowhood and subsequent poverty. His choosing to remove her from those unfortunate circumstances had led to her undying devotion.

Her eyes locked with his. "Remember, my love, you must take the child from them."

Adrenaline flowed, feeding his anger. "*Sí*, Natalia belongs to me."

She sat on the rim of the clawfoot tub, her hands clasped together. "I promise to do whatever is necessary to help you get her back."

"My sources inform me Nick and his family still live in South Dakota," Miguel said. "His friend, this other ghost, Dalton, also lives there. I will need you to become acquainted with them."

"Acquainted?"

Arms folded, he leaned against the sink. "*Sí*, it seems they are managing Carmela's restaurants. One in New York, and a new location in Rapid City."

He rubbed the prickly stubble on his chin. "As a matter of fact, they will be short a waitress soon. Do you happen to know someone with experience?"

Bianca rose and he drew her close. She moved against him. He inhaled the perfumed scent of jasmine. "I think I do."

Miguel's desire rose at her words, and he led her to the bed. While she removed her clothes, he concentrated on the flaming red rocks rooted in the distance beyond the window, their rich tone fueling his smoldering rage, a fury nothing would appease until he faced Nick again.

CHAPTER 2

BOBBY

Bobby closed the door and tossed his unopened mail onto the console. Unbuttoning his pale blue dress shirt, he crossed into the kitchen and plucked a beer from the fridge. He gulped, letting it ease his parched throat. His body relaxed, the hammering inside his head eased.

He drifted over to the window. Central Park lay bathed in the early evening light. Streetlamps lit winding pathways. In the distance, skyscrapers lined the perimeter, sentinels standing watch.

In a few months, another year would end…another year without her. During quiet moments, he could still hear her voice, a whisper in his ear. His love for Carmela remained inside the core of his soul long after sleepless nights and endless questioning by the authorities ceased.

Instructed by Nick, he denied having any knowledge of the tragic night in Tahoe, leading the government to seize the house, declaring it a crime scene and one built with drug money. It didn't matter, because he had no desire to keep the home where Carmela and so many others died.

Bobby surmised the authorities' failure to dig deeper was due to Carmela's narcotics trafficking past, which made her death insignificant.

The handling of Carmela's estate falling on him, he couldn't fathom what he would have done without his mother and Nick's support. Carmela had left everything to Natalia. Even in the throes of building their new home, they committed themselves to learn how to run a restaurant, plus teach him along the way. Now, with things settling, he preferred to raise Natalia in his beloved city. The time had come for him to move on.

His decision to bring her to New York did not come easy. She'd gone back and forth between here and South Dakota while he struggled to master the wine business and hold onto his art clientele.

Natalia was growing up, and he refused to live in the past. Doing everything possible to safeguard her happiness became his priority. Out of necessity, he hired Maggie, a nanny with impeccable references and one who would teach Natalia her mother's native language. Still, he vowed to spend as much time as he could with his daughter.

Turning to the present, his plan to fly to South Dakota tomorrow left tonight open for a chance to talk to Veronica.

Ronnie moved to New York after graduating from law school and landing a job with a prestigious Manhattan law firm. On occasion, they would go out to dinner or hang at a local club. He treasured Ronnie's friendship feeling somewhat responsible for her since Joann's marriage to Dalton and subsequent move to South Dakota.

The last few times they were together, something appeared off, and then she'd stood him up when they had planned to meet again.

He had called Ronnie earlier, insisting she drop by his apartment. Her hesitation at his invite made him uneasy. He glanced at the clock. Ronnie was due any minute.

Downing the remainder of his beer, he pitched the empty bottle into the recycling bin before changing into a fresh pair of jeans and a maroon sweater. He set a bottle of white wine, a corkscrew, and two glasses on the coffee table just as the buzzer sounded.

Bobby hit the intercom. The doorman's voice broke through. "Miss Veronica is here."

"Thanks, Hank."

Several moments later, he greeted her. A plaid wool shawl draped her shoulders. Underneath it, she wore a beige turtleneck above navy dress pants. Flats adorned her feet.

"Hey, you," she said, giving him a brief hug and a kiss on the cheek. She handed him her shawl, then smoothed her long auburn hair.

Bobby returned the kiss and hung the shawl up. "It's great to see you. Come on, let's catch up."

When they were settled on the sofa, she pointed to a picture hanging above the fireplace. "You've added another piece of art. New or hers?"

Bobby's stomach dipped. "It belonged to Carmela. No sense storing it away. I can only display so much in the Napa house. This one used to hang in Miami, but with the sale of that property, I've had to put others in storage."

She examined the canvas. "I like it."

"It's a Gustav Klimt. I love his use of color."

Ronnie chuckled. "I wouldn't recognize a Gustav whoever from a Picasso." She wagged her finger at him. "You're the expert."

He picked up the corkscrew. "Drink?"

"Absolutely."

Bobby loosened the cork and poured. Her hand trembled as she received the glass, her green eyes avoided his. She savored the wine, then scrutinized the label. "Santiago Vineyards, of course. Tastes fantastic."

"I'm trying." He poured himself a glass and settled into the cushions.

"Seeing anyone lately?" she asked.

"I've dated here and there, but it's been rough."

"I know, but you have to move forward with your life."

"Strange, that's exactly what I told myself a little while ago."

"It'll get better, Bobby. As long as you make an effort, it's all good."

"I've decided to bring Natalia home full time," Bobby said. "I hired some help, so I think it's doable."

Her face lit up. "That's wonderful. She belongs with you. There is nothing wrong with her living with your mother and Nick, but the two of you need to bond."

"We sure do. Besides, I prefer to raise Natalia here in New York. She'll be exposed to so much more than if she's tucked away in South Dakota."

He paused before continuing. "Look, Ronnie, I've always felt we can be honest with each other. I'm getting a sense something isn't right. You've stood me up twice this month. It's not like you."

Ronnie set her glass on the coffee table. "Yes, and I am sorry. Work has been a real bitch." Beads of sweat formed on her upper lip. She clamped her hands together, her knuckles turning pasty white.

"C'mon, Ronnie. What else is going on?"

She shot up, her knee knocking against the table. Bobby reached out to stop her wineglass from toppling onto the carpet.

A flash of temper revealed itself in her eyes. "I've been keeping a lot of long hours lately. Don't go making a huge deal over nothing, Bobby."

He'd never experienced this side of her before. "I didn't mean to upset you. I'm worried—"

"Why? Just because I skipped out on you a couple times doesn't mean something sinister is lurking beneath the surface."

Not wanting to agitate her further, he withdrew. "Sorry."

A faint blush fanned her cheeks. "No, I'm sorry. I shouldn't have reacted the way I did. Believe me, if there were anything wrong, I would tell you."

"Fair enough," he said. "Feel like grabbing some dinner?"

"Sounds perfect. Maybe later, we can head to a club downtown. It is Friday night, after all."

"You're on. Let me get my wallet."

In the bedroom, he removed his Glock 40 Gen 4 from the closet safe. Although things remained peaceful since Carmela's passing, he promised Nick he would remain vigilant. Killing Diego in Tahoe forced him to take a hard look at himself. It reassured him he'd be able to pull the trigger again if he needed to.

Bobby sighed and returned the Glock to the safe. No way could he get into a club with a gun. He entered the living room just as Ronnie draped the shawl around her shoulders.

"Let's bounce," Bobby said.

An hour later, they feasted on Lobster Fra Diavolo at Carmen's, their favorite Italian restaurant on the Upper West Side. Bobby observed Ronnie's restlessness, her fidgeting with the silverware, and constant glances at her cell phone. She excused herself to use the restroom twice, which he found odd.

They finished polishing off a bottle of Cuttings Cabernet Sauvignon, then Ronnie said, "I hear there's a new club downtown called Vertigo."

The slight buzz in his head, causing him to dismiss any lingering suspicions, he gulped the last of his wine. "I'm game."

Outside, he hailed a taxi for their ride across town. Within twenty minutes, they pulled up in front. Bobby paid the cabbie and escorted her to the door. With two huge bouncers looking on, they passed through a metal detector.

The interior, lit by electric blue, red, and green lights, jarred his senses. A bar ran along the length of the room while a DJ spun records below a dragon's mouth hanging overhead. The thump of the bass vibrated beneath Bobby's feet.

The pungent odor of marijuana drifted past. A packed crowd hugged the dance floor while gyrating to the music.

Ronnie tugged on his arm. "Come on, show me what you got."

They dove into the crush of people. One of Bobby's favorite songs played. For the next ten minutes, he lost himself in the music. The song ended, and another began. Ronnie stopped dancing. Bobby followed her line of vision. A guy near the edge of the dance floor beckoned to her.

"I'll be right back." She disappeared into the crowd, then reappeared next to the man. He planted his palm beneath her elbow, steering her away.

Bobby attempted to keep track of them while he made his way off the floor. Music blared amid flashing lights, splaying an array of moving colors, making it tough to see. He continued searching. His eyes traveled along the length of the bar where he spotted them at the end. They appeared to be arguing. His pulse quickened as the man seized her wrist. She wriggled free, inching backward. Bobby hurried over.

"What the hell is going on!" he shouted over the din of the music.

Ronnie spun around. "It's okay, Bobby."

Closer now, he took stock of the guy. Tall, with wavy brown hair, a close-cropped beard, muscles bulging underneath his t-shirt, and tattooed arms, he was a familiar type.

His chin jutted out, and he motioned at Bobby. "Yeah, the lady says it's okay."

"Not when you put your hands on her."

Ronnie glared at him. "Stop, Bobby. Let's just get out of here."

"Good idea," the man spat. He turned back to Ronnie. "Remember, you owe me." His eyes raked over Bobby, and he stalked off.

Bobby gripped Ronnie's hand, drawing her to the exit. When they were outside, he said, "Mind telling me who that prick was?"

"He's not important." Rushing to the curb, she hailed an approaching cab.

Bobby ran up behind her. "What did he mean, you owe him?"

She cut her eyes at him. "I'm heading home. You can either ride with me or get your own cab. Only not another word about what happened."

His body went rigid while he fought the urge to respond.

Ronnie climbed into the cab. "Coming?"

Reluctant, he sat beside her, and she gave the cabbie his address. They rode in silence until they reached his building. Bobby opened the door and stepped out.

Before he could speak, she slammed it closed. The cab sped off, red taillights fading into the night. His intuition regarding Ronnie had proved correct, and the goon at the club somehow played a part in it. Bobby trudged inside, his nerves on edge, but no less determined to find out what was wrong with Ronnie.

CHAPTER 3

CARRIE

Early Saturday morning sunlight streamed across the master bedroom. Not wanting to wake Nick, Carrie eased from their bed. Collecting a leather-bound book lying on the nightstand, she padded to the fireplace flanked on either side by two built-in bookshelves and slid the book into its proper place.

Waking at 3:00 a.m., unable to sleep, she had plucked it from a shelf. Settling onto a chaise in the sitting area, under the soft glow of a lamp, she immersed herself in one of the many classics Nick presented to her as a housewarming gift. An hour later, her lids heavy, she returned to bed.

Their ten thousand square-foot house constructed of Western Red Cedar trucked in from Oregon took over two years to complete. Carrie believed seven bedrooms, each with their own fireplace and ensuite, along with a lower level featuring a rec room, gym, cozy home theater, plus a modest wine cellar, was too much, but Nick insisted on them having all these things.

Their master suite included a huge walk-in tiled shower boasting eight body jets and a double Carrara marble vanity, all luxuries she never imagined could be hers.

She threw on a flowered silk robe over her pajamas. On quiet mornings before the children woke, she delighted in having some time for herself. Slipping out of the bedroom, Ace, their ninety-pound German Shepherd, ears erect, tail wagging, greeted her.

His wet nose nuzzled her palm, and she rubbed his head. "Good morning to you, too."

With Ace trailing behind, she crossed the radiant-heated walnut floors, making a quick detour into the great room where exposed wooden timbers graced a vaulted ceiling. A soaring double-sided Montana River Rock fireplace anchored the space between the great room and the dining room with a built-in buffet plus seating for twelve.

Multiple walls of windows let in abundant natural light while framing magnificent views of the Black Hills. Pausing, her eyes rested on the valley's expanse below, the scene sparking memories of her first visit to South Dakota. Leaves on the maples and oaks were changing. Soon they'd fan their vibrant hues against the emerald pines. Later, their branches bare, they would usher in the first snowfall.

Ready for coffee, she made her way into the kitchen, where white Calacatta marble graced the massive island and countertops, and maple cabinets gleamed beneath custom lighting.

Valentina, their au pair, petite, with shoulder-length dirty blonde hair, perched on a stool at the island reading a magazine. The twenty-five-year-old from *Vieste*, a small town in Italy, arrived with impeccable references. Nick insisted they hire someone who spoke English and Italian so their children could continue to learn the language. It didn't take long for her to fit into the family. Izzy, Michael, and Natalia adored her.

Round eyes, behind black-framed glasses, glanced up at her. "*Buongiorno*, Carrie."

"*Buongiorno*, Valentina. What do you have planned for today?"

Her fingertip nudged the glasses on the bridge of her nose. "After Izzy's riding lesson, I am taking the children to the library. They are having a special Saturday story time reading. I think they will enjoy it. Later, we will practice our Italian."

Carrie sighed. "I wish I could join you. Unfortunately, I need to stop by the restaurant and take care of a few things."

She prepared a cup of coffee and stepped outside with Ace onto the covered patio. A fireplace and recessed infrared heaters in the ceiling were used for cooler nights. An outdoor kitchen made summertime grilling easy. Beyond the patio lay a heated inground pool while the four-car garage held ample space for their automobiles plus the first of Nick's new toys, a red Lamborghini Huracan.

She stood, sipping her coffee while Ace tore off into the bluish-green of the Rocky Mountain Juniper lining one side of the property, disappearing into the woods. Inhaling the fresh air, her sight drifted across the yard to a tall oak tree. Eyes misting, she recalled the day they buried Chino, their beloved white Akita. Old age had caught up with him, and his hind legs refused to cooperate, while his breathing became labored. Nick insisted on staying with him until the end. His head in Nick's lap, Chino passed away in the middle of the night.

For the children's sake, she remained strong only to find a quiet room later, where she grieved for the dog who had saved her from Marco Valletta. She understood when Nick set out alone for the woods to shed his own tears for their loyal companion.

Six months later, Nick brought Ace home. Under his tutelage, the puppy soon developed into a fierce protector and treasured member of their family. She'd come to develop affection for him, but Chino would always hold a special place in her heart.

Watching Ace reappear between the juniper, it still amazed her how lucky she'd become. Their children meant everything to her. No words could express the depth of her love for Nick and how he had accepted Bobby as his own. Most of all, he'd given her something she never dreamed possible. A life worth living.

The last few years sped by in a blur. In the months following Carmela's death, with Bobby on overload, they dove head-first into the restaurant business while still building their home. A year later, with the restaurants doing well, they opened additional ones in Rapid City and New York City.

Her mind turned to her last trip to New York. A necessity since they helped manage *Buena Comida* there, and it was also the place her father resided.

She'd done her homework, devouring newspaper and magazine articles relating to him and his company, Paterson Brokerage House, a well-known firm on Wall Street, run by Alexander Paterson, a respected man among his peers.

Pictures of him at charity or political events throughout the city graced society and business columns. His silver-grey hair and piercing light blue eyes stood out in color photographs, confirming Bobby's eyes mirrored his grandfather's. The articles held scarce mention of his wife, only one picture, taken many years ago for their engagement announcement.

While in New York on early morning runs for restaurant supplies, she made deliberate detours to her father's Sutton Place neighborhood, where she would stand across from his townhouse.

A slight tremor in her hand almost tipped her coffee mug. No one — not even Nick— was aware of her vigils.

If given the opportunity, she'd approach him. Her burning question needed an answer. Why did he abandon her? Based on what Aunt May said, he visited Arizona not long after her birth. He should have rescued her from that hellhole!

Without warning, the deep-seated sorrow she kept hidden swept over her. Sighing, she set her mug on the patio table. Maybe now, she could understand how miserable her mother must have been, pregnant, living miles away from the man she loved in an Arizona trailer park.

Ace barked and raced toward the patio. Nick's arms wrapped around her waist. She felt his warmth against her body.

"Good morning, babe." His voice, husky and sleep-filled, washed over her. "Missed you when I woke."

Carrie placed her hands over his and leaned her head back against his shoulder. He kissed her cheek and nuzzled her neck.

"Morning. Sleep well?" she asked.

He murmured into the waves of her hair, tightening his hold on her.

Observing him while he slept, she became aware of the awful nightmares disrupting his rest. Sometimes, she heard him moan or startle awake. Ever since Carmela's death, his demons refused to back down. Those killing years were exacting their price. If only she could heal all the broken places inside him— an impossible task. He never spoke about the people he killed or how it made him feel and had never revealed the story behind the scar on his shoulder, left by a bullet wound in Tahoe.

She found it hard to envision the horrible images woven into his brain, tight-knit threads beginning to unravel. She feared someday he'd fall apart.

Nick rested his chin on top of her head. "Bobby called. He's flying in tomorrow."

Slipping from his embrace, she turned. Muscular arms outlined his gray, long-sleeved waffle t-shirt, brown leather slippers peeked from underneath his navy pajama bottoms. "I'm glad," she said. "Natalia needs her father around more often."

"He wants to take her with him to New York... permanently. Things have settled. He thinks he can handle her full-time." Nick bent and rubbed Ace's head. "Time for Natalia to live with her father. Right, Ace?"

Knowing this day would come, she paused, steadying the emotions whirling inside her. At three years old, her granddaughter delighted her. She'd inherited her mother's caramel-colored hair and mocha skin, but not her temperament. Her light blue eyes matched Bobby's. Natalia spent much of her time with them while Bobby managed his career and dealt with Carmela's estate. They'd grown used to having her here. Carrie wrapped her arms around his neck. "I guess we have to let go sometime. She is his child."

"You're right, only I can't imagine Izzy or Michael not living here," he said.

She chuckled. "Oh, really. One day we'll be empty nesters roaming around this big house."

"I refuse to look that far ahead."

"Well, it's inevitable whether we like it or not."

Nick's lips brushed hers. "I don't want to talk about it." He held up her coffee mug. "Refill?"

"Yes, please."

He disappeared, Ace on his heels.

Carrie turned away, thoughts of her father still fresh in her mind. No matter how painful, she needed to hear the truth.

She made a promise to herself. During her next trip to New York, she would not return home until she confronted him.

Loving Nick awakened her self-worth. The time had come to look her father in the eye and demand the truth.

CHAPTER 4

BIANCA

The closer they came to Rapid City, the more Bianca's apprehension increased at the prospect of putting Miguel's scheme into action. Staring through the window of his black Cadillac SUV, she read the sign. *Buena Comida*, spelled out in ornate red lettering, above a black and white striped awning graced the front of the restaurant. Ornate dark wooden doors with brass fixtures set off the entryway.

She adjusted the collar of her soft brown lambskin jacket, a gift from Miguel, and smiled. Glancing at the hem of her jeans, her smile faded. Her toes throbbing inside new Frye boots, she longed for the freedom of sandals. Unfortunately, they were not appropriate this time of year in South Dakota.

A group of young women exited the restaurant. "There, you see," Miguel said, pointing. "The shift is changing."

Sweeping back her long curls, she asked, "Which one should I choose?"

"Not so fast, Bianca. We must settle in first, then you need to find out which girl lives alone."

"*Sí*, Miguel. I understand." She glimpsed his profile. Beneath the dark stubble, his right cheek bore no scar. Handsome as he was, he did not measure up to Alejandro.

How long had it been since she lay with her lover, his hands exploring, their hips thrusting against one another? The two of them rising, riding waves of desire, until fulfilled, they rested in each other's arms. At times, her hunger for him became unbearable. If only…

"Bianca, are you listening?"

The familiar harshness in Miguel's voice prompted her back to the present. "Sorry, I was just thinking…"

"About what?"

An icy chill coursed through her. If she revealed anything about Alejandro, the consequences would prove reprehensible. She met his eyes, shuddering inside at the fire building within them. "How pleased I am to help you carry out your plans."

"Quit thinking and pay attention."

"*Sí*, Miguel." She retreated into the leather seat.

He revved the engine and pulled away. They sped along a major thoroughfare leading to the freeway.

"We will get settled in the rental outside of Rapid City," he said. "Tomorrow, you can go to *Buena Comida*, tell them your tragic tale, and make new friends."

Afraid to provoke him further, she remained silent. So far, she had never suffered a physical blow from Miguel but understood repercussions would follow if she stepped out of line.

She first caught sight of him in Mexico, her intuition telling her he could be her way out. The expensive clothes and Rolex watch assured her he wasn't just another *hombre pobre* strolling into the bar. She'd had her fill of poor men. Falling for the unfortunate widow story she invented, they lay naked in his hotel room a few hours later. She learned almost nothing about his past before Carmela Santiago. He spoke of having a dangerous profession without divulging any details.

In order to hide her own deception, she applied all her skills in the bedroom to persuade him to think only of her and forget Carmela. Foolish thinking on her part. Now, she'd grown to accept his love for Carmela would always overshadow any feelings he might have for her. Like an invisible specter, she forged a permanent wedge between them.

Leaving Rapid City behind forty minutes later, they turned up a secluded drive, stopping in front of a modest one-story frame dwelling on wooded acreage.

He deposited their suitcases in the living room and removed his coat. Muscles bulged beneath his dark turtleneck. Jeans encased his powerful thighs.

They explored the interior together. A living room, kitchen, two bedrooms, and a bathroom were on the main floor. They stepped out the rear door. A few feet away lay a steep, rocky ravine.

Back inside, she asked, "Who does this house belong to?"

"I found it online eight months ago," he said. "I corresponded with the owners by email, then signed a lease. Purchased for investment purposes, they never occupied this place and left for an extended European trip. The land is probably worth more than this house."

Miguel pointed to a staircase leading to the attic. "Let's take a look." He guided her up and opened the door.

The repulsive odor of mothballs mixed with musty wood struck them full force. He tugged on a long cord dangling from the ceiling. A bare lightbulb lit up the space. Floorboards creaked in protest as they ventured farther. Rays of sunlight filtered in through cracks in the eaves. Dust motes floated in the air.

Miguel removed a sheet spotted with stains draped over an antique bureau. Another exposed a brass bed with a thin sliver of a mattress. An old rocking chair rested in a corner next to vacant picture frames and a stack of books.

They proceeded to the far side of the room. An oval-shaped stained glass window cut off the outside view, its sill a graveyard laden with countless dead flies. Miguel examined the window frame.

"I must secure this." A grin spread across his face. "Perfect."

"For what?" she asked

"A prison." He draped his arm around her shoulder. "Once the girl is here, this will do nicely."

"You mean to keep the waitress here, then?"

His eyes narrowed. "*No*, I said the girl."

"But you cannot hold Natalia here. This is no place for her."

"I did not mention Natalia. Nick has a daughter, Isabelle. Carmela once told me they call her Izzy. There are *many* ways to make them suffer."

Her flesh crawled at his words. "But surely you would not harm a child?"

"Strange, you have no issue with me getting rid of a waitress, yet you question my intentions with a child." His brows drew together. He cupped her chin, his fingers digging in hard.

"The little girl is of no importance to me after she serves her purpose. She is the bait used to hook them so I can finish what *they* started." He released her and stomped to the doorway. "We have many things to do. Turn off the light and shut the door behind you."

Her stomach muscles coiled. She had envisioned him holding the waitress until they took possession of Natalia. Now, his deadly intentions became clear. This was more than she'd bargained for. Taking Natalia from them was one thing. Kidnapping and murdering a woman and a child quite another.

Bianca yanked the light cord and closed the door. She must remain focused on her reasons for coming to America, but she worried following Miguel's plans could jeopardize her own. Seeing Alejandro again remained the sole dream sustaining her.

Downstairs, not finding Miguel, she continued outside and down the steps. With no sign of him, she surveyed the tall Ponderosa Pines bordering thick woods, their tops brushing a pale blue sky.

Moving past them, she proceeded onto a worn trail, calling out, "Miguel, where are you?"

With each step, layers of pine needles crunched under her feet. She ducked beneath low-hanging branches. The rank stench of decaying leaves wafted on a slight breeze. A tree root caught her ankle. She pitched forward, grabbing the rough ridges of the trunk to avoid falling. The scratch of claws against bark made her look up. A lone squirrel fixed its gaze on her before scurrying farther away.

She leaned back against the tree, her eyes combing the shadowed woods. A swift zipping noise reverberated against her ear, accompanied by a loud thwack above her head. She ducked, her breath catching in her throat. Turning, she stared at a blade wedged into the trunk inches above where she had stood.

Miguel appeared, a silhouette against the leafy woodlands, the grim mask on his face expressing his displeasure. "What are you doing out here?"

"I…I was searching for you."

He wrenched the knife from the tree and slipped it into a sheath hanging at his waist. "As you can see, it is dangerous for you to wander in these woods alone. Do not do it again." He gripped her hand. "I would not want anything to happen to you."

They walked in silence, a gnawing in the pit of her gut fueling her fears. Doubts concerning her decision to lie in order to cross the border with Miguel surfaced.

When they arrived at the house, he released her and continued inside. Bianca paused in the doorway.

What would happen to her if she refused to agree with his plans? Or, if he uncovered her deception? The answers became clear when she pictured the knife.

CHAPTER 5

DALTON

Dalton considered the envelope in his hand. Arriving three days ago, it remained unopened. Determined to finally get it over with, his apprehension growing, he went to his study and closed the door. He loosened the top button of his denim shirt and sat behind the desk. Tearing the letter open, he read it, then the signature at the bottom.

"Damn it," he grumbled, pounding his fist on the hard wood. He sank into the leather chair and stared down at the pages before him. How in the heck could he explain this to Joann? Telling her he had no living relatives wasn't entirely true. With Jack on his way to the ranch, he'd have to fess up and tell her about his half-brother.

Jack's lying, stealing, and conniving were only part of the history between them. He still blamed his brother for starting the fire.

A gentle tap on the door made him look up. He shoved the letter into the desk drawer.

"Come in," he called out.

Joann appeared clad in jeans and a red checkered button-down blouse. A pair of brown calfskin boots covered her feet. "What are you doing holed up in here? You promised to take a break today."

"I know, darling. I'm sorry. Just some last-minute business." He retrieved his Stetson and led her outside. "Let's walk over to the barn. Have a peek at Sissy. Make certain she's on the mend."

From the moment Joann rode the mare, out of four he kept for riding, Sissy became her favorite. They'd sent for the veterinarian several days ago when the Palomino stopped eating.

Her fingers curled inside his hand. "I hope the vet was right, and it's only a little stomach inflammation."

"Colic is tricky in a mare," Dalton said. "Doc thinks it resulted from an intestinal muscle spasm. All her other tests were negative. So, if that's the case, she should be fine."

They arrived at the tall double wooden doors. Rick, Dalton's foreman, appeared. His easy-going swagger contradicted his tenacity for making sure things were done right. Three Border Collies, Brute, Rambo, and Duchess trailed behind him. He tapped two fingers on the pinched brim of his black cowboy hat. Younger than Dalton, his handsome face, slightly weathered from laboring in the sun, broke into a wide grin.

The dogs gathered at Joann's feet. She ruffled each of their heads before turning to Rick.

"How's my girl?"

"Palomino's much better today, Miss. She ate a bit. Not biting at her flank or kicking."

"That's good news," Dalton said.

Joann's face relaxed. "Thanks, Rick." She gestured to Dalton. "Coming?"

"In a minute. You go on ahead." After she disappeared inside, he said, "Listen, I need you to alert the men. We have a visitor arriving soon. My half-brother, Jack. When he's out and about, he needs watching."

Rick rubbed the black stubble along his chin. "Not trustworthy, huh?"

"Not in the slightest."

"No worries, Boss. I'll make sure everyone is up to speed."

Dalton clapped him on the back. "Thanks. I'm hoping he won't stay too long. Everything running smoothly?"

Rick nodded. "Going to muster cattle to the lower pasture. Taking Alejandro and a few others with me."

"Cost me a bit to get him legal. Is he working out okay?"

Rick's grin expanded, deep creases framing either side of his mouth. "He's a fast learner and a fine rustler. He's ridden drag. Never made one complaint."

Laughter escaped Dalton's lips. Riding drag, the worst position at the herd's rear, was given to low man on the totem pole.

"Think I'll move him up," Rick said. "Let him ride flank today…back up the swing riders. See how good he is at keeping the cattle from fanning out."

"I'm sure he'll appreciate it…free his nostrils and throat from dust." Dalton pointed to the dogs. "They look more than ready to go to work."

"Sure do." Rick tipped his hat, then let out a whistle. He walked off with the dogs following at his heels.

Inside the barn, light poured in from the dormers and skylights in the open design timber frame structure. Euro stalls with wrought iron railings above burnished wood lined each side. A far cry from the simple barn Dalton grew up knowing.

He stopped for a quick assessment. All the tack was stored correctly. Bridles, leads, halters, and curry combs were all in their proper place—shovels, pitchforks, plus brooms, in neat rows underneath. Polished saddles draped stands. Bundles of sweet-smelling timothy hay were stacked at the far end. His men understood he could not abide a messy barn.

Sturdy floorboards held steady beneath his weight. He tramped over scattered sawdust while several horses poked their heads out and whinnied.

Joann stood by Sissy's stall, patting her muzzle, oblivious to the musky horse scent and the faint odor of animal waste permeating the air.

How did he get so lucky? Once he got up the courage to express his feelings back in Laurel, Pennsylvania, they'd spent little time apart. He'd come to understand how Nick felt about Carrie.

During his years as a ghost, like Nick, not knowing if a kill would be his last, he never longed for someone to settle down with… until Joann. She'd brought richness to his life. Something he'd come to realize was missing.

He chuckled inside, remembering Nick's teasing when he told him of his intention to marry. Now, he couldn't imagine being without her. Red, as he affectionately called her, meant the world to him.

He slipped his arms around her waist. "See, I told you she'd pull through."

She leaned back into him. "I'm so glad she's feeling better."

The Palomino nickered and bobbed her head. Dalton snagged a carrot from a feedbag. While Sissy chomped it down, he said, "I have to talk to you about something, Red."

"Sure, what's up?"

"Let's sit by the creek."

They left the barn, strolled beyond a paddock, and sat on a hand-carved wooden bench. Sparkling clear water flowed over smooth stones lying in the creek bed. Wind slid through tall trees and grasses by the edge. Frogs croaked in the distance, overpowering the trill of birds.

When they were settled, Dalton steeled himself. "Let me start by saying, I never intended to keep this from you."

Joann assessed his face. "Should I be worried?"

"No. But you might get angry. Remember when you asked me about my family? There is something I should have told you a long time ago."

"What?"

"I have a half-brother named Jack. Seems he's headed here."

She paused a moment. "I'm sure you had your reasons. I'm not mad, just wishing you would confide in me more. For instance, you never mention your former job. I know you and Nick worked together, but I have no idea at what."

Dalton drank in the rich russet brown in her eyes. Her love filled him to overflowing. He could never have wished for a better lover and companion.

But she would never look at him the same if he told her the things he had done. Carrie knowing was one thing. She understood her man, loving him regardless of the blood on his hands. Joann knew about Carrie's past and how Travis forced her to commit murder, but Carrie skipped the part about Nick being a hired killer.

To avoid telling her his truth, he simply said, "Of course, I need to open up more, but I guess having been alone for so long, it isn't easy for me."

"That's okay. You'll get better at it."

He squeezed her hand. "Thanks for understanding."

"But your tone tells me this visit from your brother might not be a good thing."

"No, Jack's coming isn't a cause for celebration. His current situation has led him to ask if he could live with us for a while until he's back on his feet. Jack's always been a troublemaker. Claims in his letter he's changed, but I have my doubts."

"You don't trust him, do you?"

"Jack has never given me a reason *to* trust him."

"How long has it been since you saw him last?"

He removed his Stetson and set it aside. Fingers sweeping through his hair, he said, "Must be at least ten years if not more."

"Well, it's possible he has changed. You might want to give him the benefit of the doubt."

Dalton smirked. "I wouldn't give Jack the benefit of anything. Guess I'll have to wait and see."

"When does he arrive?"

"Any day now. I wish I had insisted on renovating the house. It's going to be close quarters for the three of us."

Joann bumped her body against his. "Silly, this place is big enough. We don't need the renovation. Besides, you still have the guest house Carrie and Nick lived in. It has plenty of room when company visits."

"Mmm. That's a thought. If it becomes necessary, we'll spend some time there. It will keep Jack away from the ranch and out of my business."

"Listen, hon, whatever you feel comfortable with is fine with me."

"You know how much I love you, right?"

"I sure do, sweetheart." Her arms encircled his neck, and she kissed his lips.

"Thanks for understanding, Red."

She stroked his cheek, then rested her head on his shoulder. "Always."

At this point in his life, he didn't want anything to ruin what they had built between them. He pulled her closer and kissed the top of her head.

They remained silent while fluffy porcelain clouds scattered across a cornflower blue sky. Dalton's angst eased as he held onto the hope Jack coming to South Dakota meant he had changed. Maybe he wasn't the same man who murdered their parents.

CHAPTER 6

BOBBY

It was early afternoon by the time Bobby's Uber pulled up. Overnight bag in hand, he rushed inside. He nodded at Nick, talking on his cell, then at his mother dressed in a navy pantsuit.

"It's great to see both of you," he said, setting his bag down.

Carrie hugged his neck. "Glad you arrived before I headed for the restaurant."

Ace trotted towards him. Bobby gave him a good rub. "Everything okay?"

"All is well. Rosie, our new manager, is a gem. She keeps things pretty much under control. I just need to go over some inventory with her."

"Mom, I'm sorry."

She cocked her head. "About what?"

"I feel I'm taking advantage. You and Nick do so much for me."

"We've told you at least a hundred times we don't mind."

Nick hung up his cell, a smile lighting his face.

"What's with the huge grin?" Carrie asked, pulling on her coat.

"Oh, nothing,"

"Come on, what gives? You can't fool me."

"This is between us guys," Nick said, pointing at Bobby.

Bobby blinked. "Don't look at me."

"Well, I've got to run. I'm not sure what's going on. Nick's been itching for you to get here." Car fob in her hand, she hurried out the door.

Bobby's ears perked up at the stillness. "Where is everyone?"

"Out with Valentina."

"But you know how much I miss Natty."

"Yes, I do." He draped his arm around Bobby's shoulder. "But you'll see her soon enough. I think you could use a break, and I have a little something planned." Nick grabbed his jacket from the mudroom. "Let's go."

"Where?"

"Follow me." Ace trotted up behind them. "No, not this time. *Restare*," Nick ordered.

Outside, he steered Bobby to the garage. Opening a panel, he punched in a code. One of the doors rose. With a flourish, Nick removed a gray car cover.

Bobby gasped and jumped backward. "Holy crap!" His eyes glazed over at the sight of the red Lamborghini Huracan. "You actually bought it."

"Yep, and now we're taking her out for a spin."

"A spin?"

"A buddy of mine is letting us open her up on the runway at the Black Hills Airport. With 640 horsepower, a 5.2 Liter V12, and 7-speed transmission, we're going to find out what this baby's got."

"Are you serious?"

"You bet."

Nick hit the fob. The door locks clicked, and they climbed inside. Bobby's nose filled with the scent of fine Italian leather. A charge of adrenaline shot through him while the seat hugged his body.

Nick's hands gripped the wheel. "Ready?"

"Hell yeah," Bobby said.

Nick pressed the ignition on the center console. The engine revved, the sound reverberating off the walls. He put the car in reverse and backed out. Keeping it in street mode, he swung around, squeezing the upshift paddle on the steering wheel, and headed down the driveway.

Bobby leaned over. He peeked at the headings on an array of gauges lining the dashboard. They reached the gates leading to the road. Nick switched on the axle lifter to prevent the front end from scraping the blacktop. Car motor roaring again, they exited the driveway, going from street mode to sport.

Nick drove up the ramp to the freeway. He pressed the pedal, switching lanes in an instant. They gained speed with each shift and downshift, the engine rattling Bobby's bones.

They arrived at the airport, and Bobby, almost breathless, braced himself. Nick drove the Lamborghini onto the runway. "You sure you're up for this?" he teased.

Bobby's skin tingled, goosebumps swept his arms. Focused on the asphalt stretched out ahead, he cried, "Lay it on me!"

Nick switched to track mode. He hit the gas, taking them from zero to sixty in 3.1 seconds. Bobby's heart jarred against his rib cage while the engine screamed. Nick punched the pedal again. Riveted, Bobby stared ahead mesmerized watching the automobile swallow up the road. Objects outside became a blur. Their speed increased. When they hit 200 miles per hour, Bobby's breath hitched.

Nick shifted and slowed the vehicle, then swung the car around. "Want to try her out?"

Bobby's mouth dropped. "For real?"

Nick laughed. "Yes, for real."

They swapped seats. Bobby gripped the leather steering wheel, his heart thumping. Under Nick's tutelage, he put the car in gear and started up the runway. Moments later, comfortable with the car's feel and a little more confident, he increased his speed.

His body thrummed sending a tingle through him. A lightness filled his chest. His jaw ached from the constant grin on his face. Not quite attaining the exact 200 miles per hour as Nick, he decreased the automobile's speed, coming to a stop back at their starting point.

They grinned and high-fived. "Incredible!" Bobby declared.

"Yeah, it is. Just don't tell your mother how fast we were going."

"Has she ridden with you, yet?"

"No, but I'm working on her." He checked his watch. "Hungry?"

"Starving. I'd love to grab a bite. I want to talk to you about something."

"*Buena Comida* or…?"

"That's fine. Mom's there."

They swapped seats and headed downtown. Nick parked behind the restaurant in a reserved owner's spot, and they entered through the kitchen.

Pots boiled on a massive stove, waves of steam swirling in the air. Meat sizzled in a large stainless-steel skillet, filling the room with the rich aroma of Columbian spices. Jars filled with *guasca, achiote,* and *triguisar* lined the shelves. Carlos Londoño, the Executive Chef, supervised a prep cook as he chopped red-hot peppers while Julian, the sous-chef, barked orders to a junior chef. At the far end, the remainder of the kitchen staff prepared for the dinner crowd.

Eyes crinkling above his bushy mustache, Carlos shouted over the din, *"Hola Señiors! Cómo estás?"* His thick hand holding a spoon, he lifted the lid off a large pot and stirred.

"Bien, bien, Carlos," Nick said. "What's the special today?"

"Chuleta Valluna." He pressed his fingertips to his lips in a mock kiss. *"Perfecto."*

Bobby beamed. He loved the pork Milanese and had declared it one of his favorite dishes. He grinned at the big man. *"Gracias,* Carlos. *"*

They proceeded into the dining room, where Carrie was going over the bar inventory. A sunny yellow backdrop set off an array of liquor bottles behind the mahogany bar. Paintings of Carmela's native Columbia hung on the walls. The deep red ceiling held rows of pendant lights, with shades in various hues.

They slid into a booth. Bobby glanced around, swelling with pride, while he observed the uniformed staff. Crisp white blouses paired with short black skirts adorned the women, while the men were decked out in white dress shirts and dark slacks. A few patrons lingered over a late lunch. A young woman with ebony-colored curly hair sat alone talking to Sarah, one of the waitresses, and Alice, the hostess.

Alice appeared to comfort her while the woman wiped her eyes several times with her napkin. A few moments later, the woman left.

"Pretty," Nick said, giving Bobby a wink.

Bobby threw up his hands. "Oh, no. I don't want her drama, whatever it is." He signaled to Alice. "What's up with her?"

Her green eyes blinked beneath her short blonde bob. "Poor thing. Her name is Bianca. She's new around here. Bad break-up. Seems her boyfriend deserted her. Ran off with another woman."

"Where's she living?" Bobby asked.

"A small apartment off Hill Street. Rents paid up for the next six months, and he left her some money. She's good for now. But if she can't find a job here in town soon, she'll probably move on."

"Too bad," Bobby said. "Does she have family here?"

"No one. Only family back in Mexico." Alice's eyes lit up. "But she does have waitress and bar tending experience."

"Well, we're fully staffed," Nick said. "I'm sure she'll find something."

Alice tucked a stray curl behind her ear. "It was nice seeing both of you. I better go and check on reservations for the dinner crowd."

"Hey, Alice," Bobby called out. "Let Sarah know we want two house specials and two beers."

A few minutes later, Sarah, her long brown hair gathered into a ponytail, set their beers and plates down. She flashed Bobby a smile. "Anything else I can get for you?"

"No. Thanks, Sarah."

After she left, Nick said, "There's another opportunity for you. The girl was drinking you up with her big brown eyes."

"Enough already." Bobby frowned. "I'm not looking for anything right now."

Nick's eyes filled with mischief. "Just saying." He lifted his beer.

Bobby swallowed several bites of his food, savoring the hot spices. "Listen, I need your advice."

"Go ahead, shoot."

"A good friend might be in trouble. I don't know much, so I'm stuck deciding whether or not to pursue it."

Nick's eyes narrowed. "How close a friend?"

"Close enough." Bobby sank back in the leather booth as Sarah set two more mugs of beer between them. "Thanks, Sarah."

"Well," Nick said. "Experience has taught me unless someone asks for your help, it's best to leave things alone. Unless…"

Bobby's ears perked up. "Unless what?"

"Unless it's a person you really care about."

"I was afraid you would say that."

"Say what?" Carrie stood in front of them, clutching her iPad.

"Oh, hey, Mom. Nothing, I wanted Nick's opinion."

"I get it. Guy talk." She tapped Bobby playfully on his shoulder. "So, what have you two been doing this afternoon?"

"Just hanging out," Nick said.

"Yeah, right. That's why the Lamborghini is parked out back. I guess it drove itself here."

Nick pulled her down beside him. "If you must know, we took her for a little spin."

"And where did this so-called spin take place?"

"Oh, around."

Carrie bumped her body against his. "I wasn't talking to you."

She gestured at Bobby. His cheeks bloomed red, and he avoided her eyes. "Like Nick said, around."

She burst out laughing. "You two are thick as thieves. I know you were at the airport."

Nick's eyes gleamed. "What makes you think so?"

"Your buddy, Dalton, spilled the beans. He couldn't reach you, so he called me. I told him I had no idea where you were, and he said you were probably at the Black Hills Airport, soaring down the runway in your Lamborghini. He said to call him when you get a chance."

Nick drew out his cell. "Yep. One missed call and a text."

Carrie grinned at Bobby. "So, how fast?"

The thrilling ride still with him, he blurted out, "Mom, it was incredible. Nick punched it up to 200." He jumped at a kick to his shin from Nick underneath the table.

Her eyebrow raised. She stared at Nick. "200?"

"Give or take," Nick said, eyes focused on his meal.

"So, when are you taking *me* for a spin?" Carrie asked.

Nick's arm went around her shoulders. "Whenever you're ready."

"I'm going to hold you to that," Carrie said, looking into his eyes.

Watching them, a spark of jealousy ignited inside Bobby. Why couldn't he have a solid relationship like theirs? If only things had worked out with Carmela... only Carmela hadn't been anything like his mom.

They finished their meal, then drove to the house with Carrie following in the Range Rover. Bobby could hardly wait to see Natalia. He stepped inside, and she flew into his arms and hugged his neck.

"Daddy, why were you gone so long?"

"I'm sorry, sweet girl. I had business to take care of." He carried her into the great room and sat with her on his lap.

With Nick and Carrie seated across from them, Bobby said, "Listen, Natty, I have something to tell you. I'm taking you home to New York with me."

Natalia clapped. "Goody, I'm going for a visit."

"No, you're coming to stay. I miss you too much."

"Forever?"

"Yes. You can still visit everyone here, and sometimes they'll visit us, too."

"That's right," Carrie broke in.

Izzy drifted into the room with Michael and Ace fast on her heels. She stood by Carrie.

"What's going on?"

"Hey, Bug," Bobby said. "I was just telling Natty she's coming to live with me in New York."

"Why?" Michael asked.

"Because she belongs with me."

Izzy looked from Carrie to Nick. "When will we see Natty again?"

Carrie rubbed Izzy's back. "We'll visit her, and every so often, she'll visit us."

Teary-eyed, Izzy plopped beside Bobby and Natalia. She placed an arm around Natalia's shoulder. "I don't want her to leave."

"Natty can't leave," Michael piped in, sitting on Natalia's other side.

Bobby glanced at Carrie. "I was afraid this would happen."

Carrie knelt in front of the children. "Look," she pointed at Izzy, then Michael. "Just like the two of you belong here with your father and me, Natalia belongs with her dad. He misses her. You wouldn't want Bobby to be sad, would you?"

"No," Izzy squeaked.

"Then you have to try to understand. Natalia will be fine living in New York. Take her upstairs. You can help pack some of her things. We'll come up in a minute."

After the children left, Bobby turned to Carrie. "I feel like the bad guy."

"It's rough on all of us," Carrie said. "We're used to having her here. But it's for the best. You have nothing to feel bad about."

His angst eased at her words. "Thanks, Mom."

Nick cleared his throat. "Izzy and Michael will be fine, Bobby."

A half-grin lit Bobby's face. "But y*ou* don't look so good."

"We're going to miss her, but I agree with your mother. It's the right thing to do."

"Can you help me get her ready?" Bobby asked.

"Sure," they said almost in unison.

All three went to Natalia's room and spent the next hour deciding what to pack. They'd ship the rest later. By the time they finished, the children were coming to grips with Natalia's leaving. Bobby wasn't sure about his mother and Nick. They put up a good front in helping to comfort Izzy and Michael, but the water forming in his mother's eyes plus Nick's stony silence spoke volumes. Still, he remained convinced his decision to bring his daughter home was for the best.

Later, as he lay in one of the guest rooms with Natalia asleep by his side, Ronnie popped into his head. Her refusing his help haunted him. He pictured the man at the club. That guy wasn't the type of person he assumed Ronnie would hang with.

What could she possibly owe someone like him? Surely not money. She earned a good salary as an attorney. For now, he'd take Nick's advice and hope eventually she would tell him what was going on.

CHAPTER 7

VERONICA

R onnie kicked off her shoes. She tossed her coat aside, then removed her pink silk blouse. Comfortable in her lace camisole and black pants, she withdrew a tiny vial from her purse and emptied some white powder onto the surface of the coffee table. Using a credit card, she cut two uniform rows down the middle. She rolled a ten-dollar bill into a perfect cylinder, then tucking her hair behind each ear, she inhaled a line up her left and then her right nostril.

Wiping the residue from her nose, she savored the rush coursing through her body, a treat after a demanding day at work and her best defense against Derek. The time had come for her to stand up to him.

The buzzer sounded. Ronnie slipped on her blouse before checking the peephole. Drawing a deep breath, she let Derek in. Without a word, he pushed past her. He pulled a zippered case from his brown leather jacket pocket along with a small revolver from his waistband and placed them on the coffee table.

Turning, he scrutinized her face. His forehead creased. "Starting the party without me?"

Ronnie tugged on the sleeve of her blouse. "I needed a little pick me up."

He removed his jacket, the white t-shirt underneath revealing his muscular tattooed arms. His faded, ripped jeans ended just below the shaft of his motorcycle boots. A pair of dog tags hung below a neatly trimmed beard.

"That's what I'm here for, baby," he said, flopping onto the sofa.

She attempted to retrieve the vial. Derek seized her wrist, pulling her down next to him.

His fingers dug in. "Leave it. I have plenty more. We need to discuss some business." He freed her and leaned back into the cushions. "You're making a drop this weekend."

"No, Derek, I told you I'm done. There is nothing to discuss. Find yourself another mule."

His lips drew into a grim line. "That's the coke talking. You're done when I say unless … you want me to leak the videos. Deliver a copy to HR at your job or post them on social media."

The knot in the pit of her stomach twisted. "You know I'll lose everything if those get out. My career as an attorney would be over."

"And it never will, just so long as you do what I tell you to."

Her courage slipping away with the remainder of her high, she said, "Derek, please, you promised after the drop last week, I'd be finished."

His expression turned dark, and he scowled at her. "Promises are made to be broken."

"What if I get caught?"

"You *are* a lawyer, after all. You know what to do. Besides, I have connections of my own, too. I'll take care of you if anything crops up. You should have thought more about your career before you partied at my place."

His hand pressed against the nape of her neck. Calloused fingertips pulled her within inches of his face, the acrid odor of marijuana on his breath assaulting her senses. Storm clouds forming in his eyes, he asked, "Who was the jerk at the club? I didn't appreciate the intrusion."

"No one," she mumbled.

His fingers gripped the ends of her hair, jerking her head backward. "He had some balls for no one. I better never catch the creep lurking around again." He released his grip and rubbed the tops of his thighs. "Look, your next run is coming up, and that's all you need to be concerned about." He motioned at the gun. "That's for you."

"For me?"

"Yeah. I'd feel better if you carried."

She stared at the revolver. "Derek, I don't know anything about guns. Keep it."

"I'm not saying you're gonna use it. Moving all those drugs, you never can tell what might happen. It will make someone think twice if you pull it out. You know… just to scare them."

The pounding inside her head accelerated. Her life was turning into a living hell. First drugs, now a gun. "Derek, I—"

"Chill, Ronnie," he snapped, fingering the case lying on the coffee table. "I have something special for us." He unzipped it, exposing a set of works.

Ronnie bit her lower lip while her hands kneaded the cushions. Before her lay a tourniquet, two syringes, a cooker, tiny cylinders of sterile water, a small packet of heroin, acidifier, filter tablets, and alcohol swabs.

Heart drumming against her ribs, she asked, "What's all that for?"

Derek placed his fingertip against her lips for a moment before withdrawing the cooker from the packaging. He added heroin, water, and a little acidifier.

Unable to move, Ronnie watched as he held a lighter beneath it, dissolving the drug before dropping a filter tablet into the mixture. He drew the liquid up into a syringe.

"Roll up your sleeve."

She reared back, breaking into a sweat. "No, Derek. None for me. I'll stick to coke."

"Just this once. We'll do it together. Watch me first." He set the syringe down and prepared another hit. "Here," he held out the tourniquet. "Wrap this tight around my arm."

Ronnie did as he directed. She stared in fascination while he pumped his fist, enlarging a blue vein on his forearm. He swabbed the area with alcohol, then picked up a syringe. After checking for air bubbles, he inserted the needle into his vein and pushed the plunger. A moment later, he released the tourniquet.

"See? It's easy, baby." His eyes glazed over. A smile softened his harsh features. "Come on, try it."

Her insides weakening, she rolled up her sleeve. Her life, already a wreck, couldn't get much worse. Derek adjusted the tourniquet. Her eyes locked on the drug-filled needle.

If she went down this path, there was no turning back. She pumped her fist, her eyes searching for a vein. A trail of light blue appeared in the crease of her arm. Her pulse spiked. She reached for the syringe, touching the tip of the needle to her skin before glancing over at Derek.

His head slumped forward, and his eyelids closed. Something deep inside her screamed. Images of her mother and brother emerged. She released the tourniquet and shot the heroin into a potted plant on the end table beside her. She deposited the empty syringe on the table, then rolled her sleeve down. Derek opened his eyes. To convince him she'd taken a hit, she gave him a lazy smile, leaned back, and half-closed her eyes.

"Feels good, doesn't it," he said, stroking her hair.

She squeezed his hand. "Sure does."

Derek remained in a stupor while they each snorted two lines of coke. Later, he steered her into the bedroom.

With Derek gone the following day, Ronnie lay in bed, reliving the feel of his rough hands all over her body... how she'd forced her mind into some distant place to dull the relentless buzzing inside her head. The weekend would come all too soon, bringing with it another nerve-fraying road trip, her objective clearly defined. Cross the state line, deliver the drugs, and return with the cash. Simple, Derek said. But how long before something went wrong?

If only she had been more vigilant. Drinks in clubs were drugged all the time. She couldn't even recall how she ended up at Derek's place. The next morning, when he showed her the videos, she'd run from the apartment, his laughter nipping at her heels while her stomach heaved. There were so many men and...

Sobbing, she pressed her face into the pillow. One stupid mistake could cost her everything. None of her family or friends, especially Bobby, must ever find out what a horrid person she'd become. Her only escape meant getting hold of the videos and ridding herself of Derek. But the chance of retrieving them was slim.

Wiping at her tears, she boosted herself up against the headboard. Opening the nightstand, she removed the gun, feeling its weight not only in her hand but in her mind too, recalling how Derek had shown her how to use it. She tossed it back into the draw, slamming it shut. Derek had left her little choice. Soon, she'd be his mule again.

CHAPTER 8

JACK

Jack Burgess slowed his 2003 blue Ford Focus and studied the wrought iron header above the gates. 'Hidden Creek Ranch' was spelled out in bold black lettering. Swiping his fingers through thick tufts of gunmetal grey hair, he slid the window down. He leaned and spat on the ground.

"That's what I think of this place," he mocked. He punched in the code Dalton sent and sped through the entrance. Cruising along the mile drive, he marveled at the vast numbers of cattle grazing in wide-open pastures. "Grass-fed. Impressive."

Moving on, he puzzled over how in the heck his brother was able to prosper at cattle ranching alone. All those times he needed bailing out, Dalton had been more than generous in coming to his aid.

Stopping part way, he observed half a dozen men on horseback along with three dogs. They shouted commands while the dogs maneuvered left and right, darting among the herd of cattle, driving them up a grassy hill.

He pulled up in front of a modest home, got out and stretched. "I suppose this is it."

Jack hoisted his suitcase from the trunk and set it down. Shoving the ends of his blue flannel shirt into his waistband, he sized up his surroundings. His eyes drawn to a huge barn, he ambled toward it. Shocked at the sight of the enormous structure, he paused inside the doorway and emitted a low whistle. "My little brother sure has moved up in the world."

Immaculate as it was, he wrinkled his nose at the odor of horseflesh and hay. He stepped up to one of the stalls. Admiring the Palomino's gold coat and white mane, he glanced at a plaque hanging overhead. It spelled out Sissy. Eyeing him a moment, the horse snorted and stomped her rear foot.

Jack snickered. "Exactly what I was thinking." He withdrew a pack of unfiltered Lucky's from his shirt pocket, tapped it against his palm, and slid one out. Placing it between his lips, he dug out his lighter. The pad of his thumb rubbed against the flint wheel. It sparked, producing a bright orange flame. The Palomino's eyes enlarged. She bobbed her head wildly back and forth.

"Hey, fella!"

Jack spun around. A tall, lean man, sporting a black cowboy hat and checkered bandanna, stood in front of him. He pointed at the lighter. "There's no smoking in the barn."

"Oh, sorry." Jack flipped it closed, then stowed the unlit cigarette in his pack. Stepping forward, he offered his hand. "Jack Burgess. Dalton's older brother."

The man hesitated before shaking it. "Rick. Heard you were coming."

Picking up a sour note in the man's voice, he replied, "Uh-oh, that doesn't sound too favorable."

"Depends. We have certain rules around here. How good are you at following rules?"

Jack's muscles stiffened. Who the hell does this cowboy think he is? He forced a smile. "Don't typically break them once I learn what they are."

Rick's eyes clouded over, a glimmer of malice inside them. "No smoking in the barn is one of them. I'd appreciate you not breaking it."

"Sure, no problem. Sorry for the misunderstanding. Believe I'll head up to the house." He shuffled past Rick. "My brother is anticipating my arrival."

Rick chuckled. "Yeah, he's been itching for you to get here."

Jack stalked out, a rush of adrenaline thundering through his veins. In due time, he'd teach that cowboy a lesson. Retrieving his suitcase, he sprang up the front steps and rang the bell. A few moments later, an attractive redhead opened the door.

She offered her hand. "You must be Jack. I'm Joann, Dalton's wife."

The word wife caught him off guard. He reciprocated and grinned. Pretty enough, but a definite ruffle in his plans. "Yes, it's me alright."

"Welcome, come on in."

He moved past her and into the living room. "Nice place."

"It suits us," Joann said. "Let me show you to your room." She led him upstairs to a bedroom. "It's small but comfortable."

Jack hid his disappointment. "This is fine."

"Well, I'll let you get settled. When you're ready, come downstairs. I'm preparing something special for dinner."

Jack deposited his suitcase on the bed. "I was expecting to see my brother."

"Oh, of course. I neglected to mention, Dalton's picking up supplies in Rapid City. He should be back in a bit."

"Thanks."

"If you need anything, holler."

He unpacked, hanging several pairs of jeans in the closet. He pulled a .45 handgun and an envelope from his suitcase, tucking both underneath his shirts inside the dresser drawer.

Downstairs in the dining room, he found Joann busy setting the table. She looked up.

"Dinner will be ready shortly. Thirsty?"

"Could use a cold beer if you have one."

"Coming right up." She disappeared into the kitchen.

Jack wandered over to a row of photographs sitting atop an antique oak server. A picture of Joann and Dalton in formal attire graced a gold frame.

Joann handed him a beer. "That was taken the day we were married."

"Never figured Dalton for the marrying kind," he said, twisting the cap. "You must be some special lady."

Pale pink swept across her cheeks. "Well, I guess somehow we just clicked."

His eyes strayed to the other photos, and he pointed at one. "I bet she's your daughter. Looks a lot like you."

"Yes, that's my Veronica. She's a lawyer, lives in New York City, and this one here is my son, Justin. He'll graduate college later this year."

He picked up one of the other frames. "Who are these good-looking folks?"

"That's Nick, Dalton's best buddy, his wife, Carrie, and their oldest son, Bobby."

He squinted at the photo. "Don't recall meeting them."

"They have two more children, Izzy and Michael. The older boy, Bobby, lives in New York. He's a big-time art dealer, also owns several restaurants and a winery."

"Looks kind of young to be so successful."

"Art is Bobby's real passion. The rest his little girl, Natalia, inherited when her mother passed away."

"Sounds complicated."

"No, not really."

Heavy footsteps captured his attention. Dalton's big frame swallowed up the doorway.

Jack put his beer aside and rushed forward. "Well, now, look at you, little brother." Before Dalton could react, he wrapped his arms around him, squeezing him in a bear hug. "It's good to see you after all these years."

Dalton pulled away. "I can't say I feel the same."

Joann gave him a disapproving look. "Dalton, please be cordial."

"She's right," Jack said. "I mean no harm. I'm thrilled to be here."

Dalton pointed toward the hallway. "Let's go into my study. You can tell me just how thrilled."

Jack rubbed the back of his neck. "Sure thing, whatever you say." He grabbed his beer and followed.

"Let us know when supper is ready, Red," Dalton called over his shoulder. He shut the door, then motioned at one of two chairs by the fireplace. "Take a seat."

Jack settled into the soft leather, swallowed some of his beer, and waited. He had expected this chilly reception.

Dalton peered at him. "What brings you here after all this time? I haven't heard a peep out of you in years."

"Like I said in my letter, I've fallen on hard times."

Dalton smirked and smoothed his mustache. "Hard times is nothing new for you. Who are you running from?"

"Now, hold on a minute, Dalton. Just because I need a place to stay for a bit doesn't mean some dastardly deeds been done. I'm not running, only cash poor at the moment... need a little time to get on my feet."

"How much, Jack?"

His insides stewed. Did Dalton expect to pay him off and send him on his way? Not this time. No amount of money could replace what he stole all those years ago. This land, this ranch, belonged to him. Dalton had snatched it right out from under his nose.

Jack frowned. "Is that what you think? I'm here to ask for money?"

"Well, with you, history tends to repeat itself."

"Still holding that bit of cash over my head. It was a long time ago, little brother."

"Fifty-grand is no spit in the bucket, Jack." Dalton paused. "And I don't recall you ever paying it back. You told me it was all you needed to make a new start. So, what happened?"

Jack gulped down the last of his beer, resting the empty bottle on the end table by his chair.

"Things didn't work out how I expected them to. I tried. Honest, I did, whether you believe me or not. All I want now is to regroup, take a breather, and figure out my next move."

"I'll tell you what your next move is going to be, Jack. I'm giving you the benefit of the doubt this time, only because I am still your brother. Things weren't always bad between us. You can stick around for a while and help out, but you better not cause any trouble, or I'll throw you off this ranch so fast, you won't know what hit you."

Dalton's eyes bore into him. Jack felt like a schoolboy caught playing hooky. Sweat formed on his upper lip, and he looked away. He'd taken orders from his father and brother all his life when *he* should be the one saying how things ought to go.

"Thanks. You won't regret it. Mom and Dad would be real—"

"Don't, Jack." Dalton rose, towering over him. "Don't soil their memory by letting their names pass between your lips. So long as you're around me, never mention them again. Now, I'm going to wash up. I'll see you in the dining room."

He paused in the doorway. "And one other thing. Don't you ever disrespect my wife or anybody else on this ranch, including the animals. Understood?"

"You've made things crystal clear." As soon as Dalton turned his back, he flipped him the bird.

Wiping the sweat from his upper lip, he attempted to calm the rage building inside him. Little had changed. His brother was still the same ornery son of a bitch he remembered, always causing him to feel less than, playing the good son, forcing their father to turn on him. He was convinced Dalton had persuaded his father to alter the will. But Dalton's day was coming, and he'd be sorry for letting him set foot on his ranch. Sorrier than the night of the fire. Sorrier still than on the day they had laid their parents in the cold, hard ground.

CHAPTER 9

NICK

Nick drove away from the Rapid City Regional Airport with Ace sitting in the rear of the Range Rover. Having dropped Bobby and Natalia off for their flight to New York, he admitted he would miss her more than he let on.

Natalia always brought Carmela to mind. He had never divulged to anyone the profound affect her passing left on him. While working for Ricardo, he'd watched her grow from a child into a beautiful young woman. Guilt lay heavily upon him for changing her into a monster out for revenge, and it grieved him to know how much Bobby had loved Carmela. The one positive thing to survive the massacre in Tahoe was Natalia.

Taking a detour, he decided to head to Dalton's. Forty-five minutes later, he arrived at the ranch. Brute, Rambo, and Duchess circled the car as he released Ace. Already long-time buddies, they yelped and leaped at the sight of one another.

Dalton appeared on the porch, head free of his Stetson, tufts of his thick hair skimming the top of his collar. "At least somebody's happy."

"Sounds like it," Nick said. He went up the steps, and the two men bear-hugged. "How the hell are you?"

Dalton's forehead creased. "Could be better. Come inside. I have whiskey waiting in the study."

Joann greeted them in the foyer. "Hey handsome, how's it going?" She pecked Nick on his cheek.

"All is well."

"Good. I'm just on my way out to run some errands." She checked herself in a mirror by the front door. Retrieving a comb from her purse, she ran it through her hair.

"Take the truck," Dalton said. "I won't be needing it."

She waved her hand at him. "Jack's driving me. He's waiting over by the barn."

A frown formed on Dalton's face. "Be mindful not to make any unnecessary stops."

She threw on a Red and Blue Navajo print coat. Looping the barrel buttons, she asked, "What are you talking about?"

"If I know my brother, he'll have an agenda of his own."

Nick raised an eyebrow. "Brother? You never mentioned…"

Dalton gave him a look. "I'll fill you in shortly." He bussed Joann's cheek. "No unscheduled stops, Red."

"Sure, whatever you say."

When they were settled in the study, with drinks in their hands, Dalton said, "There's a good reason I never told you I have a brother. Half-brother, that is. Same father, different mothers. My father married twice. My brother was born during his first one. When Jack's mother died, my father remarried. Jack was three when I was born. My father coddled him more than me. But he struggled to keep him on the straight and narrow."

"And now?" Nick asked.

Dalton paused, savoring his drink. "Jack is a whole other story. If it were up to me, there would be a big letter T for trouble stamped on his forehead, so when anybody saw him coming, they'd know what to expect."

"That bad, huh?"

"Never worked an honest day in his life. Has a gambling habit bigger than the state of Nevada. Lies pour from his mouth, smooth as maple syrup. We had a falling out. Haven't seen him in well over ten years. Before that, it cost me fifty thousand to get rid of him. Then, a few days ago, I receive a letter, says he's going through tough times, asked to come and stay for a bit."

Nick stared into his whiskey glass. "Strange, you have a brother who's such a mess, while I'd give almost anything to have mine here again."

"Yeah, life's a real bitch sometimes."

"You spoke of a falling out. What happened?"

Dalton refilled their glasses and sat back down. "I can't prove it, but I believe he murdered our parents."

Nick let out a slow breath. "That's heavy stuff."

"We were in our late twenties when my father became ill, bedridden almost," Dalton said. "By this time, Jack had been in numerous scrapes. To tell you the truth, I think the stress aged my mother and father prematurely."

In all the years Nick had known him, he'd never seen such pain in Dalton's eyes. He could relate when he recalled the loss of his own parents.

Dalton cleared his throat. "Sorry. It's still difficult to talk about, but I need you to hear this in case something should happen."

Nick's radar went up. "Like what?"

"You and me, we have history. I've never once doubted your friendship, so I'm asking you to give me your word on this. If things go awry, you'll take care of Jack. And none too gently. Understand?"

This was the last thing Nick expected him to say, but he honored the bond between them. He looked Dalton in the eye. "You don't have to think twice about it."

"Good. Now, I can finish. The previous house and barn were way on the other side of the ranch back then. A whole bunch of turmoil occurred leading up to the fire. Jack wasn't on favorable terms with my father, and he threatened to cut Jack out of his will. Two days later, I drove my dad to his lawyer's office in Sioux Falls where he did precisely that. After my mother, I became the sole beneficiary. He said he didn't trust Jack to run this place. The land meant too much to him."

"Several months after our little excursion to Sioux Falls, I made plans to meet up with some buddies of mine. Jack asked how long I'd be gone. I responded… can't really recall exactly what I told him. A couple hours later, I wasn't feeling too well, so I decided against going and went to bed instead."

"Around midnight, I woke to the smell of something burning. I crawled to the bedroom door. Smoke was rushing in underneath. The only option left was the window. I grabbed my baseball bat, busted the glass, climbed out onto the roof, and slid down the drainpipe. The place became an inferno."

Dalton's voice dropped. He stared off into the distance. "I'll never forget their screams. There was nothing I could do to save them. I've lived with the guilt every day of my life."

Nick glimpsed tears threatening to spill from the big man's eyes.

"Their bodies were burned beyond recognition. A horrible way to die. A death they didn't deserve."

"Where was Jack during the fire?"

"At first, I figured he was inside the house. A few minutes later, he comes running from behind the barn." Dalton paused.

"I'll always remember the look of surprise on his face. He didn't expect to see me standing there."

"So, it was intentional?"

"I believe one hundred percent he meant to kill us all. He'd become the sole heir. By law, everything would belong to him."

"Did they find out what caused the fire?"

"They declared it an accident. The report said it started from a lit cigarette. Unfortunately, my father was a smoker. And, I must admit, he fell asleep a time or two with one still burning. They believed a pile of newspapers he kept next to the bed must have lit up like a torch, only he had assured me weeks before he'd quit for good. In those last few weeks, I didn't see him light up once."

Nick leaned forward, absorbing each word. "What happened afterward?"

Dalton wiped his palms down the front of his face, clearing his eyes. "Jack was in for a shock when he discovered he'd been disinherited, and the ranch was mine. Three months later, he left."

"I was determined to keep things going, wanted to honor my father's wishes. He loved this place. Put his heart and soul into it. I labored for two years. About to lose everything and feeling sorry for myself, I drove into Rapid City one night to a bar where I met a fellow. We started drinking, and I told him my story."

"Somehow, he had heard about my shooting ability. My father taught me. I used to enter contests. Even won a bunch of ribbons and trophies." Dalton swallowed the last of his whiskey.

"Just like Ricardo did for you, this fellow offered me a way out. I trained hard, polished my craft, then began work as an independent contractor. Made it my business to know the reason why before eliminating someone. That part mattered to me a whole lot. I wasn't about to kill for the money alone. It needed to make a difference somehow."

"With cash rolling in, I not only managed to save the ranch, but I also increased the herd tenfold and put a hefty amount into investing. Did rather well."

Dalton refilled his glass. "Now, with Joann here and things running smooth, I don't want Jack messing it all up."

Nick frowned. "Too bad you can't prove he set the fire."

"Short of torturing him, no. In his letter, he claimed he's changed. So far, I'm a non-believer. According to Rick, he already spooked one of the mares with a cigarette lighter. I don't like the idea of him hanging around here. If things get iffy, we're coming up your way to my guesthouse for a bit."

Dalton stretched. "Enough about me. How are things progressing with the restaurants?"

"Going well. Keeping us busy, though."

"Lamborghini out yet?"

"Hell, yes. Me and Bobby rode the Black Hills Track." He gave Dalton a look. "By the way, thanks for spilling the beans to Carrie."

Dalton's face turned red. "Oh, sorry. I just figured it's where you might be yesterday."

"No worries, Carrie actually wants to go for a ride."

Dalton chuckled. "My kind of gal."

Nick fell silent. He debated whether to mention how his demons had returned to torment him. But he decided against it. Dalton's plate was full. Instead, he asked, "Any news on Miguel?"

"My sources tell me he hasn't come back across the border. He could be anywhere by now. I'm keeping an ear to the ground. By the way, they delivered the filly I picked out."

Nick set his glass aside. "Can't wait to see her."

They strode to the barn together. A whinny sounded from the farthest stall. At their approach, an American Paint stuck her head out.

Dalton fetched a halter with a lead rope attached. Opening the stall, he unbuckled it, and with expert hands, secured it around the horse's head. He rubbed her muzzle, clucking softly before bringing her out.

Nick admired the pinto spotted pattern of brown and white, her expresso-colored mane and tail. He let out a whistle. "She's a beauty. You chose well."

"Sure is," Dalton said. "A Paint is a good horse for beginners. How are the lessons going?"

"She started taking lessons almost a year ago," Nick replied. "All her begging and pleading paid off. I struck a deal with her. If she kept up her grades while continuing with the lessons, I'd eventually get her a horse."

Dalton laughed. "Izzy's as stubborn as you are. I'm sure she had no problem holding up her end of the bargain." He patted the horse's flank. "Rick's been working with her. She's gentle enough, almost fully broken. When did you plan on giving her to Izzy?"

"Soon as you tell me she's ready." He imagined the look on his daughter's face when he presented her with the horse and couldn't help smiling.

Dalton nodded. "Almost there." He returned the horse to its stall and removed the halter. After latching the door, he offered her a carrot. "Before you take off, I want to show you something."

He led Nick to the tack room. Three saddles were draped over stands. He pointed to the first one, a Hilason Western with hand-tooled floral and basket design stitched into the leather.

"That belongs to Red," Dalton said. "This second one, a King series, is mine."

Nick admired the detail on the gleaming brown leather.

"This last one is for Izzy. Red picked it out."

Turquoise inlay with silver studs and conchos were fastened onto the caramel-colored leather. Floral and basket tooling similar to Joann's graced the seat. Nick was at a loss for words when he spotted the initials I.D. engraved on the leather.

He met Dalton's eyes. "I don't know what to say. It's outstanding."

Footsteps rapped against the wood floor as Joann strutted toward them, sporting a wide grin, a cowgirl hat on her head. Scuffed boots peeked from the bottom of her jeans. Her red and blue Navajo jacket was replaced by a tan suede fringed one, her hands were tucked into the pockets.

Nick's eyes swept over her. "You never dressed like this back in Laurel. I'm scared you might be toting a gun underneath your jacket, Annie Oakley."

She laughed and jabbed his arm. "That's right." A look of adoration on her face, she nodded toward Dalton. "That guy has turned me into a Cowgirl of sorts, and I love him for it."

"Always had it in you, Red," Dalton said. "You just needed me to bring it out. Everything else, okay?"

"Yep. Jack took me directly to town, then home again. He's gone to the north pasture to help out." She winked at Nick. "Think Izzy will like the saddle?"

"She'll love it, but you shouldn't have bought it. You're already letting us board the horse here. The least I can do is buy a saddle."

Dalton chuckled. "Are you kidding me? What do you know about saddles?"

Nick felt a flush sweep across his face. "Well, they go on horses."

"Correct, my friend, only there is a little more to it. Not every saddle fits every horse and the needs of a rider," Dalton said.

Joann patted Nick's arm. "It's our pleasure to give this to Izzy." Hands on her hips, she continued. "We plan on doing quite a bit of riding together."

"Since when?" Nick asked.

"Oh, we discussed it many times when she rode with me on Sissy. All she talked about was getting a horse of her own."

Nick looked at the two of them. "Guess I have no choice other than to accept the gift." He checked his watch. "Time to round up Ace and head home. Let me know when you're coming my way. Can't wait to meet this brother of yours."

Slapping Nick on the back, he said. "I'm sure you'll find him interesting if nothing else."

On the trip home, Nick considered everything Dalton had told him. He became uncomfortable at the prospect of eliminating Jack. Still, he'd do whatever was necessary to protect Dalton and Joann if Jack turned out to be as evil as Dalton perceived him to be.

Each man grappled with his own issues. Dalton's were exposed while his remained hidden. His nightmares, apparent only to Carrie, caused him to wake, breathless, a choking sensation in his throat, the vision of Carmela and the faces of those he had slain over the years, taunting him, deadly intent in their eyes.

Nick pulled into the garage, then walked toward the house with Ace. A tremor traveled through him. He spun around expecting to see those men alive again, his mind torn between wanting to feel his familiar adrenaline rush which had served him so well and the need to expunge the memories of his many kills.

He stopped midway between the garage and the house. He needed to find a way to settle his past, not let his demons ruin the life he'd built with Carrie. If he wasn't careful, it could all slip away. Continuing, he went up the steps. Drawing a deep breath, he put a smile on his face, a disguise to mask all the torment building within, then he opened the front door.

Chapter 10

BIANCA

B ianca buttoned her jeans and slipped a heavy dark blue sweater over her head. She drew a tube of lip balm from her purse and swiped at her mouth. To make her story believable, she'd been living part-time in a small furnished apartment Miguel had her lease on Hill Street.

Shoving her feet into the tortuous boots, she snatched her coat from a hook by the front door and dashed outside.

Late afternoon sun reflected off the sleek black hood of the Cadillac. Miguel drummed his fingers against the steering wheel while she climbed in. He slid his DITA Aviator sunglasses below the bridge of his nose. His eyes narrowed to a pinprick.

"Must I always be waiting on you, Bianca?"

Nervous knots churned inside her stomach. "Sorry," was all she could muster. She'd gone to the restaurant for the past two weeks, becoming friendly with some of the staff who sympathized with her tale of desertion and betrayal by her boyfriend.

Miguel sped toward downtown, his eyes fixed on the road ahead. "This woman, this Sarah, you know where she lives?"

"*Sí*. The night we went out together, we stopped at her place."

"You are positive she resides alone?"

"*Sí*. I am certain."

"Have you noticed anything else?"

"The other day, at the restaurant, a handsome older man arrived with a younger one. Sarah said they were the owners."

"Why did you not mention this earlier? It must have been Nick and Bobby."

"I…I did not think of it until now."

He pounded his fist on the wheel. "Details are important, Bianca. This is no meager task we are undertaking. Did you have any interaction with them?"

"No. When I left, they were still eating their meal."

"Have you seen any of the children?"

"Not yet, but—"

"Listen carefully." His voice sliced through her words. "You must pay close attention at all times. The more information you can uncover, the better."

"I will, Miguel." She stroked his arm. "You can depend on me, *mi amor*," she said, attempting to diffuse his volcanic temper. Like molten lava boiling below the surface, anything might set it off.

When they reached downtown, he parked several blocks away from the restaurant and switched off the ignition. "Make plans with this Sarah tonight. Catch her alone. Perhaps in the rear parking lot. Be certain she does not get the chance to speak with anybody else. I will make sure the camera is out of commission."

"What kind of plans?"

"Tell her you know of a party outside of town. She has a car, no?"

Bianca nodded. "She drove it the last time we went out."

"Perfect. Drive to the house later tonight, then leave the rest to me."

Bianca chewed on her bottom lip. Things were becoming all too real. Still, she couldn't jeopardize her own plans. Crossing the border into the United States without Miguel's help would have been near impossible, not to mention dangerous. With Alejandro somewhere here, one day, she'd hold him in her arms again.

She walked the few blocks to *Buena Comida.* Inside, she waved at Sarah, then slid into a booth.

Sarah strutted over, ponytail swinging from side to side. "Hey girl, how are you doing?"

"Pretty good. I might have some job prospects."

"That's great. So, I guess you'll be hanging around then?"

"For now. I'm hoping things will work out." She ordered *Aguacate Relleno de Salmón.* She'd taken a liking to the avocado stuffed with cooked peas, corn, onion, carrots, salmon and seasoned with cilantro. She ate slowly, savoring the rich spices sliding across her tongue, making sure to finish near the end of Sarah's shift at four o'clock.

Bianca glanced around. Only a few customers remained, and the manager was nowhere in sight. By the time she finished eating, she'd become the sole patron, and the shift change had been completed. She paid cash for her meal before signaling Sarah. "Getting off soon?"

"In a bit. I agreed to help restock stations."

"I will wait and walk outside with you," Bianca said.

Thirty minutes later, they strolled around to the rear of the restaurant. Except for the evening shift employees' cars, the lot was deserted.

"I was invited to a party tonight, Sarah. Would you like to come?"

"I'm pretty beat. I waited on a large group earlier today. I think I'll go home and crash." She hit the unlock button on her key fob.

Bianca frowned. "There will be some nice people there. Friends of my ex. It is my first gathering since… the break-up."

Sarah hesitated. Undoing the clip on her ponytail, she shook her head, causing waves of long brown hair to fall below her shoulders. "And I'm the one who's been telling *you* to start going out more." She tapped Bianca's shoulder. "Okay, come on. Let's stop by my place. I need to change and freshen up, then we'll run by yours."

"I do not own any fancy dresses." Bianca pointed to her jeans and sweater. "This will have to do."

Sarah laughed. "No worries. We're about the same size. You can borrow something of mine. When does the party start?"

"Around seven."

"Good, we have plenty of time. Get in, and we'll go get pretty."

They arrived at Sarah's modest apartment on the corner of a dead-end street. Bianca surveyed the empty block. Inside, Sarah directed her to the closet while she showered. After she shut the bathroom door, Bianca sent Miguel a text telling him they would arrive a little before seven. He responded back with further instructions. Rummaging through Sarah's pocketbook, she drew out her cell phone and placed it in the nightstand draw.

Removing a red dress with some beading along the sleeves and a plunging neckline, she undressed and slipped it on. She checked herself in the full-length mirror. The dress showed off her ample cleavage and flattering figure. She wound her long hair into a knot, letting a few curls hang loose.

Sarah emerged, wrapped in a towel. "Wow, you look great! All you need are some heels. I'm not sure if any of mine will fit. Try a pair on."

Bianca rummaged through a pile of shoes lying on the floor of the closet, settling on a pair of red heels. They were a bit snug but doable.

Sarah sat at her dressing table and applied fresh make-up. She passed a brush through her blow-dried hair, then threw on a simple peacock blue shift, adding gold earrings, a gold chain with a four-leaf clover pendant, and a bangle bracelet. Glancing in the mirror, she smiled and said, "Well, not as killer as you, but not too shabby either."

Bianca's throat went dry. The air around her grew heavy. She wanted to run away, take her chances with Miguel so Sarah might live. For a moment, her knees threatened to buckle beneath her.

"What's wrong?" Sarah's voice cut through her rising panic.

"N…nothing," she said.

"You look like you're about to be sick."

Bianca forced a smile. "Nerves. I'm not used to going out without him."

"You need to start fresh. Think of tonight as a first step. I'll be right there with you." She picked up a bottle of perfume from her dresser.

"Here, try this."

"Thank you. You are such a good friend, Sarah." Bianca dabbed some on her wrists and behind each ear. The sweet blossomy scent of roses permeated the room.

"Okay, it's a little past six. How long is the drive?" Sarah asked.

"I am afraid it's over thirty minutes outside of town."

Sarah pulled a coat from the closet and tossed a long button-down cardigan to Bianca. "Good, then we have plenty of time to quiet your nerves."

Bianca gathered her things, and they headed out. She endured a mind-numbing drive while Sarah, radio blasting, chatted non-stop about their chances of getting lucky tonight. The closer they came to the house, the more the pressure building inside Bianca's chest swelled. She retreated farther into her seat under the crushing weight.

They snaked up the driveway and stopped. Darkness settled around them. Miguel's car sat outside. Light shone through the front windows of the house.

"Looks like we made it before anyone else." Sarah chirped. "Might work out, though. First dibs and all when the guys show."

They went up the steps. The door opened wide, and Miguel appeared, hands behind his back. Smiling, his face turned at an angle to hide his scar. He stepped aside and said, "Please come in."

Sarah tugged on Bianca's arm and whispered in her ear. "What a mysterious-looking guy. He's a bit older, though I love the accent."

The door shut behind them. Within seconds, Miguel's gloved hand cupped Sarah's mouth, his other arm came around her shoulders, pinning her against him. Her purse dropped to the floor. Eyes wide, she fought in a futile attempt to break free.

Bianca crept along the far wall, pressing her back against it. She could smell the fear in the room, foul and repulsive, wrapping itself around them. Sarah's eyes pleaded with her, and she looked away.

"Hold still!" Miguel ordered.

Tears spilling down her cheeks, Sarah stopped struggling. He released his hand from across her mouth. Her bottom lip quivered, and her breath heaved in and out.

"Please, please, let me go," she whimpered. "I won't tell anyone."

Miguel gripped her tighter. "I am afraid that is not possible."

"What do you want from us?" Sarah screeched.

"Us?" He grew silent for a moment. "Oh, I see." He cut his eyes at Bianca. "Tell her why you brought her here."

Frantic, Bianca tried to speak. Her throat closed while tremors racked her body.

"Never mind," Miguel growled. In one swift move, he placed his hand below Sarah's chin and the other behind her head, twisting it up, then sideways, snapping her neck.

The sickening crack felt like a blow to Bianca's gut as Sarah went limp. Shaking uncontrollably, she slid down the wall, collapsing onto the floor. A wave of nausea swept over her. Her pulse raced while her heart battered against her ribcage. She now understood how ruthless and evil Miguel really was.

Miguel eyed her. "Get up! What is wrong with you? Come help me."

Whimpering sounds invaded her ears. A moment went by before she realized they were coming from her.

"Bianca, I won't ask you again. Bring her purse." He grabbed Sarah by the hair and dragged her body outside.

Forcing herself to stand, she picked up the purse and followed him. Sarah lay face up on the ground. Her eyes, frozen with fear, were wide open, staring blankly at the dark sky.

Snatching the purse from Bianca, Miguel riffled through it, extracting her keys. "You did as I told you with her cell phone?" he asked.

Bianca nodded. "It is at her apartment."

Miguel popped the trunk of Sarah's car and dumped her inside, along with her purse, and slammed it shut. He flung his keys at Bianca. "Take the Cadillac and follow me. We need to get rid of the body."

Limbs shaking, Bianca climbed into the SUV. Headlights shone in the rearview while he swung Sarah's automobile around. She started the engine and pulled behind him, her eyes on his red taillights.

They drove a harrowing hour and a half, then pulled off the freeway onto a winding road. A few yards past a sign reading 'Crystal Lake,' Miguel drove into the sloped woodlands. Moonlight reflected off water in the distance.

Bianca parked a few feet away. With the engine still running, Miguel got out. He motioned for Bianca to slide her window down.

"Open the tailgate."

He removed a large towel from the Cadillac's rear and proceeded to wipe Sarah's car's interior and exterior. Reaching through the open window, he put the automobile in neutral before slamming the door shut. Planting himself behind the vehicle, he pushed it toward a steep slope. The car picked up speed and plunged into the water.

Unable to look away, Bianca watched it slip beneath the murky surface.

Miguel strode back to the SUV. "Get in the passenger seat."

She let him slide behind the wheel. They drove for a while before he spoke. "I cannot have you falling apart when I need you the most, Bianca. Can I count on your promise to help me or not?"

Clasping her hands in her lap to stop them from shaking, she said, "*Sí*, you can. Back there…at the house, I did not think everything would happen so fast."

"Fast? I have waited almost three years for this. You had better gather your strength, or things may become complicated."

They rode the rest of the way in silence. When they arrived, she could detect the weariness beneath the shadows on his face. He trudged ahead and went inside the house.

Bianca followed at a slow pace. A glint of light caught her eye. She bent, reaching for the object. Her breath hitched. Sarah's necklace laced her fingers. Shoving it into the pocket of the cardigan, she hurried up the steps.

Miguel's clothes were strewn about the bedroom floor. She removed Sarah's sweater and sat on the bed listening to the shower run. Glancing down, the red high heels caught her attention. She cast them off, kicking them underneath the bed with her bare feet.

Raising her wrist, she inhaled Sarah's perfume. Her eyes filled. She sucked in her breath, resisting the urge to scream. How could she put Sarah's murder behind her? Surely, Miguel expected… no, would demand it. So much bitterness flowed through his veins, all because of Carmela Santiago's death.

A few moments later, Miguel, a towel snug around his waist, drew her to her feet. Water dripped from the ends of his hair. He shoved his hand down the front of her dress and cupped her breast. He pressed against her, but her desire waned. Sex was the furthest thing from her mind.

"Take it off," he said.

Within minutes, she lay naked beneath him, his hips thrusting, driving himself deeper and deeper inside her. The pleasure she once experienced with him dissolved, replaced by the image of Sarah's body. Forcing herself to look into his dark eyes, terror rooted itself within her, surging up in waves, growing stronger each minute. She steeled herself. Miguel must not see her terror. It was the thing that drove him when he detected it in others.

Poor, innocent Sarah was gone. Taking a life meant nothing to him. How many more would perish before he finished with his plan of revenge?

He left her bruised and broken as she pulled the covers around herself. She needed to find Alejandro before *she* ended up beneath the black waters of a lake.

CHAPTER 11

CARRIE

Carrie hurried through the rear entrance of *Buena Comida*. After greeting Carlos and the kitchen crew, she continued into the dining room. Chatter from the lunch crowd swelled. The wait staff scribbled orders and served refreshments. Others balanced trays of food, navigating around tables. Busboys sailed in and out of the swinging doors, bearing tubs of soiled dishes. Rosie, the manager, waved from behind the bar, luminous brown eyes catching hers.

"Hey, Carrie."

Long skinny rows of braids were gathered at the nape of her slender neck by multicolored beads. The white-uniform blouse complimented her smooth dark skin. High cheekbones gave her a slightly regal look. Her slim figure and energetic nature belied her fifty years.

Rosie came to them with loads of experience. They had been lucky enough to lure her away from a five-star restaurant and relied heavily on her expertise.

Carrie dropped onto one of the few empty bar stools. "How are things going?" She wriggled out of her jacket and readjusted the sleeves of her print silk blouse.

Rosie placed several bottles of alcohol on the shelf behind her. "Except for one MIA, we're good."

Carrie paused, her eyebrows knitting. "Who?"

"Sarah didn't show up and never called. I swear this younger generation nowadays…no sense of responsibility at times. Girl, you wouldn't believe the excuses I've heard when someone does call in."

"Has it happened before?"

"With Sarah? Not that I can recall. I tried her cell and left several messages on her voicemail. I told Alice if we don't hear from her by day's end, she should run by Sarah's place."

Carrie surveyed the room. In the far corner, she recognized the woman sitting alone at a table. She'd been hanging around the restaurant lately, and she remembered her speaking with Sarah on occasion.

"I'll be right back, Rosie." Nodding at several regulars, she made her way over to her. "Hello, how are you today?"

Bianca glanced up from her bowl of *sancocho*, a soup consisting of meat, corn, potatoes, and yucca. "Fine." She scooped up a spoonful of white rice, dumping it into the soup.

Carrie extended her hand. "I'm Carrie D'Angelo, one of the owners."

Bianca set her spoon down and shook Carrie's hand. "Bianca Flores."

"Sorry to interrupt your meal. Can I speak with you for a moment?"

She pointed to the chair across from her. "Please, sit."

"I notice you've been coming in quite often," Carrie began. "I observed you speaking with a few of the staff."

"*Sí*, they have been very understanding."

"Understanding?"

Her eyes watered. "My boyfriend deserted me some time ago. We were to marry."

"Oh, I'm so sorry. Perhaps you're better off without him."

"It is what Sarah keeps telling me. Is she here today?"

"Well, I was about to ask if you had heard from her."

"I did see her yesterday. We talked briefly. She invited me to a party last night, but I was not up for it."

Carrie leaned back into her chair. "A party? Where?"

"She did not say. Is there something wrong?"

"Sarah didn't show up today, and she hasn't called."

Bianca's brow creased. "Oh?"

"If you hear from her, please let me or someone else on the staff know?"

"Of course. I am sure Sarah is okay. Maybe the party went on a little too long."

"Could be," Carrie said and rose. "But I would feel better knowing she's alright. Nice meeting you, Bianca."

"Nice meeting you, too." She lowered her head and continued eating.

Carrie finished consulting with Rosie on a few matters, then drove home. Nick seemed distant lately. She wanted to spend time with him and the children, make sure they all ate dinner together.

*   *   *   *

Following a meal full of Izzy and Michael's chatter, she relaxed with Nick on the patio, drinking wine while Valentina helped the children bathe and get ready for bed.

Carrie set her glass aside and leaned into the cushions of the love seat. "Are you okay?"

He offered a half-smile. "Fine. Why do you ask?"

"It's just… you seem a little off."

Nick swallowed some wine. "Babe, believe me, I'm fine."

Dare she mention the moaning in his sleep, the night sweats she observed? Why was he holding back? Deciding to push further, she said, "You're not sleeping well."

He stared into his glass before meeting her eyes. "I think about the past…some of the things I've done. You can't help, and I refuse to burden you with it. In time, I'll figure it out."

"Maybe you need to talk to someone."

"Talk to someone?" he scoffed. "Are you kidding me?" He drained the last of his wine and fell silent.

"I just meant—"

"Carrie don't be ridiculous. I can't talk to anyone about this. What? Tell them, hey, I used to kill people for a living, and now I'm having nightmares." He drew the bottle of wine from the patio table and poured a second glass.

Pressing her lips together, she glanced away. Of course, he couldn't speak to anyone on the outside. She stroked his arm. "You're right, only I hate seeing you suffer. I want to help, but I'm frustrated as to how."

He found her hand and squeezed it. "And I love you all the more for it."

"There is one person you can confide in. Dalton."

"I considered it. But it's not a good time. Dalton's having issues of his own. Seems his older brother, Jack, showed up unexpectedly. Loads of history there, none of it favorable."

"Oh? He never mentioned a brother."

"And with good reason. I won't go into all the particulars, but I have a feeling Jack's stay isn't going to be pleasant for him or Joann."

Carrie's cell buzzed. She picked it up and read the name. "Hi, Alice. Did you stop by Sarah's? What? Yes, I agree, it is strange. Please call me if you hear anything." She hung up and looked at Nick.

"Sarah didn't show up for work today. No one's heard from her."

"Not like her," Nick said.

"I agree. Alice went by her place. Her car is gone, and she didn't answer the door. I have this awful feeling."

"Pull up her employee records. Find out if her family has had any contact with her."

Carrie finished her wine. "Okay. But they live in Colorado. I hate to alarm them."

"If it were Izzy, would you want someone to call?"

"I see your point." She went inside to the den and sat at the desk. Hesitating for a second, she marveled at how far she'd come. The days of her being computer illiterate were behind her. When they agreed to help Bobby, a few courses brought her up to speed. She searched for Sarah's information, then picked up the landline.

A few minutes later, she returned to the patio. "Well, they haven't heard from her. I told them I'd keep them posted. If she doesn't show up tomorrow, I'm going to file a missing person's report."

Nick sighed. "Hopefully, that won't be necessary."

Carrie sat, snuggling close. She rested her head against his shoulder. "Do you remember our first night on the patio drinking wine at Dalton's house? We were pretty much strangers."

He kissed the top of her head. "I sure do. One of the best nights of my life."

"Nick, no matter what you've done in the past, I believe all those things were destined to happen because they brought us together. You saved me from Travis. If that brings you any comfort at all, hold on to it and what we have built over the years."

She raised her head and met his eyes. "I love you."

"What would I do without you?" he said softly. Bending, he kissed her gently at first, then with more urgency, his hand sweeping through her hair and down her back. Pulling her to her feet, he led her upstairs.

Their desire for each other renewed, she clung to him in the darkness, determined to heal the wounds lying deep within his soul. She wouldn't let his demons win. At least not tonight.

*   *   *   *

The following day, with no word from Sarah, Carrie filed a report. The detective advised her to expect interviews with her employees and anyone else connected to Sarah.

When she arrived at *Buena Comida*, Bianca rushed over to her. "Mrs. D'Angelo, do you remember me?"

"Of course. Bianca? Right?"

"*Sí*. Have you heard from Sarah?"

"Sadly, no. I filed a police report."

"Is it serious?"

"I'm afraid, so. It's been over twenty-four hours during which we've been unable to contact her. You may have been the last person to see her. I'm sure the police will want to talk to you."

"Anything I can do to help, Mrs. D'Angelo."

Carrie tapped her lightly on the shoulder. "I appreciate that."

"Here, let me give you my number."

She put Bianca's number into her phone, then made her way into the small office at the rear of the dining room where Rosie entered inventory into a computer, her red-polished fingernails flying across the keyboard. The long braids were gone, leaving her hair hanging in coiled ringlets around her face. She glanced up at Carrie.

"File the report?"

"Yes. I hope they find her, and she's alright."

Rosie stopped typing and sighed. "Don't go getting your hopes up. I'm uncomfortable with the idea of her having gone to a party no one else here attended. It goes against the norm. They're a pretty tight-knit group."

"It is strange, isn't it? With young people, you can't always be certain what they'll do."

"True," Rosie said. A broad smile creased her otherwise seamless skin. "I can remember some of the dumb stuff I tried to hide from my mama and daddy when I ran the streets."

Carrie laughed. "You…running the streets?"

"Girl, you have no idea how bad I was at times. It's a wonder I finally pulled myself together and got my degree." She eyeballed Carrie. "What about you? Have a wild past you're hiding?"

A flutter hit the pit of Carrie's stomach. She broke eye contact and pretended to check her watch before answering. All those awful memories of Arizona and of course, Travis, were better left private, scars invisible to the outside world but never forgotten. "No, nothing out of the ordinary," she said. "I was only fifteen when I gave birth to Bobby. Some people might call it a mistake, but I never regretted it."

"Bobby's a good guy. You're lucky." Rosie leaned back into the chair. "Look, I don't want to jump the gun, but we're minus one in the dining room without Sarah. We'll need another server, and Jim just informed me he'll be giving notice. He's going back to California. It will leave us short a bartender, too."

Carrie rubbed her temples. Employee turnover in the restaurant business was always an issue. "Let's give it until the end of this week, at least. Then we'll revisit the situation."

"You're the boss," Rosie said. "By the way, the parking lot camera is out. I'll have it repaired as soon as possible."

* * * *

The week sped by while the police began interviewing the employees. Sarah's parents flew in, and Carrie offered her home to them, but they insisted on staying at Sarah's apartment in case she returned. Carrie couldn't imagine what they were feeling. When she lost Bobby all those years ago, at least she knew what her mother had done. Sarah's parents were living with the agony of not knowing what happened to their daughter.

As much as she hated to do it, she agreed with Rosie, and they posted a sign in the window. Later that day, Bianca applied for a job. They decided with Bianca's server and bartending experience, she'd be an asset.

"Poor thing," Carrie said, watching Bianca leave. "Her one good friend is missing. She told me she felt bad applying for the position, but if she didn't find a job soon, she'd have to leave and look elsewhere. All her paperwork is in order, so I guess we're set."

"I'll put her behind the bar tomorrow," Rosie said. "Time will tell if we made the right decision."

Carrie gave Rosie a quick hug before slipping on her coat. "I want you to know how much we appreciate you."

Rosie chuckled. "My paycheck is proof enough. The fact is, you, Nick and Bobby, are some of the finest people I've worked for."

"If you're ever unhappy here—"

"Oh, don't you worry," Rosie cut in. "Trust me, you'll be the first to know if I'm feeling unappreciated." She ushered Carrie toward the door. "Now go on home to that handsome husband of yours. Gotta get me one just like him someday before I'm too old," she said with a wink.

"It's never too late," Carrie said, winking back before heading out. Having run some errands earlier, she had parked out front. On the sidewalk, she paused in mid-stride. Sarah's smiling face beamed at her from a utility pole, one of the many missing person leaflets plastered all over downtown. The wind whipped around the corner, stirring a pile of fallen leaves. A chill ran through her. Sarah could be anywhere out there, hurt, or suffering, or… stopping her mind from going any further, she looked at the poster again, then up at the sky. "Please bring Sarah back," she whispered before getting into her car for the drive home.

CHAPTER 12

MIGUEL

Miguel studied Bianca's sleeping face. Had he made a mistake, including her in his plans? While she displayed a tough exterior, she turned out to be a weak-minded woman who could not stomach the necessary evils of this world.

He flung the covers back and tugged on a pair of jeans. Morning light flooded the kitchen while he prepared a pot of coffee. Bianca had done well in securing the job at *Buena Comida*, the first step in her gaining their trust while gathering the information he needed, but she had an interview with the police later today, and it troubled him. If she broke down, all his plans would fall apart.

"Buenos Días, Miguel."

Bianca padded over to him, sleep still settled in her dark eyes, her pink bathrobe cinched tight around her waist. A mannerism unfamiliar to him.

Even though she denied it, things had changed between them since the night he eliminated Sarah. He did not think it would matter to him, but somehow it did.

"Buenos Días." He poured some coffee and passed the cup to her.

"Gracias."

She drew out a chair while he placed cream and sugar on the table and sat across from her. "Are you ready for today?"

Bianca averted her eyes while she stirred sugar into her coffee. "*Sí.*"

"There are many questions they could ask. You need to be prepared to give them the right answers. Let us practice one more time."

Bianca squirmed, then gulped some coffee.

"How long have you known Sarah?"

"Almost a month."

"When did you see her last?"

"At the restaurant."

He slapped his palm on top of the table. She flinched and drew back.

"No, Bianca. You must be more precise in case anyone spotted you in the parking lot."

"Miguel, you are making me nervous." She tugged at the sash on her robe.

His brow arched. "You cannot afford to be nervous. Now continue."

"I last saw Sarah in the parking lot of the restaurant."

His ire rising, he tried to calm himself. "And?"

"She invited me to a party."

"And where was this party?"

"She did not say. She was invited by some new people she met."

"Did you attend the party?"

She shook her head.

Miguel gritted his teeth. "You *must speak*, not nod."

"No. I was too tired."

"Had she ever mentioned any of these so-called new people before?"

Bianca started to shake her head, then caught herself. "No, not to me."

"Did she mention a steady boyfriend?"

"No."

"Look, Bianca. I am not trying to make this difficult. Whatever you say, you cannot arouse their suspicions or lead them here to me. I do not think you relish spending the rest of your life in prison."

"Prison? No, of course not."

Miguel eased up from the table. "Come here." He trailed his palm along her cheek. "I do not wish to be cruel. I care for you. But I must be sure we will always protect each other."

She held his hand in hers and kissed his bare chest. "Of course. You are never to doubt my love for you. The night Sarah died, I did not do so well. I needed time to process everything."

"And now?"

"I can see your plan more clearly. You did what was necessary. There was no other way I could apply for the job at *Buena Comida*."

"Good," he said. "Stay focused today. All will be fine. The next time Nick's wife arrives, you must become acquainted with her. Inquire about the children in a casual conversation. I need to know where the daughter attends school and if Natalia is with them or with her father."

Miguel paused, then undid the sash on her robe. His hand traveled up between her thighs, and she let out a moan. He lifted her up onto the counter. His fingers traced her hard nipples, and she arched her back. Forcing his tongue between her lips, he kissed her long and deep, then unzipped his jeans. She wrapped her legs around his waist. When he entered her, she cried out, her fingers digging into the muscled flesh on his shoulder blades. His desire intensified. He thrust his hips, and they peaked together.

Finished, he eased her off the counter. This was the Bianca he had become accustomed to. He pulled her closer, and she rested her body against his.

If only he could count on her. These last years filled with waiting for his time to settle things were long, hard ones for him. Nothing on earth could deter him from avenging Carmela's death.

Of course, when everything settled, if Bianca did not prove to be the strong woman he needed, one who could stomach his way of life, he'd make her death quick and painless.

But right now, he needed her. Miguel stroked her hair. *"Mi amor,"* he said. "You will not let me down."

She looked up, her eyes once again filled with fire. "I promise," she whispered.

CHAPTER 13

JACK

Jack wandered over to the barn, a cigarette in his hand. Having seen Joann lead one of the horses inside earlier, it was time to cozy up to the woman of the household. So far, in his opinion, they were getting along well. During their trip into town, he made certain to remain a gentleman, loading the groceries and opening the truck door for her.

He maintained polite conversation until the drive home proved rather unsettling when he checked the rearview mirror. A Lincoln Sedan followed a close distance behind. When it swung up a side road, the twist in his gut eased.

Vigilant on his journey up from Nevada, he remained confident nobody was chasing his heels. An acrid taste tinged his tongue knowing Dalton wouldn't bail him out this time.

He drew in one last drag before crushing the lit cigarette beneath his shoe. Inside the barn, he ignored the odor dredging up memories from his youth. Made to do daily chores under his father's watchful eye, he could never understand how anyone tolerated life on a ranch with all the hard work involved.

Joann was settling Sissy in her stall. She secured the latch and approached, boots tapping on the wood floor, a bridle in her hands.

"Morning, Jack." She hung the bridle on one of the hooks by the far wall.

Giving her his best smile, he said, "How was your ride?"

"Wonderful. Got in some quiet time. I snuck off today, just Sissy and me. Your brother doesn't care for me riding alone. He generally sends someone with me when he can't come himself."

Jack held a finger to his lips and winked. "Mum's the word. He'll never hear it from me. I understand why you'd like a little solitude. I'm the same way at times."

They strolled out together. Joann stopped to brush some trail dust off the bottom of her jeans. "Can I ask you something, Jack?"

"Sure, anything."

"It was obvious Dalton wasn't thrilled you were coming. I don't like seeing my man upset. Can you enlighten me a bit?"

Jack hung his head and stared at the ground for a moment. "I won't lie to you. I have a troubled past I'm rather ashamed of. Heck, one of the main reasons for wanting to see my brother is to show him I've changed." He cleared his throat and met her eyes. "Those bleak times are behind me, only I'm afraid it's going to take some convincing where Dalton is concerned."

"I'm certain he'll come around," Joann said. "Dalton's softer than you think."

"Sure hope you're right. I wouldn't want to move on, knowing he still thought ill of me. He's the only family I have left after…"

Joann touched his arm. "What is it, Jack?"

"Like I said, I simply want to resolve our differences before I move on."

"I think it would be good for the two of you to reconcile." Her eyes grew soft. She headed for the house.

The seeds of sympathy were sown, and Jack was confident they'd grow. People in Vegas would soon lose patience. His palms leaking sweat, he pulled out his pack of cigarettes and lit one. Taking a deep drag, he exhaled and followed the stream of smoke with his eyes. He'd heard about what happens to those who owe the kind of money he did. He cringed inside at the image of a broken arm, leg, or smashed fingers and a whole host of other tortuous methods used to collect a debt.

But he needed to remain confident. His debts would be settled, things would turn around—no more running and hiding. No more living a hardscrabble life, depending on the kindness of others to get by. The time to cash in his chips was drawing near, and his brother was one of those chips.

CHAPTER 14

BIANCA

Bianca checked the ice bin before moving on to the small tubs of lime and lemon wedges. She had aced the police interview more out of fear of Miguel than the law. Since Sarah's death, her intuition told her he had become aware of her lack of desire, prompting her to try to convince him her passion remained the same. She couldn't afford to have him think otherwise.

A male customer signaled for a refill. She poured him a shot of Johnnie Walker Black Label. Before she could pull her hand away, he covered it with his.

"You're a charming young lady. A refreshing change from Jim. Whatever happened to him?"

She drew her hand back, forcing a smile. "He left for California."

"California is nice. Ever been?"

"No, maybe someday, I will." Working at *Buena Comida* for a little over a week, she managed to keep flirtatious men in check so far.

"By the way, love your accent." He winked and downed the shot.

To her relief, Beth approached with drink orders. Bianca mixed gin, simple syrup, plus lime juice for a perfect gimlet, then shook and strained it into a cocktail glass. She added two draft beers to the tray and a mojito.

"How's it going?" Beth asked.

"Good. I am getting used to things."

"That's great." Beth picked up the tray and headed for a booth in the far corner.

Bianca wiped up a spill before readying some dirty beer mugs for the kitchen while the lunch crowd thinned. About to take a break, she stopped when Carrie walked through the swinging doors of the kitchen holding the hand of a cute little girl with long black hair and a backpack slung across her shoulders.

Carrie pointed to a booth. "Start your homework. Your father will be here soon." She unbuttoned her navy wool blazer and sat at the bar, tossing her handbag onto the stool next to her.

"Hello, Mrs. D'Angelo. I did not realize you were coming in today."

"I hadn't planned on it, but Rosie called. Two deliveries came up short again, and one of the cooks is out. We were in town already, so I decided to swing by."

"Can I get you something?" Bianca asked.

"A glass of white wine would be heaven. Maybe some Pinot Grigio?"

Bianca poured the wine and set the glass down. Fascinated by Carrie's eyes ever since the first time they spoke, she couldn't help focusing on them. She'd never seen ones such deep blue, almost violet in color.

Carrie picked up the glass and sipped. "Tastes wonderful after such a hectic day." She paused. "Is something wrong?"

Bianca felt herself blush. "I am sorry for staring. You have beautiful eyes."

"It's okay, Bianca. Thank you. I'm used to people commenting on them."

Bianca pointed to the booth. "Is she your daughter?"

"Yes. That's Isabelle. We call her Izzy. I have a girl and two boys. My husband and I are also grandparents."

"No! Impossible."

"It's possible, alright," Carrie said. "I had my son, Bobby, when I was quite young. He has a little girl of his own named Natalia. He's also a part-owner here."

"I have not met him."

"No, he lives in New York with Natalia. She used to live with us." Carrie sighed. "We do miss her, but she belongs with her father."

"If you do not mind my asking, what about the child's mother?"

A shadow passed over Carrie's face. "She died when Natalia was an infant."

"Oh, it is terrible when a child loses a parent."

"I agree."

"How old are your little ones?"

"Izzy is nine, and Michael is six."

"Such fun ages," Bianca said. "I have no children of my own, only several nieces and nephews back in Mexico. I miss them sometimes."

"I'm sure you do. It must be tough living here without any family."

"I wish I could bring them here for a better life. There are good schools here in America. They are nice, no?"

"Well, Michael is still being homeschooled, and Izzy used to attend public school. Seems she became bored. Her teachers suggested we take a different route. We were lucky to find a

Montessori school nearby. It employs a more child-centered approach and... I'm sorry, Bianca. I'm rattling on." She took another sip of wine. "Glad to see you're settling in. The customers really like you."

"Thank you. I do my best."

Carrie finished her wine and glanced out the front window. "I need to get going. My husband just pulled up." She scooped up her purse, then called to Izzy, who collected her books and hurried over to the bar.

"Izzy, say hello to Bianca."

Her green eyes sparkled. "Hello, it's nice to meet you, Bianca."

"It is nice to meet you, too, Izzy."

Bianca watched them walk out. What a perfect life Carrie had. Such a handsome husband and children. Some people were born lucky. She imagined Carrie never had to suffer at the hands of a man like Miguel or do without. Sighing, she removed the empty wine glass and placed it on the dirty rack.

Rosie appeared and sailed past. "Be right back. Need to run an errand," she called over her shoulder.

Bianca stepped from behind the bar. She glanced around. Most of the wait staff were gone on a meal break before the dinner rush. Only a few lingered inside one of the booths. She made her way to Rosie's office and couldn't believe her luck when she discovered it unlocked.

She examined the call sheet lying on the desk. Names, addresses, and telephone numbers for the employees were printed in neat columns. At the top were Carrie, Nick, and Bobby's phone numbers. She snapped a picture with her cell. A shelf across the room held a photograph of Izzy and Carrie in a silver frame. She snapped that, too and quickly returned to the bar.

Thirty minutes later, on break, she relaxed in a quiet corner of the restaurant. Miguel will be pleased with all the information she learned today. All she wanted more than anything was to get the entire business over with.

Opening her purse, she dug behind the lining and drew out one of the letters. A letter written by Alejandro filled with promises for their future together. Smoothing the worn pages, her eyes misted. She traced the last line with her fingertip. Her lips mouthed the words, *'Estoy esperando por ti mi amor.'* I am waiting for you, my love.

The night of the fight in Mexico played in her mind. A man had flirted with her in front of Alejandro, who became furious. Within minutes, an argument ensued between the two outside the bar, Alejandro knocking him to the ground where the back of his head hit the hard cement causing his death.

Later, they learned he was the son of a prominent man in Mexico City, leaving Alejandro no choice but to flee. With the money they saved for their wedding, he paid to cross the border into the United States, promising to send for her.

His letters began arriving while he searched for work in his new country, void of a return address for fear someone in Mexico would question her and come looking for him. When his letters stopped, her faith in him never wavered. Alejandro would never forsake her.

Once Miguel had Natalia, she could leave him to begin her search. With America such a vast country, trying to locate Alejandro could take a long time, but her love for him would sustain her. Leaving behind her family in Mexico was worth everything to be with him again. She folded the letter, tucking it back into the lining with the others.

Feeling the void left by Sarah, Bianca scanned the room. Would someone discover the car... the body decomposing inside? A shiver ran through her. If she wasn't careful, she could end up like Sarah.

That awful night still vivid in her mind, she cautioned herself not to let Miguel become aware of how much the murder had affected her. At times, the sound of Sarah's neck snapping replayed itself in her dreams.

Several nights she had woken, drenched in sweat, her body shaking as she peered over at Miguel, fast asleep.

Bianca returned to the bar. Best not to dwell on what could happen and concentrate on the present. The sooner Miguel finished things, the better. She could feel herself inching closer to Alejandro.

CHAPTER 15

BOBBY

At eight in the morning, Bobby, dressed in a t-shirt and pajama bottoms, perched on the edge of Natalia's bed. He delighted in his daughter's sleeping face. Sweeping away, the lock of curls spilling across her forehead, momentary tears stung his eyes. If only Carmela could see their sweet little girl.

He had made the right decision in moving her home. She got along well with Maggie, and with his determination to keep Natalia's heritage alive, she taught her Spanish while Bobby learned along with her. In between helping to manage the restaurants, working with his art clientele, and occasional flights to the Napa winery, he devoted his free time to Natalia.

They took walks in Central Park, went on outings to the zoo, and visited puppet shows at Penny Jones and Company Puppet Theater in the West Village. He couldn't wait until she became old enough to be introduced to the many art museums he frequented. Planting a light kiss on her cheek, he went into the kitchen. It was Friday, one of Maggie's days off and he anticipated spending it with Natalia.

His mother was due to fly in later this morning, her sudden desire to visit piquing his curiosity. Bobby had assured her the restaurant was running smooth, and Natalia had settled in. Still, she insisted on coming. Rather than argue, he stopped protesting. He prepared a cup of coffee, sat, and opened the New York Times. A sleepy Natalia tiptoed toward him. Pulling her onto his lap, he planted a kiss on top of her head.

"Morning, Natty. Did you sleep okay?"

She rubbed her eyes. "Yes. Is Maggie here?"

"No, it's her day off. But Grandma will be here soon."

"Grandma is coming?"

"Yes. How about some breakfast? Cereal or pancakes, maybe?"

"Pancakes, please. With Mickey ears."

He placed her in a chair at the table. "Mickey ear pancakes coming right up."

Bobby mixed batter and poured it onto a heated skillet. He formed a circle, then joined two smaller ones on the top edge to form ears. The aroma of a pancake sizzling filled the kitchen as Mickey Mouse's head took shape.

Reaching for a plate from the overhead cabinet, he flipped the pancake onto it and carried it with a fork and maple syrup to the table. "Here you go. Milk or orange juice?"

"Milk," she replied, grinning.

While she ate, he threw on jeans and the navy cashmere sweater Carrie bought him one Christmas.

After Natalia finished most of her pancake, he dressed her, then brushed her hair, letting it fall in loose waves landing just above her waist. When the buzzer rang, Natalia rushed to answer it. She snatched the small stool Bobby kept for her by the door, climbed on, and pressed the intercom button. "Good morning, Hank."

An audible chuckle could be heard before Hank's voice came through the speaker.

"There is a lady here to see you. Sez, she's your grandma."

"Let her up, please, Hank," she said, hopping off the stool.

A few minutes later, the doorbell sounded. Natalia tore open the door and threw herself at Carrie. "Grandma, you're here!"

Carrie set her overnight bag aside and gathered her close. "I've missed you." She kissed Natalia's cheek and stroked her hair.

"You smell good," Natalia said, giggling.

"I hope so." Carrie let go of Natalia and gave Bobby a hug. "How are things going?" She removed her long winter coat, revealing a pair of beige slacks and a cream-colored sweater. Brown leather boots covered her feet.

"We're both doing great."

"Wonderful."

He hung her coat in the foyer closet. "I'll put your bag in the spare bedroom."

"I don't mind staying at a hotel."

Bobby looked at Natalia. "We want Grandma to stay here with us, right?"

Natalia jumped up and down. "You have to, Grandma."

"Okay then, I'll stay."

Over the next hour, the three of them sat on the floor of Natalia's room, pretending to drink tea out of miniature porcelain cups. When they finished their tea party, Carrie said, "I have a present for you, Natty." She retrieved her overnight bag. Removing a package wrapped in multicolored paper, she handed it to Natalia and sat back down.

Bobby's eyebrow arched. "Mom, you didn't have to bring her anything."

Carrie pointed her finger at him. "She's mine to spoil. It's what grandparents are for, so deal with it," she said, laughing.

Natalia tugged at the red ribbon and tore off the wrapper. "Daddy, look." She held up a doll with long auburn braids dressed in riding apparel. Also, inside the box lay a plastic horse with a golden yellow mane and tail.

"Your mommy used to love to ride horses, sweetheart," Carrie said. "Maybe one day, you can ride, too."

Bobby's heart swelled at the sight of the gift his mother brought. Despite all the hurt Carmela caused her, she'd never held a grudge, just one of the things he loved about her. He looked at Natalia. "Natty, what do you say?"

"Thank you." She set the doll aside and hugged Carrie's neck. "I love it."

"You play with your doll for a little bit while I talk with Grandma."

Bobby dropped onto the sofa in the living room and Carrie sat in a chair across from him.

"Listen," he began. "I need a favor. You can say no. You do enough for me already."

"What kind of favor?"

"Can you watch Natty later tonight for a few hours?" He hesitated, deciding what to tell her. "I need to see a friend."

A sly smile curled her lips. "Oh, might it be a lady friend? I'm glad you're getting back out there."

"I hate to disappoint you. No, nothing like that. This person may be in trouble."

She clasped her hands together and leaned forward. "Bobby, look, I won't pry, but before you get involved in someone else's problems, remember you have a daughter to consider."

He swiped at the lock of hair dipping below his right eye. "I'd never do anything that might harm Natalia or me. I just need to check on this friend and make sure they're okay."

"Do I know this person?"

"No," he lied, not wanting alarm bells going off in his mother's head if he told her it was Ronnie. Since the night they went to the club over two weeks ago, he hadn't seen her, and she failed to answer his calls. He'd received only one text saying she was busy with work and would speak to him soon.

"I don't mind taking care of Natty. Just remember what I said."

"Thanks. By the way, what made you fly in today other than to see us?" She shifted in the chair, her eyes avoiding his.

"Mom?"

"I promised I would never lie to you again. There is something I need to do here in New York."

"What?"

She moved to the windows overlooking the park. Bobby followed and stood next to her, waiting for an answer.

Without looking at him, she said, "I came to confront my father... your grandfather."

A wave of adrenaline coursed through him. "My grandfather?" She'd hardly mentioned him before, other than to say she never knew him. "Who is he? How did you locate him?"

"He wasn't hard to find. Aunt May explained things about his relationship with your grandmother. It seems he's a pretty prominent person. He runs a major brokerage firm here in the city."

"Wow! Why didn't you tell me before now?"

Letting out a sigh, she faced him. "Because I wasn't ready to. I haven't even told Nick yet. This is something I must do. Just like you needed answers all those years ago, so do I."

He touched her arm. "How can I help?"

"For now, when you speak to Nick, don't mention it. He has enough going on."

Bobby folded his arms. "What do you mean? He seemed fine the last time I saw him."

"Yeah, he puts on a good front, but he's hurting, Bobby."

Panic gripped him. "Is he sick?"

Her eyes watered. "Physically, no, but his mental state is not good. His past is catching up with him."

Bobby peered out at the skyscrapers in the distance. "I can't imagine the body count he's dealing with."

"Please, don't say anything, Bobby. He'll shut down even further. I suggested he talk to Dalton. He would understand, only it seems he has a long-lost brother visiting with issues of his own."

"I'm sorry for what he's going through," Bobby said. "He's been good to me, always treated me like a son. It hurts to know he's suffering."

"I'm glad we talked. I needed to tell someone." They stood in silence for a few moments before Carrie spoke again. "I have to ask you something?"

Bobby's stomach twisted, almost certain of what she was about to say. "Sure."

"How did Carmela die…what happened? Did Nick…?"

Bobby's heart lurched. Whenever anyone mentioned Carmela's name, the ache inside returned. He forced himself to push it away and focus.

Carrie wrung her hands. "I mean, he has a scar from a bullet wound, and I have no idea how he was shot. No one will talk about Tahoe. I know it's hard, but it may help me to understand things."

He met his mother's eyes. It wasn't his responsibility to tell her what Nick wouldn't, but he needed to ease her anxiety. "No, Carmela got in the way when no one expected it... caught in the crossfire, you could say. But not ours."

"You were right there, weren't you, Bobby?" she said, trying to keep her voice steady. "It must have been awful."

"It was more horrible than you can imagine." His eyes filled, blurring his vision. "In those last minutes, when I held her, I *knew* she loved me." He swiped at his tears and took a deep breath.

Carrie's arms encircled him. "I'm sorry. I'm only trying to understand. I wish I could make all the hurt go away." She stepped back and studied his face.

"I really don't want to revisit that night," he said. "It's too painful. But promise me, if you need my help with Nick or with your father, you'll tell me."

"Yes, I promise." She stood on tiptoe, cupped his face, and kissed his cheek. "I'm sorry. I know how much you cared for Carmela. You're a wonderful son, Bobby. How did I ever get so lucky?"

Warmth rushed to his cheeks. "And I couldn't have asked for a better mother."

*   *   *   *

Just before sunset, Bobby hailed a taxi for the trip across town to Ronnie's place. He exited the cab into the cool, brisk air and hurried inside. About to press her buzzer, the door flew open. The sour expression on Ronnie's face didn't go unnoticed. He hid his shock at the sight of her pale face above the blue-flowered bathrobe and her apparent weight loss. A faint bluish tint stained her lower eyelids. He braced himself for the worst.

"Bobby, what are you doing here?"

"How'd you know?"

"I watched you get out of the cab."

"Can you at least let me in?"

"Sorry." She stepped aside.

He eyeballed the duffle bag sitting on the entryway floor. "Going somewhere?"

"As a matter of fact, yes. A weekend thing with some friends. I was about to shower."

Alarmed at the sight of her once neat apartment now in disarray, he advanced into the living room where clothes were strewn haphazardly across the sofa. Empty wine bottles and half-eaten food containers littered the coffee table. He eyeballed the residue of a white substance against the dark wood. He pointed at the table.

"Ronnie, what the hell are you doing?"

Hands clutching her hips, she narrowed her eyes. "Frankly, if I choose to do a little coke, it's none of your business!"

"When you look like crap and your place is a mess, I'm making it my business. I thought you were smarter than that."

"Quit trying to play the hero. I'm not your damsel in distress."

He forced down his rising anger. "I care about you. I only want to help."

"Help? Then, stop interfering. I'm a big girl. I can take care of myself."

"It looks like you're doing a hell of a job at it," he shot back.

She stomped to the door and tore it open. "Please leave, Bobby."

Drawing in a breath, he tried to placate her. "Ronnie, talk to me. I would never judge you."

"That's a load of crap. What do you call all those things you said a few minutes ago? Sounded pretty judgmental to me coming from someone who used to sleep with one of the biggest and sleaziest drug lords in the country."

His heart skidded in his chest, her words wounding him to his core. "How could you say that to me? I wasn't aware of the drugs until way later."

"Oh, boo hoo, Bobby! Don't come around here laying your holier than thou attitude on me. Stay out of my affairs."

"Ronnie, this isn't you. Tell me what's wrong."

"For the last time. I don't want or need your help. I'm perfectly fine."

"No, you're not."

He paused in the doorway and searched her eyes, catching a glimpse of fear inside them. Something or someone had a hold on her. "We've always been honest with each other, so go on, Ronnie, get mad. I don't care. I'm here for you whenever you're ready."

Outside, his heart broke. Ronnie was headed down the rabbit hole, and it appeared there was nothing he could do to stop her.

CHAPTER 16

VERONICA

Ronnie slammed the door and dissolved into tears. She slid onto the floor, her back pressed against the hard wood.

What had she done? She never meant to say those horrible things to Bobby. He still loved Carmela. He'd never forgive her.

Her life was a mess, and she had no clue how to fix it. Coke remained the sole comfort getting her through the day.

She eased up and stared at the duffel bag. Ten bricks of cocaine lay inside, each brick a kilo worth twenty-five thousand dollars to be delivered to an address in Baltimore. Derek would pick up the cash tomorrow.

This was her fourth drop, each one more nerve-rattling than the one before. Monitoring her speed and checking the rearview for cops were among the many pitfalls of a mule. Images of the criminals she encountered became etched in her mind.

Ronnie showered and changed into jeans and a white blouse. She placed the revolver inside her purse, then threw on a blazer. Collecting the duffel, she left her building and tossed it into the trunk of her car. Leaving the city lights behind, she headed for the New Jersey Turnpike, where she'd pick up I95.

Three hours later, under an ebony sky speckled with stars, she pulled up to a line of row houses. Easing out of the car, she slung her purse over her shoulder, and double-checked the address, then scanned the street before removing the duffle.

Insides trembling, she climbed up the steps and pressed the bell. A face appeared from behind the front window curtain. Moments later, the lock snapped, and the door swung open. A dark-skinned woman dressed in tight jeans and a t-shirt reading, 'Always Available,' stared at her. Heavy make-up covered her face, long spider-like false eyelashes blinked at her.

"You, Derek's girl?"

"Yes."

"Come inside."

Ronnie jumped at the snap of the lock behind her. The woman led her up a hallway and into a kitchen at the rear of the house. Three men seated around a table held playing cards, revolvers in full view. The pungent odor of marijuana hung in the air. A fluorescent light buzzed overhead.

"This here is Derek's lady," the woman said before exiting back down the hallway.

One man looked up. Shaggy blond hair spilled over his eyes. He grinned, exhibiting rows of yellow teeth. "Got the blow?"

"Yes, right here." She set the heavy duffle on the floor.

He pointed. "Open it, please."

She bent and unzipped the bag.

"Take out the bricks."

"Look," Ronnie said. "It's all there. I need to get back to New York."

One of the other men snapped his fingers at her, his hooded eyes traveling the length of her body. "Do what the man says. You'll be done soon enough."

Her hands shaking, she withdrew each brick, stacking them on the table. When she set the last one down, the third man covered her hand with his own. A toothpick hung from the corner of his mouth. Curly brown hair framed his face while a hawkish nose jutted over his thick lips.

"Nice," he said.

Ronnie's skin prickled. Sweat seeped between her shoulder blades. She slid her hand away.

The tip of the man's tongue darted out as he shifted the toothpick to the opposite side of his mouth. He drew a switchblade from his pocket and slit one of the bricks open. Dipping the knife into the white powder, he placed the blade beneath his nose and snorted.

His eyes popped wide open. "That's some good shit Derek dropped."

"Now, can I have the money?" Ronnie asked.

The man wiped the blade on his shirt, then closed the knife. He slipped it back into his pocket and eased up.

Ronnie took a step back. "Please, I…"

His beefy hand encircled her arm, steering her into the bedroom.

"Let go!" Ronnie cried, yanking herself free.

His eyes narrowed. "Cool it. I'm getting the cash." He knelt and dragged a briefcase from underneath the bed and set it on top. "Here it is. Want to count it?" He fingered the clasps, and the lid flew open. Stacks of bills lay in neat rows.

"No, I trust you."

He slammed the case shut. Instead of handing it to her, he placed it at the foot of the bed.

"How about a little fun before you hit the road?"

Ronnie backed away, only not quick enough. Before she could react, he shoved her onto the bed. She tried to get up, and he pushed her down again.

The toothpick dropped from his mouth. He yanked the knife out, warning her. "Don't make this difficult."

"Please, please, don't do this," she pleaded, her heart threatening to burst from her chest.

"Unbutton your blouse."

Ronnie froze, her mind reeling as he towered over her. She searched his eyes. Everything in them told her this was going to happen.

"I won't ask you again," he growled. "Do it, or I'll rip it off."

Slowly, she undid the buttons on her blouse. He dropped the knife and climbed on top of her. His hands groped her breasts while his hot sour breath fanned her face. Ronnie turned her head. Feeling for her purse, she slid her hand inside while he continued to fondle her.

She gasped as he grunted and dug his fingers between her legs. Gripping the gun, she pulled it out, and jammed it into his ribs.

"Get off me, you son of a bitch, or I'll pull the trigger!" she screamed. Hot tears raced down her cheeks. His body stiffened, and he lifted himself up.

Ronnie held the gun with both hands. "Back the hell away."

He smirked at her, then obeyed. "Killjoy," he quipped. "Didn't really want a skinny broad like you, anyhow. You need some meat on those bones. Take the money and get out." He zipped his jeans and left.

Ronnie rose on shaky legs. Adjusting her clothes, she kept the gun close. She grabbed the briefcase and eased out of the bedroom. The men and the coke were gone. Only the woman remained.

Ronnie slipped the gun into her purse and hurried past, ignoring her when she shouted, "Sorry about that."

She tore down the front steps, unlocked the car, and threw the briefcase behind the seat. Hands glued to the wheel, she concentrated on the road ahead as she made her way back to New York, arriving home just as the sun broke over the horizon.

Inside, she dropped the briefcase in the front hall, then she stripped and headed straight for the shower. She scrubbed her body hard, turning parts of her flesh bright pink. Curling her arms around her middle, she leaned against the white tile. She stared at the red marks on her breasts and wept.

Wrapping herself in a towel, she dove under the flowered quilt on her bed. Squeezing her eyes shut, she tried to wipe out the image of the man who attempted to rape her. When he arrived for the money, she'd tell Derek she quit being his mule. No matter what the threats or consequences, she was done. Exhausted, she drifted off to sleep only to startle awake at the persistent sound of the buzzer.

Ronnie snatched her robe and dashed to the door. Derek grabbed the briefcase and swept past her, a broad grin on his face. She followed him into the living room and perched on the arm of the sofa while he counted the money.

"It's all here. Good work." Drawing a packet of coke from his pocket, he threw it onto the coffee table.

"Good work!" she barked at him. "One of those big goons tried to rape me. Wouldn't let me leave."

"One of the many hazards of the job, baby." He gave her a broad smile.

She bolted up. "That's all you have to say, Derek. Don't you even care about what happened to me?"

His expression turned serious. He picked up a stack of bills from the briefcase. "Here," he said, tossing the cash at her. "This ought to make you feel better."

Ronnie caught the bundle and flung it back at him. It sailed over his head and landed on the floor. "I don't want it. What I want is for you to care. The beast could have raped me! If it wasn't for the gun…"

"Okay, calm down. I'm sorry, but what do you expect me to do about it?" He sauntered over to her. "Good thing you didn't shoot anybody. They're some of my best customers."

She couldn't believe his response. "Your… your customers? Is that all you're concerned with?"

"Don't act all high and mighty just because you almost got screwed. You know this is how I earn my living." Derek shut the briefcase. "You did great, Ronnie. Next time be more careful. Maybe bad things won't happen." Without saying another word, he slipped out the door.

She collapsed onto the sofa in disbelief. Derek didn't care about her at all, not one bit. If she was hurt, murdered even, while transporting his drugs, he'd find another mule to take her place.

Ronnie glanced at the packet of coke he'd left on the coffee table. She dug in her purse and removed a credit card. Sprinkling some of it out, she cut two lines. She plucked a crisp twenty-dollar bill from the packet of cash and rolled it into a perfect cylinder, then drew the coke up into one nostril, then the other.

Her head buzzed. Warmth spread through her body as she rubbed the excess from her nose. The turmoil inside her quieted.

Sinking back against the cushions, she picked up the throw pillow lying next to her and wrapped her arms around it. Her spirits rising, she felt invincible. If only she'd done a line before going into that house. Her fear would have evaporated, and she could have conquered anything. She hugged the pillow tighter. A couple of hits was all she'd need for her next drop.

CHAPTER 17

CARRIE

Carrie adjusted her sunglasses and pulled on her red leather gloves. Turning her collar up against the frigid afternoon wind charging across the Hudson River before tearing down Sutton Place, she sought refuge inside a doorway, her eyes glued to the entrance of a brownstone on the opposite side of the street.

This past year she'd performed this trip more times than she could count, watching people come and go along with delivery persons toting sacks of groceries to the rear of the home. Never able to muster up the courage to cross and ring the bell, she waited, hoping her father would appear.

In her mind, she'd rehearsed what to say. Nothing sounded right. What does one say to the father who abandoned her to a childhood of misery? Questions lingered inside, along with deep-seated anger.

He could have saved her, freed her from the torture her mother put her through. Only, if he had, would Bobby be in her life at all? She couldn't imagine her world without him. All her bad memories were made bearable because of Bobby.

Carrie shivered, the cold staking its claim on her body. She drew back into the doorway telling herself, five more minutes and she'd hail a cab. Her pulse slammed when a man emerged attired in a tan wool coat, a plaid scarf draped around his neck, his silver hair ruffled by the breeze as he jogged down the steps. He appeared taller than in the pictures she'd seen.

Unable to move, she drew in a deep breath, attempting to calm herself. Forcing one foot in front of the other, she crossed the street and followed at a discreet distance, mesmerized by his walk, how his stride was steady and confident, his shoulders squared.

On 57th Street, he stopped in front of a pub called Neary's and ducked inside. Her resolve steadfast, she yanked the heavy door open.

A long, sleek, dark mahogany bar lined one wall. Red tablecloths draped the tables while tufted red leather booths hugged the walls. The aroma of corned beef and cabbage mingled with the sharp scent of whiskey. A few hours before the dinner rush, the place was relatively empty.

She removed her sunglasses, searched the room, and located him seated at a booth toward the rear with two other men.

"Can I help you, Miss?"

A young woman stood before her. "How many, please?"

"Just me, thank you."

She showed Carrie to a table by the door and placed a menu down.

"Excuse me," Carrie said. "I prefer not to sit close to the front door. It's a bit chilly outside. With people coming and going, there's certain to be a draft."

"No problem, follow me." She led her to a booth near her father.

"Just an Irish Coffee, please," Carrie said, pulling off her gloves.

"Sure thing."

Carrie took off her coat. Within a few moments, she discovered all three men were reflected in a mirror across the room. She could hear their conversation. The waitress set whiskeys down in front of them before delivering her coffee.

One, a stout middle-aged man in a dark blue suit, pointed his finger at her father. "Look, you did what he asked. Everything went fine." He raised his glass and gulped. "Don't you like making money?"

"It's not about the money." Anger laced her father's voice

Carrie pulled out her cell and pretended to make a call, her ears trained on them.

Her father leaned forward. "Twice was more than enough. I don't relish the prospect of going to prison. Do you?"

The second gentleman swept a hand through his burnt-copper hair and crossed his arms. A pair of brown-rimmed frames circled his eyes. "For what *we* stand to gain, maybe. Besides, you're flush. If things cave, you can well afford a fancy lawyer."

Her father smacked his palm on the table. "This is blackmail, short and simple. I can see where this is leading. I've given him what he wants, but he's still demanding more. We had an agreement, gentlemen. I've kept my end, now he needs to keep his or—"

"Or what?" The man in the blue suit pushed his chair back. "We're not going to debate this any longer. You know his terms. You either satisfy them or suffer the consequences."

Both men rose and headed for the exit. Carrie lowered her head as they went by. She slipped her cell inside her purse. Those men were threatening her father. What could he be involved in? Maybe this wasn't the right time to confront him.

Her father knocked back his drink and moved past without so much as a glance. She signaled the waitress and tossed a twenty-dollar bill on the table.

Shoving her arms into her coat sleeves, she gathered her things and hurried outside, catching sight of him as he rounded the corner and disappeared. A gust of icy wind blasted her face causing her breath to hitch. She rushed after him. Arriving at the end of the street, she turned in his direction, still debating if she was doing the right thing.

Without warning, he stepped out of a doorway and blocked her path. Carrie went numb inside.

"Why are you following me?" he demanded.

"I…"

"Come on now, young woman, who are you, and what do you want?"

Slowly, she removed her sunglasses. All those years, she waited for him to rescue her. Sure, one day, she'd open the trailer door and see his face. A face she had no memory of, now, here he was, standing before her.

Her voice breaking, she forced the words out. "I'm your daughter."

His mouth fell open. He took a step back. "My… my daughter? I don't understand." The lines around his eyes creased. He gave her a blank stare.

"It's me, Carrie."

He clutched at his chest, and for a moment, he looked like he might keel over. "Carrie?"

"Yes, and here's what I want. I need you to explain why you abandoned me. Let me grow up with a mother who beat me almost every day of my life because she couldn't stand the sight of me."

His posture went limp. The color drained from his cheeks, but his eyes never left hers.

"Why?" he said. "Why would Helen do such a thing?"

Her vision blurred. She wiped at her tears and told him the truth. "Because … I reminded her of you."

CHAPTER 18

JACK

Jack finished loading supplies into the pick-up truck. Hoping to demonstrate his sincerity to Dalton, he had offered to run some errands for him. Reluctant at first, Dalton agreed and handed him a list of items to be purchased in Rapid City.

Slamming the tailgate shut, he climbed into the truck. The passenger door flew open. Jack jerked his head. "What the fu…?"

"Hello, Jackie boy." Pigeon eyes, ringed by pouches of flesh, peeked out of a round face. Sunlight reflected off the top of the man's bald head.

"Mel? What the hell are you doing here?"

Giving Jack a playful jab on his arm, he said, "I could ask you the same question."

"I told you when I left Vegas, I'd be in touch."

"Left? More like cut and run." He drew a cigar from his shirt pocket.

Jack waved his hand. "Not inside the truck."

Mel paused. With a smirk on his face, he slipped the cigar back into his pocket. "Not yours, huh?"

"Of course not. Belongs to my brother."

"Oh, the big bad brother you've mentioned over a dozen times. And how are things progressing?"

"Slow, to say the least. I didn't count on him taking a wife."

"Getting rid of one more shouldn't be an issue for you. That is unless…"

Heat creeping up his cheeks, Jack rubbed the back of his neck. "Unless what?"

Mel shot him a look. "Maybe this is all too much for you. People in Vegas are growing impatient. You agreed to pay off what you owe."

"And I'll keep my end of the bargain. The two-million-dollar policy I took out on my brother will more than cover it, and the land the ranch sits on is worth a lot of money. Plus, whatever liquid assets he has become mine."

Mel's forehead wrinkled. "I bet your brother's unaware of that policy."

Jack turned away and stared ahead. "Of course. His signature was forged. A good buddy posed as him with a phony ID and all the crucial information. I promised to take care of him when I cash in. I just need a bit more time."

"From what you told me, mishaps have occurred on the ranch before. Should be easy to get things over with."

"Come on, Mel. It can't appear like history repeating itself. I don't want the authorities poking around. I need a fresh angle. A sudden accident or something along those lines. Don't worry, I'll figure it out."

Mel made a fist and clamped his other hand around it. The sound of knuckles popping filled the truck. "I'm not worried, but you better be. If you can't remedy this situation, that brother of yours may pay the price." He opened the door and eased out. "See you soon, Jackie boy."

Air escaped Jack's lungs as Mel walked away. He smacked his palm on the steering wheel and swore. This was supposed to be simple. He would return to the ranch, tragedy would befall Dalton, and everything would become his. But with Joann in the picture, things were tricky.

Driving toward the ranch, he wished he'd never gone to Vegas all those years ago. Taking a job in one of the casinos and quickly acquiring a taste for gambling, he did quite well for a while, even joining in on mob-run private games.

But his luck changed, causing Dalton to bail him out numerous times before cutting him off after the last fifty thousand. Now, with his debts amounting to half a mil, and a promise to pay it all back plus interest, he needed that insurance payout.

He arrived at the ranch and backed the truck up to the barn. His head pounding, he unloaded the supplies. What he required now was a foolproof plan. His brother and Joann needed to go. Too bad for her. She had been more than kind since his arrival.

"All okay, Jack?" Dalton stood before him. He tilted his Stetson back. "You look a little pale."

"I'm fine. Got everything on the list."

"Make any unscheduled stops?"

Jack's insides boiled, but he forced a fake smile. "No. Straight to town and back."

Dalton eyed him. He removed a pair of gloves from his rear pocket and tossed them to Jack. "Think you could give Rick a hand with some fencing repairs down by the south pasture?"

"I'll get right on it."

"Before you go, I need to say something."

Jack leaned against the tailgate. He pulled on the gloves while expecting another insult.

"Look, I know I've been tough on you, but over the years, you've given me good reason to doubt you. I was pretty upset when your letter arrived. I could have turned you away. Instead, I decided to give you a chance."

"Little brother, I told you I've changed. I want to heal things between us, and I thank you for helping me. If you hadn't taken me in, I'm not sure what I would have done."

Dalton smoothed his mustache. "Don't make me regret it." He walked off into the barn.

Pushing down his rage, Jack climbed into the truck and drove to the south pasture. Dalton's attitude would never change. It only served to reinforce his plans. If he didn't act soon, Vegas would give the order, and he couldn't let that happen.

He spotted Rick tightening some barbed wire around a fence post. He wandered over to him, knee-high grass rustling against his jeans. Rick stretched the wire tight with one gloved hand, then, using his other, caught the wire in the v-groove of a curved nail puller. Securing it behind one of the barbs, he pulled it through.

Jack cleared his throat. "Dalton sent me to help."

"Know anything about fencing?"

Jack wanted to knock the cowboy hat right off the man's thick skull. "I grew up on this ranch. Fixed many a fence."

Rick squared his shoulders. "Good, let's get to it."

He handed him the battery-powered stapler and the end of some wire. Jack yanked the wire towards him. Experience had taught him if you stretched it too tight, it could break at the far end and snap back the other way. Tapping on the wire to produce a humming sound assures one it's good enough to staple and need not be tightened anymore.

"Well, is she tight enough?" Rick asked.

Jack imagined how Rick might look with a length of barbed wire wrapped around his face, thick piercing barbs sunk into his flesh. He hesitated, putting this last thought aside and said, "Tap the wire for me."

Rick tapped. A slight hum floated in the air. "Sounds good," Rick said. "Drive a staple into the post."

They finished and proceeded to the next section. Aware of how much Dalton favored Rick, Jack held his temper in check. He needed to get this cowboy on his side. Putting on his best smile, he said, "My brother sure depends on you. Finding people to work a ranch can prove difficult."

Rick raised an eyebrow. "Is that so?"

"Stands to reason in these times, most ranches are drying up. Young folks don't choose this kind of life anymore."

"I guess," Rick said. "You have to be suited for it. Me personally, I prefer it. Couldn't work for a better man than your brother."

Jack's stomach soured at his words. Of course, everyone loved Dalton. Even the hired help sang his praises. "Yeah, he's something alright."

With scant conversation between them, they completed the last section of fencing just before dusk. Jack's body ached. He hadn't performed any manual labor in more years than he could count.

Working a ranch wasn't his vision of an ideal life. Unlike his father and Dalton, he derived no satisfaction from it. They had acted like it was a crime not choosing to raise cattle. His dreams were bigger. He preferred to get as far away as he could from the stench of hay, manure, and the soil he could never shake from his worn boots or clean from underneath his fingernails.

Rising at dawn to a pink-streaked sky in summer, he dreaded the blistering rays of sunlight climbing up over the horizon and shivering on horseback in winter amid gusts of icy wind blowing across the valley while they rounded up cattle for slaughter.

Driving away from the pasture, he stopped and gazed at the spot where the home he'd grown up in once rested. Now covered in tall grass sprouting up from Houdek Soil, the land bore no evidence of the tragedy that had befallen them all those years ago.

He never set the fire, but he also never made any attempt to save them. Arriving home from town late, unsteady on his feet after a night of boozing with friends, he'd gone inside intending to crash. Catching a whiff of smoke down the hall, he approached his parents' bedroom where bright flames licked at the carpet from beneath their door.

Jack stared at his hands, recalling the scorching heat as he tugged at the doorknob. All the arguments from the previous weeks surfaced. Bitter words had passed between them. Panic overtook him, and he raced outside, hiding behind the barn.

The crackling of the wooden frame igniting swelled while thick, choking smoke and screams filled the air. He had covered his ears, collapsing onto the ground. Moments later, he visualized his parents burning to death. In an instant, the consequences of his having done the wrong thing loomed.

Clutching the side of the barn, coughing and wheezing, he made his way toward the blaze illuminating the night sky, shocked to see Dalton standing outside, tears pouring down his face, repeating, 'I couldn't save them.' All along, he'd assumed his brother wasn't home.

After the burial, accusations flew between him and his brother. Dalton believed he planned the fire. Guilt planted itself inside him only to be replaced by bitterness at the reading of the Will when he learned his father had cut him out completely. He left the ranch for good, but the anger stayed within him.

Could he have saved them? He'd never know the answer, but Dalton would always blame him for starting the fire.

Jack pulled away and rode to the house more resolved than ever to push matters ahead. Without Dalton's forgiveness, things could never be right between them, and his brother would never hand over the cash he needed to clear his debts. Seething inside, all he wanted was Dalton and that bride of his gone.

CHAPTER 19

BIANCA

Miguel stopped several blocks from Izzy's school. "The children will be letting out soon, Bianca." He pointed at the grocery store. "I will wait for you in there. A man like me would look suspicious, parked outside. You know what you must do."

"*Sí*. Discover how the little girl travels home."

"Be careful. She may recognize you." Miguel left and headed inside the store.

Several minutes later, Bianca positioned herself diagonally across from the building. A line of automobiles formed in front while a school bus pulled into the circular drive. She had a perfect view of the exit.

Children emerged. Some clambered aboard the bus while others raced to cars. She kept her eyes on the doors. The crowd of children diminished until finally, Izzy appeared.

Dressed in a royal blue ski jacket and school uniform khaki pants, she ran toward a silver Audi SUV, her long dark hair trailing behind her. A young woman with short-cropped blonde hair and glasses climbed out. She hugged Izzy and opened the rear door where a small boy sat in a car seat.

Pulling away, she drove to where Miguel waited. She moved into the passenger seat while he opened the rear and set a bag of groceries inside. He slid behind the wheel. "So, what have you learned?"

Bianca relayed the information to him. "I am not certain this person picks her up each day. Or, if the little boy is always with her."

Miguel tapped his fingers on the steering wheel. "Then you must determine if this is a regular routine."

"And if it is?"

"I will deal with it. All I require is the girl, but if I have to eliminate the woman and take both children, so be it."

"But, Miguel, both children?"

"You understand very little," he barked. "If Carmela were alive, she would want me to do everything in my power to exact revenge. No matter what the cost."

Bianca weighed his words. Things were getting out of control. First, Sarah, and now he might murder another woman and kidnap *two* children. Afraid of angering him further, she stared ahead. Nothing could dissuade him from this madness.

"You are working the late shift this week?" he asked.

"Yes. I must be there by four."

He turned to her, his eyes two orbs of dark coal. "For the next week, you will maintain your vigil until we are certain what the little girl's routine is."

*   *   *   *

With the restaurant full, the dinner rush kept Bianca busy. The aroma of Columbian dishes cooking streamed from the kitchen while snatches of conversation drifted above the soft Latin music emanating from the speakers. The tables and booths filled, while customers waited for available seating at the bar. Setting down glass after glass, she was determined to keep up with the demand.

Rosie came toward her, eyes sweeping the length of the bar. "Need assistance?"

"I am fine. Everything is covered."

"There's no crime in asking for help, Bianca."

"*Si*, but it is not necessary."

"Okay, then. Everyone seems to have their orders. If you change your mind, let me know."

After Rosie left, she placed a draft beer in front of a customer. A couple at the other end were escorted to their table. A pretty woman with red hair and a tall, handsome gentleman with a mustache and cowboy hat slid onto the empty stools. She remembered seeing them here before having dinner with the D'Angelos.

The man signaled to her. "The lady will have a glass of Santiago Red Rosé, and I'll have a shot of Johnnie Walker Black."

She prepared their drinks and set them down.

"Thanks, hon," the woman said. "You're Bianca, right?"

"*Si*."

"Carrie has mentioned you a few times… what an excellent employee you are and how lucky she is to have you."

"Thank you. That is nice to hear." She turned toward another customer and began preparing a drink.

"I'm glad Alejandro is working out so well," she heard the woman say.

"So am I," the man responded. "I was skeptical at first. He knew next to nothing about horses and cattle, but Rick says Alejandro's one of the best rustlers he's got."

Bianca froze. The trembling in her legs climbed up her body. Could it be *her* Alejandro they were speaking of? Horses, cattle? What did it all mean?

Alice came to escort them to their table. The man tossed down a generous tip, and they followed her.

Hands shaking, she scooped up the cash and stuffed it into the jar below the bar. She couldn't take her eyes off the couple now seated in a booth.

They spoke his name, music to her ears. Alejandro could be here in South Dakota. Her heart rocketing inside her chest, she smiled, then stopped her mind from going further. How could she find out for sure? She didn't dare ask. Alejandro might have given little information about his past.

It sounded like he'd secured a job. If so, she refused to jeopardize it. He must be working hard, saving money so he could build a new life for them, unaware she was already here.

Hoping he might be near, she allowed herself a tiny bit of happiness. She needed to learn more about this couple. With most of the customers seated and only a few loitering at the bar, she signaled Alice.

Pointing, she said, "Can you tell me who those two people are?"

Alice's face lit up. "Just about everyone around here knows Dalton Burgess. For years, all the single ladies tried to snag him. He ended up marrying the woman with him. She's not from South Dakota. Sure is nice, though. Her name's Joann."

"They live here in town?"

"No. Mr. Burgess owns a cattle ranch about forty-five minutes from here called Hidden Creek." She eyed Bianca. "Why all the questions?"

Bianca looked away and gathered some dirty glasses. "Just curious. He left a big tip."

Alice giggled. "Yeah, he's one of our best tippers."

Her excitement mounted. Could this Dalton be the same man Miguel had mentioned? If so, dare she say anything to him? With the possibility of Alejandro being on the ranch, she decided to keep the information to herself for now.

* * * *

Bianca's shift ended, and she relaxed in the small apartment on Hill Street waiting for Miguel to pick her up. The usual fatigue from working late eluded her after hearing the couple at the restaurant speak Alejandro's name.

Alice mentioning Hidden Creek Ranch made her mind swim with possibilities, but caution must take precedence. If Miguel became suspicious, she was sure she'd never see Alejandro again.

Her cell phone buzzed. He was waiting for her several blocks up the street. Collecting her purse, she hurried to meet him.

"How were things at the restaurant?" he asked while they drove.

"Very busy. I did well with tips tonight."

Miguel chuckled. "Tips? You do not need tips. I can buy you whatever you want."

"I know, *mi amor,* but I like earning some money of my own."

"You are a good person, Bianca. Perhaps too good for me."

"Why do you say such a thing? We are meant for one another. I felt it the moment you walked into the cantina in *Mérida,*" she lied.

"Did you? Or were you hoping for a rich man to cure your hardship?" He swept his fingertips lightly over her cheek. "There is nothing wrong with you wanting a better way of life."

"Miguel, please, I would not be with just any man."

"And what about one like me? If you had known what I am capable of, would you have come away with me?"

Her stomach plummeted. Inside, her answer was a resounding no. Instead, she replied, "Yes. A thousand times, yes. I love you. What happened with Sarah has not changed my feelings for you."

They wound up the drive, and Miguel parked in front. He shut the engine. His hand inched up, squeezing the back of her neck.

"Are you that naïve to think Sarah is the only person I have ever killed?"

"Miguel, I…"

"I have murdered many in my time…all with no regrets. Carmela issued the orders, and I followed them. She sanctioned each one without remorse. Only the death of her beloved father touched her. Another reason to make Nick pay."

Bianca shuddered at the hate simmering in his eyes, blacker than the midnight sky, strong enough to form into solid concrete and stand on its own. She had made a dreadful mistake leaving Mexico with Miguel, but it was too late to change anything now.

He turned away and got out of the car.

Bianca followed behind, willing herself to remain calm. Miguel must never uncover her plan to find Alejandro. She understood, if he did, he'd kill her too.

CHAPTER 20

ALEX

Alex steadied his breath. Sitting just feet away from him in the coffee shop on East 56th Street, he could hardly believe she was here. Her features were startling. Carrie had his mother's eyes and even some of her mannerisms. What would she think of the beautiful granddaughter she had denied if she were alive today?

People sitting around them tapping on computers and cell phones amid the whir of espresso machines became distant distractions while he listened to the torrent of abuse she endured as a child living in the Arizona trailer park with the woman he once loved.

Having learned about her cruel upbringing, how on earth could he sit here and try to defend what he'd done all those years ago?

When she fell silent, he asked, "Where is your mother now?"

Her lip trembled. "She was murdered. They never caught the person."

Shocked at her answer, he fought to compose himself. Taking a breath, he said, "Please believe me when I tell you I was unaware of Helen's mistreatment of you."

"And if you had…been aware?"

"I would never have allowed it to happen."

Her eyes filled. "Then how could you—"

Alex held up his hand. "Please, let me explain. Certain events took place that were out of my control. I loved Helen…but circumstances worked against us."

"So, what my Aunt May said is true. You chose your family's wealth over my mother."

Hanging onto his composure, he glanced around and lowered his voice. "No, Carrie, that isn't true. I cared deeply for your mother."

Attempting to console her, Alex reached and placed his hand on hers. She quickly pulled it away. The anguish he lived with almost daily returned, making him wish he could erase all she had suffered.

"Your mother and I were seeing each other for about eight months when she told me she was pregnant with you. By then, my parents had arranged for me to marry someone else."

"Arranged?"

"Kate, my wife, came from a family we'd known for years. We practically grew up together. Both sides encouraged the marriage." Unable to meet her eyes for a moment, he looked away, searching for the right words.

"I told my parents about your mother. Yes, they threatened to cut me off, but it didn't matter to me, not with what was at stake." He paused. How unbelievable this all sounded to him now.

"While I was abroad on a business trip with my father, my mother contacted Helen. She informed her I wasn't going to marry her. If she wouldn't have an abortion, she'd best accept a check and leave New York. She even announced my engagement in the local papers and began making wedding plans with Kate."

Her eyes swept over him, a puzzled expression on her face. "But it's not what Aunt May told me. She said *you* wanted my mother to have an abortion, that *you* demanded she go."

"Look, there is no reason for me to lie. My mother… your grandmother, drove Helen away. Now, whether she spoke the truth to May or not, I can't say. I'm telling you exactly what happened."

"When I returned, I was furious. I tried to find your mother. Months went by with no trace. I was beside myself, knowing she had probably given birth. Finally, one day, the private detective I hired found her, and I flew to Arizona. There you were, this tiny, beautiful baby girl, lying in your crib." He hesitated, his throat thickening at the memory.

"But Helen had changed. She believed I put my mother up to everything, including keeping the engagement hidden from her. I tried to tell her I never spoke about Kate because I had no intention of marrying her."

"But what could she have gained by lying to Aunt May?"

Alex sighed. "I'm not sure, possibly to justify the person she'd become. We fought the entire time. Things turned rather ugly between us. I could see Helen drank a bit too much, and she wasn't thinking clearly."

Carrie pointed her finger at him. "But *you* left me with her anyway."

"But I didn't think she would harm you. In retrospect, I should have paid more attention."

She bolted up from her chair. "So, I've been right all along. You didn't love me enough to take me with you."

With the shock of seeing his daughter gripping him inside, he struggled to remain calm. Instead, his panic grew when she slipped into her coat and reached for her purse. "No, Carrie, wait. I haven't finished explaining what happened."

Her eyes bore through him. A muscle in her jaw twitched. "I think I've heard everything I needed to hear."

She dashed to the exit. Alex scrambled to his feet and caught up to her outside, tugging at her coat sleeve. "Carrie, please, stop. Let me explain."

Wrenching her arm away, she shouted, "Don't touch me! I don't want to listen to any more of your sad story or what kind of trouble you're in."

"Trouble? What are you talking about?"

"I overheard those men in the restaurant. Are you going to deny there's something wrong?"

His heart thumped, and he sought to maintain his composure. "They're associates of mine. We're having a minor disagreement about a business venture."

"More half-truths," she said. "Besides, I wasn't expecting too much from you. I just wanted you to explain why you left."

Desperate, he spread his arms, ready to plead with her. Pedestrians glanced sideways at the two of them. A taxi horn blared above the din of the traffic.

"And, I was trying to tell you before you tore out of the coffee shop," he said. "This is no place for us to talk. Come home with me. I need you to hear the rest. Maybe, then you'll—"

"I'll what? Forgive you?" Her gloved hands clenched. A tear erupted from the corner of her eye.

He moved closer. She drew back and shook her head. "Don't."

"Carrie, listen, I want you to meet Kate so you can understand everything."

"So, you did marry her after all." She glared at him. "Well, I hope the two of you have been happy together all these years."

"There is much more you're unaware of. Look, you have every right to be furious with me, but please hear me out."

A thick lock of her dark hair spilling down the front of her coat caught his attention. The ache inside his chest ripped at his core. Alex held back the impulse to reach out, sweep it back behind her shoulder. A small gesture he might have had the chance to perform long ago when she was a child.

"I have no interest in going to your home or in meeting your wife." Her voice cracked. "I've... heard enough from you." She pulled her collar up against the biting wind and pushed past him.

Rushing to catch up with her, he reached inside his coat. "Here, take my card."

Angry eyes peered up at him. "For what?"

"My number is on it." Alex tucked it into her coat pocket. "Just in case, but I'll understand if I don't hear from you."

Without another word, she hurried away, disappearing into the crowd moving along the sidewalk. Alex's head throbbed. His heart ached with the weight of his guilt. The blame for all the horror she endured rested on him.

Afraid his knees might buckle, he caught hold of a lamppost. What if he never saw Carrie again? He'd lost her once already.

Shoving his hands into the pockets of his wool coat, head down, he braced himself against the howling wind. His breathing labored, he trudged home, the image of his daughter churning in his head.

Earlier, he'd taken notice of the diamond wedding band on her finger. A possible sign her life had turned out okay, but at this moment, all he wished to do was help her heal. Her meeting Kate might be a part of that healing.

Filled with unease at Carrie's mention of his conversation in the restaurant, he prayed she wouldn't discuss it with anyone else. These were dangerous men. Men he had no business getting involved with in the first place. He'd never rid himself of them. They would keep coming back for more, an endless treadmill he couldn't get off.

Before mounting the steps to his home, he glanced over his shoulder one last time. Hoping to see Carrie, he scanned the street. Dusk settled in, making him aware of the many sleepless nights lying ahead.

CHAPTER 21

BOBBY

Bobby kept his eyes fixed on the taillights two car lengths ahead. What was he thinking following Ronnie?

Silent since their last argument, the apology he expected from her never materialized. It pained him when he recalled her cruel words regarding Carmela. Still, he chose to forgive her and drop by her apartment, take a drive to Brooklyn for a bite at one of their favorite restaurants and try to heal the rift between them, but things quickly changed.

As he parked across from her building on West 57th Street, Ronnie appeared, carrying a sizeable maroon-colored duffle bag. She placed it inside the trunk of her car. The gnawing in his gut returned. He decided to follow her and called Maggie, glad when she agreed to stay with Natalia past her regular hours.

Friday night traffic vacated the city at a crawl. Bobby turned on the radio, willing himself to keep calm in the middle of a crush of automobiles. He eyed the bumper stickers on the one in front and found them far from entertaining.

Traffic improved when they exited the Lincoln Tunnel and sped up a ramp to the New Jersey Turnpike. Bobby weaved in and out, wondering what lay inside the duffle bag. Choosing not to assume the worst, he pumped up the volume on the radio.

As he drove, he reflected on his mother's return from her initial meeting with his grandfather. Her refusal to divulge any details made him curious. He tried to press her further, but she declined to discuss it.

Later, he found a business card lying on the hall closet floor with Paterson Brokerage House printed on it and Alexander Paterson's name. Instead of returning it to her, he slipped it into his wallet.

This man was his grandfather, and his desire to contact him grew. But he needed to proceed with caution. He didn't want to do anything to upset his mother.

Bobby drew himself back to the present. Several hours later, he drove over the Delaware Memorial Bridge, where Ronnie proceeded on I95 for a few more exits.

Did she know someone in Delaware? He couldn't recall her ever mentioning anyone. Within minutes, he found himself on the seedy side of Wilmington.

Sunset approached by the time she pulled to the curb in front of a small bungalow. He maneuvered into a spot across the street several car lengths away and waited.

Ronnie exited and hoisted the duffle bag from the trunk. She set it down, then drew a revolver from her purse.

Bobby's breath caught. Bringing a gun along could only mean one thing. She needed to protect herself. The contents inside the bag were probably illegal. Could it be drugs, money laundering, or something else?

He watched her check the chamber, then shove it back into her purse. She mounted the front steps with the duffel bag, rang the bell, then disappeared inside.

His body went rigid. Trepidation sweeping his core, he pulled out his Glock and set it on the seat next to him. Up until now, the odds of having to use it remained far from his mind. His foot tapped against the rubber mat below. He rubbed his palms together, uncertain of what to do.

Should he approach the house? A move like that might put her in jeopardy. The prospect of something happening to Ronnie heightened his anxiety.

He picked up the Glock and gripped the door latch. About to step out, he stopped when Ronnie reappeared, scurrying down the steps with an olive-green duffel bag trimmed in light tan. An exchange had been made.

His questions mounting, he tailed her back to New York City. Expecting her to park and walk into her building, to his surprise, she remained inside her car. Minutes ticked by. She made no move to get out.

A man dressed in jeans, sneakers, and a blue hoodie strutted up to the driver's side window and tapped on the glass. Ronnie opened the door, and they walked to the trunk. Bobby controlled the urge to dash across the street.

Nick had advised him long ago restraint and caution meant everything in a dangerous situation. To act without thinking things through could make all the difference in the outcome.

Ronnie handed him the duffel, and they spoke for a few minutes. He slipped something to her and took off up the block while she went inside her building.

Bobby weighed his options. Should he confront her now or wait? She would know he'd been following her. It could drive her farther away.

Armed, he decided to take a chance. He left the car and hurried after the man with the duffel. Where he was headed might provide additional information concerning Ronnie.

At 59th and Columbus Circle, he descended the steps to the subway station. Bobby pulled out his Metro Card. At the bottom, he swiped it and went through the turnstile. Alarmed, when he didn't catch sight of the man, his eyes searched the platform.

The distant rumble of an approaching train grew louder. Bobby took a few quick steps, almost colliding with the man when he stepped from behind one of the steel girders.

"Sorry," Bobby said. Head down, he continued walking to the other end.

The train thundered into the station sending scraps of debris sailing along the platform and up into the air. The familiar odor of creosote, mingled with brake dust and electrical smoke, filled Bobby's nostrils. The doors slid open.

He observed which railway car the man boarded and made his way one car back from him. They pulled out of the station with a few passengers spread out among the seats. Bobby leaned against the connecting door where he could keep track of the man. The train rocked and swayed, then delivered a sudden jolt forcing Bobby to anchor himself to keep his balance.

As they neared West 96 Street, the man with the duffel went to the doors. The train tore into the station, lurched, and stopped. The doors slid apart, and Bobby continued his pursuit.

Advancing up the steps and out onto the street, the icy wind struck him full force. Eyes watering, he struggled to keep the man in sight. A block later, he retreated into a bar called the Red Devil.

Bobby turned his collar up and went inside. Unaccustomed to the dimly lit room, he blinked, then focused, locating him all the way in the rear, handing the bag over to someone.

Bobby recognized him immediately. The same guy who accosted Ronnie at the club took possession of the duffel.

Proceeding to the bar's front corner by the wall, he perched on a stool, keeping his head down while the two men went past and exited the bar.

Every fiber of his being numbed. He ordered a whiskey neat, putting it away in one shot, then ordered another, not wanting to believe what he had seen.

How could Ronnie have gotten mixed up in this? She was playing a risky game. Transporting illicit goods, crossing over state lines, and carrying a weapon all pointed to one thing. Ronnie was a mule. And when things begin to unravel, as they were bound to do, most mules never live to tell their tale.

CHAPTER 22

CARRIE

Carrie scrutinized the guest list on the computer screen, careful to make certain she hadn't left anyone out. Somewhat despondent from her trip to New York, she decided to arrange an employee appreciation party. With Sarah still missing, she hoped it might help to lift everyone's spirits.

Nick wandered in and peeked over her shoulder. He let out a slow whistle. "Looks like your list is growing."

"I realize it's a bit long. I called Joann, and we agreed to combine Dalton's employees with ours, make it one huge celebration. Fall is moving fast. Before the rush of the holidays are upon us, now is the perfect time to do this."

"Sounds like a good idea." He kissed the top of her head before sinking into the chair across from the desk. "Care to tell me what else is going on?"

She looked up from the screen. "What do you mean?"

"Ever since you came home from Bobby's, you seem a bit off." He frowned and folded his arms. "Missing Natty?"

"Well, of course, I miss her, but she's where she belongs."

"Then, what is it?"

"What do you suppose happened to Sarah? I mean…the police don't have a single clue."

"The more time passes, the odds of finding her alive decrease," Nick said.

Gooseflesh broke out on Carrie's skin at his words. She didn't want to believe Sarah was dead. Tapping her French-tipped fingernails on the surface of the desk, she said, "Her parents left for Colorado yesterday. I promised them I'd keep in touch."

"I can only imagine how they feel," Nick said. "Not knowing is worse than knowing what happened to their daughter." He leaned forward. "What else is going on with you?"

Carrie perched on the edge of the desk in front of him. "I planned on telling you this sooner or later."

His brow furrowed. "So, I suppose this is later?"

"Don't be angry. I needed to know how things would play out first." She went on to explain her encounter with her father.

He held out his arms. "Come here."

She collapsed onto his lap and rested her head against his chest. "I wanted to believe he loved me all those years ago."

He stroked her cheek. "Babe, listen to me. People don't always do what's right. At least he didn't turn you away. Maybe you should have gone to his house... given him a chance to explain."

Carrie raised her head. "How do you think I would feel, staring into the face of the woman who destroyed my mother's life?"

"If he wanted you to meet her, there must have been a good reason."

She swallowed hard. Just the mention of meeting her father's wife fueled her hostility. "Besides, I'm not sure what else he's mixed up in." Sighing, she lifted herself up.

"What do you mean?"

"Well, when I followed him to the bar, I overheard a conversation between him and two other men. They sounded threatening."

"Did you ask him about it?"

"Yes. He insisted they were business associates, that it was a minor disagreement. Only it didn't sound like it to me."

Nick rubbed his eyes and stretched. "Well, if he won't discuss it, there's little you can do. But please think about how you waited all your life to find him. It's not like you to give up so easily. Next time you visit Bobby, you might want to hear his side of things before you write him off."

Talking about her father made her head throb. "Let's drop this for now. I promised Izzy I would spend the day with her since she's off from school."

"Girls only, I'm guessing?"

She winked. "Absolutely."

*　　*　　*　　*

Several hours later, with their nails painted along with a relaxing pedicure, Carrie and Izzy were stationed at the front counter in their favorite ice cream parlor. Izzy pressed herself against the glass, her green eyes squinting at the rows of containers filled with assorted flavors. The waffle cones sugary scent lingered in the air. The whir of a blender mixing a milkshake drowned out the chatter of the children and adults standing in line behind them.

After considerable debate, Izzy ordered a Chocolate Sundae while she chose a plain cup of vanilla with rainbow sprinkles. They grabbed their order and slid into a booth. Izzy tugged off her jacket before slipping a maraschino cherry into her mouth. She swallowed, then dipped a spoon into her ice cream.

"Good, huh?" Carrie asked before digging in herself, savoring the taste of the granular sprinkles dissolving on her tongue amid the creamy vanilla.

Izzy grinned and sunk her spoon in again. "The best." After a few more mouthfuls, she said, "Mom, can I ask you something?"

"Sure. You can always ask or tell me anything."

"Most of my friends talk about their grandparents. I know Daddy's parents died a long time ago. What about yours?" She picked up her napkin and wiped away a drizzle of chocolate syrup from the corner of her lower lip.

Carrie propped her chin in her hand. She stared at her daughter. It was only logical for her to be curious. After what happened with Bobby, she had promised herself a long time ago she wouldn't lie to her children. "I guess you're old enough for me to tell you I didn't grow up in a home as nice as ours with parents who loved me."

Izzy's forehead wrinkled. "What do you mean?" She continued eating her ice cream.

Carrie took a deep breath. "My mother had a lot of problems. She drank too much alcohol. It made her very sick."

"What about your father?"

"My mother and father didn't live together."

"Oh. Like a divorce? Some kids in my class have parents who are divorced. They don't live together either."

"Kind of like that except they never married."

Izzy stuck her spoon into her cup and stopped eating. "Why not? Didn't they love each other?"

"Yes, but sometimes, even when two people love each other, things don't always work out."

"Where is your mom now?"

"She died a long time ago. Way before you were born."

"What did she die of?"

Carrie paused. She couldn't bear to tell her about the murder. "She got terribly ill."

"From the alcohol?"

"Yes. It's not good when you drink too much."

"That's sad." Izzy picked up her spoon again.

"Yes, but it was many years ago."

"What about your dad?"

Carrie set the rest of her ice cream aside. "My father...your grandfather lives in New York."

Her face brightened. "Does he live near Bobby? Does he know him? Does—"

"Slow down, Izzy. No, Bobby hasn't met him." She patted her hand. "Listen, someday you'll meet him, but not right now."

"Why? Why can't I meet him?" She scraped the last of the chocolate syrup from the bottom of her dish.

"It's not a good time. But I promise one day you will..." She stopped and followed Izzy's gaze. Her eyes were locked on a gentleman standing at the counter dressed in a leather jacket, jeans, and a baseball cap pulled down on his head.

"Mommy, that poor man. His face is messed up."

"Hush. It's not polite to stare. He probably feels self-conscious enough."

"Sorry, Mommy."

"Come on, it's time to go. I hope you had a nice day."

"It was fun. I can't wait to show Daddy my nails."

On their way out, Carrie stopped near the front to pay the bill while Izzy strolled over to the man. "What kind of ice cream are you getting?" Carrie heard her ask.

"What is your favorite?" he replied.

"The Chocolate Sundae."

"Maybe I will have one, too. Thanks."

"Izzy, let's go," Carrie called over her shoulder.

As they drove home, Izzy said, "I think I made that man feel better. I told him what my favorite ice cream is."

"That's nice." She brushed Izzy's cheek. "We always tell you to be kind to everyone, even if they're different from you." Carrie concentrated on the road and thought about Izzy's questions. One day she'd face her father again. But her wounds still raw from their last encounter, she sensed it wouldn't be any time soon.

CHAPTER 23

MIGUEL

Miguel relaxed inside the Cadillac SUV outside of Rapid City, eating his Chocolate Sundae. He smiled, then slipped another spoonful of the velvety smooth ice cream into his mouth. Izzy was correct. It tasted excellent.

His trip into town had been necessary. In order to make the attic escape-proof, the stained-glass window needed to be secured. While parked across the street from an ice cream shop loading his supply of lumber, he couldn't believe his luck when he recognized Izzy with her mother from the photo Bianca had taken.

Miguel speculated on how much Nick told his wife about their confrontation in Tahoe. An accomplished ghost would not disclose anything. To discuss your kills was taboo.

Deciding to get closer, he made sure they were deep in conversation before going inside. Watching them, he wished the attic was ready. When Izzy noticed him, he turned away.

The mother paid scant attention when later, her daughter addressed him. Forcing them off the freeway crossed his mind, but he'd have to hold them both or kill the woman. Izzy was the important one, his bargaining chip in the whole matter.

Finished with his ice cream, he tossed the empty cup out onto the curb. At the rental house, he unloaded the car and placed a large sheet of plywood in the attic. Fetching a hammer and nails, he boarded up the window, then added a deadbolt to the door.

Scrutinizing his work and satisfied the room was secure enough, he went downstairs. Miguel paused in the bedroom doorway. Having worked a double shift at the restaurant, Bianca lay sleeping. The comforter, drawn all the way up, left only the top of her head visible.

Closing the door, he continued into the kitchen and prepared a pot of coffee. He poured a cup and sat, thumbing through the newspaper. Every so often, his eyes wandered to Bianca's purse resting on the counter.

He never had any cause to look inside, but today something nagged at him, like a magnet, pulling him toward it. Finishing off the last of his coffee, he got up and opened her purse. At first, he discovered nothing of relevance. Only her wallet, a comb, and lipstick, until he discovered a part of the lining was loose.

He tugged at the corner, his fingers probing. To his astonishment, he pulled out a bundle of letters addressed to her in Mexico. Settling into a chair, he opened one and started reading.

With each sentence, a rush of adrenaline soared through his veins. The base of his skull throbbed while a hammering rose inside his head. By the time he completed the last letter, every muscle in his six-foot-two frame was wound tight.

Bianca was not who she claimed to be. Portraying the destitute widow, playing on his sympathy and using him to cross the border into the United States. All in the hope of reuniting with her lover. The depth of her treachery was intolerable. Collecting the letters, he deposited them back inside the lining of her purse. His fingers gripped the edge of the counter as he weighed his options.

"Miguel?"

He whirled around. Bianca tiptoed across the linoleum, her pale green taffeta nightgown revealing the mounds of her breasts. She pressed herself against him and caressed his cheek. Her perfume, once so enticing, repulsed him.

"What is it?" she asked.

He studied her slender neck, the delicate flesh taunting him to squeeze the life out of her. How easy it would be to make her suffer right now. He visualized her begging him to stop, her eyes pleading, hands clawing at his wrists—her last, frantic gasp for air, before collapsing to the floor.

"Miguel, please, tell me what is wrong."

"Nothing," he said, pulling himself back from the brink. "I have many things on my mind. I saw the girl, Izzy, with her mother."

Bianca stepped back, her eyes wide. "Where?"

"In Rapid City. While running errands, I happened to notice them. Izzy spoke to me."

Her brow creased. "You have put yourself at risk. If her mother—"

"Quit speaking nonsense," he barked. "I am always careful. It was unfortunate I still needed to secure the attic. Otherwise, I might have followed them and snatched the girl." Miguel considered the uncertainty in her eyes. "I hope you are ready for this. I will depend on you much more than before."

Bianca removed a cup from the cabinet, filling it with coffee. Adding cream and sugar, she stirred while staring off into the distance.

"Did you hear me, Bianca?"

"*Sí.* I heard you. I am afraid something will go wrong."

Fuming inside, he said, "Then you had better pray it does not."

He examined every inch of her, focusing on the waves in her long hair, her deep brown eyes, and sculpted lips, before looking away. There would be no mention of the letters yet. Not until his plan was complete. Then she would pay for her transgressions against him.

"I will do my best as always." She sipped. Hot steam rose from her cup, dissipating into the air. "You can rely on me, Miguel."

He strode out of the kitchen, the bitter taste of her betrayal on his tongue. When the time came, Bianca Flores would no longer walk this earth. She would regret her deception with her last dying breath.

CHAPTER 24

NICK

Downstairs in the game room, Nick racked the billiard balls and drew a cue stick from the rack. While he chalked the tip, he glanced over at Dalton at the opposite end of the pool table. "Glad you came over today. Ready for me to kick your ass in a game of eight-ball?"

Dalton chuckled. "Give it your best shot."

Crouching by the left side of the table one diamond away from the corner pocket, Nick placed the cue ball two diamonds up, then set up his shot. With the stick gliding effortlessly through his fingers, he struck the cue ball half a tip below center, sending it directly at the middle where it clipped the solid yellow number one on the left, drove it into the side pocket and scattered the rest of the balls.

"Show off," Dalton said.

Nick sunk two more balls before Dalton dominated the game by sinking four striped balls in a row.

Nick pointed his cue stick at him. "Somebody's been practicing."

"Yeah, maybe a little."

Within minutes, Dalton called the eight-ball shot and won. He dropped his cue stick into the rack and gestured at Nick. "So, who kicked who's ass?"

Nick placed his stick alongside Dalton's. "I didn't realize I was being conned by a ringer."

Dalton smirked. "Sure glad the ladies are upstairs. Wouldn't want them to have witnessed the beating I gave you."

"Careful, or your head won't fit through the door," Nick teased. He stepped behind the custom-built mahogany bar beyond the dual-sided fireplace, where glass shelves, lit with pastel blue lighting, held numerous bottles of expensive alcohol. "Drink?"

"Yes, as a matter of fact, I might have two since I won."

Nick poured Johnnie Walker Blue Label into two tumblers and they settled themselves on thick, cushioned bar stools.

Dalton's eyes swept the room, taking in the videos game machines, air hockey, and ping- pong table beneath the beamed ceiling. The other end featured a dartboard and poker table. Pictures of famous sports figures lined the walls. He caught a glimpse of the adjoining room holding a home theater with plush seating and nodded. "You and Carrie sure did a hell of a job designing all this. I'm rather envious. This game room beats anything I've seen lately."

Nick swallowed some whisky. "You can build your own."

"Red would never go for it. I gave up trying to persuade her to add onto the ranch house a long time ago. She's happy with the way things are."

Nick rubbed the back of his neck and glanced around. "Building this place was pure hell at times, but well worth it in the end. I can't count the number of disagreements Carrie and I had. She never asked for anything this enormous and grand." He studied his drink. "But she deserves it and more."

"She's an exceptional woman," Dalton said, and downed his whisky.

"Don't I know it." Nick finished his and poured two more. Hoisting his glass, he said, "Here's to *our* exceptional women."

"I'll second that." Dalton sipped, then set his glass aside and leaned his elbows on the bar. "Any word on the missing waitress?"

"Unfortunately, no. The police have no leads. Sarah seems to have disappeared without a trace, along with her car."

"Ran off, maybe?"

Nick shook his head. "Not the type to run off. Plus, her cell phone was left behind. I hope they find out what happened to her one way or the other. I don't know what I would do if it were Izzy."

"Yeah, a tough road for any parent to travel."

"By the way, is the horse ready?"

Dalton nodded. "Yep. You can bring Izzy out to the ranch whenever you want."

An unusual silence settled between them. Nick drew a deep breath. "Listen, I'm not certain if this is the ideal time or not..."

"For what?"

"With Jack being here, you have enough on your mind, and I don't need to add to it."

Dalton squinted. "After all these years, you should know better. You can always talk to me about anything at any time."

Nick met his eyes. "Do you ever think about some of the things we've done...all the killing, especially the night in Tahoe?"

"Look, I see where you're headed with this. Ever since Carmela died, you've been blaming yourself for it. The woman brought on her own demise, Nick. Your hands are clean as far as she goes."

"That's just it," Nick said. "The day I shot Ricardo, Carmela changed. Trust me, she was a good person until she witnessed the shooting."

Dalton groaned. "If you choose to believe that, then I can't change your mind. Remember, no one forced Carmela to do the evil things she did. Not to mention Ricardo teaching her narcotics trafficking, and how eager she was to learn. We'll never know how many were hooked, overdosed, or how many families she ruined because of her drug running."

The whisky did a slow burn in Nick's stomach. "What about all the others?"

Dalton squeezed Nick's shoulder. "Don't do this to yourself. The people we killed got what they deserved. Truth be told, I've done a whole heap more than you, and I sleep like a baby knowing there's one less son of a bitch roaming around, messing things up for good folks."

"I always thought so too, until…"

"Until what?"

Nick rubbed his temples to relieve the pressure building inside his skull. "I've been having nightmares."

"About what?"

"Being hounded by dead men. It's so bad, Carrie is aware." He swiped his fingers through his hair and paused. "The other day, I felt them all around me."

"Are you telling me you're letting those no-good pieces of scum haunt you? Men like that … and I mean every single one … are right where they belong."

Nick stared into his whisky, then up into his friend's eyes. "How do you do it, Dalton? How can it not haunt you?"

Dalton slapped his palm on the bar. "It can't, and it never will because I simply have to ask myself one question."

"What's that?"

"Is this world better off without them in it? You and I both know the answer. I'm no saint, and neither are you, but we do uphold a certain code. Our kills are justified. We only harm those who do evil. Even the men who perished in Tahoe, worked for Carmela and would have murdered us. Don't kid yourself. There are plenty more out there right now who shouldn't be walking upright."

Nick paused. Dalton's words causing him to reflect on the years he spent working for Ricardo. He had always believed the man saved him, but now reality set in. He'd been indoctrinated, programmed to do his bidding, and the one time he refused, Ricardo wrote him off.

Dalton jabbed Nick's arm. "Hey, come back."

"What?"

"I lost you for a second."

"Sorry, I was thinking about Ricardo and how easily he brainwashed me."

"Ricardo caught you at your lowest point. He knew precisely what to do."

"You're right," Nick said. "But I'm struggling and…"

"And what?"

Tightness bound his chest. He inhaled against it. "Even with all the nightmares and images, sometimes, I miss the adrenaline rush. I wonder how normal that is."

Dalton's bushy brows drew together. "The way the world is now, who's to say what is and isn't normal. But I believe the rush comes from the bitterness of the past. Yours from losing family members and a job you loved through no fault of your own. Mine from losing family, too. The rush we feel during a kill shot only serves to make us better at what we do. We couldn't have become ghosts without it."

Nick cocked his head. "You too?"

"Hell, you thought you were the only one. And yes, like you, I do miss it, but I try to focus on what's important, right here, right now."

Nick's fingers curled around his glass. "It makes me wonder if men like Miguel Medina experience a rush."

Dalton's expression grew grim. "More likely than not. But Miguel is a different breed altogether. I've heard things over the years. His standards are much lower. Using a knife is proof enough. I shudder to think how he enjoys twisting a blade into someone's guts. Our kills are clean and quick. If he were on our side, it goes without saying he'd carry his own weight. Against us, he's a formidable enemy."

"All I know is if I hadn't gotten that knife away from him in Tahoe, I wouldn't be sitting here today," Nick said.

"Look," Dalton continued. "I love you like a brother. You have to make peace with all this, or it will destroy you. Carrie and your children can't afford for you to get swallowed up in all of it. Hell, I can't either."

"Are you still in the business?" Nick asked.

"Not since marrying Red a year ago. On the last hit, I realized how distracted I'd become. All I wanted to do was finish and return home to her." Dalton seized the bottle and splashed some more into his glass, then gulped it down. "Distractions are not a healthy thing in our trade."

"Amen to that," Nick said. "And, thanks for listening."

Dalton winked. "Anytime." He stood and inhaled. "Something sure smells great. Let's go and see what the ladies are cooking."

"Be there in a minute." Nick picked up their empty tumblers, rinsed, and dried them. Dalton made a lot of sense. Now, all he needed to do was convince himself.

CHAPTER 25

JACK

Jack poured a shot of Macallan Old Fine Oak Scotch. Inspecting the bottle, he admired his brother's excellent taste in liquor. He leaned back into the soft brown leather armchair, then swung his booted feet up onto the coffee table.

"Man, this is living." He gulped the drink and poured another, glad he had the place to himself for a change. With Dalton and Joann off visiting Nick and Carrie, he could sit and envision the ranch and all its holdings belonged to him.

Still unable to come up with a solid plan regarding his brother and Joann, he played out several scenarios in his mind, concluding the best course of action if possible, might be two at once, over and done. Unless other opportunities presented themselves.

He rose and wandered to the photographs he'd seen on his arrival. Raising the picture of Nick, Carrie, and Bobby, he examined their faces.

"What a beauty she is." He reflected on the women who had shared his bed over the years. Some were worth their looks, others not so much.

"It's a woman's duty to satisfy a man, give him what he needs," he declared. Smiling, he traced Carrie's face with his fingertip. "I can only imagine what Nick's getting from you." A chuckle escaped his lips.

Setting the photograph aside, he went to Dalton's study and jiggled the doorknob. "You think a lock will keep me out, little brother?" He'd picked many a lock in Vegas. Could be time to pick this one.

His head jerked when he heard a car pull up outside. Could they be home already? He dashed up the hallway, snatched the bottle of scotch, and returned it to the wet bar. After rinsing the shot glass, he climbed the stairs. Halfway up, the doorbell rang.

Annoyed, Jack trudged back down. Someone had the gate code. He pulled the door open. A young woman with auburn hair and green eyes stared at him. A purse was slung over one shoulder, and she gripped a brown duffel bag in her hand. A small valise lay at her feet.

With an uncertain look in her eye, she said, "I'm Veronica, Joann's daughter."

"Well, of course. I recognize you from your picture. I'm Jack, Dalton's older brother." He extended his hand.

The corner of her mouth twitched as his hand clasped hers. "Oh, Dalton never mentioned a brother. It's nice to meet you, Jack."

He looked at the duffel. "Here, let me carry the bag for you."

She waved his hand away, a slight blush rising in her cheeks. "No, that's okay. You can carry the other one for me."

He lifted the valise. "Come on in, Veronica."

"Please, call me Ronnie. Everyone does."

"Okay then, Ronnie."

She followed him into the living room. "Is my mom or Dalton at home?"

"I'm afraid not," he said, setting the valise down. "They're out visiting. Were they expecting you?"

"No. I wanted to surprise them." She swiped at a strand of hair resting across her left eyelid and glanced at the stairs. "I usually stay in one of the spare bedrooms. I'd like to freshen up. It's been a long trip."

"Where from?"

"New York."

Jack raised an eyebrow. "I'm sure someone could have picked you up from the airport if they were aware you were coming."

"Oh no," Ronnie said. "I didn't fly. I've been on the road for several days. Mom will pitch a fit when she finds out. She'd rather Dalton send his jet."

Jack's pulse spiked. A spasm struck the pit of his stomach. The son of a bitch has his own jet!

He steadied himself and picked up the valise beating Ronnie to the stairs. "Now, I insist you let me carry both bags up. It's the least I can do after your long trip." Her hesitation piqued his curiosity, and he offered her a teasing smile. "Come on, hand it over."

Pausing a moment, she relented and gave up the duffel.

His arm dropped at the unexpected weight. "Whoa, what's inside here, a load of bricks?"

Her face blanched. "My laptop, work files, and some personal things. The files make it heavy."

"Right, Joann mentioned you're a lawyer."

They climbed up and on to the second spare room. Jack set the bag on the bed. "I don't know where my manners are. Can I get you something to eat or drink?"

"If it's no trouble, I could use a sandwich."

"Sure thing. Come down when you're ready."

Jack shut the bedroom door and headed for the kitchen. Ronnie's demeanor told him a whole bunch. Something odd lay inside that duffel for sure. Chances are it wouldn't pass through security at the airport. Why else would she drive all the way from New York when she could have flown.

While preparing Ronnie a sandwich, the jet popped into his head. If she hadn't mentioned it, he never would have known. No way could Dalton afford a jet off running a cattle ranch. His brother was keeping secrets.

"This is so nice of you." Ronnie stood in the kitchen doorway. Her dark green sweatshirt hung loose. Tan khaki slacks swam on her slight frame.

From his viewpoint, she didn't look too healthy. "No problem. Anything to drink with your sandwich?"

"A cold beer would be nice," she said, flashing him a smile for the first time.

Jack handed her a beer, then snagged one for himself. They retreated into the dining room and sat across from one another. Ronnie bit into her sandwich before twisting the cap off the beer.

Jack studied her for a moment. He surmised he might pick up some more useful information regarding Dalton.

"Do you live nearby?" she asked.

"Vegas, actually." Jack raised his beer and drank.

"I've never been. Always wanted to go."

"It's not for everyone."

She sipped her beer. "I'm not really interested in gambling, but I'd like to see some of the shows."

"Vegas has excellent entertainment and darn good restaurants. Pricey, though," Jack said.

"I'll have to check it out sometime."

"So, working on any big legal cases?" He asked. "Heard there's loads of crime in New York what with all the drugs and such." She raked her fingers through her hair and paused. He'd struck a nerve.

"I've handled a few criminal cases. Nothing too significant," she said between bites.

Deciding to switch gears, he said. "Since I've been here, I see how hard my brother works keeping this ranch profitable. Can't figure how he's able to do it. We haven't had the chance to catch up."

"Well, I know he's worked other jobs."

"What kind?"

"He traveled a great deal for a while. Mostly with Nick. They've been friends for years. I don't know if you've met him yet."

"No, but I'm certain I will soon."

"I think it was some type of government work." Finished with her sandwich, she pushed the plate aside. Her eyelids drooped, and she rested her chin in the palm of her hand.

Jack smiled. "Sounds like Dalton. He's a true patriot."

Ronnie tilted her head and pursed her lips. "It was before he and my mother married. Seems he's home more often now." She shoved her chair back. "If you'll excuse me, I'm exhausted. I think I'll take a shower and nap before they get home. Thanks again for the sandwich and beer."

"You're welcome."

She reached for the plate and the empty beer bottle.

"I'll get that," Jack said. "You go take it easy."

He cleared her dish and the beer bottles, then plopped onto the sofa in the living room. So, besides a plane, Dalton worked a government job. His brother sure had a fascinating life, and it appeared this Nick might play a part in it. He was correct in guessing Dalton's money came from more than cattle ranching.

Sounds of the shower running caught his attention. He crept up the stairs. Ronnie was in the bathroom down the hall. Jack slipped into her bedroom and spied the duffel on top of the flowered comforter. Ears primed for her possible return, he unzipped it.

He slapped his cheek. This girl was something else. Living in Vegas had taught him most people are not what they appear to be. No way in hell Joann or Dalton was aware of her running drugs. For the life of him, he couldn't figure out why an attorney was moving narcotics.

His heart thumping, he picked up a brick of cocaine. This could solve part of his problem. Jack drew another, readjusted the rest, and zipped up the bag. He hurried to his room and locked the door. Familiar with seedy types back home, he knew two bricks were worth at least twenty thousand each, if not more. He could hand them over to Mel, a down payment on what he owed. If nothing else, it would buy him some time.

He shoved the coke underneath his mattress and went downstairs. Eyeing the door to Dalton's study again, he was convinced the answers he lacked about his brother lay sealed inside. With Ronnie here, he didn't dare take a chance and pick the lock. Plus, Dalton and Joann could return any minute now.

Thanks to Ronnie, he'd learned some interesting facts today. Those facts might be helpful. He turned away from the door and went back into the living room.

"In due time, little brother, I will discover how you're able to afford a jet plane." Dalton appeared wealthier than he could have imagined. All he needed to do now was discover the source.

CHAPTER 26

VERONICA

Ronnie bolted up from the bed and switched on the lamp. Catching a brief nap was what she had needed before driving to the Grey Hound Bus Station in Rapid City. Unloading the drugs would soothe her frayed nerves. Wanting to make the drive before her mother and Dalton returned home, she dressed, snatched the duffle bag, and charged downstairs. Jack was nowhere in sight. She sprinted to her car. At the end of the driveway, she removed a small vial from her purse. She inhaled two hits, then drove through the gates of the property.

For the first time, Derek had given her two duffle bags. One to be delivered to Indiana and the other to South Dakota. The handoff in Indiana went off without a hitch. Tonight, she'd drive into Rapid City and rid herself of the second bag.

On the way to her drop, she grew curious about Jack. Dalton had never mentioned a brother. His pleasant manner appeared genuine. Was she right in perceiving something sinister underneath his exterior?

Ronnie checked the time. She drove to the far end of the nearly empty station parking lot, pulling into a spot away from the streetlamps. She kept her purse close, just in case. A few minutes passed before a black sedan drove up alongside her. A man, his face half-hidden by shadows, got out. He tapped on the glass, and she slid the window down.

"You set?" he asked.

Without looking his way, she replied, "Yes." Ronnie popped the trunk, and he removed the duffle before slipping another one in. He tossed hers into the sedan, then sped away. Heart roaring, she waited a minute before leaving the parking lot. Relieved, when she arrived at the ranch and didn't see Dalton's truck, she rushed inside.

"There you are."

Ronnie froze. Jack stood in the hallway.

"I thought you were resting."

"I…needed to make a quick run." He eyed her as she patted her purse. "Drug store for aspirin."

"I'm sure we have some in the house."

"I prefer a certain kind." Sweeping past him, she asked. "My mom home yet?"

"No. But I think I hear the truck coming up the drive now."

He followed her into the living room. Within minutes the front door opened.

Joann rushed in. "Ronnie!" She wrapped her arms around her.

When Joann finally let go. Ronnie kissed her cheek. "Hello to you, too."

"Why didn't you tell us you were coming?"

"I wanted to surprise you." She moved around Joann and pecked Dalton's cheek.

A broad grin lit his face, and he reciprocated. "I recognized your car when we pulled in. Did you drive all the way from New York?"

"I enjoyed the ride. It's nice to have a bit of solitude."

Dalton stepped back. "You're looking a little thin, Ronnie."

"I agree," Joann said. "Haven't you been taking care of yourself?"

"I'm fine, Mom. Keeping late hours at my job. I sometimes skip a meal."

Joann wagged her finger. "Your health is important. You better get back on track."

"I promise I will."

"How long are you staying?" Joann asked.

"I'm afraid I have to take off in the morning."

Joann frowned. "Carrie and I planned a party for tomorrow evening. Our employees are all coming. It's kind of an appreciation thing between the restaurant and the ranch. Can you at least stay one more day?"

Ronnie hesitated. "Works piling up while I'm gone."

"Oh, come on, Veronica. An extra day won't hurt. Bobby's even flying in with Natalia."

Whenever her mother called her Veronica, things tended to blow up a bit, which led to her probing. At this point, the fewer questions, the better for her. "Okay, I'll stay."

"Thank you," Joann said. "It means a lot to have you here. We don't get to see each other often."

"I know, Mom." A yawn slipped out, and she rubbed her eyes. "If you don't mind, I'm going to turn in early."

Joann's expression softened. "Have you eaten anything?"

"Yes, Jack was kind enough to prepare something for me when I arrived. I'm fine. Just tired."

"Red, leave her be for now. She needs to rest." Dalton said.

"Just a mother's concern," Joann said, frowning."

Ronnie kissed them both on the cheek again and headed upstairs. Inside the bedroom, she dug into her purse and retrieved the vial of coke, inhaling two hits before stripping off her clothes. She pinched her nostrils, mind buzzing as she crawled into bed. Her angst diminished, then abruptly resurfaced. How could she face Bobby? Even if she apologized, he would never forget her ugly words. Tears formed behind her lids while her phone buzzed.

Derek was on the line. She drew a shaky breath. "Hello, Derek."

"Don't you hello me, you bitch!"

She sat straight up. Her body shook. "What's wrong? I finished both drops."

"Yeah, you finished them all right. I just got a call. You were short two bricks in South Dakota."

She broke out in a sweat. "That's impossible."

"Apparently not."

"Derek, I swear to you. I never touched..." Her heart lurched. Jack was the only other person home before her mother and Dalton arrived.

"You get your ass back here, Ronnie. And you bring those two missing bricks with you. Because of you, I've lost my connection there. They don't trust me anymore. The cartel is making good with them on the money. Now I have to make good with the cartel."

"Cartel?" She bit her bottom lip. "You're working with a cartel?"

"Where on earth do you think the narcotics come from? The drug fairy? I move a certain amount for the cartel, and we split the money."

"I can't leave here now. My mother would ask too many questions."

"I don't give a damn about your mother. You either get back to New York with the bricks in forty-eight hours, or I release those videos of you all over social media and deliver a copy to your job. And if you're so concerned about your mother, maybe she'd like to see them, too."

"Derek, please. I need a little time to find out what happened."

"What I said is final. Don't disappoint me, Ronnie."

The line went dead, and she stared at the phone. No way could those s be leaked. Her entire life would be in ruins. She wouldn't have the courage to face her mother or anyone else again.

Sinking against the pillows, her mind in turmoil, she glanced at her purse lying on the bed, her gun tucked inside. There was only one thing left to do. Get the dope from Jack.

CHAPTER 27

BOBBY

B obby examined the card, debating whether to make the call. Something must have gone terribly wrong between his mother and his grandfather. Even so, he felt entitled to meet him.

With limited time left to deliberate before leaving for South Dakota, he dialed the number. His palms sweaty, he readjusted the cell phone. On the fourth ring, a man answered.

"Hello."

Bobby braced himself. "Yes...hello. Is this Alex Paterson?"

"Yes, who is this?"

"I'm afraid we haven't met. I'm your grandson, Bobby. Carrie is my mother." Silence greeted him.

"Are you still there?" Bobby asked, fearing he'd made a mistake.

"Yes, yes, of course. I'm just a bit shocked. How did you ... I mean, did *she* give you my number?"

"Not exactly. Your card fell out of her pocket. I should have given it back, but she was upset after meeting with you. I wasn't sure what to do."

"How much did your mother tell you?"

"Very little. She refused to talk about it."

"If you're agreeable, can we meet? I would like the opportunity to explain things."

Bobby bit the inside of his cheek. This was unexpected. He checked his watch. "I have some time before catching a flight later today, but you would have to come here. My daughter is napping."

"Text me the address, and I'll leave now."

Bobby hung up, sent the text, then paused. Introducing his grandfather into their lives might be a mistake. If he had caused his mother additional anguish, he didn't want him around either.

Thirty minutes later, Bobby opened the door, his composure slipping as he did a double take. Standing before him was a tall, well-dressed man with silver hair and light blue eyes. It was like looking into a mirror thirty years from now.

"Bobby, I'm Alex." He offered his hand.

After a brief handshake, Bobby led him into the living room.

"Nice place," Alex said. "Seems you've done well for yourself." He pointed to one of the paintings. "Do you mind?"

"No," Bobby said.

On closer inspection, he said, "Gustav Klimt. One of my favorite artists." He turned, scrutinizing another above the sofa. "I'm not familiar with this artist, but I like it."

"It's by Carolyn O'Neill, an Australian painter."

"Well, it seems you inherited my passion for art."

Bobby ignored the comment. "Please, sit."

Eyeing a frame resting on an end table, he picked it up. "Your daughter?"

"Yes. Natalia when she was a baby. She's three now."

His eyes watered while he fingered the photograph. "She's beautiful."

"Thanks."

Alex set the photo down and eased into an armchair opposite the sofa. "You'll have to excuse me. This is all a bit overwhelming."

Bobby's spine stiffened. "What happened between you and my mother?"

"Listen, I'm not going to lie to you. Our meeting ended on a bad note. I didn't get the chance to explain what transpired all those years ago before she became upset."

"That doesn't make any sense. My mother said she needed answers."

Alex lowered his head and stared at the floor. His shoulders sagged, and he let out a breath. "True, but when I asked her to come and meet my wife, she refused."

Bobby bolted up. "Meet your wife! Why? All you have to do is explain things."

"Because she is a significant part of the circumstances surrounding what happened. I know it was a lot to ask, but nevertheless, the right thing to do."

"I'm confused," Bobby said. "Can't you just tell her? Your wife shouldn't have anything to do with it."

Alex stood and faced him. "Sadly, that isn't true." He locked eyes with Bobby. "I want to have a relationship with your mother, and you, too, of course. And I'd love to meet Natalia."

Bobby crossed his arms, his eyes not veering away. "It's all about what you want, isn't it?"

"No, not at all. It's ... it would be easier—"

"Exactly. Easier for you. Do you have any idea what my mother went through after you abandoned her?"

Alex's face pinched. "Yes, she told me how awful your grandmother treated her."

"But," Bobby said. "You really don't know the whole story concerning her, or *me* for that matter."

"Then tell me, please, Bobby, I'll do anything to remedy some of the damage I've caused."

Bobby smirked. "I think that ship has sailed, and there isn't enough time to tell you everything today. I have a flight to catch to South Dakota. My mother has no idea I called you. I need time to figure things out." He walked to the door and opened it.

Alex followed, hesitating on the threshold. "Please let me know when I can meet with you again. Whether you believe me or not, Bobby, I care deeply for your mother. I realize I don't have the right to ask for anything from either of you, but please consider giving me a chance."

"Like I said, I'll think about it."

Bobby closed the door, his stomach in knots. He could only imagine how his mother reacted when asked to meet his grandfather's wife and couldn't fathom why meeting her was vital.

He went to Natalia's room. She lay sleeping, her hair splayed out on the pillow. He sat on the bed, the movement waking her.

"Hi, pretty girl. Ready to go to Grandma and Grandpa's house?"

She rubbed at her eyes. "Are we going on the airplane?"

"Yes. Come here." He pulled the blanket down and perched her on his lap. Too much was happening in his life again.

Between worrying about Ronnie and meeting his grandfather, the party at his mother's tomorrow might be a nice distraction. Sooner or later, he would have to deal with both.

Natalia snuggled against him. He thought about his father. According to his mother, he was not a good man, and she had suffered plenty at his hands. Alex seemed nice enough, but how could he be sure it wasn't all an act?

The only way to uncover the truth would mean taking him up on his offer. When he returned from South Dakota, he'd contact Alex again. His mother needed answers, and he wanted to be the one to get them for her.

CHAPTER 28

THE PARTY

Dressed casually in black pants and a cobalt blue sweater, her hair done in a French braid, trailing down her back like a thick cord of dark silk, Carrie surveyed the buffet tables lining the perimeter of the great room.

The savory aroma of cooked meats and fresh fish mingled with the sweet scent of baked goods. A fire blazed in the dual-sided fireplace for guests to enjoy from either the dining or great rooms. Extra seating with tables draped in plain white cloths were stationed about. Soft jazz music emanated from the recessed speakers.

Appetizers, consisting of marinated grilled shrimp, crab cakes, salmon, and clams, along with oysters on the half-shell, were located side by side. She eyed the platters of cheese from the local Dimrock Dairy and plucked a square of Colby, popping it into her mouth.

She advanced past another buffet table bearing sides of potato and pasta salads. A line of pans loaded with roasted portobello mushrooms and sautéed green beans were next to cuts of Filet Mignon, racks of barbecue ribs, baked chicken, and buffalo burgers. Hot dogs and hamburgers were available for the children.

Traditional South Dakota dishes would also be served. She made sure there were favorites like pheasant, broiled walleye, and grilled lamb and beef cubes known as chislic.

The dessert table held assorted cookie platters, fresh fruit salad, apple pie, warm cinnamon rolls, and local specialties such as Kuchen, a pastry filled with creamy custard, and poured over peaches and Kolache, another pastry stuffed with candied fruit.

Wanting something fun for the children, she ordered an ice cream bar. Chocolate, caramel, and strawberry sauce, along with candy, fruit, and nut toppings, were displayed. Cans of whipped cream and bowls of maraschino cherries were arranged on the side, and lastly, homemade fudge from Turtle Town in Hill City.

Nodding her approval to the caterers, she proceeded to survey the fresh-squeezed lemonade and bottled soda, juice, and water. A few feet away, a bar was set up with beer, wine, and assorted liquor.

She strolled outside onto the patio where Nick adjusted the outdoor heaters. A fire, spitting sap, crackled in the outdoor fireplace.

"You and Joann have outdone yourselves," he said, reaching for her. "This is going to be a fantastic night."

Carrie smoothed the collar of his long-sleeved polo shirt. She wrapped her arms around his neck. "I hope so. My main purpose is to lighten the mood a little." Her body tensed for a moment. "I wish Sarah were here."

"So do I. But we all need this break. Our restaurant staff and Dalton's ranch hands work hard."

"Don't you two ever get enough of each other?" Dalton's voice boomed as he stepped through the open sliders, a broad grin on his face. His denim shirt, tucked into his jeans, revealed an antiqued western silver belt buckle that shone in the firelight.

"Never," Carrie said, letting go of Nick. She went and kissed Dalton on the cheek. "Where's Joann?"

"Red and Ronnie are checking out the spread inside."

Carrie's heart lifted. "Oh, I'm so glad Ronnie's here. We miss seeing her."

Dalton's grin evaporated. He peered over his shoulder before saying, "Yes, but try not to look shocked when you see her. She's lost quite a bit of weight. Claims it's work. I get the feeling it's not the whole story."

Nick set another log on the fire. "What do you think it is?"

"Not sure. I haven't said much because I don't want to alarm Red any further." He smoothed his mustache and paused. "By the way, you'll finally get to meet my brother. Joann insisted I bring him. Probably for the best. I have concerns when it comes to leaving him alone at home for too long."

"Looking forward to it," Nick said, winking at Dalton.

Carrie pointed her finger at Nick. "I caught that. Joann told me he's been pretty decent so far."

"Jury's still out, though," Dalton said.

They walked inside. Joann and Ronnie were standing by the bar, a glass of wine in their hands. Carrie tried to conceal her shock at Ronnie's appearance. Her face was pale and drawn, and the deep maroon, pocketed cardigan over her white blouse gobbled up her rail-thin frame. The dress pants beneath it swam on her. She pressed a small leather clutch under her arm.

"Ronnie, it's good to see you," Carrie said, giving her a brief hug.

Nick draped his arm around Ronnie's shoulder. "We've missed you. Hope we get to see you more often in the future."

Ronnie sipped her wine and smiled. "It's great to be here. I heard Bobby was coming?"

Carrie spotted the slight tremor in Ronnie's hand. "Yes, he flew in late this afternoon and should be down any minute.

Valentina will keep track of all the children tonight so we can relax a bit."

"How many more?" Ronnie asked.

Eight belong to our ranch hands," Joann said. She nudged Ronnie's side. "Maybe someday you'll make me a grandmother."

Ronnie blushed. "Not anytime soon, I'm afraid."

Dalton nodded at Nick. "Let's go find Jack."

Carrie looped her arm through Joann's. "Come on, I hear cars pulling up out front. Time to play hostess."

*　　*　　*　　*

Ronnie finished her wine, then beckoned the bartender for a refill while guests filed in, heading for the bar and buffet tables.

Feeling no desire to mingle or eat, she drifted outside to the patio and sat by the fire, her mind in turmoil. Derek's threats unnerved her. With Dalton and her mother home, there had been no way for her to confront Jack about the missing cocaine.

"I didn't realize you were here." Bobby strode toward her, handsome as ever, dressed in black jeans and a grey turtleneck. He perched on the arm of the chair across from her, a drink in his hand.

"Actually, I was kind of forced to come." She looked away and sipped her wine.

He sat down next to her. "It's okay, Ronnie. I'm not mad at you."

"You should be. After all the horrible things I said."

"Ronnie, look at me."

Unwilling, she stared down at the floor. "I...can't. You've always been good to me. You didn't deserve to be treated that way."

He squeezed her shoulder. She looked up and into his eyes, the kindest eyes she'd seen in a long time. "I'm truly sorry for hurting you, Bobby. It would kill me to lose our friendship."

Running his finger along her cheek, he said, "All is forgiven, but we need to talk someplace private." He led her past the swarm of guests. Bobby greeted Rosie and several employees before entering the study and closing the door. Ronnie tossed her purse down and eased into an armchair while he leaned against the desk.

He finished his drink and set the glass aside. "I believe you when you say you don't want to lose our friendship, Ronnie. But friends are honest with each other, and right now, I need you to be honest with me."

"I'm not sure what you mean."

"I think you do. I've known for a while now something's wrong, and I found out exactly what it is."

Failing to stop her bottom lip from quivering, she set her glass down. "So, tell me then."

"You're trafficking drugs for that jerk at the club."

Bile burned her throat. She gulped, forcing it down. Shielding her face, she bent her head and wept. "I...I'm so ashamed."

Bobby knelt beside her. "What's he got on you?"

She rocked back and forth, her mouth dry, her chest tightening. The time had come to tell him everything. Dropping her hands, his face a blur through her tears, she said, "Videos. Awful videos of me having sex with different men."

Bobby stood. He rubbed the back of his neck and paced. "But how? I don't understand."

"I met Derek at a club one night. He must have drugged my drink. I don't remember much of anything. I woke up the next morning at his apartment, in his bed, naked. When I began questioning him, he showed me the videos, threatening to release them on porn sights, social media, plus send copies to my job if I refused to traffic drugs for him."

She sprang up from the chair, her face inches from his, she cried, "I didn't know what else to do! I thought it would be a one-time thing, and he'd hand them over."

His eyes swept over her. "You're not telling me everything."

She backed away. "What do you mean? I just told you what happened."

"Ronnie, have you looked in a mirror lately? You're using."

A nerve quickened in her gut. "So, what if I am. You have no idea what it's been like for me. It's only a little coke to help me through all this."

Bobby frowned and folded his arms. "I think it's more than a little. I won't argue the point right now while I decide what to do about Derek and those videos."

"No, Bobby, you can't!" she wailed. "I don't want you caught up in all of this. You have Natalia to consider. Derek's a dangerous guy. He's tied to a cartel."

He held both her hands in his. "I've run across worse men than Derek. I care about you, Ronnie. I won't stand by and let him destroy you."

"But—"

"Trust me, Derek will never let you stop running drugs or using coke until he's finished with you." His eyes locked on hers. "Do you understand what I'm saying? You'll die, Ronnie. You know too much about his business. He'll kill you."

Her breath caught. Chills rippled across her flesh. She tore her hands away and reached for her purse. Searching inside, she removed a small vial.

Bobby knocked the vial out of her hand. "Don't! Coke's not the answer. You need to start being smarter. He's controlling you with that garbage."

"I'm ruined anyway. It doesn't matter." Trying to steady the tremor in her voice, she told him about Jack, the missing coke, and Derek's threats.

He cupped her chin. "I'm not going to let anything happen to you. I want you to stay here in South Dakota with your mother. Call your job and ask for time off."

"Stay here? I can't, Bobby. I have to get the coke from Jack and return it to Derek. I appreciate your wanting to help, but what could you possibly do?"

"You can't leave for New York just yet, and the less you know, the better." He handed her his cell. "Put Derek's number and address in here."

She opened her mouth to speak, but he pressed his fingertip to her lips. "No more talking. No more worrying and don't say anything to Jack. Everything will be taken care of."

Ronnie did as he asked, then handed him the phone.

"Now," Bobby said. "Fix your face, and when you're ready, come and join the party." He picked up the vial of coke, slipped it into the pocket of his jeans, and left.

Ronnie collapsed into the chair. Confessing everything to Bobby put him in between her and Derek. If anything happened to him, she would never forgive herself. She plucked a tissue from her purse and dabbed at her eyes. Right now, she had no other choice but to trust him.

*   *   *   *

Bianca smoothed the front of her flowered dress. She teetered for a moment in her three-inch heels before stepping into the great room. Being inside a home as lavish as this made her uneasy. Her assumptions regarding Carrie were correct. How fortunate some people were, their lives overflowing with riches.

Moving along the buffet tables, she filled her plate, then snatched a glass of champagne from one of the waiters circulating around the room. Seating herself with a few *Buena Comida* employees, she relished the filet mignon and portobello mushrooms.

Alice gulped her wine and winked. "This is the life. Maybe someday we'll meet a wealthy, handsome man like Mr. D'Angelo, who'll sweep us off our feet. I wonder how they met."

Bianca flashed her a smile between bites. Sure, money was nice, but love, much more important. She didn't blame Alice for her remarks. She'd never been in love with a man the way she loved Alejandro.

Finished with her plate, Bianca lifted her glass of champagne and rose. She surveyed the room. The Dalton ranch employees had been invited also. Alejandro might be among them. She drifted toward voices emanating from a stairway leading to the lower level.

Careful not to spill her drink, she navigated the steps. People were spread out, some playing video games or air hockey, while others shot pool.

Feeling a tug at her wrist, she glanced down.

"I remember you from the restaurant," Izzy said. "Your name is Bianca, isn't it?" Her long hair was curled, and she wore a pretty pink sweater with a design on the front and jeans.

Bianca's throat pulsed. She forced a smile. "That is right. Are you having fun?"

"Yes, loads. We even have an ice cream bar upstairs."

"Really? I must have missed it."

"Izzy D'Angelo! I have been searching for you everywhere. Come upstairs with me. You are not supposed to be down here with the adults."

A young woman with short-cropped blonde hair charged at them. Bianca recognized her as the person who picked Izzy up at school.

"Valentina," Izzy said, frowning. "I was talking to Bianca. She works at *Buena Comida.*"

"You heard me. Now, come along." She looked at Bianca. "Sorry."

"It is okay. Izzy was just saying hello."

They headed upstairs, and Bianca followed, her heart pounding at the thought of Miguel and his plans for Izzy.

She wandered outside to the patio. People were gathered around the fireplace, drinks in their hands. Voices filled her ears as she drifted past the pool. Puffs of steam wafted along the surface of the water in the chilly air. Light from a full moon spilled across the Bluestone pavers and shrubbery encircling the yard.

A man wearing a cowboy hat stood near a pathway, his back to her. Something stirred inside her. Could it be? A tingling spread across her breast. She moved closer. The surrounding noise faded into the night. Her legs threatened to give way.

"Alejandro?"

Bianca ran to him. She set her champagne glass down on the stone wall by the edge of the path. Her arms encircled his neck. She pressed her face against it, feeling the warmth of his skin on her cheek.

"*Mi amor,*" she whispered over and over, her lips leaving a delicate trail of kisses. Gazing up at him, she traced her fingertip along his brow. "I thought I would never find you."

She felt his body go stiff. He stared at her, a shocked expression on his face and a hollow look in his eyes. Gently, he removed her arms from around his neck and drew her into the shadows.

"Bianca, please. You must not do this here."

Tears welled up. "What are you saying? Are you not happy to see me?"

Removing his hat, he swept a hand through his thick dark hair. He squinted over her shoulder as if expecting someone. "Of course, I am glad you are safe. What are you doing here?"

"I work at the owner's restaurant."

"No, I mean, how were you able to cross the border?"

How could she explain she used another man to enter the country? "I saved money and paid to cross. What does it matter? I am here with you now."

He cocked his head. "You were fortunate, Bianca. Mexico is full of *ladrones* who promise everything and deliver nothing."

"*Sí,* I was lucky," she said, fumbling with the collar of her dress. "But what about you? I did not know what to think when your letters stopped."

"You deserve answers, but we cannot speak any further right now."

Her jaw clenched. This was not her Alejandro. Not the same man who held her in his arms and declared his love.

"Do you know how much I longed for this day?" she said, her voice breaking. "I have dreamt of nothing else since you left Mexico. Even when your letters failed to arrive, I still believed in you."

His eyes met hers. "I am sorry. I should have written to let you know I managed to find a job working for a respectable man at a cattle ranch."

The tension inside her waned for a moment. "But that is a good thing. We can be together now."

He touched her lightly on the shoulder. "I did not think I would ever see you again, Bianca. My life has changed, and your life must change now, too."

Warmth crept up her neck while she fumbled for words. "What are you saying? I do not understand."

He looked past her and raised his hat. Avoiding her eyes, he sat it on his head again and adjusted the brim. Lines on his forehead creased. "Please do not cause a scene, Bianca."

A short, pretty, blonde-haired woman approached. She wore a loose-fitting, simple, long-sleeved black dress, which showed off her baby bump. A pair of flats adorned her feet, and a flowered scarf hung from around her neck. She reached for Alejandro's hand, the glint of a gold band flashing. Releasing a girlish giggle, she stared at Bianca. "Is he talking you to death? My husband has a habit of doing that."

Bianca drew a deep breath. The air around her became toxic as the woman spit venom with each word she spoke. Her heart buffeted against her chest. "Husband?"

"Yes, I'm sorry. I don't think we've met. I'm Pam...Pamela, Alejandro's wife."

Alejandro cleared his throat. "This is Bianca, an old friend from Mexico."

Bianca bit her lip to stop herself from screaming. What did he say? An old friend from Mexico?

Pamela held out her hand. "I'm pleased to meet you, Bianca."

She declined the handshake. "I see you are expecting a child."

Pamela lowered her hand and patted her stomach. "Yes, we're very excited. Our little boy will arrive in two more months."

Bianca locked eyes with Alejandro. This was all a terrible dream. Soon she would wake, and none of this would be real.

An awkward silence settled between the three. Pamela glanced at her, then at Alejandro. "Well, it's getting a bit chilly. What do you say we head back?" she said, pulling him away. "Nice meeting you, Bianca."

Unable to move, she fumed as they strolled down the path hand in hand. Heat exploded inside her. Alejandro had chosen a *gringa* over her. How quickly he must have forgotten their love for each other. Quick enough to marry and have another woman carry his child.

She tried to collect herself. What a fool she'd been to fall for a man who cared little about her. Her heart, once filled with love for Alejandro emptied, replaced with a wound so raw and deep it scorched her soul.

Snatching up her drink, she drained the last of the champagne, then hurled the empty glass at the ground. Fragments scattered across the pavers and shimmered in the moonlight. Alejandro had brought her world to an end, her future swallowed up by the blackness of his betrayal.

She stormed across the lawn, pausing to glare at the magnificent estate. Strings of patio lights twinkled against the dark night. Music and laughter poured from inside, the guests immune to her shattered dreams and broken heart.

Tall windows cast silhouettes of the children lining up in front of the ice cream bar. What right did the D'Angelos' have to live this glamorous life without worry or fear? Why should she be the only one to suffer?

She continued inside, her eyes settling on Izzy. Her fingers curled, digging into her palms. Soon, Miguel would shock the little girl's parents back into reality, and she would witness their undoing. Hers would not be the only life torn apart.

*   *   *   *

Jack traipsed along the rear of the property. Ever since his arrival, he'd been dodging Veronica. Before departing the house earlier, she had shot him a look. Being unable to confront him about the cocaine must be twisting her insides.

Moving farther, he came upon a man and a woman deep in conversation, oblivious to his presence. He retreated behind some shrubbery to listen. From what he could hear, things were not going well.

Shortly, a third person arrived, a pretty and very pregnant blonde. She walked away with the man, and he recognized him as one of the cattlemen from the ranch. The other woman stayed back, her feelings apparent when she threw her glass onto the ground.

Jack chuckled to himself. The woman had strong feelings for the young man, which weren't reciprocated. She'd come all the way from Mexico only to learn he'd married someone else.

He watched her stomp off, then continued along the path. The house and the property were fantastic. One could only imagine the money invested in building all this. Meeting Nick had also been an eye-opener.

In conversation, when he had pried him on how he made his living, he replied they were part owners in a restaurant. Alarm bells rang in Jack's head at his response. It must be a helluva restaurant for them to afford this place. Something was amiss.

He ruminated on his failure to turn up anything unusual in Dalton's study. Picking the lock while Joann, Dalton, and Ronnie went riding this morning, he hadn't found a clue as to where most of his brother's money came from. Rummaging through desk drawers and a file cabinet revealed nothing more than documentation pertaining to the ranch.

Checking behind pictures and rolling up the area rug in hopes of finding a hidden safe were wasted efforts. Dalton covered his tracks. Asking him outright about the jet crossed his mind, but at this point, arousing his brother's suspicions could mess up his own plans.

He stepped onto another pathway leading to the house. Halfway there, he was surprised to discover a tall, good-looking young man standing a few feet ahead, arms folded, staring at him. Jack recalled seeing him earlier.

"Jack Burgess?" he asked.

"Yeah. I don't think we've met."

"No, we haven't. Bobby D'Angelo"

Jack squinted at him. "Oh, Nick and Carrie's son." He held out his hand. Taken aback when Bobby declined to shake it, he said, "Is there a problem?"

"That depends. I believe you have something belonging to a friend of mine. I'm asking you to return it."

Jack's muscles coiled. Who did this guy think he was? "Now, listen here. I have no idea what you're talking about, and I would appreciate it if you would step aside and let me pass."

"I'm not going to argue with you. Give the coke you stole back to Ronnie or—"

"Or what?" Jack drew his shoulders up.

Bobby smirked. "How stupid are you? Those drugs belong to a cartel, and they are already aware they're missing."

Jack shuffled a step back. "Not my problem. Ronnie should have kept a better eye on her narcotics."

"See, that's where you're wrong, Jack. You've *made* it your problem. All I have to do is make one call to let them know where you are."

"Listen, I need those drugs. Not for myself, but as part of a payoff for someone in trouble."

"Too bad. Ronnie means a lot to me, and I'm not going to let her take the fall for what you did."

Jack rubbed the stubble on his chin. He locked eyes with Bobby. "I bet that sweet mother of hers doesn't have any idea what her daughter is doing."

In one swift move, Bobby's hands gripped the front of Jack's collar, his fingers twisting, digging the fabric into his flesh. "Dalton wouldn't appreciate your saying anything to her. Ronnie is his stepdaughter. All bets say he'll stand by her and Joann before you."

"Okay, okay. You don't have to get rough. I didn't mean any harm. Like I said, I was trying to help a friend."

Bobby dropped his hands. "By no later than tomorrow morning, Ronnie better find the coke back in her possession without another word from you to her or anyone. If not, I make the call." He turned and strutted away.

Jack straightened his collar and spat. "Son of a bitch."

Giving the coke to Ronnie meant he couldn't bargain for extra time. Mel would turn up soon again, and he wouldn't take kindly to any more excuses.

He trudged along, his mind percolating. This D'Angelo kid had some nerve. Joann mentioned he was a fancy art dealer who owned restaurants and a winery. Bet there was more to his story than she let on. Must have picked up a whole mess of tricks from that father of his.

Jack stopped at the end of the path. People milled about on the patio. He continued across the lawn, his mind filled with questions about Nick, Bobby, and Dalton. Folks around here were sure keeping secrets. The time had come for him to do some digging.

CHAPTER 29

BOBBY

Bobby folded the last of Natalia's clothes and deposited them into his suitcase. He swung around as Carrie burst into the room and scooped his daughter up into her arms.

"Grandma's going to miss you."

Natalia hugged her neck. "Me, too."

Carrie frowned at him. "I wish you could stay longer."

Bobby zipped the suitcase and set it on the floor. "Sorry, I'm swamped right now." He pulled out his cell phone. "Could you take Natty downstairs? I need to make a call?"

"Sure. No problem." She gave Natalia another squeeze. "Let's go say goodbye to Grandpa."

Bobby shut the bedroom door and dialed Derek's number. He answered on the second ring.

"Who's this?"

"A friend of Veronica's. We met a while back at Vertigo."

"Oh, you're the dick from the club."

Bobby gripped the phone, wishing he could reach out and smash the guy's face. "It's debatable as to who is the dick."

"What the hell do you want?"

"I know you've been threatening Ronnie by holding those videos over her head. I'm also aware of the missing coke."

"You take it?" he growled.

"It doesn't matter who took it. I'll return it to you under certain conditions." Loud laughter stung his ear, making him flinch.

"You think this is a negotiation, Bro?"

"No, I'm positive. You'll get the coke back in exchange for the videos, and you'll also stop using Veronica as a mule. No further contact, ever again." Before he could answer, Bobby continued, "And if you don't like these terms, I'm afraid there *will* be consequences." Heavy breathing moved through the line while he waited for Derek's response.

"Do you actually think I'm just gonna agree to everything? What are *you* bringing to the table? Where's the incentive? The coke already belongs to me."

It was Bobby's turn to laugh. "You want incentive? How about letting you continue to do business?"

"Listen, punk, you can threaten me all day long. I'm connected."

"I don't give a damn about your connections. You screwed up, Derek, by messing with Ronnie. You see, you'll be surprised to find, she's got connections of her own." Bobby waited through the silence on the other end.

"Two hundred thousand and my coke back, then you get the videos, and I leave her alone."

"Who's the one negotiating now?"

"Deal or not?"

"Deal. I'll call you with the time and place within the next twenty-four hours." Bobby ended the call and dialed Dalton's number.

"Hey, I need to see you before I head to New York with Natalia."

"Sounds serious," Dalton said.

"It is. I'll meet you at *Buena Comida*."

* * * *

A few hours later, Bobby and Dalton were seated at the bar. Alice sat in a booth with Natalia, engrossed in a game on her tablet.

"Is Ronnie still here?" Bobby asked.

The lines around Dalton's mouth creased. "Yeah, she's with Red. They went riding a bit ago. What are Nick and Carrie up to?"

Bobby laughed. "Recovering from the party last night. Rosie is coming in later, so they're going to chill at home."

"I think everyone enjoyed themselves," Dalton said. "It was a much-needed diversion."

"Look," Bobby began. "You've always been good to me, and since Ronnie is important to you, I felt it was right to come to you with this."

Dalton rested his arms on the bar, his eyes fixed on Bobby's. "What's this about?"

He explained Ronnie's dilemma, including Jack stealing the coke, plus the deal he made with Derek. He believed Dalton needed to know everything.

"I'm hoping you won't judge Ronnie too harshly. None of this was her fault. Creeps drug drinks all the time in clubs." Bobby hesitated. "Actually… I would appreciate it if you didn't say anything at all to her about this. I told her I'm handling things, only I may need your help."

Dalton signaled for a shot. Bianca set a shot of Johnnie Walker Black down and flashed him a smile.

"What can I get you, *Señor* D'Angelo?"

"Nothing, thanks," Bobby said. They waited until she left to serve another customer.

Dalton sighed. "One look at Veronica and I was certain there was something seriously wrong. I wish she had confided in me, but I understand her embarrassment with the whole business." He downed the shot. "She could have been locked up or worse, murdered, running drugs. If I can stop this Derek character, then there's one less dirtbag going around creating mayhem in the world."

Clear on what Dalton meant, Bobby's stomach muscles tightened.

Dalton signaled for another shot. After Bianca moved away, Bobby said, "And Jack?"

"I'll deal with that dummy when I'm ready. Right now, we'll fly back to New York together on my plane. I'll bring Rick with me. I don't want you too deeply involved in this. You do the handoff, and I'll take care of the rest."

"I have to pick up the coke and the cash from Ronnie," Bobby said. "I'll need to withdraw money from my account."

Dalton polished off his drink. "Which I guarantee I'll return to you." He slapped Bobby on the back. "Thanks for watching out for Ronnie. My plane will be ready. I'll say I'm dropping you off then heading to Texas to look at some livestock."

*   *   *   *

By late afternoon, Bobby arrived at Dalton's ranch. He went upstairs to speak to Ronnie while Joann took Natalia to the barn to see the horses. The toll trafficking and cocaine use had taken on her became even more striking as she stood before him. A white towel wrapped around her wet hair exposed her sunken cheekbones, while her bathrobe, though cinched tight, hung loosely off her shoulders.

"Did Jack return the coke?" Bobby asked.

"Yes…but how did you—"

"Never mind that."

She reached into the closet and hauled out two duffle bags. "Money from the drops and the coke." While he unzipped them, she paced.

"Bobby, I don't like you being involved in all of this."

"Too late. This will all be over soon."

"What are you going to do?"

He gave her a reassuring smile. "I don't want you to worry. I'll call you when everything is over." He stopped in the doorway. "Promise me one thing, Ronnie."

Her eyes brimmed. "Anything."

"No more coke."

Eyeing her purse, she picked it up and emptied the contents onto the bed. A small packet of white powder lay among her cosmetics. She handed it to Bobby.

"That's all of it."

"Good. Stay here and get well." He held up the packet. "You don't need this poison anymore." Bobby studied her for a moment. "Besides, you look like crap. I want the old Ronnie back." He kissed her cheek and left.

The plane ride to New York, giving them time to plan, Dalton instructed Bobby to contact Derek and set up a meet for this evening.

"Whoa," Bobby said. "I need time to withdraw the money."

Dalton signaled to Rick. He drew a canvas bag from the overhead compartment and set it between them. Without a word, he dropped back into the leather seat, long legs crossed, cowboy hat pulled down over his eyes.

"The money is in here," Dalton said. "Text me this creep's information. All you need to do is hand it over to him, get the videos, and leave the rest to us."

"I appreciate it," Bobby said. He opened one of the bags Ronnie had given him and added the cash to the stacks inside. "Thanks for helping me out with all of this."

"No thanks necessary, son. I love Ronnie like she's my own. And as for you," he wagged his finger and winked, "Nick would never forgive me if I didn't get involved. I owe him my life… literally."

Bobby couldn't imagine what the two men had endured over the years. The bond between them ran much deeper than what one viewed on the outside, and he liked knowing they always had each other's backs.

Glancing over at Rick, he swallowed hard while memories of Tahoe emerged. Of course, this wasn't as dangerous, but Dalton's intentions generated uneasiness in the pit of his stomach, especially since Rick had been one of the men present that awful night. Still, he trusted both men to take care of things.

Later in the evening, while Maggie took care of Natalia, Bobby called Derek and arranged to meet at Jimmy's Corner, a busy establishment near Times Square. He'd text Dalton after the handoff and head back home.

Bobby transferred all the cash and the coke into one large canvas duffel, then grabbed a cab. He strolled into the bar, reassured he'd taken his Glock in case.

Jimmy's, a bona fide tribute to boxing, exhibited posters, photos, and mementos of famous boxers on its walls. Music blared from an old jukebox as patrons, two deep lined the bar. Bobby squeezed in between them. He ordered a beer on tap and made his way to the rear, where he sat at a small table.

With Derek's impending arrival, he fought to keep his temper in check. Nothing could go wrong tonight. Dalton depended on him. He drank his beer and waited.

A few moments later, Derek approached.

"Hello, punk," he jeered.

Bobby motioned to the chair opposite him. "Let's dispense with the niceties."

Derek laughed and dropped into the chair. "I don't get it. You got a thing for Ronnie?"

"I'll ask the questions. Where are the videos?"

He reached inside his jacket, removed two CDs, and slid them across the table.

"Nothing on your phone?" Bobby asked.

Derek stroked his beard. "Nada. See for yourself." He handed him his cell.

Bobby scrolled through and handed it back. "You could have more than one, but I guess I have to take you at your word." He pulled the duffel from underneath the table.

Derek bent to retrieve it. Bobby held on. "This means no further contact with Ronnie. Ever. Understood?"

"Sure, that sweet ass of hers just made me a bundle. Unless this bag is light, she'll never hear from me again."

Bobby let go and left without glancing back. "Prick," he muttered under his breath. "You have no clue what screwing with Ronnie has cost you."

CHAPTER 30

DALTON

Dalton's gloved hand switched on the table lamp. He set his Stetson aside, then opened a small black case and retrieved the Dead Air Odessa 9 suppressor. Adding one baffle at a time, he adjusted the length and secured it to his 9mm. Finished, he smoothed his mustache and eased onto the upholstered chair facing the front door of Derek's apartment.

He glanced at his cell. "Bobby sent a text. The creep should arrive soon."

Rick removed his cowboy hat, depositing it on an end table. Before positioning himself near the door, he adjusted his leather gloves, pulling them snuggly up over his wrists, then readied his Glock.

Gaining entry had been easy with the proper set of picks. Searching the sparsely furnished rooms, Rick discovered a plastic case of CDs, three burner phones, plus a minor stash of drugs and works. Clothes and bare necessities were inside a bedroom, but no personal effects were displayed, making it obvious this place was designed for a quick exit, a typical dealer's crash pad.

Dalton wished Veronica had spoken to Bobby sooner. If anything happened to her, Red wouldn't handle it well. Her children were the most important things in her life. Hell, she'd raised them all by herself.

There was no jealousy on his part. He accepted being second and respected her for it. Some women put a man before their offspring. By his way of thinking, it showed a lack of nurturing.

"I'm truly sorry to keep dragging you into my mess," Dalton said.

A lazy smile emerged on Rick's lips. "Your mess will always be mine too, Boss." He leaned back, one leg straight, the other bent at the knee, the sole of his boot pressed flat against the wall. "Besides, taking care of the ranch is fine, but every so often, I get a craving for a bit of excitement."

Dalton chuckled. "I think I've had near enough excitement to last me a lifetime."

"I can tell," Rick said. "Marrying has settled you somewhat."

"True. It still bewilders me how the love of a good woman tends to reshape you a bit. Before me, Nick is a fine example of that." He moved to the edge of the chair, the 9mm resting in his lap. "I've never pried but always wondered about your situation."

Rick dipped his head and stared at the floor for a moment. "Well, I guess the married life isn't in my wheelhouse if you get my meaning. I do have a lady I care for and visit on a routine basis. The same one I brought to the party, but I can't quite seem to make things permanent."

"I never expected to be married," Dalton said. "But if it's any consolation, you'll know when the time and the person are right. Just sort of happens naturally."

Rick nodded. They both fell silent a moment.

"I never ask for too many details about a job," Rick began, "but this guy, this Derek fella, is he that bad?"

"He's a small fish at best. One who feeds off the weaker fish at the bottom of the pond," Dalton said. "People like him cause the destruction of the innocent. He made the wrong decision when he chose to swim in my particular pond and feed off someone extremely important to me."

"You need not say anymore. I've come across people like him all my life."

Footsteps echoed in the hallway outside. Dalton signaled to Rick, then switched off the lamp. His eyes, gradually adapting to the darkness, were locked on the front door. A key turned in the lock, and it swung open, hallway light flooding the room. Derek stepped in. Rick's arm reached around his neck. The barrel of his gun jabbed against Derek's back. He kicked the door shut.

"What the hell?" The canvas duffel in Derek's hand fell with a thud to the floor.

Dalton turned on the lamp. "Now, don't struggle, son." He motioned to Rick. "Bring him over here."

Rick shoved him forward into the living room, guiding him to a chair opposite Dalton. "Sit."

Derek eased down, his eyes bulged, the tendons in his neck breached the surface. He glanced up at Rick, then over at Dalton. "What do you want? If it's money, I have plenty in that bag over there on the floor."

"No," Dalton said. "This is not about money."

Derek blinked. His complexion paled in the evening light. "Oh, I get it. You're from the cartel and here about the missing coke from the connect in South Dakota." He pointed his finger. "It's right over there. See for yourself."

"Wrong again," Dalton said.

He squirmed. His face filled with fear. "Then, what?"

"I'll tell you what." Dalton rose, towering over him. "It's about drugging women and blackmailing them into doing your bidding." He gestured at the CD case on the end table. "What's on those? The latest motion pictures, or music, maybe?"

"They're not mine. I'm holding them for a friend."

"So, if I pop one in your disc player over there, I won't see any drugged naked women having sex with men?"

"I have no idea what the hell you're talking about." Derek gripped the arms of the chair, his knuckles turning white. "Look, if you don't want the money, I can give you drugs."

"Is your head that thick?" Dalton asked. He opened the case and removed a CD.

"Wait," Derek cried. "Okay, you're right. The truth is the cartel made me do it. It's an easy way to get women to transport drugs."

"You wouldn't recognize the truth if you tripped over it," Dalton scoffed. "Now, let's start again. Does the name Veronica sound familiar to you?"

"If you mean, Ronnie, yeah."

"Finally, an ounce of honesty. How do you know her?"

"She buys from me. Ronnie loves her coke."

"You have her running drugs?"

"Once in a while. She practically volunteered."

"I'm sure she did since you were threatening to release videos of her."

Derek squirmed deeper into the cushions. Beads of sweat formed across his forehead. "Look, I'm sorry about Ronnie. I—"

Dalton jabbed the barrel of his gun into Derek's forehead. "Those real dog tags?"

Derek chewed his lower lip. "Fake," he squeaked. "But I have a lot of respect for the military."

"Yeah, I bet you do." Dalton yanked them off his neck. "You're a disgrace, nothing but a punk and a bully. Now, I want to know if you have any more videos of Veronica or any other poor misused young lady?"

Derek pointed to the CD case. "Except for those, I handed over all the ones with Ronnie in them to a guy I met earlier at the bar. Probably working with you."

"That's correct," Dalton said.

"Look, I'm done with Ronnie. I'll never bother her or anyone else again."

Dalton pushed the barrel harder against Derek's forehead. "And I'm going to make sure."

He clutched his arms to his chest. "Please, mister, please don't."

"Oh, don't worry. I'm leaving it all up to you. Hand over your cell phone."

Derek dug into the pocket of his jeans. "Here, take it."

Dalton motioned to Rick. He pointed to the works and packets of drugs on the table. Rick gathered them up, dropping them into Derek's lap.

"What's this for?" he asked.

"This is your lucky day," Dalton began. "I don't generally do this, but I'm giving you two choices. Number one, I put a bullet in your head. Simple and quick. Number two, you shoot yourself up with enough poison to overdose."

Mouth gaping, he looked from Rick to Dalton. "There must be some other way. Just tell me what I can do to fix things."

Dalton's pulse slammed in his neck while he watched Derek fall apart. "This is non-negotiable, son. You've done considerable damage. You choose now before I run out of patience." Dalton sat across from him, his 9mm still aimed at Derek.

Derek, his hands trembling, tried to open one of the packets. His fingers fumbled, and it dropped back onto his lap.

Rick stormed over. Grabbing the packets of drugs and the works, he set them on the end table, then prepared a shot. He handed the syringe to Derek along with the tourniquet.

Derek pushed his sleeve up and stopped. "I…I can't do it." Tears coursed down his cheeks, glistening on his dark beard. "Please, I don't want to die." He dropped the syringe into his lap.

Dalton waved the gun at him. "Would you rather I use this?"

Derek squeezed his eyes shut. "No," he said, his voice barely above a whisper.

Rick fastened the tourniquet around Derek's arm, found a vein, picked up the needle, and administered the shot.

In a few moments, Derek's pupils constricted. His head flopped from side to side. "Hey, that's enough," he mumbled while Rick prepared another one. He tried raising up. His arms flailing while Rick hovered over him.

Pushing his knee into Derek's groin, Rick held his arm. Within a few seconds of the next shot, he went limp. Rick wrapped Derek's fingers around the needle still in his arm before letting his hand drop. He set the works and the remaining drugs in his lap. After a couple minutes, he pressed his thumbs to Derek's eyes, lifting his lids, then felt for a pulse on his neck.

"Pulse is threading. He's almost gone. It's not necessary, but I could give him one more shot?"

"Let's wait," Dalton said, a bit stunned by Rick's actions.

Derek's body jerked, and he appeared to seize. White foam ran from the corner of his mouth. They waited until a bluish tint washed over his lips. Rick checked for a pulse again.

"He's gone."

Dalton rose to his feet and removed the suppressor, returning it to its case. "That's one less piece of scum walking around." Going over to the canvas handbag, he unzipped it and tossed the drugs to Rick. "Mind flushing these?"

Rick finished getting rid of the cocaine before collecting the CD case and burner phones, depositing them inside the canvas bag. He stuck his Glock behind him in his waistband, opened the door, and scrutinized the hallway. "All clear."

Dalton put his gun away and picked up the bag. In the elevator alone, they removed their gloves. Rick leaned against the wall opposite him. "You certainly surprised me today," Dalton said. "I'm almost afraid to ask, but where did you learn to prepare a shot of heroin?"

Rick tilted his cowboy hat back, his eyes growing distant for a moment. "Calvin, my younger brother, was an addict. He got mixed up with the wrong crowd. Witnessed him doing it over and over." Pain crept across Rick's face.

"I'm sorry," Dalton said.

"Don't be. It was long ago. I tried helping him more times than I care to count. Poor boy loved those drugs better than anything or anyone else. So much so that one day, they overpowered him, and he died." Rick paused, leaving the hum of the elevator descending echoing between them. "I loved Cal, but he was too far gone. Some people just can't be saved."

Dalton sighed. "If I had known, I would not have given Derek a choice. For you to prepare those shots and think of your brother..." He paused a moment. "Do you have any idea how much I respect and appreciate you?"

Rick stared at the floor. "No words, please. They're not needed. Working for you on the ranch saved me after Cal died. I've gotten more joy out of being a cattleman than anything else."

"And the extra stuff?" Dalton asked.

Rick looked up and winked. "Oh, days like this and that night in Tahoe are necessary now and again. Spices things up a bit. Especially if it serves some good. Know what I mean?"

Dalton grinned. "I sure do."

The elevator doors opened on the lobby floor. A woman with a baby in a stroller waited. Dalton stepped out while Rick held the door for her. She pushed the stroller inside, then turned to him. "Thank you. It's hard to find a gentleman sometimes in this city."

Rick tipped his hat. "You're welcome."

They flew back to South Dakota the same night. Satisfied Ronnie was out from under Derek, Dalton poured a drink while observing Rick asleep in the seat across from him. Tonight, he'd learned a bit more about his life. You just couldn't figure some people out. Loyal to a fault, but, in some ways, still a mystery. Besides Nick, he sure was glad to have Rick by his side.

CHAPTER 31

VERONICA

Ronnie hit the speed dial number for Bobby. Her eyes drifted to the New York newspaper spread out on her kitchen table. It wasn't plastered across the front page, merely a short column on the fourth, reporting the death by overdose of a suspected drug dealer.

"Hey, it's good to hear from you, Ronnie. How are things at the ranch?"

"I'm not at the ranch, Bobby. I arrived home late last night."

"Oh? I thought we agreed you were going to spend more time there."

"No. I was worried about this thing with Derek. Have you read today's paper?"

"Been busy at the gallery, haven't had a chance. I—"

"Derek's dead." She waited through the silence at the other end, her heart galloping.

"Bobby, did you hear what I said?"

"Yes. Does it say what happened?"

"Apparently, he overdosed."

"Well, at least he won't bother you anymore."

"Be honest, Bobby. Did you have anything at all to do with this? I know you were going to contact him."

"Yes, and I did. We met, and he handed over the videos in exchange for the dope and some extra cash. I threatened him a bit, and he agreed to leave you alone for good."

The gnawing in the pit of her stomach intensified. "And then?"

"What do you mean?"

"Look, Derek used on occasion, but he wasn't stupid enough to overdose."

"Seriously, Ronnie? You think I had something to do with Derek's death?"

She paced, her free hand sweeping through her hair. "The night of the party, you said I didn't have to worry any longer, and everything would get taken care of. Those were *your* words, Bobby. What am I supposed to think?"

"And I explained what transpired between Derek and me, and it's the truth. I wouldn't lie to you. Listen, I'm not about to mourn for some lowlife who overdosed on his own junk."

Ronnie paused, dropping onto the sofa. She should be relieved, but somehow the coincidence became too glaring not to question. Was she formulating things in her mind concerning Derek's death, challenging what Bobby told her? He wasn't capable of murder any more than she was."

"I'm sorry. You're right. I am glad he can't hurt me anymore." Hesitating a moment, she asked, "What about the videos?"

"I destroyed them, of course."

"What if...what if there were others at his apartment?"

"I doubt it. I made things clear when we met. Put your mind at ease. Derek's gone, and so are the videos."

Tears of relief spilled from her eyes. "I can't thank you enough for what you did, Bobby."

"I'll always have your back. Now, get rid of the newspaper. No more dwelling on the past."

Her anxiety lessening, she said, "How about getting together for dinner?"

"Wish I could. I have something I need to take care of later. Tomorrow night's okay if Maggie agrees to stay later and watch Natalia. I'll let you know."

"Tomorrow won't work. Since we won't be seeing each other for a bit, I have something to tell you."

"Something positive, I hope."

"Yes. In South Dakota, I realized I need help with my addiction. These withdrawal symptoms are hell... another reason I had to fly home before someone, especially my mother, caught wind. I've arranged for treatment with a detox center in upstate New York. I leave tomorrow morning."

"I'm proud of you, Ronnie. The fact you recognize you need help is a good first step."

Tears threatened to well up. "If it wasn't for you, I don't think I would be doing this."

"But you are, and it's wonderful. Stay in touch. I'm here if you need me. I mean it, Ronnie. Even if it's just to talk."

"I will. Take care and kiss Natalia for me."

The call with Bobby made her feel almost whole again. Following his instructions, she gathered up the newspaper and tossed it into the trash. In the bedroom, she yanked open the nightstand drawer and swept up three remaining vials of coke.

She lined them up on the bathroom vanity—time for a new beginning. Since the night of the party with Bobby, she'd been coke-free. Determined to remain so, one by one, she emptied their contents into the toilet and flushed.

CHAPTER 32

BOBBY

Bobby scrolled through his texts and reread the one from his grandfather asking to meet again. After sending a brief message to Dalton regarding Ronnie going into treatment, he finished up at the gallery, then prepared to head to the Empire Steak House.

Although a rarity, he was glad to be dressed in a dark wool suit since there wasn't time to go home and change. He put on his coat and hailed a taxi outside. While the cab inched across town, he braced himself for the upcoming meeting. No way would it end without him learning why his grandfather abandoned his mother all those years ago. She deserved to know the truth.

The cab pulled in, and he glanced at the elaborate red awning above the entryway. Drawing in a deep breath, he went inside.

He checked his coat and gave his grandfather's name. The maître d´ led him through the elegant dining room where tables set with fine china rested beneath a domed ceiling under an elaborate crystal chandelier.

The aroma of steak and seafood filled the air. Patrons dined on high-end delicacies, the din of their conversations muffled by the thick cushioned walls. The back of the room boasted an enormous chiller constructed entirely of glass, displaying numerous bottles of expensive wines and champagnes.

They proceeded past a long bar and up a broad staircase to the second level. Bobby observed the lavish but empty surroundings. Had his grandfather reserved this spot for the two of them? Having done some homework on his own, he'd read about the brokerage firm and some of its affluent clients, assuring him of his grandfather's wealth.

The maître d´ pointed to a tufted leather circular booth and set a menu down.

"Would you like anything from the bar, sir?"

"Yes. Gin and tonic with a twist of lime."

"Right away." He retreated down the staircase only to return a few minutes later with the drink. "Anything else while you wait for your party, sir."

"Thank you, no." Bobby checked his watch. His grandfather was ten minutes late. He sipped the smooth gin while he browsed through emails on his phone.

"Glad you agreed to come."

Bobby looked up. Dressed in a grey suit, with a drink already in his hand, Alex slid into the booth across from him.

"You reserved this space for the two of us?" Bobby asked.

"It's more private. We can have a real conversation."

"Oh, it's going to get real, alright." Bobby laid his phone on the white tablecloth. "To be quite honest with you, I only agreed to come because I don't like seeing my mother upset."

Alex's face flushed. "I wish things hadn't gone the way they did with your mother. She wouldn't budge on her decision not to meet my wife."

"Can you blame her?"

"No, not really, but…"

The waitress approached. "Good evening, gentleman. Ready to order?"

Both men studied the menu, with Bobby ordering the broiled Chilean Sea Bass and Alex the New York Sirloin.

Alex said, "They are *known* for their steaks."

Bobby shot him a look. "I'm well aware, but I've eaten enough steak while visiting South Dakota recently."

"It's where your mother lives, isn't it?"

"Yes, and she's happily married."

"I'm glad she has someone who cares for her."

"Well, apparently, *you* didn't." Bobby clasped his hands together and sought to maintain his composure. He didn't want things going south… he wanted information.

"Listen, my mother's life now doesn't negate her past or mine either. The trauma she experienced, being abused first by her mother and later by my biological father, might never have happened had you been there for us."

Alex fingered a folded napkin. "I can't go back and change things Bobby." He gulped his drink. "What would you have me do?"

"Tell me everything. I can at least bring my mother some comfort if there is any in what you have to say. She needs some form of closure. Hell, so do I."

"Okay, but on one condition. We eat this meal together with no further talk about the past. I want to hear about the present. All about yours and your mother's life today, then you do for me what she wouldn't?"

Bobby cut his eyes at him. "What?"

"Come home with me and meet Kate." He smoothed his maroon striped tie.

"Oh, that again." Bobby drummed his fingers on the table and considered his grandfather's offer. He wanted the truth, and if it meant meeting his wife, he'd do it.

"Okay," Bobby said. "Agreed."

As they dined, he told his grandfather about his mother and Nick. How good he was to her and to him. He spoke about Izzy and Michael and his life with Natalia omitting Nick's past profession as a hired killer, Carmela's drug dealing, and specific other details.

"Sounds like all of you are doing quite well. Sorry about Natalia's mother, dying so young." He looked away for a moment. "Illness can be a terrible thing." Alex finished his last bite of steak and set his fork down. "But I'm sure there's more you're simply not telling me. Am I correct?"

"Nothing too important," Bobby responded, polishing off his second drink.

"I won't pursue it. Don't have the right to. I hope someday you'll tell me," Alex said with a wink."

Bobby paused. Did his grandfather know more about them than he let on? Was he testing him to see how much he'd reveal?

"Why would you suggest I'm holding some things back?" Bobby asked.

"Because, at some point in our lives, we all do it. Whether it's to protect ourselves or someone we care about. I'm not judging, just stating a fact."

Bobby's nerves rippled at his grandfather's words. They rang true. To protect Ronnie, he'd withheld the truth about

Derek's death from her, though he was one hundred percent positive it was Dalton's doing.

Alex paid the check, then stood and pulled on his wool coat. "Shall we go?"

"Sure."

They made their way to Sutton Place, a few minutes from the restaurant. His grandfather glanced over his shoulder several times, his uneasiness apparent.

When they stopped in front of a stately brownstone, Bobby asked, "Is everything okay?"

Alex raised an eyebrow. "Perfect. No worries."

They stepped through an ornate front door and into a double-height entry foyer where a sweeping filigreed spiral staircase ascended.

They continued into a great room. An intricately woven Isfahan rug graced gleaming wood floors while a fire blazed beneath a carved marble mantel. Expensive overstuffed sofas and chairs anchored the space. Sculptures were exhibited on several side tables and recessed areas, some lit from behind or below, along with various works of art.

Alex pointed to a sofa near the fireplace. "Please sit. I'll let Kate know you're here." At the far end of the enormous room, he pressed a button and disappeared into an elevator.

Bobby wandered around, inspecting the magnificent artwork and sculptures, the collections almost taking his breath away. There were works from many prominent artists, and out of habit, he began to calculate their worth. His grandfather appeared to be wealthier than he imagined.

His spine tingled. A new sense of belonging swept over him. They had much in common. As his grandfather had said, he'd inherited his love of art, a talent asleep inside him, waiting for the right moment to reveal itself.

Engrossed in the paintings, he didn't hear the elevator door open at the other end.

"Impressed?" Alex called out.

Bobby studied one last piece before turning around. His grandfather approached with a woman. In the soft evening light, he couldn't quite make out her face. They moved closer. His jaw almost dropped.

He struggled to mask his shock. She was not what he expected at all.

"Bobby," Alex said, "I'd like you to meet my wife, Kate."

CHAPTER 33

NICK

Nick zipped his brown leather jacket and climbed behind the wheel of the Range Rover. Carrie slid into the seat next to him and adjusted the hem of her heavy wool sweater. She checked on Izzy sitting in the rear. Two long braids trailed down the front of her shoulders while her green eyes peeked out from underneath her bangs. Her dark blue quilted coat was buttoned up against the late October weather.

"Make sure your seatbelt is on," Carrie said."

"I'm all buckled up. Why isn't Michael coming with us?"

Nick winked at Carrie. "Because we have a surprise for you?"

Izzy clapped her hands. "A surprise! What is it, Daddy?"

"It wouldn't be a surprise if we told you. You'll learn soon enough."

Almost as excited as Izzy, Nick couldn't stop grinning. Buying her a horse had been on his mind for a good while. Ever since she'd ridden at Carmela's with Bobby and again with Joann on occasion, she'd been pestering them for one.

By the time they arrived at Dalton's ranch, Izzy could hardly contain herself, talking non-stop, trying to guess what they had in store for her. Dalton and Joann greeted them by the barn doors. They climbed out of the Range Rover. Nick crouched, meeting Izzy's eyes.

"Remember, I promised if you kept your grades up and continued your riding lessons, I would buy you a horse."

Izzy's eyes popped open wide. Her cheeks reddened. "You bought me a horse!" she squealed. "Where, where? I want to see it."

"Hold on," Nick said. "First, you need to thank Uncle Dalton and Aunt Joann. They helped picked her out."

Izzy jumped up and down. She ran and hugged Joann, then Dalton. "Thank you." Her eyes shining, she asked, "Is it a girl, horse?"

Dalton pushed back his Stetson and laughed. "Yes, a mare, Izzy." He opened the barn doors while Nick took hold of her hand, leading her past the other horses to the last stall. The mare poked her head out and whinnied when Dalton opened the stall.

Rising on tiptoes, Izzy reached up and rubbed her muzzle. "Hello," she said softly. "I'm Izzy." The horse's ears pricked up, and she bobbed her head.

Izzy turned to Nick. "What's her name?"

His heart dipped, then soared as he caught the light in her eyes. "I think it's up to you to choose a name for her."

"Wait," Dalton said. "Let me bring her out so you can have a proper meeting." He prepared the horse and led her over. "She's called a Paint because of her brown and white markings. A nice gentle breed for you to begin riding on your own."

Izzy stroked the mare's flank. "She's so pretty." She turned and wrapped her arms around Nick's waist. "Thank you, Daddy. I promise I'll take good care of her."

He bent and kissed the top of her head. "I know you will. Now, how about giving her a name?"

She stared at the horse for a moment and pursed her lips. "Bella. Her name is Bella, for beautiful in Italian."

"Good choice," Carrie said. She smoothed Izzy's bangs.

Joann smiled. "That's a fine name. It suits her. Now, we have another surprise for you." She reached for Izzy's hand. "Follow me, sweetheart."

They all strolled to the tack room together, Dalton bringing up the rear with Bella. Joann pointed to the turquoise trimmed leather saddle. "This is for you," she said to Izzy. From your Uncle Dalton and me."

Carrie's mouth dropped. "It's stunning. Nick tried to describe it to me. It's even more beautiful than I imagined."

Izzy looked from Joann to Dalton. She traced her finger across the initials. "Thank you, I love it. Can I ride Bella now?"

"Sure, sweetie," Joann said. "We'll get you saddled up, and you can ride her around the training pen. I'll ride beside you. You need time to get used to each other."

Fifteen minutes later, oblivious to the cool breeze, Nick and Carrie straddled the top of the fence while Izzy rode Bella around the pen with Joann on Sissy and Dalton standing watch across from them.

"My God, she's a natural," Nick said, swelling with pride as Izzy took the horse into a steady trot. "The years are passing so quickly. I remember the first time I held her in Lugano."

Carrie bumped against him. "Mmm, are those tears I see in your eyes?"

"Just look at her, babe. How did we get so lucky?" He draped his arm around her shoulders, and she stroked his hand.

"I sometimes wonder myself. Between Bobby, Izzy, and Michael, we've done pretty well." She took out her cell phone and proceeded to film. "I'll send this video to Bobby. Thanks to

Dalton, he's an excellent rider, too. I'm sure when he visits, he'll want to go riding with Izzy."

Carrie stopped filming. She looked up at Nick. "Thank you," she whispered and pecked his cheek.

"For what?"

"For the life you've given the children and me. The list is too long for words."

"No, I should be the one saying thank you. If it wasn't for you, I'm not sure where I would have ended up." He cupped her chin and kissed her tenderly on the lips.

Dalton ambled over to them. "Still with the mushy stuff?"

Carrie giggled. "Always."

"Mind if I steal him for a bit? Got a nice bottle of scotch I'd like to open."

"Go on, you two. Do your guy thing. I'll stay here."

Nick jumped down and followed Dalton inside. When they were settled in the study, with drinks in their hands, Dalton proceeded to tell him about Veronica.

Stunned, Nick said. "I would never have guessed Ronnie might be involved in something like that. Does Joann know?"

"God, no." Dalton knocked back his drink and poured another one. "It wasn't Ronnie's fault, and she's in treatment now. I'm not sure what might have happened to her if Bobby hadn't intervened. He's grown into such a fine caring young man."

"He sure has," Nick said. "It's amazing how he was able to reach the other side. I suspect he gets it from Carrie. Both damaged, yet exceptionally strong-willed."

Dalton smoothed his mustache. "I still have to deal with that idiot brother of mine. He stole the coke for a reason. I know he hasn't been straightforward with me. Captured him picking the lock and rifling through my office.

Nick raised up in his seat. "What?"

"Yeah, he didn't realize the overhead smoke detector outside the door is really a camera, plus there's one hidden inside here.

"What do you think he was searching for?"

"I'm not quite sure, but I plan to find out." He set his glass down and sighed. "Up until then, he almost had me believing he'd changed."

"I'm sorry. That's too bad."

Dalton waved his hand. "Don't be. I should have known better. But there is another reason I wanted to talk to you. How are you holding up?"

Nick finished his drink. He held out his glass, signaling Dalton to pour him another. He leaned forward and stared at the floor before taking a sip. "I thought a lot about what you said concerning our kills." He met Dalton's eyes. "We did do some good. The world's better off without those men still walking around. But..."

Dalton's brow furrowed. "But what?"

Nick paused and swallowed a sip. "I still think about Carmela and my part in things."

Dalton let out a long breath. "Wish I could convince you otherwise. I already told you how I felt about her and what she did."

"I'm working on it," Nick said. "Maybe one day it will settle." He consumed the rest of his drink. It slid past the back of his throat, producing a slow burn as it traveled down. He wished the guilt he bore over Carmela, like the whiskey, would gradually wash away.

Since his talk with Dalton, his demons slept. How long they would remain sleeping, he wasn't sure.

His mind cleared again when he pictured Izzy riding her horse. Right now, he needed to focus on the positive things in his life and be thankful for the safety, love, and security of his family.

CHAPTER 34

MIGUEL

Miguel tucked the end of the sheet laying on top of the slim mattress, then covered it with a yellow blanket and patchwork comforter. He tossed two pillows near the brass headboard and began unpacking the portable heater.

Footsteps echoed on the stairs. Bianca appeared, her hair cinched tight at the nape of her neck with a pearl clip. The white blouse with *Buena Comida* embroidered above the pocket skimmed the waist of her short black skirt.

"It is almost time for me to leave," she said. "What are you doing?"

"What does it look like I am doing?" he scoffed. Tearing the cardboard away, he lifted the heater and placed it across from the bed. Ignoring her, he searched for an outlet.

"There." Bianca pointed to the far corner of the room.

He stared at the outlet and rubbed his chin. "I will need a longer cord."

"What is wrong?" she asked. "You seem distant lately."

"Nothing." He inspected the outlet. "The time is almost here to kidnap the girl. I have many things on my mind."

Shivering, she wrapped her arms around her body. "Something is not right between us. You have changed, Miguel. What have I done to disappoint you?"

The sound of her voice gnawed at him. He wanted to rip her limbs apart. But he needed her. Once he took possession of Izzy, Bianca must take care of matters like food, water, emptying the bucket, and such, while he focused on dealing with Nick. If things did not work out, he'd kill Izzy. Bianca was destined to die either way.

Miguel scanned the room for any missed details. Bianca approached and squeezed his shoulder. Miguel jerked away. Tears clung to her dark lashes.

"*Mi amor*, talk to me," she pleaded.

"Dry your eyes," he said. "This is no time for weakness. I have so much ahead of me, and yet you whine and pester."

"Please, I will do anything you ask. It is this coldness, this distance I feel between us." She lowered her head. "We have not made love in a long time." A slight blush fanned her cheeks.

"Is that what you want?" He pointed to the attic stairs. "Then move."

Bianca's mouth fell open. She staggered back a step and stared at him.

He gripped her arm. "Go down. *Now!*" he commanded, shoving her toward the doorway.

"But I simply meant—"

"Now, Bianca or I will throw you down the steps."

She hurried through the door with him following behind. At the bottom of the stairs, he eyed her uniform. "Remove your things." He motioned toward the bedroom. "You will be late for your shift today."

Sitting on the end of the bed, he derived pleasure at the trembling in her body while she undressed. Never again would she take him for a fool.

"Loosen your hair," he ordered.

Hands visibly shaking, she withdrew the pearl clip, then slipped underneath the quilt.

Miguel tore the covers away. His eyes roamed over her naked flesh. What a pity to have to destroy something so lovely. He stripped and pressed his body against hers. He seized fists full of her long tresses. His fingers clenched, the word *mentirosa,* liar, repeating in his head.

She squirmed beneath him. "Miguel, you're hurting me. Please, *stop!*"

He glared into her frightened eyes. "Stop? I thought this is what you wanted." He forced himself inside her, driving deeper with each thrust, disregarding her painful cries until he finished.

Bianca lay still, a whimper escaping her lips now and again. He lifted himself off her and snatched up her clothes, hurling them at her. "There, that should make you feel better. Get dressed. I will drive you to work."

An hour later, after dropping Bianca a few blocks from the restaurant, he spotted a white Range Rover pull in several car lengths away across the street. Focusing on the man behind the wheel, he tugged his baseball cap down over his forehead. Raising his collar, he sank into the seat of the Cadillac.

Every nerve in his body twitched at the sight of Nick emerging from the SUV. His pulse slammed in his neck. A flashback of their fight in Tahoe returned. Seething inside, he rubbed the scar along his cheek. Nick opened the rear door on the passenger side, then strolled into the hardware store holding the hand of a little boy. "Must be his son," he spat.

A deep longing rose at the memory of lying with Carmela on the last night before she died. Miguel stopped himself from crying out. He'd lost a part of his soul when she perished. Time and again, he asked himself why. Why did she leave the safety of the house? What was she thinking right before a bullet ended her life?

Now, just feet away, the man responsible for her death still lived and breathed—something Carmela had been denied. If not for him, they would be together with Natalia.

Tempting fate, he waited until Nick returned with the child. He slid all the way down as Nick drove past, then inched up, catching sight of his car in the rearview mirror traveling along the busy main thoroughfare.

Hands clamped on the steering wheel, he followed in Nick's direction. Why not finish things now? Put a bullet into his skull, seize his boy and imprison him until Bobby brought Natalia.

Heat burst inside his body at the prospect, but to do it here, increased the chance of something going wrong, and there would be too many witnesses. He must keep his impulses in check.

Nick must suffer. A quick death would not suffice. He needed to learn the dire cost of his actions. Kidnapping his daughter will prove more powerful than swift vengeance.

Miguel turned the corner and drove in the opposite direction. His heart hammering, he pulled to the side of the road and smacked his palm on the wheel. Queasiness gripped the pit of his stomach, forcing him to draw in a deep breath. He could not let his emotions interfere with his plans, one of the first lessons every ghost must master. Your life depended on maintaining a level head and a cold heart.

This was no time for him to regress to the young, inexperienced hellion from the slums of *Soacha,* Columbia, who once acted without thinking matters through.

Driving on, the anger coiled inside him started to unwind. Letting go of his reaction upon seeing Nick, he reflected on his cruel treatment of Bianca, and with it came the realization he needed to reassure her. If he pushed her further, she might fall apart like on the night he murdered Sarah. She needed to keep her wits about her.

Her betrayal must be put on hold for the time being. Meanwhile, he would gather last-minute necessities before abducting Izzy.

Miguel settled his emotions, confident he would even the score with Nick, have Natalia with him once again, and rid himself of Bianca Flores.

CHAPTER 35

BIANCA

Glassware clinked while Bianca prepared for her shift, organizing and rearranging various liquor bottles and stemware. While setting the straws and stirrers within reach, a wave of dizziness swept over her.

She gripped the edge of the bar to steady herself. Miguel's behavior earlier in bed led her to reflect on the sudden change in his demeanor. Convinced the rage smoldering inside him resulted from his hatred for Nick, she still believed it couldn't possibly have anything to do with her.

Hiding her grief over losing Alejandro had not been easy. The future she envisioned vanished along with him. She had depended on Miguel to relieve her suffering, but the ugly episode earlier today made her question him. Surely, once Natalia became theirs, his heart would soften again.

The lunch crowd streamed in, forcing her to smile and begin mixing drink orders. When the rush died down a little before two o'clock, she signaled Rosie for someone to relieve her. On her way through the kitchen, she greeted the staff before stepping out of the rear exit. Buttoning her coat against the cool breeze whipping across the parking lot, Sarah's face loomed before her once again. She clutched her middle and squeezed her eyes shut.

"Bianca?"

Her eyes flew open. The breeze diminished while the heaviness inside her chest swelled. Alejandro stood smiling, a few feet away clad in a denim jacket, jeans, and brown cowboy boots, his head bare. Marveling at his tanned face and broad shoulders, she drank in his full lips, high cheekbones, and dark brows while wondering how much a woman could ache before breaking apart.

His smile faded. "Are you okay?"

"I…" A burning struck the back of her throat, cutting off her voice.

"Bianca, please, speak to me."

Her knees quaking, she asked, "What are you doing here?" She tried to swallow, but her mouth had gone dry at the sight of him.

"I did not mean to hurt you." He inched forward. "Give me a chance to explain."

He caressed her cheek, the touch of his hand piercing her heart. She stepped backward. "What is there to explain? You made matters clear the night of the party. You have a wife and a baby arriving soon. That is *my* reality now. The agony I must learn to live with."

"I did not plan any of it. I had every intention of being with you again someday." A frown deepened the lines at the corners of his mouth. "I fell on hard times until I was lucky enough to secure work on *Señor* Dalton's ranch. I never worked with horses and cattle, but he agreed to teach me."

"He taught you so well you forgot all about *me*," she declared, her voice rising.

"Please, understand," he pleaded. "I became terrified when he discovered I had entered the country illegally. The prospect of being sent back to Mexico…they would have killed me, Bianca. *Señor* Dalton helped me get papers allowing me to continue to live here in the United States legally."

"How nice for you to have help from someone and find a wife in the process, too." she mocked.

"When I met Pamela, I was lonely. Things happened fast."

"Did you not think, perhaps in Mexico, I was lonely too?"

His shoulders drooped. "I did not want you to sit and wait for me, so I stopped sending letters. I felt it best for you to move on."

"How could I move on?" she wailed. "I have loved you more than anything else in this world."

Powerless to stop herself, she cradled his face in her hands, drowning in the warmth of his brown eyes. The same eyes which once looked at her with such love and promise.

"You have broken my heart, Alejandro. I believed in us. For the past few years, I have thought of almost nothing but you."

His arms tightened around her. She rested her head against his chest and wept, wishing she'd never left Mexico, never discovered the truth.

He stroked her hair. "Please don't cry. Your life is not over. You will find someone again. A man who is better than me. I am truly sorry... for everything."

She pushed him away and wiped at her tears. "So, you will continue to stay with her, then?"

"What can I do? Pamela is my wife. She is carrying our child."

"Do you love her?"

He rubbed the back of his neck and stared at the ground. His silence a proven declaration of his love for that *gringa,* she said, "Well, there is nothing left to say. I need to go back inside."

"Wait, please. I must know you will be okay. Where are you staying? Do you have enough money? You never explained how you were able to enter the United States."

"*Si*, I told you I paid to cross the border."

His dark brows arched. "I do not believe you. A woman as beautiful as you would never make it across without—"

"Without what?" She cut her eyes at him. "Being raped or murdered."

"I can't help it, Bianca. I am doubting your story."

"Too bad. I do not care whether you believe me or not." She hurried toward the kitchen door.

"I have seen you with him," he called out.

Bianca froze. She whirled around. "Who? What are you talking about?"

"The man in the Cadillac." His eyes met hers.

For a moment, she contemplated telling him she had a lover of her own who brought her across the border. Someone dangerous, a killer in fact, who wouldn't hesitate to murder them if he became aware of their past.

She flicked her wrist, dismissing him. "He is a friend, nothing more."

"A friend who helped you cross?" he said, folding his arms. "I found it odd when he dropped you several blocks from the restaurant. Did you not wish to be seen together?"

"Oh, so now you are spying on me?"

"No, I just happened to see you."

Heat flushed through her body. She stamped her foot, then shook her fist at him. "You have *no right* to question me, not after what you have done. Go away, Alejandro. Go home to your *gringa* and leave me alone."

"Maybe next time I will ask him what he is to you," he shot back.

Panic gripped her at his words. "Nothing good will come of it. You would be wise to stay out of my affairs. Now, please go."

Stiffening her spine, she tore the door open and stormed inside without glancing back. She swept by Alice setting a tray piled with dirty dishes on the counter.

Eyes full of mischief, she caught Bianca's arm. "Who's the cutie?"

Bianca continued through the swinging kitchen doors with Alice following at her heels. Two customers perched on stools at the far end of the bar while the tables and booths remained empty before the dinner hour.

"Come on, I saw you out in the parking lot. That guy attended the party. He works at the Dalton ranch."

Bianca massaged her temples. "Just someone I knew in Mexico."

"Someone special?" Alice asked, grinning.

Bianca wanted to scream, to shout yes, he was someone special. The man she had loved most of her life. Instead, she answered, "No."

"That's good because I'm pretty sure he's married."

Her eyes watered. Hearing Alice mention the word married deepened the wound lying inside her.

"Hey, I'm sorry." Alice's shoulders slumped. "I didn't mean to upset you."

"It is okay. Everything is fine. He reminded me of home. I miss it sometime."

"I can only imagine," Alice said. "Being far away from family is tough."

Wishing to end the conversation, she replied, "I am okay. It does not happen often." She turned and collected the remainder of the dirty glasses, loading them into a rack, and preparing them for the kitchen.

Alice picked up the rack. "Here, let me take it for you."

"Thank you." Alice vanished through the swinging doors. Glad to be alone, she spotted a few drops of water on top of the bar. Grabbing a rag, she rubbed, wishing she could erase the memory of Alejandro as easily.

When closing time arrived, and Bianca was more than ready to leave. She said goodnight to the staff and dashed up the street where Miguel waited for her.

With every stride, she imagined Alejandro's eyes on her, sensing he lurked nearby. What if Miguel discovered him? A shiver ran through her. She opened the door of the Cadillac. The sickly, sweet scent of roses invaded her nose, just like…Sarah's perfume. Her stomach flipped. Miguel leaned over and handed her the bouquet.

"Here, these are for you."

Bianca hesitated, the memory of that dreadful night replaying in her mind. She wanted to run in the opposite direction.

"Something wrong?" he asked.

Faking a smile, she said, "No. Thank you. They are beautiful, *mi amor*." She accepted the flowers and settled into the seat of the Cadillac.

Miguel drove in the opposite direction of the house while she cracked the window. She inhaled the fresh air and discreetly searched for any sign of Alejandro.

"Where are we going?" she asked.

He offered her a rare smile. "I have a surprise for you." Tension lingered inside her. Were the roses truly a gift or a purposeful reminder?

Resting his arm on the console between them, he said, "We cannot be seen together here. I know it is late. Relax and enjoy the ride."

Forty-five minutes later, they rode into Deadwood, miles from Rapid City, in the northern Black Hills. Old fashioned lampposts lit the cobblestone streets. Rustic buildings bore a resemblance to a western town. Hotels and rows of restaurants were sandwiched between shops and casinos.

"What is this place?" she asked.

"It was once occupied by cowboys, gunslingers, and other ruthless men," Miguel said.

"Gunslingers?"

"Yes, cowboys who carried guns and were expert at drawing them quickly from a holster when necessary."

Bianca frowned. "Oh."

Miguel squeezed her hand. "You have been working hard. I thought it would be nice to have a late dinner here and do some gambling before checking into a hotel."

A warning sparked inside her. Why the abrupt change?

As if reading her mind, he said. "This is my way of saying I am sorry for earlier today."

Still hesitant, she replied, "I know you are under a great deal of stress. I must try to do better by you." Lifting her hand to his lips, he kissed her palm. "We will forget about everything for the rest of the night and enjoy our time here."

Her apprehension faded. Letting herself relax, she smiled and said, "Thank you, *mi amor.*"

Seeing Alejandro again had revived the embers of the fire dying inside her, but to continue to live in the past would only hamper her relationship with Miguel. Alejandro had a new life without her, and she must begin to build her own. Later, exhausted from work and the day's events, she left Miguel gambling in one of the casinos and retreated to the hotel room. She removed Alejandro's letters from the lining of her purse. One by one, she tore them into small pieces. Dropping the tatters into the toilet, she flushed them away. She must hold on to this new beginning with Miguel and believe in their future together.

CHAPTER 36

BOBBY

Deep scars covered the right half of her face and neck, broad ridges of crimson and white. The opposite side appeared to be virtually unblemished. Her vibrant auburn hair, cut short, let reveal one earlobe with a sizable diamond sparkling in the firelight. A long-sleeve print blouse concealed her arms while a pair of dress pants and simple leather flats clad her feet. Bobby suspected her clothes hid additional scarring. Alex maneuvered her wheelchair into place before seating himself on the loveseat beside it.

One perfect ocean blue eye beneath full lashes met him, while the other remained buried under knobby folds of skin. "It's good to finally meet you, Bobby," she said.

Embarrassed by his initial reaction, Bobby forced a smile, then stooped and shook Kate's hand. Her fingers were rough yet delicate in his. A light floral scent wafted past.

"It's okay. I know you're quite shocked," she continued, pointing to the sofa. "Please sit."

Still somewhat rattled, Bobby eased down.

Kate folded her scarred hands. "Your reaction is normal. I don't want you to feel uncomfortable." Her eye swept over him.

His cheeks burned. "I didn't mean to…"

"Nonsense. Now, please put it out of your mind. Alex has been telling me all about you. In fact, he's been singing your praises almost non-stop." Her look of adoration at the mention of his grandfather's name was unmistakable.

"I know things haven't gone particularly well between your mother and grandfather," she said. "My hope is if you have any influence at all, you can convince her to come and meet me." A smile curled the edge of her mouth. "I've known about her for a long time now."

"I…I don't understand," Bobby said.

She glanced at Alex, then back at Bobby. "Because it's time she learns I am the cause of your grandfather deserting her."

"But she knows the two of you were getting married when my grandmother was pregnant with her."

Pain in her eyes, she looked at Alex. "Do you prefer to tell him the whole story, or should I?"

He rested a gentle hand on her shoulder. "It's my responsibility."

"When I last saw your mother as an infant in Arizona," he began. "I had already decided to break things off with Kate. I was determined to make amends with Helen, your grandmother. But she had grown hostile toward me. She refused to believe I played no part in my mother's plans to drive her away."

"Meanwhile, Kate was overseas on a European vacation when I received news about the accident. The car she was riding in crashed and caught fire. I left Arizona immediately. She barely escaped with her life, but as you can well imagine, her suffering has been immeasurable."

His eyes moist, he scanned Bobby's face for a moment. "Kate was not expected to survive, but after undergoing many operations and several years of rehabilitation, she pulled through. Awed by her strength, I remained by her side through it all. She faced everything head-on when she could have easily given up."

"When she recovered, I chose not to call off the wedding. At first, Kate refused to move forward. She believed I was marrying her out of pity. The fact is, I was convinced we were meant to be together."

Kate reached for his hand. "And I have loved him all the more ever since."

Bobby couldn't detect an ounce of bitterness over what had befallen her and surmised there wasn't anything superficial about her. Here sat a woman whose soul shone through the hideous scars covering her body.

"I'm sorry for all you have suffered," Bobby said. "But please understand, my mother suffered too. Physically and mentally." He eyed his grandfather. "What happened to Kate still doesn't excuse your abandoning her."

Alex let out an exasperated breath. "I did return to Arizona, Bobby. My biggest mistake was going too late. Many years had elapsed before I summoned the courage to confess everything to Kate. She convinced me to go see Helen and try to build a relationship with your mother. By the time I arrived, your grandmother had been incarcerated for selling you, and your mother had disappeared. I even drove to the prison, and on the third attempt, Helen finally agreed to meet with me."

Bobby squinted at him. "What did she say?"

"That she wasn't sorry for what she did because your mother caused her nothing but trouble. She had no idea where she'd gone, and she didn't care. I realized then how much I failed your mother *and you*. I hired people to try to find the two of you, only you both vanished without a trace."

Alex went and sat on the edge of the sofa next to Bobby. "I know my decisions haven't always been the right ones. I'm not looking for sympathy, just hoping you and your mother will come to understand and include me and Kate in your lives someday."

Wiping his sweaty palms down the front of his jeans, Bobby tried to digest everything. What was he supposed to say now? Shrouded in silence, the three of them stared at the fire.

Finally, Kate spoke. "Bobby, your grandfather knows he should have told me way before he did. But he can't change any of it."

Bobby stood, his stomach clenched tight. He wrestled with his decision to speak. "Well... since you've been honest with me, I'll tell you what happened after my grandmother sold me away to strangers."

"You don't have to do this," Alex said.

Bobby focused on the fire, locking his eyes on the flames. He hadn't spoken about Laurel, Russ, or Claudia in many years. Not since... telling Carmela.

"I was abused, like my mother," Bobby began. "The man who bought me mistreated my stepmother and me." He continued, pouring out his words, disclosing almost everything."

Kate gasped. "I'm so sorry."

Alex rose, his arm came around Bobby, and he squeezed his shoulder. "My fault, all of it." His voice breaking, he said, "I... I couldn't locate you, but I thank God your mother did."

"How *did* she find you?" Kate asked.

Bobby moved out from under his grandfather's arm and stepped back. "If I can persuade her to meet Kate, I'll let her decide whether or not she chooses to tell you."

Alex placed his hand on the wheelchair. "This is a fairly recent necessity. I'm praying your mother will change her mind soon since Kate's prognosis is—"

"Alex." Kate raised her head, her expression stern. "I think enough has been said already," she admonished."

"Of course," Alex said, his face flushing red in the firelight.

Bobby cleared his throat. "I have to go." He bent and kissed Kate's cheek. "It was good meeting you, and I want you to know I don't blame you for any of it."

"I hope you'll come and visit again soon, Bobby. I'd also like the chance to meet your mother."

He paused in the doorway. "I can't promise anything, but I'll see what I can do."

A perfect full moon lit the front steps as they descended them together. At the bottom, Bobby turned and said, "I'm glad you convinced me to come here today. I understand things better, but you need to know where I'm coming from."

Alex raised an eyebrow. "And where's that?"

"I can only imagine what you and Kate have been through, but it shouldn't have taken you over fifteen years to try and find us. My mother and I both carry a lot of weight from our pasts. Her guilt over losing me has never truly left her, and it probably never will. And if it wasn't for Nick treating me like a son and helping to strengthen my self-esteem, who knows where I might be today. So, for now, I don't think forgiveness is on the table."

Alex's shoulders drooped. "I can't blame you one bit. The only thing I want now is to see your mother and you again." He shrugged. "Maybe meet my grandchildren, and of course, Nick."

About to hail a taxi, Bobby hesitated when two men crossed the street toward them.

"Do you know them?" he asked.

Alex averted his eyes. "From work. We conduct business together."

Both men approached his grandfather, ignoring Bobby altogether. One wore horn-rimmed glasses, his face pinched above thin lips. "I feel like you're avoiding us?"

"Gentlemen, please," Alex said. "Another time."

A look of contempt flashed across the man's face. "Heard that excuse more than once."

Alex rubbed his hands together. "I'll have it for you by week's end. I would appreciate it if you would go on about your evening."

Bobby studied the second man as he thrust his hand deep inside the breast of his long wool coat before adding, "Week's end or you no longer get what you need." He winked at the two of them. "Enjoy the rest of your night."

They continued up the block. One of them glanced back before they rounded the corner.

Bobby glared at Alex. "Care to explain?"

"Nothing to worry about. I'm handling it."

"I recognize a threat when I hear one."

Alex looked away. "Everything's under control."

Bobby threw up his hands. "Okay, suit yourself. It's just another thing you're hiding." He stepped to the curb and hailed an approaching taxicab.

"Bobby, wait." Alex rushed over to him. "Will you get back to me sometime soon?"

"I'll talk to my mother, but I can't go against her wishes if she refuses to see you again."

"Fair enough," Alex said, stepping away.

Inside the cab, Bobby pondered the evening's revelations. Poor Kate had endured so much, and even upon learning of Alex's past relationship, she still encouraged him to find them. His respect for her growing by the minute he decided to talk to Nick. Maybe he could make some headway in convincing his mother to meet with Kate.

The only other problem was finding out why those men were threatening his grandfather and what, if anything, to do about it.

CHAPTER 37

NICK

Nick weighed his conversation with Bobby from the previous night while working out in the gym downstairs. Following a quick shower and shave, he threw on jeans and a long-sleeve pullover before heading for the great room. Mid-morning wind whipped around the eaves outside the house, generating a faint whistle, a warning an early snowfall wasn't far off.

Unsure of Carrie's reaction, he chose to tread lightly. Any mention of her father set her in a tailspin. He found her cuddling on the sofa with Izzy and Michael in front of the fire, all of them still dressed in their pajamas watching a Disney movie. Valentina sat nearby reading a book while Ace sprawled asleep at her feet.

"A lazy day?" Nick asked.

Carrie glanced away from the television. "A much-needed one. Come join us."

Hating to break up the scene, but feeling it was necessary, he said, "Babe, we have to talk."

Worry lines framed her mouth. "What's wrong?" She eased up out of the tangle of her children's arms and legs.

"Mom, stay," Izzy said, pouting.

"Please," Michael chimed in.

Carrie grinned and ruffled his hair. "I'll be right back. You can tell me what happens next." Slipping her feet inside her pink fuzzy mules, she followed Nick into the kitchen.

Nick removed a beer from the built-in cooler underneath the counter. He straddled a stool next to her at the island. "I know you don't like talking about your father, but Bobby called, and I think we need to make a trip to New York."

Her face pinched. "What has Bobby got to do with him?"

"Don't get angry," he cautioned. "They had quite a conversation. He didn't give any details, but he feels you should meet with your father again."

"I've already done that. I have no desire to see him right now." She jumped up and tried to rush past him.

Nick caught her hand. "Hold on. I think it's important you consider it. Bobby met your father's wife and—"

"What!" She jerked her hand away. "Are you serious? Why would he do such a thing?"

"Please, wait, let me finish. It might be time for you to bend a little when it comes to your father."

Her nostrils flared. "Bend a little? Where was he when my mother kept beating the crap out of me?"

He gestured at the stool. "Please."

She plopped down next to him, arms folded. "Go on, I'm listening."

A smile tugged at the edge of his mouth.

"You find this amusing?"

He rubbed her arm. "Of course not. You're beautiful even when you're angry."

"Don't change the subject, Nick. I'm waiting."

"Okay, just hear me out." He twisted the cap off his beer and swallowed a few sips. "Bobby saw how agitated you were after seeing your father, and since you wouldn't talk about it, right or wrong, he made it his business to find out why."

Drumming her fingers on the granite top, she said, "I love him to death, but he needs to quit poking his nose in other people's affairs."

Nick chuckled. "I'd say when it comes to Bobby, that's an admirable trait. He can't help himself."

Her eyes flashed. "What else?"

"He talked with the two of them, and he feels we need to meet Kate and listen to their story. Then you can decide for yourself if you want to have any further contact. Bobby also said when he was leaving, two men approached and threatened your father. Might be the same ones you saw that day."

She rested her chin in her palm, a faraway look in her eyes.

"If he is in some kind of trouble, maybe I can help," Nick said.

"No. Not with all you're dealing with. If something should happen to you because of him, I'd blame myself."

He swept his palm lightly across her cheek. "I've spoken with Dalton, and I'm beginning to come to grips with things. I won't pressure you, but I have a feeling we need to do this. Besides, it's time I met him anyway." He finished off his beer and tossed the empty bottle into the trash. "You decide."

Her brows knit together. "Okay, it might help to find out everything that happened back then, but I can't guarantee I'll remain calm when I see him."

"Fair enough," Nick said. "I'll book a flight for New York, and we can leave tomorrow morning." He kissed the top of her head. "Let's finish watching the movie before we pack."

CHAPTER 38

CARRIE

Carrie sat opposite Bobby in the living room while Nick held Natalia on his lap. Sunlight streamed in, illuminating a canvas on the far wall. Landing in New York several hours ago, Carrie still seethed. Heat rising inside her body, she tugged at the collar of her beige cable knit sweater.

"Bobby, how could you go behind my back like that?"

Hands clamped together, he leaned forward. "If you had explained why you were so upset, I probably wouldn't have done it. He came here and…"

"He was here?" She stood and glared at him.

"After you left, I found his card on the closet floor. I called him, and he agreed to come and talk to me. It was almost eerie, like looking into a mirror and—"

"When did this happen?" she cut in.

Deep crimson swept Bobby's cheeks. "The day of the party. And before you say anything else, I didn't mention it when I came to South Dakota because I wasn't sure what to do."

"Well, from what Nick told me, you must have figured it out." Her pulse raced. "He said you met his wife."

Bobby glanced at Nick. "Yes, and I feel you should too."

"Why? Will it change what he did… how he deserted my mother and me?"

"Of course not." He got to his feet and faced her. "I told him as much before I left. I didn't want to go to his house, but we made an agreement."

Nick set Natalia on the sofa next to him. "What kind of agreement?" he asked.

"I would tell him about our lives, mine in New York, and yours in South Dakota in exchange for him telling me what happened all those years ago." He eyed Nick. "Don't worry, I skipped the bad parts."

Bobby touched Carrie's shoulder. "Mom, please don't be mad. I think you'll get some of the answers you're looking for."

"And did you?"

His expression wary, he shrugged and stared at the floor. "To some degree, yes."

"Bobby, look at me." Her heart softening, she said, "I realize you meant well, but I still wish you hadn't done it."

"So, now what?" he asked.

Nick stood and stretched, his muscular arms straining against the fabric of his long sleeve polo shirt. "It's her choice. We can meet with them or not."

"There is one other thing I need to say if you do decide to go," Bobby said.

Carrie studied him. "What?"

"When you meet Kate… she's been through a lot, and well…"

"Not as much as we've been through in the past," Carrie huffed.

"Mom, please. Just be kind."

"Don't worry. I can't really blame her for what he did."

She wandered to the windows overlooking Central Park with Natalia trailing behind her. Naked trees dotted the landscape, their bare branches spread out beneath a pale blue sky. Her eyes followed the traffic snaking along the street below. For so long now, questions regarding her father had plagued her. If she decided to meet with him again, she needed to prepare herself for his answers.

With her back to them, she said, "Bobby, Nick told me about the two men. They're probably the same ones I saw. Did your grandfather disclose anything about them to you?"

"No. But it was clear they were threatening him."

She lifted Natalia up into her arms. Smoothing her long curls, she kissed her forehead.

"What do you think, Natty? Should Grandma visit her daddy?"

Natalia's blue eyes brightened. "Yes, Grandma. Go see him."

*   *   *   *

They climbed the front steps of the brownstone together. Carrie hesitated when they reached the top. "I'm not so sure about this."

Nick's hand found hers. "Time to learn the truth."

She pressed the buzzer. Alex opened the door, his face brightening into a smile. "I'm so glad you agreed to come." He held out his hand. "It's good to meet you, Nick."

The two men shook. "I want you to understand this is a lot to ask of her," Nick said.

"I realize that." He stepped aside. "Please, come in. May I take your coats?"

Carrie declined the offer. "I'm not sure how long we're staying."

Struck by his home's grandeur, she immediately began comparing it to the miserable trailer in Breezy Meadows. Her jaw clamped, she pursed her lips and squeezed Nick's hand.

They stepped into an enormous great room. Startled at first by the sight of a woman sitting in a wheelchair angled toward the fireplace, she stopped. This must be what Bobby meant. Her father's wife was wheelchair-bound. Carrie moved forward as Kate turned her head.

Almost rearing back, she caught herself, the sight of the woman's face making her ashamed of the things she had said earlier.

"Hello, Carrie. I'm Kate." She extended her hand. "It's good to finally meet you."

Carrie shook her hand and said, "Yes, I guess it's a long time coming."

"And you must be, Nick."

"Yes." He gave her hand a gentle shake.

Alex pointed to the sofa. "Please sit. Can I get you anything?"

"Nothing, thank you," Carrie said. "We're having dinner later with Bobby."

"Ah, yes, Bobby," Alex said. "You raised a fine young man, Carrie."

"No thanks to you." Regretting the words, the moment she uttered them, she looked at Kate. "I'm sorry, it's just…"

Kate raised a scarred hand. "You have every right to be angry." She paused, positioning the chair to face them. "All we want is for you to hear what happened all those years ago. Not to gain your forgiveness, but to let you decide whether you want to have a relationship with your father and me. It's something we both wish for but know is entirely up to you."

Unsure of what to say, Carrie fidgeted with one of her earrings. She clasped her hands together to stop them from shaking. Here she was ready to condemn her father, but meeting Kate made doing so difficult.

"I agree," Nick began. "The two of you need to explain your side of things."

Alex nodded. Over the next twenty minutes, he paced while relating how Kate's accident played a major role in his decision to conceal his past with Helen and the child they had together.

When he finished, Carrie remained silent. She'd waited so long to face him with the slim hope his reasons for deserting her would make sense, but they didn't. There was no release.

Alex sat across from them. "Carrie, please say something. Anything," he pleaded.

Nick placed his hand over hers, and her eyes met his. He gave a slight nod. "Go on, Carrie. Tell him what you're feeling."

Pent-up rage surfaced and formed a thickening in her throat. She drew a breath, forcing her voice to remain steady. Measuring her words, she said, "You have no idea how much I... no, *we* needed you... all the suffering Bobby and I endured because no one helped us. I see now why my mother became who she was. She loved you, but *your* mother made her feel like she wasn't good enough, leading her to drown her hurt and shame in alcohol and drugs."

Tears building behind her eyes, she sought to contain them, refusing to break down in front of them. "You could have fought harder for me. Instead, you chose to walk away for over fifteen years."

"But I tried to find you. And yes, I did take too long, but with Kate's life at stake, I was too cowardly to tell her everything. I'm sorry you had to endure such awful treatment from your mother." He paused. His eyes locked on hers. "Haven't you ever made a wrong decision?"

Carrie's breath caught, his words piercing her heart. "So, you want to know if I ever made a bad decision," she sneered. "Is that some kind of an accusation?"

"Carrie," Nick cautioned.

She brushed his hand away and jumped up. "I got pregnant with Bobby at fifteen years old. After I told his father, he disappeared. I wanted the baby more than anything else in this world. I thought, finally, here is someone who will love me no matter what."

"After Bobby was born, I had trouble nursing. I was young and inexperienced. My mother offered no help because she never loved me, and she never loved Bobby. She'd been clean for a while, so I left him with her. I went to get formula and came right back." Her hands clenched at the memory, nails digging into her palms. "I'm guessing Bobby told you how that story ended. Talk about a wrong decision."

Alex's face paled. "Carrie, I didn't mean…"

Hands clamped on her hips, she continued. "Well, since we're laying everything out on the table…my mother ended up in jail, and Bobby's father came back. I left Arizona with him. Guess I made bad decision number two because, for the next sixteen years, he knocked me around pretty good. Of course, I continued to stay with him, believing I deserved it after losing Bobby. Wouldn't you agree I needed to be punished for leaving my son with a drug-addicted alcoholic?"

Kate gasped, a look of horror on her face.

Carrie paused, waiting for a response. Over the next few moments, except for the crackling fire, the room lay silent.

"But you found him again, didn't you?" Kate asked. "That's what matters most. Bobby said he would leave it up to you to tell us the rest."

"Oh, now there's a fascinating story," Carrie muttered. "Purely accidental." She cut her eyes at Alex. "Unlike you, I had neither the money nor the resources to find him."

Nick shot Carrie a warning look. "I think enough has been said for now."

She caught herself and stopped. Her father wasn't entitled to know the rest. What transpired in Laurel and South Dakota belonged to them and only them.

Nick's arm went around her. He gave her shoulder a gentle squeeze. "I think we should get going." Focusing on Alex and Kate, he said, "We came here today because I felt it was important we listen to both sides. Carrie needs time with all of this. Whether or not she chooses to have a relationship with the two of you is entirely up to her. I won't influence her one way or the other.

"I appreciate that," Alex said. He looked at Carrie. "I wish I could change what happened, but I can't. I hope you will believe me when I say not a day went by without me thinking of you. And it still holds true today."

He leaned toward her and attempted to kiss her cheek. Carrie quickly moved away from him. "I'm not ready for that." she snapped.

They said goodbye to Kate and walked to the door. Nick stopped and addressed Alex. "I'm going to be blunt with you. I love Carrie and my children more than anything else in this world. We've created a home and a family together. Today, you've gotten a glimpse into the heartache she still carries with her. I believe your intentions are genuine, but I won't tolerate you hurting her again. If she decides to let you into her life, you're either all the way in, or you're not."

Alex stared at Carrie. "I understand. I don't expect you to forgive me. All I want is a chance."

Her mind numb, she didn't respond. Continuing down the steps with Nick, she hailed a taxi. Inside the cab, she glanced back at her father standing on the sidewalk, a forlorn look on his face. Closing her eyes, she rested her head against Nick's shoulder.

"I know you're upset, but I'm glad you agreed to come," he said. "You've suffered long enough, without knowing the truth."

She lifted her head, eyes searching his face. "Question is what will I do with it?"

Nick kissed her forehead. "Take it slow. You'll figure it out." He draped his arm around her shoulders. "You good?"

"Always, so long as I have you." Carrie snuggled against him, resolved not to think about any of it for the rest of the night. Hearing the whole story, confirmed Kate wasn't to blame for any of it, and she could only imagine what she had gone through after the accident.

Nick was right. She needed to let things sit before considering any kind of relationship with her father. There would be plenty of time to determine what came next for them.

CHAPTER 39

JACK

Jack stood next to Rick while they assessed the carnage around them. Spread out across the pasture, five of Dalton's prize Black Angus cows lay lifeless, their eyes wide open, bullet holes in their skulls. Dark crimson splotches stained their bloodied hides, the stench attracting numerous black flies. A kettle of Turkey Vultures circled above in anticipation. Alejandro and two of Dalton's other men rode up on horseback.

Rick tilted his hat back and let out a slow whistle. "Boss is gonna be real pissed about all this." He swung toward Jack, a flash of irritation in his eyes. "Any idea who the heck would do something like this?" he growled, his suspicions evident in the tone of his voice.

Jack squared his shoulders at Rick's words. "Me? No, of course not. It's obvious my brother must have enemies." Recalling Mel's warnings, his gut twisted into knots. People in Vegas had lost patience, the cows sending a clear signal they wanted their money.

They turned at the sound of a vehicle approaching. Dalton's pickup raced across the field, bouncing along the uneven ruts. Coming to an abrupt stop a few feet away, he killed the engine and jumped out. He examined the dead cows. Shaking his head back and forth, he lumbered over to them.

"What the hell happened here, Rick?"

"Haven't a clue, Boss. Never heard the shots. I was just asking Jack if he might know."

Dalton folded his arms and glared at Jack. "Well?"

He raised, then lowered his shoulders. "I'm just as bewildered as you. Unless…"

"Unless what?"

"Maybe you have some enemies you're not aware of." His palms broke out in a sweat. He shoved his hands into the front pockets of his jeans, forcing himself to maintain a neutral expression.

Dalton ignored his answer. "Take care of this mess, please, Rick. Couldn't be dead for more than a couple hours. Get Alejandro and a few others to help with the butchering. Divide it up between the men. No use letting this meat go to waste."

"You got it, Boss."

The three of them froze at the sound of a galloping horse. Joann charged toward them. She reigned Sissy in, halting a few feet away from the dead cows. Sissy whinnied and took a few steps backward.

"Damn it!" Dalton swore. "Of all times for her to ride this way. It's the last thing I need right now."

She dismounted as he approached.

"I'm sorry you had to see this, Red," he called out. "Please go on back to the house."

Her face drained of color "I don't understand. Who would do such a thing?"

"Rustlers," Dalton said. "Looking for free meat. Rick scared them away only not soon enough, I'm afraid."

"Has this ever happened before?"

"Not in a long, long time. It's pretty rare. I don't want you worrying. It will be handled."

Her eyes swept over him. "Handled how?"

"Red, please. We're used to these things happening sometimes on a ranch."

"Is it safe for me to ride?"

Dalton hesitated. "I would prefer you didn't right now. One of the men will escort you back to the house."

She nodded toward the cows. "What are you going to do with them?"

"Rick and the boys will butcher them and split the meat. The main thing is no one got hurt."

Uncertainty etched on her face, she said, "Well, I guess that's something to be thankful for. She put one booted foot into the stirrup and swung her other leg over Sissy's saddle. "We'll talk more later?" she asked.

"Sure, Red." Dalton signaled one of his men. After she left, he pointed at Jack. "You, come with me."

"You don't need me to stick around here and help?"

"I said come with me!" Dalton barked through clenched teeth.

They climbed into the pickup, Dalton drove like a madman until they arrived at the house. Once inside, he steered Jack into his study and slammed the door.

"Geez, little brother. Take it easy."

"Sit, Jack. We're going to have a talk about a few things."

Jack dropped into the chair across from Dalton's desk. He'd never seen his brother this mad before. Crossing and uncrossing his legs, he felt a tingling in his feet. A muscle below his eye twitched. He rubbed at it and waited.

"I thought this time things would turn out different," Dalton said, his voice hard enough to split a rock. "But I've got five dead cows in my pasture, which tells me you've been lying from the first day you set foot on this ranch. It's time for you to come clean."

Jack cleared his throat. "Look, I didn't have anything to do with killing those cows."

"And I believe you. But I bet you know who's involved, so you better fess up."

"Why do you always talk down to me? I came here with the best of intentions and —"

"The best of intentions! Was one of those intentions, breaking into my office and rifling through my stuff?"

Jack's heart thumped. How had his brother found out?

"Or," Dalton continued, "What about the coke you stole from Veronica?"

"I gave it back," he blurted before he could stop himself.

"Sure, after Bobby threatened you." Dalton pounded his fist on the desk. "I asked you straight out the day you arrived, how much. You swore up and down you didn't owe any money. Now, spill it, Jack."

"You ain't so innocent either, little brother."

"What the hell are you talking about?"

"I did some digging, and first off, that Bobby fella, Nick's son, was tangled up with some big-time drug trafficker. From what the newspapers said, the authorities investigated him too. Something about a mass shooting in Tahoe."

Dalton smoothed his mustache, his eyes narrowed. "That's old news, Jack. Bobby was found innocent of any wrongdoing."

"Look, all I know is some folks around here seem far wealthier than average people. Living in big fancy houses and riding around on private jets."

Dalton's brow furrowed. His face flushed a deep crimson. "So, what! None of it has anything to do with you. I've earned every penny I have, and if I want to buy a jet, I damn well will."

"Can't be from ranching alone," Jack said. "I know it, and so do you." Dalton's face grew dark. A vein pulsed in his neck. Had he gone too far?

Dalton's eyes locked on his. "After what you did to our parents, I don't owe you any explanation with regard to the life I live."

The guilt and shame Jack carried swelled. His chest heaved. He fought to keep control. "I...I never started the fire," he said, his voice shaking. "I went out drinking that night. By the time I came home, it was already burning."

"I've heard that story before," Dalton snapped.

Jack gripped the arms of the chair. "I swear to God it's true. I went up the hall to their bedroom door." He stared down at his shaking hands. "It was too hot to open." Tears building behind his eyes, he looked up at Dalton. "Memories of Dad and me arguing came back. I wasn't thinking clearly. I panicked and ran behind the barn. When I realized I'd done the wrong thing, I ran back to the house. Then, I saw you standing outside."

Dalton's eyebrow quirked upward. "Must have been quite a surprise for you."

"Of course. You had told me earlier you were going out. It's the reason I never checked your room. You gotta believe me, Dalton." He racked shaky fingers through his hair. "I live with what I did every day of my life. Could I have saved them? I'll never know for sure, but I *didn't* set the fire."

Tears coursed down his cheeks and dripped off his chin. Ashamed, he covered his face with his hands and wept. Moments later, he looked up. Dalton sat silent, his face a mask.

"Dalton, I'm telling you this not so you'll forgive me because I will never forgive myself. I wanted you to hear the truth about what happened. A lit cigarette *was* the cause of the fire, not me."

Dalton leaned back into his chair. He clasped his hands together. "Do you want to know the truth, Jack? For all the heartache you caused our mother and father, and me for that matter, you might just as well have started the fire."

"But—"

"No buts, Jack. I won't discuss it with you anymore. All I want to know is how much. How much do you owe this time and to who?"

Pain gnawing at his stomach, Jack wrapped his arms around his middle and rocked back and forth. "Half a mil," he said, his voice shaking. "A group in Vegas."

Dalton sucked in a breath. "Give me the name of the person I should contact."

"That's not a good idea. These are some rough fellas."

"I can be pretty rough, too. A name, Jack," he said, snapping his fingers. "Now."

He'd never seen this look in Dalton's eyes before, like someone had flipped a switch.

"DeLuca. Frank DeLuca."

Dalton shoved a pen and paper toward him. "Write down his number."

Jack removed his cell phone and scribbled.

"Now," Dalton said, nodding toward the door. "Get out of my sight. You stay put on this ranch until I settle things in Vegas. When I get back, I'll settle things with *you.*"

Jack eased up. Hesitating at the door, he turned back toward Dalton. "You can't reason with a man like DeLuca. He'll want the full amount I owe and nothing less."

Dalton's face pinched, a flush sweeping over it while his fists curled on top of the desk. "If that's true, you better start looking for somewhere else to hide because you'll be finished here."

Jack shut the door and stomped up the stairs to his room. Fury raging inside, he opened the drawer and drew out his .45. At this moment, nothing would give him more pleasure than to put a bullet in his brother. Blood rushed to his head.

Fingering the trigger, he imagined Dalton sprawled on the floor. Steadying himself, he tossed the revolver back into the drawer and flopped down onto the bed, his mind in turmoil.

Jack felt a hardening form in his gut. Coming clean to Dalton hurt. At the same time, it didn't matter anymore whether he believed the truth or not about the fire. That was his choice.

He let out a long breath and stared up at the ceiling. Did Dalton think he could deal with Frank DeLuca, convince him to forgive the debt? Going to Vegas could get him killed.

Jack sat straight up. A smile curled his lips. With Dalton gone, he'd collect on the policy. As for Joann left running the ranch, well, accidents do happen.

His mood lifting, Jack relaxed against the headboard. Things might turn his way after all.

CHAPTER 40

NICK

Bobby sat across from Nick, cups of coffee in their hands. "I don't think you told my mother the truth before she left yesterday." He smirked and sipped. "What gives with you staying behind?"

"I knew she needed to get back home because of a private party scheduled at the restaurant," Nick said. "Rosie could handle it, of course, but just like you and your gallery shows, she needs to make sure everything is up to her standards." He shrugged. "I told a half-truth."

Bobby laughed. "I figured you telling her you wanted to spend more time with me wasn't your whole agenda."

Nick poured himself a second cup of coffee. "I do miss Natalia. *You,* not so much," he said, sarcasm rich in his voice.

Bobby wiped fake tears away. "And here I thought you missed me." He looked at his watch. "Maggie took Natalia out early this morning. This is my quiet time, even though my daughter is on my mind every other minute."

"That's the way it is when you have children." Nick sat. His face turned serious. "Tell me about the two men outside your grandfather's house."

"Nothing else to tell. Like I said, they threatened him. One guy asked if he was avoiding them, then my grandfather said he would have it by the end of the week. I don't know what *it* was. The other guy tucked his hand inside his coat."

"What do you mean?" Nick asked.

"Indicating he had a weapon." Bobby's brows knit together. "When I questioned my grandfather about it, he tried to brush it off. He said they were business associates."

"Your mother saw those men, too. I think it's time I find out what's going on, especially if she decides to have a relationship with your grandfather."

"What are you going to do?"

Nick gulped the rest of his coffee. "Call and ask him to meet with me."

Bobby went to the sink and rinsed his cup. "Want me to tag along?"

"Absolutely not. No need for you to get tangled up in someone else's issues again."

"Again?"

Nick eyed him. "I know all about Ronnie and your part in things."

"Yeah, but—"

"Enough," Nick said. "I'm proud of you for helping Ronnie, but you kept me in the dark. That's not like you. I'm not mad, just disappointed to be left out of the loop."

Bobby leaned against the sink. Wiping his hands on a dishtowel, he said, "I'm sorry. I knew Dalton could take care of things, and…" He broke eye contact.

Nick folded his arms. "So, your mother mentioned something."

Bobby fell silent and stared at the floor. Reading his body language, Nick surmised he'd touched a nerve. "Look, I want you to know, I'm much better. I talked with Dalton. It made me realize I did do some good." He studied Bobby a moment. "And what about you? Are you really okay?"

His face filled with remorse, he said, "For the most part. What I did in Tahoe was justified. I only wish I had gotten there sooner. Maybe, Carmela would still be alive."

Pain hit the bottom of Nick's stomach. "Look, we can't change what happened. You handled yourself well. Did all you could, and at least Natalia is safe and nowhere near Miguel Medina."

"That's for sure," Bobby said. "Any word on him?"

"Dalton has his ear to the ground. Last we heard he was in Mexico. I believe he'd think twice before coming back to the United States." He pulled out his cell phone. "I'm going to give your grandfather a call."

*　　*　　*　　*

An hour later, Nick sat next to Alex in a bar a few blocks from Sutton Place. At mid-morning, except for one other person sitting at the opposite end, it was empty.

Nick rested his feet on the brass rail while the bartender set two shots down. He turned his head and detected Alex's worn expression, the deep worry lines etched on his face. If anyone appeared like they were in a predicament of sorts, he sure did.

"Look," Nick said. "An incident has come up twice. Once with Carrie and again with Bobby. Are you in some kind of trouble?"

"Nothing I can't handle. Simply a business matter."

Nick frowned. "If something were to happen to you in the middle of trying to reconcile with Carrie, it's going to hurt her even more. I'm willing to help if it keeps you from being in harm's way."

Alex cast a skeptical eye. "What do you mean?"

Nick swallowed some whiskey. "I won't give you any details. Just know I can make whatever it is go away."

His eyes evading Nick's, he sipped his drink before saying, "We don't really know each other, do we?" Beads of sweat formed on his brow. He tapped his fingers on the bar.

"True," Nick said. "I understand your hesitation, but you owe it to Carrie to at least explain what's going on."

"Will you discuss it with her?"

"Carrie and I don't keep things from each other. It's caused trouble in the past, and I would rather it didn't happen again."

Alex paused. "I feel embarrassed about it all." A slight flush stained his cheeks. "Never in a million years did I think I'd do something so foolish."

"We all do things we regret," Nick said. "But if it's for a good reason, maybe it's not so foolish."

Alex drained his glass. "How much do you know about insider trading?"

"I know it's illegal." The muscles in Nick's jaw tightened. This was the last thing he expected Alex to say. "Why would you take a chance on doing prison time? You seem wealthy enough."

"Oh, it's not about money, though I wish it had been."

Confused, Nick said, "Enlighten me, then."

Alex signaled the bartender for another drink. He gulped it down and set the glass aside. "You've met Kate, and you are aware of what she went through because of the accident. What you don't know about is her current illness." A note of despair creeping into his voice, he continued. "How much suffering one person is supposed to stand is beyond me."

"How bad is it?" Nick asked.

Hands clamped together, Alex rested them on the bar. "If the drug doesn't work, terminal." His eyes watered, and he blinked several times.

"Sorry," Nick said. "I can't imagine what the two of you are going through, but what does this have to do with insider trading?"

"My firm has clients of all types. One owns a pharmaceutical company. After Kate was diagnosed and her treatments stopped working, I contacted him to ask if she could try any new drugs. He told me his company had worked on one that showed promise, only it wasn't approved for trial here in the United States."

Nick sipped his drink. "So, in return for the drug, he asked you to alert him whenever you received information on certain stocks?"

"Correct. Kate's been taking the drug for the past six months, and her condition is showing improvement. As a matter of fact, she has needed the wheelchair less and less." He paused and rubbed his temples. "But I refused to give them any more information."

"Does Kate know what you did for her?"

Alex reared back. "No. She would have refused to take the drug. Kate believes this client gave it to me out of the goodness of his heart." A sigh escaped his lips. "I can't tell her I jeopardized everything to get it."

"And the two goons threatening you?"

"They work for him. I won't get any more of the drug unless I cooperate." The lines around his eyes deepened. "I've been stalling, but now…" His voice trailed off.

"What?"

"I don't think I have a choice. At least this way, Kate will have a chance."

Nick's radar went up. "Why does this guy think he's untouchable? He broke the law, too."

"He has some connections in the government. I'm sure Kate is not the only one he is supplying with a non-FDA-approved drug. I appreciate your wanting to help, but there really isn't anything you can do."

With Kate's treatment hanging in the balance, Nick didn't have to think too hard. He narrowed his eyes. "There is always something to be done."

"Why would you try to help me? We barely know each other."

Nick drained his glass. "Make no mistake. I'm doing this for Kate. Your heart is in the right place, and I can't fault you for trying to save the woman you love."

"I'm not sure what to say."

"There are conditions to my helping you," Nick said.

Alex's brows drew together. "Like?"

"You'll need to hold them off for a while. Give me the information on your client. I'll make sure Kate will continue to get the drug she needs without *you* breaking the law."

"But what …"

Nick held up his hand. "No questions."

Alex rubbed his chin and stared at the floor a moment. "Agreed. I'm ashamed to say I did give them something on a new tech stock yesterday. It will satisfy them for a bit." A note of softness crept into his voice. "I don't know yours and Carrie's full history, but I get the feeling you love her as much as I love Kate."

Nick stood up, and the two men shook hands. "Carrie might not admit it, but she still needs her father. Don't ever hurt her again."

*   *   *   *

The next day, Nick flew back to South Dakota, armed with all the particulars on Alex's client. Turning up his collar against the frosty air, he waited curbside at the airport for Carrie. His cell phone rang.

"You back in town?" Dalton's voice was unusually stiff.

"Just got in. What's up?"

"How do you feel about flying to Vegas tomorrow afternoon?"

"Vegas? Haven't been in years. Should be interesting."

"That I can guarantee," Dalton said. "Fill you in later."

Nick slipped his cell phone into his pocket as Carrie pulled up. He tossed his bag onto the backseat and climbed in, the familiar scent of her perfume instantly erasing any fatigue. The buttons of her navy wool coat were open, revealing the white turtleneck sweater underneath. Jeans concealed her shapely legs. He leaned over, brushed back her hair, and kissed her cheek.

"Missed you," he said. "Everything good at home?"

She glanced at him before pulling away from the curb, a spark in her violet-blue eyes. "Fine, except for Izzy, pestering me every other minute to ride Bella. I'm glad she loves to go riding, only she can't do it every single day, and Michael asked if he could drive your Lamborghini."

Nick laughed. "Might have to build a barn of our own and give Michael driving lessons."

She punched him playfully on the arm. "Very funny."

Careful not to upset the mood between them, he said, "I called your father to find out about those two men. He agreed to meet with me."

She pursed her lips. "I had a hunch there was more to your staying in New York an extra day."

"Sorry," Nick said. "I wasn't sure how you would feel about it. Your father is a touchy subject." He filled her in while they drove.

"How can someone be so evil?" Carrie asked. "Holding back a drug that could prolong or save Kate's life is incomprehensible."

"I know. It's disgusting. Your father got tangled up trying to help her. I can't blame him for it. I'd move heaven and earth to save you."

Carrie smiled. "Let's hope that isn't necessary. Those days are behind us. I just want you to be careful when dealing with my father's problem."

"Don't worry, I will." He leaned back into the seat. "Any rush to get home?"

"Not really. Why?"

"I rented an overnight stay in a cabin at Horse Creek." He gave her a devilish grin and winked. "Thought you and I could get in some alone time." His hand squeezed her thigh.

She gave him a sideways look. "Sounds good, but I don't have anything with me. Plus, Valentina —"

"I called Valentina," he cut in. "And you don't need anything for what we'll be doing."

Her cheeks flamed red. "Nicholas D'Angelo, what do you have on your mind?"

"I think you know."

Taking her hand off the wheel, she reached for his. "I'm game." She said softly.

*   *   *   *

An hour later, oblivious to the glow from the golden logs lining the walls of the cabin enfolding them, they lay on a comforter in front of the fire. Nick's hands skimmed over her soft naked skin. Exchanging hot, open-mouthed kisses, he relished the warmth of her body against his own. His lips left hers and traveled along her neck and around the mounds of her breasts.

They climbed higher, the crack and pop of the sap an accompaniment to their soft moans and whispers. Nick pulled her closer and entered. She arched her back in response, fingers threading through his hair, then skating down his muscular back, gripping his waist, pulling him deeper inside.

When they were satisfied, he slipped beside her and pulled the comforter around them. She rested her head in the crook of his arm. "I'm glad you arranged this detour," she said. "We need to reconnect more often than we have lately."

"I agree." He cupped her chin and kissed her lips. "No matter what happens, always remember how much I love you."

She pushed up on one elbow, her eyes fixed on his. "You're scaring me. Is there something I should know?"

He swept back the lock of hair falling across her cheek. "Of course not. I meant, with our busy lives, I might not say it enough. I treasure you and the family we created together." He pressed her hand to his lips and kissed her palm. Glad their hunger for each other never waned with the ebb and flow of daily living, he cherished these moments. His life had no meaning without her.

Sometimes in the few quiet hours, thoughts of what if would invade to taunt him. What if he'd been loyal to Ricardo? What if he'd never found her? What if, back then, she rejected his love? Carrie was much more than he deserved, but somehow, the tangled tapestry of their lives had brought them together.

At this moment, he refused to admit to the nagging feeling in the pit of his stomach. Could he be imagining things, or was it almost too quiet?

Pushing it away, he said, "Now, how about going someplace nice for dinner?"

Her face relaxed into a smile, and he ran his fingertip along the crease at the corner of her mouth, the tiny beautiful flaw he still found so endearing.

As they gathered their clothes and dressed, he convinced himself his angst grew from the restlessness of the demons sleeping inside him. His transgressions were in the past, and so long as Miguel Medina stayed away, his family remained safe. He hesitated at the cabin door.

"Everything is fine. You have nothing to worry about."

Her arms went around his neck. "I believe you," she said.

They walked out together, his mind settling, and his body satisfied by the depth of their love for each other.

CHAPTER 41

DALTON

Dalton and Nick sat across from one another, enjoying a late lunch of roast beef sandwiches and cold beer on the flight to Vegas. Dalton ruled out bringing Rick along. After dealing with those slaughtered cows, he believed it wiser to leave him behind to keep an eye on Joann and the ranch. He filled Nick in on Jack's dilemma, and Nick, in turn, told him about his meeting with Alex.

"Sorry to get you into this," Dalton said between bites. "If I'd known about Alex, I wouldn't have asked."

A soft chuckle escaped Nick's mouth. "Not a problem, since I might be asking you to make a trip to New York."

"No worries. I love New York."

"I have to check on a few things first."

"Like what?"

"I need to find a weak link in the chain. Someone at the pharmaceutical company who'll talk. If this guy is giving Alex drugs that are not FDA approved, I can only imagine what other illegal stuff he's doing."

"I'll make a few calls. Let's see what pops up."

"Thanks," Nick said. "So, who are we going to see in Vegas?"

Dalton finished off the last of his beer. "Supposed to be some big shot. From what I understand, he's running most of the unlicensed private gambling. Just the thing my idiot brother tends to get involved in."

"Killing cows in lieu of payment doesn't add up," Nick said. "Now, breaking a leg or two does."

"I agree, but they probably messed with me because Jack doesn't own anything of value and breaking his legs will not get them their money. Since I've done it before, this was a direct message for me to bail him out."

Nick pushed back his empty plate and stretched. "Big mistake."

"You bet your ass it was," Dalton said, the image of the dead cows flashing before him. "You do something like that, and you're messing with my livelihood."

"So, what's the plan?"

"I'll try and reason with him… give a little, but there is no way I am going to hand over the full amount Jack owes."

Nick raised an eyebrow. "What about the next time?"

"There won't be a next time. Part of the deal is to let Jack know he doesn't have a seat at the table anymore when it comes to private games."

"Is this guy in Vegas connected?"

"Not sure."

"Might make it more difficult if he is," Nick said. "Could put obstacles in the way."

Dalton grinned. "Nothing we can't get over. There's plenty of heat in the cargo hold."

Later, as the jet descended onto the runway at McCarran Airport, a deep sadness overtook Dalton. Any shred of hope Jack was a reformed man had vanished. It no longer mattered whether his story about the night of the fire held true or not. Jack had worn out his welcome, and when this bit in Vegas finished, he'd let his brother know he needed to leave the ranch.

Dalton and Nick made their way across the hotel lobby to the private elevator while the bellhop followed with their bags. Stepping out on the thirty-second floor, they continued over a suspended walkway above a reflecting pool to one of the penthouse suites.

Dalton slipped his card into the computerized slot and opened the door of the 3,000 square foot suite. Floor to ceiling windows faced east overlooking the Strip. Polished marble floors led to a formal living and dining room with seating for ten and carpeted in a modern geometric pattern. Premier artwork hung from the walls. A separate lounge area with a bar anchored the far end. Two master bedrooms lay on opposite sides. A private solarium with a garden and fountain graced the outdoor terrace.

"Everything to your liking, sir?" the bellhop asked.

Dalton cracked a smile. "What's your name, son?"

"Jimmy, sir."

"Everything is perfect, Jimmy." He dug out his wallet and slipped him a hundred-dollar bill.

"Thank you, sir. You have twenty-four-hour concierge service." He pointed to a phone on the end table. "If you need anything, lift the receiver and press the number nine."

"Will do," Dalton said. After Jimmy left, he tossed his Stetson onto an end table and turned to Nick. "Is this up to your standards?"

Nick surveyed the room. "I've seen better. Guess I'll have to put up with it." He laughed at the look on Dalton's face. "How much did this set you back?"

Dalton shrugged. "Five grand a night. I figured we haven't been here in a while. Why not be comfortable."

"No complaints here. Which bedroom do you prefer, my King?"

"Very funny. Either one is okay by me."

Nick picked up his bag. "In that case, I'll take the one on the right."

"Meantime," Dalton said. "I'm going to give this guy a call while we settle in. He went into the other bedroom, pulled out his cell phone and punched in Frank DeLuca's number.

"This is Frank. Who is this?" The voice had a granular tone to it.

"Dalton Burgess. Jack's brother. We need to meet."

"About what?"

"The money he owes you. I'd like to try and work something out." Silence followed by an audible chuckle came through the line.

"Look, Jack knows the deal. You play the game, you lose, you pay the money. There is no working things out."

Dalton kept his temper in check. "I understand where you're coming from, but I think you need to hear me out in person."

"Why is that?"

"I want to give you a fair chance to accept my offer."

"Fair? Buddy, this is Vegas. Nothing is fair. But you've got me curious, so I'll listen to whatever you have to say. There's a bar off the strip called Mickey's. Let the bartender know you came to see me. Be there at ten."

Before Dalton could answer, the line went dead. Dealing with Frank DeLuca wasn't going to be easy. Tossing his cell onto the bed, he unpacked, then went into the suite's main room and straight to the bar. He poured a shot into a crystal tumbler.

Nick came out of his room and caught the grim look on Dalton's face. "Not a good talk, I presume."

"About what I expected. We meet him later tonight at a bar off the strip." He raised the bottle of scotch.

Nick declined, then grinned and rubbed his palms together. "Gives us time for some gambling. It's been quite a while since I tempted Lady Luck."

Dalton drained his shot glass. "Can't remember the last time I participated in a good game of Blackjack."

The two men headed for the Casino floor. The acrid scent of cigarette smoke swam in the air. The jangle of row upon row of backlit slot machines beckoning patrons filled the vast room. Dozens of players sat on stools, drinking, smoking, their eager hands touching screens and pressing buttons. Uniformed casino workers walked the patterned carpet. Domed security cameras dotted the high ceiling.

They made their way past the tables where the click of a roulette wheel could be heard above the dealer calling for last bets while players placed chips onto the green felt. Shouts erupted from a crowd gathered around a table shooting craps.

Once inside the high limit gaming area, they seated themselves at the $500.00 limit blackjack table along with two other players. While being plied with pricey cognac, they played, losing some hands and winning others.

Hours later, Dalton scowled at his watch. "Had enough yet?" he asked. "I'm about ready for dinner."

Eyeing Dalton's face and the paltry stack of chips in front of him, Nick said, "Think so." He glanced at his ample pile and smirked. "Sorry, you didn't do so well."

"Just remember how good I am at shooting pool. Now let's order up some room service and relax before it's time to go."

* * * *

Dinner arrived, but Dalton's appetite had waned in anticipation of his meeting. He wanted this whole mess of Jack's over with. If Frank refused to accept less than the half-million owed him, things were going to get messy. He glanced away from his plate and watched Nick devour the last of his meal. Had he done the right thing bringing him here to Vegas?"

Nick wiped his mouth and looked up. "I can feel your eyes all over me."

Dalton stroked his mustache. "I know you told me you're feeling better. Still, I think I should have handled this on my own."

"Don't be ridiculous," Nick said. "I'll always have your back and you mine. Besides, I'm sure you can come to some kind of agreement with this guy."

"And if not?"

"Then we'll handle it the way we always do."

Dalton sighed. "Okay then, let's go see if we can stop this whole thing from blowing up."

* * * *

They arrived at Mickey's promptly at ten. Dimly lit and in need of a serious update, the place screamed seedy. Slits exposing white stuffing were visible in the black leather stools lining the length of the bar. Several men sat at tables, plying worn-out-looking women with drinks while a picture faded in and out on a television mounted across the room. A drunken patron, his head face down on the bar, mumbled incoherently.

Dalton wrinkled his nose at the stench of cigarettes, sweat, and stale beer. He looked at Nick. "Drink?"

"I'd be afraid I would catch something incurable," he mumbled.

Dalton chuckled. "Just kidding."

They approached the bartender. Grey-haired with a ruddy complexion and multiple stains plastered on the front of his shirt, he smiled, revealing tobacco-stained teeth. "What can I get for you fellows?"

"Name's Dalton Burgess."

"He's expecting you." He motioned toward a door at the back of the room. "In there."

Dalton rapped on the door. A voice called out, "Come."

This room was a far cry from the front. Plush seating lined the edges while the middle held two round tables. A small, fully stocked bar stood tucked into a corner. Two burly-looking men addressed them.

The taller one stepped closer. "Sorry, gotta frisk you, fellas."

"I expected as much," Dalton said.

They raised their arms while the two men patted them down, removing both 9mms. Backing away, they placed them on the bar before flanking the rear exit.

A side door opened. A pudgy man with brown hair above silver sideburns appeared. Dark, half-moon shadows rested beneath his eyes, his neck invisible behind the folds of his double chin. A paunch pushed against the fabric of his suit jacket, the one button threatening to pop. He lumbered toward them, a somber expression on his face.

"Is all this really necessary?" Dalton asked.

"I'm afraid so."

Dalton recognized the gravelly voice from the phone call, the man sounding like he had spent time chewing rocks.

"Frank DeLuca." He came toward them, stopping in midstride. "Holy crap. I can't believe it." His eyes swept over Nick. "Little Nicky from the neighborhood." His brow puckered. "It's Frankie Boy. Don't you remember me?"

Dalton passed looks between the two. "You know each other?"

"We go way back. Right, Nicky?" Frank said.

He offered Nick his hand. Refusing to shake it, his face like iron, Nick said, "Yeah, way back."

Frank hesitated, then dropped his hand. "No use in rehashing the past, Nicky. Certain decisions were made for various reasons."

"Decisions made by you, Frank," Nick said.

Frank's eyes flashed. "It's best to let things lie. What's done is done. We need to deal with the here and now."

"Yeah, sure, Frank," Nick said.

"Good. Then we understand one another."

In his mind, Dalton cursed Jack once again for having to end up here in this room. By the look of things, odds were the history between Nick and Frank wasn't finished.

CHAPTER 42

JACK

Jack strolled into the barn just as Joann led Sissy from her stall. With Dalton away, he wanted to feel her out about his brother's situation.

Dressed in jeans and a tan quilted jacket, she called out, "Morning, Jack," while saddling the horse.

"Heading out?" he asked.

She chuckled. "More like sneaking out. Rick's off picking up supplies. I told him I'd stay put until he got back, but I'm capable of riding alone."

"Don't think my brother would agree. Not since dealing with those slaughtered cows," Jack said.

Joann shrugged. "According to Dalton, rustling is rare."

He followed behind as she set her beige cowgirl hat with the beaded trim on her head, took Sissy's reins, and led her out of the barn.

"It's been a long time since I've gone riding. Mind if I join you?"

"Sure, you can saddle up, Rio. Dalton doesn't want anyone riding Thunder. His horse is very special to him."

"No problem." He looked down at his feet. "Can't ride in these shoes. Let me run up to the house for a quick change."

Upstairs in his room, Jack changed into his boots and threw on a heavier jacket. He opened his dresser and felt for the .45, tucking it into his waistband. Changing his mind, he put it away. If something were to happen to Joann, it had to look like an accident.

Back at the barn, he readied Rio, then led the dark chestnut outside. He mounted, the feel of the leather reins rekindling old memories of time spent riding with his father and Dalton, his muscles aching from a long hard day of ranching and herding cattle.

The two rode toward the first trail. They maintained a slow gait, riding side by side beneath a cloudless blue sky while a slight breeze blew across the surrounding pastures.

Jack eased up on his reins a bit. "Dalton say how long he'd be gone?"

Extending a gloved hand, Joann patted her horse's side. "Good girl, Sissy." She glanced at Jack. "No, he didn't. Said he was going to look at some new Angus to replace the ones that were shot."

"Makes sense," Jack said.

"Funny Nick went with him," she said. "I didn't think he had any interest in looking at cows."

Jack's ears perked up. "Maybe it's not where they went."

She brought Sissy to a stop. "What do you mean? I told you where he went and why. Dalton doesn't lie." Her brow arched. "Do you know something I don't?"

"No, of course not, but flying around in a jet is awfully expensive."

Irritation flickered across her face. "Look, Jack. I don't know what, if anything, you're implying, and I don't want to ruin our friendship, so let's leave Dalton's business alone."

"Sure, I didn't mean any harm."

Joann clucked her tongue and squeezed her legs against Sissy's side, urging her to go faster, moving ahead of Jack until Sissy broke into a gallop. Plumes of dust swirled up from the sun-warmed earth filling Jack's nostrils. He held back a sneeze, then rode after her, cursing under his breath.

Up ahead, cows grazing in a paddock filled with mixed grasses raised their heads at the sound of the horses' hooves beating a path along the trail. They stared, curious, as they flew past.

Almost to the creek, Joann slowed the horse and came to a stop. She looked back at Jack, coming up behind her. "Hope that wasn't too much for you. Sissy enjoys a good run now and then."

He forced a smile. "Not at all. I kind of enjoyed it."

They proceeded down a rise and along the side of a creek. Rows of tall cattails framed parts of the bank. When they reached the shallow end, Joann dismounted and led Sissy to the water. Nodding at Jack, she said, "I'm sure they're both thirsty."

He followed suit, guiding Rio a distance away. While the horses drank, Joann meandered a few feet from the bank. She stooped to pick some fuchsia-colored Joe Pye Weed, inspecting the large domed clusters of tubular disk flowers. When her hands were full, she sat on the grass.

Jack heard the sound before she did. The unmistakable hiss of a prairie rattler, a venomous pit viper. Not daring to move, he scanned the ground, spotting the snake as it slithered through the tall grass toward Joann. Gray-green skin with round brown blotches ran down the middle of its back. Sissy whinnied and bobbed her head.

Joann eyed the horse. "What's wrong, girl?"

Sissy stepped farther into the water, her nostrils flared, and she continued to whinny. Jack crouched, pretending to inspect Rio's flank. Luck had finally arrived. A bite from that snake could kill Joann. Two bites for sure if he could agitate it enough.

Joann rose, moving steadily toward the rattler. His heart racing in anticipation, Jack braced for her scream.

The crack of gunfire split the air. Rio whinnied, then reared up on his hind legs. Jack's head jerked toward the sound while Sissy bolted across the creek and into the woods on the other side. Rick stood on the rise next to his horse, a rifle in his hands.

He calmly slipped the rifle into the leather scabbard underneath the stirrup's fender, mounted the horse, and rode toward them.

Her face devoid of color, Joann dropped the flowers and stared at the dead snake, then up at Rick. "Oh, my God. I didn't see it! I didn't see it!" she cried.

Rick jumped down and walked over to her. "It's okay. No harm was done, but you need to stay alert." Turning to Jack, a look of pure hatred in his eyes, he said," Isn't that right, Jack?"

Still holding tight to Rio's reins, he returned the stony look. "Yeah. Sorry. I was tending to Rio. Didn't see the damned thing."

"Didn't hear it either, I guess," Rick shot back.

Joann patted Rick's arm. "Thank you. Dalton warned me about rattlers. I must be more careful." Her eyes wide, she pointed to the other side of the creek. "What about Sissy?"

Rick let out a chuckle. "She's been around long enough. She'll find her way back to the barn."

Worry lines crossed her face. "Are you sure?"

"If it will make you feel better, I'll take you back to the house while Jack goes to look for her."

"Yes, it would, but you have work to do. Jack can take me."

"I'm afraid not," Rick said. "You're my responsibility while the boss is gone. Besides, you promised me you wouldn't ride unless one of the other ranch hands or I went with you."

Color flamed her cheeks. "Since Jack came, I thought it would be okay."

"Like I said, you're my responsibility, not Jack's."

A rumble started low in Jack's stomach before soaring up like a thunderbolt to his brain. This cowboy's time was overdue. "Now, look here," he said. "I'm capable of watching out for her."

Rick nodded toward the dead snake. "Yeah, I can tell." He mounted his horse and reached for Joann's hand. She climbed up and sat behind him, hands wrapped around his waist.

"Thanks for going after Sissy, Jack," Joann said.

"You're welcome. I'll be along in a bit." Fists clenched, he turned away. If only Rick hadn't interfered, he'd have one less problem to worry about. He rode Rio across the creek and into the woods to look for Sissy. Bringing her to the barn would bode well for him with Joann.

Thirty minutes later, he found her at the edge of the woods. Though tempted, he refrained from giving her a good kick in one of her legs. Instead, he grabbed the reins and headed back.

He reached the barn where Rick stood outside, a sour expression still on his face. Jack climbed down off Rio and handed Sissy's reins to him. "Here she is."

Stony silence greeted him as Rick took the reins and led her inside. Jack followed behind.

"The least you could say is thank you."

Rick stopped dead in his tracks and spun around. He tipped his cowboy hat back on his head and folded his arms. "Do you expect me to believe you didn't hear or see that rattler?"

Jack let out an exasperated breath. "I told you I was tending to Rio. Whether you believe me or not, I'm thankful you happened to arrive in time."

Rick's eyes narrowed. "I didn't just happen to show up. The minute one of my men told me they spotted you riding with Joann, I went looking for her. So, you can play your bull crap on someone else."

"You think I meant to harm my brother's wife. Why? I have no cause to hurt Joann."

"Oh, I think you do. I'm not sure yet why, but this is your last warning. Under no circumstances are you to go riding with her again."

Jack's head throbbed. If he had his .45 on him right now, he'd do this cowboy in. "And if I do?"

Rick moved closer, his legs planted wide. Hands on his hips, his eyes swept over Jack. "I promise you'll regret it."

Feeling the heat from Rick's body, he stepped back and led Rio to his stall. Glancing over his shoulder, he said, "You may run this ranch for my brother, but you don't run me."

Rick gave him a stiff smile. "Make sure you give the horse a good rub down once you put the tack away." He went past Jack to Sissy's stall.

Later, after a mostly silent dinner with Joann and no sign of Dalton's return, Jack wandered outside to smoke a cigarette. Leaning against the railing at the far side of the property, he gazed up at the stars and ruminated over the day's events.

A couple of simple snake bites should have killed Joann. Now, he counted on things in Vegas going against Dalton even more. Frank DeLuca was no one to mess with. Even if he brought

Nick along, Dalton would be foolish to think he could intimidate him the way he did his own brother.

He finished his cigarette and lit another, filling his lungs with chilly night air, smoke, and nicotine. The time had come for things to turn his way. Two million dollars waited for him. He could envision the money and what he would do with it. If Dalton didn't die in Vegas, he'd make sure he'd die right here on this ranch.

CHAPTER 43

MIGUEL

Miguel surveyed the pantry. Cans of soup and dry goods lined the shelves, quick and easy meals for Bianca to prepare. She still had to continue to work at *Buena Comida*, gaining insight and information. By the end of the coming week, he would be ready to move forward. With Izzy secured in the attic, he could negotiate the return of Natalia and then eliminate Nick.

Grabbing a bottle of tequila and a glass, he wandered onto the front porch. Ignoring the arctic air staking its claim in the hills, he sat and poured an ample amount and swallowed. The heat from the alcohol spread through his chest. He smiled while he considered Nick's reaction upon learning he had taken someone he loved.

But then, his smile faded away. Surely, Nick would do anything to get his daughter back, but did it include giving up Natalia? How could a man trade one child for another? Tracing his scar with his fingertip, the fire simmering inside him flamed anew.

His silent promise to the memory of Carmela must be fulfilled and those standing in his way extinguished. Regardless of the outcome, Nick will die, and Izzy along with him. Next on his list were Bobby and Dalton Burgess. The three had wrought destruction in Tahoe and changed the course of his life. Soon, he would change theirs.

"How are you today, *mi amor?*"

Bianca stood in the doorway, pulling her robe tight against the chill. She'd worked a late shift and slept until almost noon.

He held out his hand and motioned for her to come to him. "*Bien.*"

She sat on his lap and rested her head against his shoulder. "Why do you sit outside in the cold when I can keep you warm in our bed?"

A low chuckle escaped his throat. He swept his fingers through her dark curls, a quiet storm swirling inside him. She believed her deception stayed hidden from him. His palm cupped her chin, and he raised her head. The eyes looking back at him so adoringly were a contradiction of what lie beneath them.

He had seen her with her lover behind *Buena Comida*. A silly cowboy, a mere ranch hand. Too distant to discern the words spoken between them, he waited and followed the man without being discovered. When he disappeared behind the gates of a place called Hidden Creek Ranch, he'd done some digging.

To his delight, he found it belonged to Dalton Burgess. It was as though Carmela had reached out from beyond and played a part in aiding him. He now possessed the whereabouts of all three men—Nick in the Black Hills, Dalton on his ranch, and Bobby in New York.

He had driven along the perimeter of the property, watching herds of cattle grazing, and found it amusing—what a cover for a killer. The world viewed him as a successful rancher, while in fact, he killed to supplement his living. As for Bianca's cowboy, he'd deal with him and Bianca later.

"What is it, Miguel?"

"Your eyes, "he said, releasing her chin.

A smile curved her lips. "What about my eyes?"

"I sometimes wonder how they see me."

"With love, of course." Her fingers rubbed the back of his neck. "I see the man who loves and cares for me. The man who I desire for all time."

"And what else?" he asked. Confusion swept her face. She bit her lower lip. He watched the muscles in her throat contract as she swallowed hard. "What about the man who murdered a poor innocent girl?"

Bianca pushed away from him and stood. "Why must you spoil things? I am trying so hard to be the kind of woman you want."

He raised an eyebrow. "And what kind of woman are you?"

Eyes glistening with tears, she said, "I love you, Miguel. Whether you choose to believe me or not. I thought our trip to Deadwood had made things better between us." A tear splashed down her cheek. "There is something between us I cannot fight because I do not know what it is."

He looked away and poured another shot of tequila. A murder of crows took flight above the green pines, circling, squawking, black wings flailing against a pale sky. "You would do well to put such thoughts to bed, Bianca. We have too much ahead of us."

She wiped her face and stared at the ground. "I will try."

"No," he warned. "You will do it. This is no time to wallow in emotions which will leave you unsatisfied and unfocused."

He downed his drink, rose, and leaned against the railing. "You are certain of the girl's schedule?"

"She is picked up at the same time from school each day, then driven straight home except for an occasional stop at the library."

"Good. I will have her here soon. While at home, you will be responsible for the girl's meals and such."

"*Sí*, I understand."

"Has there been any more talk about Sarah?"

Her face pinched. "No. But everyone has been interviewed several times. They have not come up with anything regarding her disappearance."

"Good. It is one less thing I need to worry about. I think you should stay in the apartment on Hill Street for the next few days. Invite some of the staff over one night. Things must appear normal where you are concerned. When I have the girl, you will stay here with me."

"*Sí.*" Visibly shivering, she padded to the door and went inside.

Miguel turned and looked up. The crows still circled above, their cawing growing louder. All at once, they soared higher, their black wings spread wide. Then, without warning, they dove down into the woods and became silent.

Miguel smiled. *"Un buen presagio,"* he whispered. "A good omen."

CHAPTER 44

NICK

Ice ran through Nick's veins. His vision narrowed, the man standing in front of him, becoming a pinprick in his sight. Their eyes locked. Nick took a step forward. "Where have you been hiding all these years?"

Frank shrugged. "Me? Hiding? Just out of the country for a while. Got relatives I was longing to see."

Weaponless and trapped, Nick eyed his 9mm lying on the bar. "Must have been a long trip."

"Long enough." Frank twisted his diamond pinky ring. "Those were good times back in the old neighborhood. Except, of course, what happened to Mike. Did they ever catch the son of a bitch?"

Nick hesitated a beat, the mention of his murdered brother tearing at the old wound inside him. A wound that never healed. "Yeah, he's doing life."

"Well, it doesn't bring Mike back, but at least it's something." He loosened his tie and unbuttoned the top of his shirt, letting out a quick exhale, almost a snort, through his nose.

"Look, I never meant for it to go down the way it did, but you left me no choice. That was a sad day for the NYPD. Still, you're looking pretty good."

Adrenaline surged through Nick, the rapid beating of his heart hammered in his ears, while his spine went stiff. "I always knew it was you, Frank. It had your stink all over it."

Frank's eyes turned to slits. The dense layer of skin beneath his double chin quivered while his face turned a deep scarlet. "You understood how things worked, Nicky. Refusing to cooperate caused your fall from grace, not me."

"That's debatable." Nick drew in a slow, steady breath. He prided himself on his patience. Seeing Frank again was more than testing it. Nodding at Dalton, he said, "Go ahead and discuss what you need to."

Dalton shifted and cleared his throat. "Look, I know Jack owes you a boatload of money. His gambling's got him in trouble before, and because he's my brother, I've always bailed him out."

Frank's face relaxed. "Good. When can I expect full payment?"

"That's not going to happen," Dalton said. "Not this time. I'm willing to give you half. That's only fair considering my slaughtered cows, and in return, I want Jack banned from all strip and backroom games for good."

Frank looked at the other two men and smirked. "Is this guy for real? He thinks I'm going to cut a deal." The men chuckled under their breath. Frank went to the bar and poured some whiskey. "I'd offer you some, but I don't think the occasion is quite right." He swallowed it, then banged his fist on the bar. "First of all, I don't know anything about some slaughtered cows. That's not my style. Second, if you want to keep your brother in one piece and banned from the games, you'll pay me in full."

Dalton looked him up and down and smoothed his mustache. "And if I don't agree?"

"Then you better spend some quality time with your brother because he won't be walking upright much longer."

"I'll think about it," Dalton said.

"Don't think too long. I've run out of patience." Frank jerked his head at the two men. Each one picked up a weapon and released the magazines, letting them drop to the floor. Releasing the safety lever, they ejected the round left in the chamber and handed Frank the guns.

Frank handed one to Dalton, the other to Nick. "Not sure whose is whose. I guess you'll figure it out." He eyeballed Nick for a moment. "From the expression on your face, I shouldn't say it was good seeing you. But I'm not one to hold a grudge, so anytime you're looking for some high-end action, you know where to find me."

"Oh, I'm sure we'll be seeing each other again," Nick shot back.

Frank licked his lips. "Meaning?"

"You do want your money, don't you?"

A flicker of a smile crossed his face. "Now you're talking my language. See you soon." He turned and left through the side door.

*   *   *   *

Nick kept a stony silence on the ride back to the hotel suite. Once inside, he went straight to the bar. Filling a tumbler half-way with scotch, he took several long swallows.

"Never seen you like this before," Dalton said. "You caught me off guard. What's the story with you and Frank DeLuca?"

Exhausted, his nerves on edge from keeping himself in check, Nick poured another drink and dropped onto the sofa. "Lots of history. Frank and I grew up running the streets together. Back then, he wasn't too bad. But money talks, as they say. We were barely seventeen when he hooked up with some older mob guys."

Dalton eased into the chair opposite him. "You mean they were connected?"

"Yeah," Nick said. "They flashed cash. The kind of money a teenager could never earn on his own. Had Frank running small errands for them at first. Once they knew he could be trusted, they pulled him all the way in."

"Frank tried to get me on board along with Michael." He met Dalton's eyes. "I won't lie and say I wasn't tempted. But when my brother was killed, it changed the way I looked at everything. I made a promise to his memory to do good and stay on the right side of the law."

"Understandable," Dalton said.

"You know the story about my getting kicked off the force," Nick continued. "The money and drugs we confiscated belonged to the mob."

Dalton leaned forward, his hands clasped together. "Why did you go ahead with the bust anyway?"

"Trusting the brass was my fatal mistake. I wasn't aware payoffs went all the way to the top at the department."

"Frank had that much power?"

"No, not then. Frank followed orders, overseeing the distribution, and collecting the money for them. During the investigation and before the raid, Frank hinted I should stay away, said the bust would never stick. Only he left out the part about my being set up. I always suspected his hand in it. Now I know for sure he knew what they planned before the bust ever happened. With me there, they couldn't run their game anymore. I was a thorn in a corrupt department's side."

"When everything went down, I fought hard to keep my gold shield. Frank became the last thing on my mind. They won in the end. I spiraled down until I met Ricardo."

Dalton nodded. "He caught you at your weakest."

"With my parent's accident in the middle of it all and the loss of my shield, I was too bitter by then. Staying on the right side didn't matter anymore."

"Well, I have no intention of giving Frank his money. And as much trouble as Jack has caused, I still can't let Frank get hold of him."

Nick swallowed the rest of his whiskey. "And I can't let Frank live, so I guess we're both on the same page. Let's try to make this quick and easy. I still have business in New York."

CHAPTER 45

ALEX

Uneasy with his decision to let Nick help, Alex blinked at the morning sun streaming in the window on the 44th floor of his brokerage firm on East 59th Street. Hands in the pockets of his blue wool suit, he studied the tall skyscrapers in the distance. He didn't doubt Nick's sincerity, but what if things went wrong?

Putting Nick's life in jeopardy because of his decision to help Kate had him on edge. He needed to find out more about Nick. The only way to do that would be to take a chance and fly to South Dakota.

He picked up his cell and called Bobby. He answered on the third ring.

"Hello."

"Bobby, it's your grandfather. I have a favor to ask of you."

A long sigh wafted through. "Go ahead."

"I want to fly to South Dakota to see your mother and Nick."

"Not a good idea," Bobby said. "I'm not sure they would want you to come at this point."

Alex paused. Never since Kate's illness had he felt like begging, but he needed this. "Bobby, please call her for me. If it's okay, tell her I need to talk about my coming there. It's important."

"I can't promise anything. I'll ask her to get in touch with you."

"Today, please, if possible." Alex went and sat behind his desk, fingers drumming against the top, he waited. Twenty minutes later, his cell rang.

"Carrie?"

"Yes, Bobby asked me to call you. Is Kate alright?"

"As well as can be expected. I didn't mean to alarm you. I...I wanted to ask if I could come to see you."

"Why? The last time we met, I think I made myself clear about how I feel. I need time."

"Of course, but I met with Nick, and I have questions."

"Questions about what?" Her voice had an edge to it.

"Look, I'm going to be honest. I took Nick up on his offer, only I'm having second thoughts. If anything happens to him—"

"I think it's too late for that," she cut in. "Nick is determined to help because of Kate."

"And I'm more than grateful, but I need to sit and talk with you. Please say yes. I can fly in this afternoon."

He waited through the silence until she said the words he wanted to hear.

"Okay. Text me your flight information, and I'll send a car for you."

Relieved, he said, "Better yet, give me your address. I'll reserve a car."

* * * *

Alex took in the landscape of the Black Hills. Their hues fading, leaves lost their grip among the branches and floated to the ground in the chilly breeze. The limo pulled up to the gates of the property, and he gave the driver the code.

They wound up the drive surrounded on each side by tall ponderosa pines. Struck by the beauty of the stunning stone and timber home, he climbed out of the limo. He paused a moment before going up the steps, soothed by the fact his daughter had come so far from the run-down trailer in Arizona.

His pulse ticked higher. Almost breathless, he rang the bell. The sound of footsteps running toward the other side of the door made him take a step back. It flew open, and a little girl with dark hair and green eyes dressed in a flowered shirt and jeans peered up at him. A German Shepherd ran up behind her, barking incessantly. She wagged her finger at him. "Quiet, Ace. Hit it." The dog stopped, his rump dropping to the floor.

Her face beaming, she looked up at him. "I'm Izzy. Are you my grandpa?" she asked.

"I believe so," he said, tears welling in his eyes. "I'm your Grandpa Alex."

"Can I give you a hug?"

"Of course." He bent, and her small arms hugged his neck. Alex reveled in the joy of the moment. He breathed in and stroked her hair.

She let go and beckoned to him. "Come in, Grandpa. Mommy and Michael are waiting for you."

She led him down a hall, which opened onto a magnificent great room where a soaring timbered ceiling and full-length windows greeted him, the view of the valley below nothing short of spectacular. Bright flames licked the logs inside a double-sided fireplace anchoring the room.

Carrie smoothed her long hair and rose from the sofa, her cornflower blue sweater heightening the violet in her eyes. A young boy stood next to her, his hand gripping her black jeans.

Alex walked toward them. "And who might this be?"

"That's Michael," Izzy chimed in. "Say hello to Grandpa, silly."

His voice, barely audible," Michael said, "Hello."

"Don't you want to give him a hug?" Izzy asked. She went over and attempted to pull him toward Alex.

Carrie shot her a look. "That's enough, Izzy. Leave your brother alone."

"It's alright," Alex said. "Maybe next time."

Carrie's eyes swept over him. "Well, you're real sure of yourself," she said, her voice hollow.

Her remark gnawed at his soul. Had he made a mistake in coming here? "I only meant…never mind. Can we talk?"

"Izzy, you and Michael go upstairs for a bit. I need to talk to your grandfather."

Izzy's hands clamped her hips, "But I want to stay."

"You can visit later. Please don't give me a hard time, or there will be no riding Bella tomorrow."

Her face fell. "You'll wait for me, Grandpa, won't you?"

"Of course," Alex said. With the children gone, he turned to Carrie. "I have no words for what I'm feeling right now. How old are they?"

Their eyes met, and she broke contact. Brushing past him, she called over her shoulder, "Izzy is nine, and Michael is six. Come into the kitchen."

Alex followed and waited on a stool by the island while she prepared coffee. "Is Nick home?" he asked.

Carrie set cream and sugar down, then poured two mugs. She handed one to him and sat on the opposite side of the island. "No, he's not. I'm not sure when he'll return."

"Oh." He rubbed the light grey stubble on his chin. "Thank you for letting me come. I really appreciate it."

Her demeanor stoic, Alex caught the stiffness in her body language. How could he ever penetrate the wall she had built to keep him out?

"What was so urgent you needed to fly here today?"

Afraid of saying the wrong thing, it took him a moment to find his voice. "I don't know Nick well, but I sense he's a good man. When I agreed to let him help me, it was on the condition that I don't ask him for any details. I want to be honest and tell you it bothers me somewhat."

She lifted her mug and shot him a look. "Nick can handle himself. You don't need to worry about him."

"What do you mean, Carrie? I don't know anything about his background, what he did or does for a living." He glanced around. "I mean, look at this place."

Her cheeks flushed. "That shouldn't matter to you. Nick loves us. Be glad we are well taken care of."

Alex let out a breath and massaged his temples. "Of course, I'm glad you have a good husband and a wonderful home, except the people I'm involved with could do great harm to him."

She set her mug down and smirked as if she were mocking him. He had warned her of the gravity of the situation, and it didn't faze her one bit.

"Didn't you hear what I just said? Don't you believe me?"

For the first time, her face softened a bit. "I'm sorry," she blurted out. "I'm not making light of things. Like you said earlier, you don't really know Nick. I won't discuss his background except to say he worked for the government at one time, and he's highly trained in certain areas."

His scalp prickled at her words. Could Nick have been with the CIA or some type of assassin? He shifted uncomfortably. "Then, this whole situation doesn't worry you at all?"

"Of course, it does. I don't want Nick getting hurt, but at the same time, when he makes up his mind to do something, there's no changing it."

"Where is he right now?"

"He flew to Vegas with a friend of his for a few days."

His tension eased. At least nothing was happening in New York. Alex sipped his coffee and paused for a moment. "I guess I just need to trust him."

"You should, and you can," Carrie said. In an instant, her stiff posture returned. "Now, if you want to spend some time with your grandchildren, I will go and get them."

He broke out in a smile. "Absolutely."

*   *   *   *

Later, on his flight back to New York, Alex was glad he decided to come and talk to Carrie. No real breakthrough had occurred between them but meeting his grandchildren for the first time lifted his spirits, a lightness he hadn't felt in years.

Izzy was a delight. A tough but sweet little girl. Michael seemed more reserved. He held back a bit in the beginning. By the time he prepared to leave, he had become more talkative and willing to give up a hug.

Alex couldn't wait to see them again. Maybe this would open a door for him with Bobby, give him a chance to meet Natalia, too.

Carrie was another matter. More than anything in this world, he wanted her to forgive him and build a relationship. Alex studied the night sky filled with stars outside the window of the jet. Today became the first step in his determination to break through to Carrie. He needed to find a way to make her see how much he loved her.

CHAPTER 46

NICK

White-hot rays of sun beat on the hood of the rental car with a vengeance while Nick and Dalton sat across from Sheri's Brothel watching various men go in and out. Desert broom and cactus dotted the landscape. A small dust devil swirled in the far distance, spitting sand in the air. Using the GPS tracker Nick slipped underneath Frank's car the previous night, they had tailed Frank DeLuca and his two men to this spot over an hour ago.

"Any ideas?" Dalton asked.

Nick tapped his fingers on the steering wheel. "Too busy for a kill here, and I really don't relish staying in Vegas much longer to figure out his daily routine. If we can take the two bodyguards out, killing Frank will be easy.

Dalton raised an eyebrow. "Am I correct in thinking you want to make things more personal with Frank?"

"Hell, yes. The son of a bitch almost ruined my life. I can only imagine what other misery he's caused over the years."

"How do you feel about the bar?"

Nick swiped his hand through his hair. "Not comfortable with it. The bar has too many unknowns. Too cramped a space, and we would have to worry about customers, not to mention the bartender."

A puzzled expression on his face, Dalton said, "Out in the open?"

"Not exactly. I checked and found out Frank has his boys park on the private top deck at the same casino we're staying at. If we block the camera, we can come and go by the door leading to the penthouse parking deck without being seen. It's the perfect spot. After all the action at the brothel, they'll probably return to their suite before going out again."

Dalton's eyes lit up. "You might be right."

"Call Frank and tell him if he agrees to keep Jack out of the games, you'll pay him the full amount. Set up a meeting for ten tonight at his bar. We'll eliminate his boys on the deck and grab Frank."

"What about his being a made man?" Dalton asked.

"It's perfect. They'll think it's mob connected. The bosses will fight among themselves, trying to figure out who to blame."

Nick pulled away and drove toward the strip. "We'll use a wireless jammer to temporarily knock out the surveillance cameras. I'll park the rental on a different deck."

Dalton smoothed his mustache, a wiry smile on his face. "Sounds like a plan."

*　　*　　*　　*

While eating dinner in their suite, they were interrupted by a knock at the door. Dalton answered it and retrieved an envelope from a young clerk. He tipped him and returned to the table.

"What's that?" Nick asked.

"Could be something, could be nothing," Dalton said, tearing it open. He removed a single sheet of paper, read it, then handed it to Nick. "This ought to help with your New York problem."

Nick scanned the paper. "Holy crap!" He looked at Dalton. "Is this true?"

Dalton swallowed his last fork full. "Pretty reliable source. I told you I'd make a few phone calls. While you were napping on the plane, I made one of those calls to an old flame of mine." His eyes twinkled. "She worked in the industry and used to be employed at the pharmaceutical company Alex gets his drug from. She left because she didn't like some of the stuff she heard going on. Things she hints at in the letter. The guy she mentions still works there. He's the person we need to meet with."

Nick chuckled under his breath.

"What?"

"You never cease to amaze me. I don't recall you mentioning anyone in New York. How long did that last?"

"Not too long. About a year and a half. We spilt on friendly terms." He winked at Nick. "She didn't like all the distance between us. I was handling a lot of kills during that time."

Nick tucked the letter back into the envelope. "Thanks. This will help." He checked his watch. "Time to go."

Both men put on jackets, knit caps, and black leather gloves before attaching silencers to their 9mms. Nick slipped some towels from the bathroom into a duffel bag. They made their way to the door of the upper deck. Dalton turned on the handheld wireless camera blocker to disrupt and jam the signal before they stepped out. Nick surveyed the deck. Four spots were reserved for the Penthouse Suites. Frank's car sat in the one closest to the door. Except for one other vehicle, the remaining spots were empty. Nick counted on them staying that way. He set the duffel down, and they crouched beside Frank's car and waited.

Ten minutes later, the door opened, and two of Frank's bodyguards appeared. Lit cigarettes in their hands, neither paid attention as they joked with each other.

Dalton nodded. They pulled out their weapons and came from behind the car.

One of the men whirled around. "What the fu—"

"Don't move," Nick said. "Hands up."

Two bullets, one from each silencer entered each man's forehead. Their bodies jerked, cigarettes dropping as they fell to the ground.

Dalton searched their pockets for the keys, then opened the trunk of Frank's white Cadillac DTS. They dumped the bodies inside. Nick slammed the trunk shut. The door to the deck opened and he spun around, pointing his weapon at Frank.

Frank's eyes went wide. "What the hell is going on?"

Nick motioned with his gun. "Get in the car." He opened the rear door of the Cadillac and shoved him inside. Dalton grabbed the duffel and slid behind the wheel while Nick sat beside Frank, his gun aimed and ready.

"Come on, Nicky," Frank said. "Is this really necessary?"

"I'm afraid so." Nick relished the fright in Frank's eyes as Dalton headed for the desert.

"Listen, forget about the debt. Jack can go free and clear. I'll make sure he doesn't gain entry to any of the games."

Nick smirked, then winked at Frank, but remained silent.

The lights of the strip faded under the night sky. A full moon accompanied them. When they were far enough away, Dalton pulled off the main road, driving farther into the vast desert, and stopped.

"Get out of the car, Frank," Nick ordered.

Frank fumbled with the door handle. "Please, don't do this."

"I said out of the car, *now!*"

His body shaking uncontrollably, Frank climbed out. He stumbled a step or two before his hands latched onto the rear fender.

Nick followed, his weapon aimed at Frank. "You have no idea what you cost me. I lost everything just so you could keep up your bribes and drug running."

A sliver of moonlight shone on Frank's face, revealing the terror in his eyes. "Come on, you know I was following orders."

"And I was doing my job. Doing what was right."

"It wasn't personal, Nicky."

"It wasn't personal?" Nick shot back. "We grew up together, Frank. You knew the reason I became a cop, how much my career meant to me. And to make matters worse, you came to Marie's wedding, watched me give her away, knowing full well the money was being planted."

Spreading his arms wide, he took a tentative step forward. "But look at you! Seems you made out okay. Let's just put all of it behind us. We can work something out." His bottom lip quivered, and he dropped to his knees. His hands clasped together, he pleaded. "Please, Nicky. Let me fix things."

"Impossible, Frank. I became a hired killer because of what you did, and tonight, I'm adding you to my body count."

Frank's face filled with horror. Beads of sweat gleamed on his forehead in the moonlight. Tears poured down his cheeks. "You're making a terrible mistake. I'm connected. They'll come for you."

Nick waved his 9mm at him. "And I'm a ghost, Frank. They will never know who or why."

"What can I do? Please, tell me?" Frank cried.

Nick stared into the eyes of the man begging for his life. He aimed at Frank's forehead. The familiar adrenaline rush soared through his body. "Nothing," he said and calmly pulled the trigger twice.

Frank fell backward onto the desert sand, eyes open, his mouth gaping. Dalton helped Nick remove the bodies from the trunk. They laid them next to Frank, then drove back to the casino in silence. Nick took the towels from the duffel, and they wiped down the Cadillac.

Within the next hour, they checked out, dropped off the rental, and boarded Dalton's jet for New York.

CHAPTER 47

CARRIE

Carrie sat in the office with Rosie. Problems had stacked up one on top of the other. The dishwasher stopped working, two food deliveries were incomplete, and an employee was caught stealing.

Tugging at the collar of her black turtleneck sweater, Carrie said, "What else is going to go wrong today?"

Rosie's brown eyes widened. "Girl, please. Don't go there." She went to a small fridge in the corner and removed a bottle of Pinot Grigio, placing it on the desk. Grabbing a corkscrew, she opened it and poured two glasses, handing one to Carrie. "At least the repairman is on his way. The dishwasher should be fixed soon."

Raising up her glass, Rosie said, "Here's to better days at *Buena Comida*."

Carrie lifted hers and sipped the chilled wine. Her muscles unwound a bit. It wasn't only the issues at the restaurant putting her on edge. Nick hadn't returned from his trip. What was he up to?

He had told her Dalton needed help with a problem Jack caused. She believed him, but at the same time, it worried her. Old patterns of his coming and going were something she didn't want to think about.

There was a tap at the door, and Alice poked her head in. "Sorry, there is someone here to see you, Mrs. D'Angelo."

"Who?" Carrie asked, rising from her chair.

"Joann Burgess."

"I'll be right back," she said to Rosie, the wine glass still in her hand."

"Take your time. I'll start on payroll."

Carrie strolled over to Joann. It was late afternoon with the restaurant nearly empty.

"Hey, you didn't tell me you were coming." Her lips brushed Joann's cheek.

Pointing to the bar, Carrie said, "Come, sit." Something was off. Joann wasn't her usual easy-going self.

Joann slid onto a stool next to her. Her eyes studied Carrie's for a moment.

"Wine?" Carrie asked before signaling to Bianca.

"No, ginger ale would be fine."

Bianca smiled. "Coming right up." She scooped ice into a glass, then squirted soda into it.

"Thanks," Joann said.

Bianca turned away and went about wiping the other end of the bar before racking dirty glasses.

Carrie took a sip of wine. "What's up?"

"Well, Jack's been with us for a while now. Yesterday, we went riding together, and he questioned me about Dalton."

"What do you mean, questioned you?"

"He asked if Dalton mentioned anything besides looking at some cows… he made a statement about it being expensive to fly the jet."

The pit of Carrie's stomach grew heavy. Dalton had never revealed his past to Joann. Even though she felt it might spell trouble in the future, it was never her place to tell Joann anything regarding Dalton.

"I know Nick flew with him," Joann continued. "Were they going anywhere else?"

Old feelings of lying and hiding back in Laurel surfaced inside Carrie. Uncomfortable being deceptive with her best friend, she sipped her wine and tried to remain casual.

"Nick didn't mention anything."

"Carrie, hon, look. I started thinking and what Jack said makes sense. Maintaining and flying a jet costs a lot of money. Cattle ranching alone can't cover those expenses."

"Have you ever asked him about it?"

Joann clasped her hands and leaned forward. "No, I haven't, and that's my fault. We've been so happy together. I think deep down I didn't want anything to spoil it."

She attempted to lessen Joann's fear. "Dalton and Nick made some excellent investments over the years. Their kind of money makes money."

"I guess so. But have you ever seen proof?"

"Proof?"

"Yes, like paperwork, files, bank statements?"

"No. I trust Nick. I don't feel the need to pry or ask too many questions. He provides a good home for me and our children."

"But aren't you just a little bit curious, Carrie? I mean, when two people get married, everything should be out in the open between them. Dalton not telling me about Jack makes me wonder what else he's keeping from me."

Carrie set her wine glass aside, knowing she was walking a fine line with Joann. "If you have questions, you need to talk to Dalton when he gets back. I'm sure it will settle your mind."

Joann's face relaxed. "I guess you're right. I shouldn't expect answers from you."

Carrie glanced at her watch. "Oh, damn. I need to pick Izzy up from school, and I haven't finished things here yet."

"Doesn't Valentina usually pick her up?"

"Yes, but Michael wasn't feeling well this morning. He ran a slight fever, so she's home with him."

Joann's eyes sparked and she grinned. "I can pick her up for you, bring her to the ranch to visit Bella."

"No, it's out of your way."

"Don't be silly. I'm not in a hurry, and with Dalton gone, I would love the company."

"Tell you what. It's Friday, so there's no rush for homework. If Michael is okay, I'll come by later. We can have some girl time. Otherwise, Izzy can stay over if that's okay with you?"

"Sounds good. Let me know and I'll fix dinner."

* * * *

Joann left and Carrie called the school to let them know Joann would be picking Izzy up, and then she sent her a text as well. She smiled to herself, remembering her old argument with Bobby about not letting Izzy have a cell phone. Now, she not only had her own phone but a horse, too. Her little girl was growing up so fast.

Over the next couple of hours, she finished up with Rosie, then called Valentina to inquire about Michael.

"Is everything okay? How is Michael."

"Much better," Valentina said. "His fever is gone."

"Oh, good. I'm going to Joann's. Izzy and I will be home later."

Carrie sent a quick text to Joann, then headed for Dalton's ranch. On the way there, she recalled their earlier conversation. She never told Joann everything all those years ago, never exposed Nick's working for Ricardo or his being a ghost.

But how far would Dalton go in revealing his past? Glad she and Nick cleared things up a long time ago and had no lingering secrets between them, she hoped they could do the same. Carrie sighed and settled back into the leather seat. It wasn't any of her business. She could only hope Joann would be satisfied with whatever he told her. For now, she looked forward to a well-deserved break and spending time with her friend.

CHAPTER 48

MIGUEL

Miguel glanced at his cell and frowned. On his way to grab the girl, he had no time for an idle chat.

"What is it, Bianca?" he snapped.

"Miguel, there has been a change?"

"What do you mean?"

"Izzy will not be in the usual car. *Señor* Dalton's wife is picking her up from school. She was here talking to Carrie. Before she left, she offered to pick Izzy up and bring her to the ranch."

Miguel rubbed the stubble on his chin. This could play right into his hands. "Do you know what kind of vehicle she is driving?"

"*Sí*. It is a silver Ford F150. His wife has short red hair."

"Okay. I will handle things."

"But Miguel…"

"I know exactly where the ranch is and what road they will take." There was a moment's silence on the other end.

"You do?"

"I have driven there before. If there is nothing else, Bianca, I need to go. You are to come home right after your shift."

"*Sí,* Miguel."

Before she could say anything else, he ended the call, pleased at Bianca's surprise. What would she think if he told her the rest? How ready to explode, he had followed her ex-lover, then taken his high-powered rifle and slaughtered a few of Dalton's cows.

Miguel climbed into the Cadillac and opened the small valise sitting on the passenger seat. He took out a syringe, slipped it into his pocket, then removed several zip ties and tossed them next to the valise. Satisfied, he pulled on his black gloves and headed for the school. Soon, Nick would know how it felt to lose something dear to him.

Miguel parked on the opposite side of the street and down the block from the school entrance. He slumped into the seat and raised a pair of binoculars. The children started to emerge, and he scanned the waiting vehicles.

Sure enough, a silver truck waited with a red-haired woman inside. The girl ran to it and got into the rear passenger seat. He lowered his binoculars, pulled away, and followed them.

Outside of town, the traffic thinned, and they turned off the main road and onto another one with a sign reading 'private property.' Miguel knew they were nearing Dalton's ranch.

The truck slowed and his adrenaline soared. Dalton's wife must have detected him. He sped up, almost touching her bumper. The vehicle swerved, and he continued to tap the rear end. A steep ravine came into view up ahead. He gunned the engine and drove up alongside the truck, forcing it off the road. It swerved and skidded. The tires on the right-side screeched then lifted. Screams came from inside.

Miguel backed up and watched the truck plunge down into the tall grass below, coming to a stop when the front end smashed into a tree.

Leaping from the Cadillac, he made his way down. Dalton's wife lay slumped over the airbag. Izzy struggled with the rear door, calling for help when she saw him.

He yanked the door handle. It sprung open, and he helped her out. A small knot was forming on the front of her forehead. Tears streamed down her face and dripped onto her quilted blue coat.

"Please, help my aunt!" she cried.

Miguel bent, he stared into her eyes. "Don't worry, Izzy. I will. But first, you must come away from the truck. He took her hand, led her up from the ravine and toward his car.

Izzy stopped. She pulled her hand free. Eyes red and blinking, she said, "I remember you from the ice cream shop."

"That is right. You have an excellent memory."

"But how do you know my name?"

Miguel grabbed her hand again and steered her to the car. "That is not important right now. You must come with me."

"No, no. Help my aunt first, please." She broke free and tried to run. He whipped around and snatched her up by her waist.

She kicked and screamed. "Put me down!"

He ignored her struggling and threw her onto the back seat. "Don't fight me," he warned.

Her eyes grew wild, while her fingernails raked his face. "Let me go!"

Miguel touched his cheek. Streaks of blood trailed across his palm. "You little bitch!" His hand pressed against her throat. "That was a mistake," he sneered.

He pulled the syringe out, tore off the cap with his teeth, and plunged it into the side of her neck. Within seconds, her body went limp. He secured her hands and feet with the zip ties and slammed the door shut.

Pulling his 9mm from the glovebox, he hurried to the ravine. The more damage he could inflict, the better. His heartbeat quickened with the thought of what he was about to do. First, Dalton's cows, now his wife. Making his way to the truck, he glanced up at the darkening sky. "This is for you, Carmela." He continued down into the ravine.

CHAPTER 49

NICK

Nick and Dalton sat across from a mousy little man at the back of a New York restaurant. Every few minutes, from behind his wire-rimmed spectacles, Basil Stilton's eyes darted around the room. Twisting the white cloth napkin in his hands, he said, "Look, I think I made a mistake in agreeing to meet with you. I could get in a lot of trouble."

"Calm down, Basil," Nick said. "Nobody is going to get into trouble."

"But if they find out, I gave you the information…"

Dalton smoothed his mustache and grinned. "Listen, we just need the owner to stop harassing someone. It's not about anything else. Now, my friend told me you have proof of what's been going on at the company illegally."

"I do, yes, but…" He licked his lips and blinked. "I need your assurance that this doesn't lead back to me. I don't like some of what is going on at Greystone Pharmaceuticals. It's hurting people."

"It's all the more reason you should want to do the right thing." Nick said.

Basil leaned in and twisted the napkin again. "They're exporting unapproved drugs."

"But," Nick said. "Bypassing our government here and sending non-approved FDA drugs overseas isn't illegal."

"Correct," Basil said. "Except when an unapproved drug is first exported, the drug company must notify the FDA and continue to maintain records, and the export must comply with the laws of the importing country. You have to obtain a CPP rider."

Dalton gave him a look. "Help us out here, Basil. What's a CPP rider?"

"It's a Certificate of Pharmaceutical Product which states the drug conforms to the World Health Organization's requirements. The company has to have one for each drug it wants to export."

"So, they never applied?" Nick asked.

"No." He removed his wire rims. "And then I started hearing things."

Dalton frowned. "What sort of things?"

Basil reached down into a briefcase sitting on the floor beside the table. He removed a folder, placing it in front of Nick.

"That some of the drugs," he pointed to the folder. "Namely, the ones inside there are being sold on the black market for undetected profits. Worse still, some people are dying instead of getting well, but black marketeers don't care. They'll sell them anyway."

Nick and Dalton exchanged glances. "And the company doesn't care?" Nick asked.

Basil wiped a sheen of sweat from his brow. "Correct."

Nick opened the folder, his eyes traveling over the documents inside. "Help me to understand why a company would take such an enormous risk."

"New drugs are being developed all the time," Basil said. "Competition between drug companies is monumental. You're talking billions of dollars in profits if you manage to develop the right one. Greystone hadn't come up with anything significant in quite a while, and we were being outpriced by the others with some of our long-term staples."

"Those copies of memos and company emails inside the folder are proof what they're doing is harmful." He set his wire rims back onto the bridge of his nose. "Look, I'm a scientist, not a murderer. I walk into the lab every day trying to develop drugs and better cures for disease. I don't want their blood on my hands."

Nick studied him for a moment. Basil was one of the good guys, and he took comfort in knowing they were still out there. "Don't worry, this will never come back on you."

Basil lifted his briefcase and rose to his feet. "I hope you're right." He nodded, then left by the rear exit of the restaurant.

Back at the hotel, Nick and Dalton reviewed the contents of the folder. With each memo and email he read, Nick grew more furious.

"As if they don't make enough money already." He rose and paced the room.

"How do you want to play this one?" Dalton asked.

"I know what I would like to do, but Alex needs a certain drug for Kate. I can't take this guy out. But I can make him think I will."

"Probably not the only pharmaceutical company doing this," Dalton said. "You might not be able to stop him from continuing to export, either."

Nick paused and rubbed the back of his neck. "That part is true. The main thing is to ensure Kate still gets her drug, and Alex is off the hook for good."

Nick pulled out his cell and dialed the number Alex had given him. A male voice answered on the second ring.

"Milton Greystone."

"Mr. Greystone, you don't know me, but I think we should meet," Nick said.

"Why?"

"Let's just say I'm a friend of Alex Paterson's. There is something I need to discuss concerning him."

"Sorry, the name's not familiar."

Nick's body tensed. "Let's not play games, Mr. Greystone. I believe you'll find what I have to say interesting. We need to meet today."

"What did you say your name was?"

"I didn't. Just so you're comfortable, I'll even come to your office or wherever you prefer."

"Well then, my office on East79th, today at five."

*   *   *   *

Nick stepped out of the elevator on the forty-first floor of Greystone Pharmaceuticals promptly at five with a folder in his hands. His feet sunk into the plush beige carpeting leading to Milton Greystone's office. A pretty blonde dressed in a business suit behind a desk gathered up her purse.

Devouring Nick with her eyes, she smiled and asked, "Mr. Greystone's five o'clock?"

"Yes."

She led him to double wooden doors, knocked, and turned the brass knob. "You can go right in."

Nick moved past her as she called to a gentleman, focused on a computer screen, sitting at an enormous mahogany desk. "Anything else this evening, Mr. Greystone?"

Without glancing up, he said, "No, Judy. Have a good evening."

The door closed softly behind Nick, and he approached the desk. Milton Greystone, a thin, wiry-looking man dressed in a brown suit, blue shirt, and cream-colored tie, squinted up at him. He removed a pair of reading glasses and set them down.

Pointing to a chair in front of the desk, he said, "I presume you're the gentleman who called me earlier?"

"That's right," Nick said, flashing a grin.

"Since you know my name, don't you think it's only fair you tell me yours?"

Nick shook his head. "No, not really. What's important right now is the reason I came to see you."

Greystone sat back into his chair. "You mentioned Alex Paterson."

"Yes."

"Well, what about him?"

"Seems you've been supplying his wife with a certain drug in exchange for insider trading information."

Greystone leaned forward. He drummed his fingers on the desk. "Whoever told you that is lying."

"I don't think so." Nick fought to control himself. He could bank on exactly what type of person he was dealing with—a self-centered, narcissistic, entitled creep. "Look, I'm not here to waste my time or yours. You've been threatening Alex by sending a couple of creeps around to frighten him." He tossed the folder onto the desk. "You're exporting drugs illegally, and I know some of those drugs are capable of killing people."

Greystone's brow quivered. He opened the folder. His eyes scanned the papers while his face turned ashen. "Where did you get these!" he demanded.

"I'd settle down if I were you," Nick said. "I'm not one of your minions you can boss around." He stood and lunged at Greystone, grabbing the collar of his shirt. Papers scattered, falling to the floor, as he pulled him up and over the desk, slamming him against it.

"What the hell do you think you're doing?" Greystone screeched.

"I'm warning you to stop harassing Alex. I could blow the whistle on you and your company, but then Alex wouldn't get what he needs. So, in the future, you will not ask for any more information, and you will supply him with the drug for his wife." He released Greystone and stepped away.

Eyes bulging, he glared at Nick. "And if I don't agree?"

"I can guarantee you won't live much longer. It won't matter how many bodyguards you surround yourself with. You'll be looking over your shoulder every minute of every day. After you're gone, everyone will know about your illegal dealings. A nice legacy for your family, don't you think? The government would strip them of everything."

Greystone eyed the folder. "And those?"

"I have copies of everything. Those memos and emails are insurance. And as much as I'd like to take you out now for the despicable things you are doing, I won't as long as you do what I asked."

Greystone inched around his desk. Fingers gripping the edge, he collapsed into his chair.

"How do I know I can trust you?"

Nick cut his eyes at him. "You don't. That's the price you're going to pay."

Greystone's face sagged. "Tell Alex he can have the drug for as long as Kate needs it. I won't hassle him anymore."

"See how easy that was," Nick said. He turned, strode to the door, and stopped. "How the hell you even sleep at night is a mystery to me. Don't ever do anything to hurt Alex or his family, or you will see me again." He left without looking back.

*　　*　　*　　*

By the time Nick reached the hotel, it was dark. Dalton greeted him at the door.

"How'd it go?"

"I believe Mr. Greystone won't be bothering Alex anymore. Short of eliminating him, I don't think he'll stop exporting. But that's not my fight. I accomplished what I had to for Kate's sake."

Following a quick meal from room service, they decided to fly back to South Dakota rather than stay another night. While he and Dalton prepared to leave for the airport, his cell phone rang. He didn't recognize the number.

"Hello."

"I have your daughter, *mi enemigo.*"

The voice on the other end iced his blood. Hairs rose on the back of his neck. His body went stiff.

"Miguel?"

"*Sí.* Izzy is with me."

The line went dead. The horror of what he had heard sank in. Air refused to enter his lungs. Terror swept over him in a sickening wave. He looked at Dalton. For the first time in his life, Nick came face to face with fear.

CHAPTER 50

IZZY

Izzy blinked. Her vision blurred, and she rubbed her eyes. Pushing herself up into a sitting position, she surveyed her surroundings, then stared at the bare light bulb hanging from a long cord. Her forehead throbbed. She fingered the knot and winced. Nothing looked familiar. Where was she?

Wrinkling her nose at the repugnant odor of mothballs, she swung her legs over the side of the bed. A portable heater hummed against the silence. Her blue quilted coat lay in a heap on the floor alongside her backpack. She picked them up and rifled through both, then tossed them aside. Her cell phone was gone.

Moving past the antique bureau, floorboards creaking beneath her feet, she made her way to the only door.

The memory of riding with Joann in the truck surfaced. The vehicle tumbling. Her aunt slumped over the wheel. The man…the man with the scar on his face reaching for her.

Izzy twisted the knob and pulled, her heart galloping while she yanked at it again without success. "Hello," she shouted. "Is anybody there?"

Whirling around, she spied the boards hammered in place at the other end of the room. Could there be a window behind them? She ran and tugged at the nailed boards, panicked when they wouldn't budge. Running back to the door, she kicked against it, screaming, "Let me out! Let me out! Please let me out!"

She waited through the quiet on the other side. All she wanted to do was go home. Tears erupted as she continued to pound on the door again.

Heavy footsteps sounded, and she moved away. Locks clicked, and the door opened. The man with the scar stepped inside and shut it behind him. She eyed the sheath hanging from his waist, the handle of a knife visible.

"I see you are awake."

"Please, Mister, I want to go home. Where is my aunt? Is she okay?"

"Never mind about her," he snapped. "Worry about yourself."

He moved out of the shadows. The bulb lit his face. She reared back at the sight of his scar and the ugly red marks running along his other cheek.

He glared at her and touched them. "Yes, *you* did this."

Her legs wobbled. "I didn't mean it. You were hurting me."

His face twisted into an ugly scowl. "You are a fighter, just like your father."

"My...my father? You know my daddy?"

"Yes. Quite well."

She swallowed back the lump wedged in her throat. "Then call him. He'll come and get me."

He advanced, towering over her. She caught the scent of his cologne mixed with sweat. Black eyes below heavy dark brows cut through her.

"Oh, I have done so already."

Her heart soared. "When is he coming?"

"I am afraid he is not."

Izzy's stomach twisted at his answer. That couldn't be true. Her daddy would never leave her here with this awful man. "You're lying!" she cried. "He's coming. I know he is."

Folding his arms across his chest, he stared down at her. "This wonderful father of yours, let me tell you something, Izzy, he is just like me."

She shook her head. "No, never. He's nothing like you. He's good and kind."

His laugh tore through her. She backed farther away, lost her balance, and fell onto the hard floor.

"No, little one," he mocked. "Your father is a killer. A man who enjoys murdering people. I know firsthand." His fingertip traced the scar on his cheek. "Even though I managed to get away, he left me with this."

Izzy covered her ears. She didn't want to hear this man saying bad things about her father. He was only trying to scare her.

"You can close your ears all you like. It will not change who he is. Your father has killed many, and I am sure he has enjoyed doing it."

In a flash, his fingers wrapped around her arm. He dragged her to the bed. Ignoring her kicks and screams, he tossed her onto the mattress. "You will listen to me, or I *will* hurt you! Do you understand?"

Teardrops dripped off her trembling chin. "Yes."

He sat on the edge of the bed. "You have no idea what kind of man your father really is, but I am telling you the truth. Why do you think you are here?"

Her mind spun. She didn't know why this man had taken her to this awful place. "I…I don't know," she stammered, terror spiraling through her.

"Because your father took something from me, and I want it back."

Wiping at her tears, she asked. "What did he take?"

"He took *my* little girl. She belongs with me. Not with your family."

She studied his face. This crazy man wasn't making any sense.

"What little girl?"

"Natalia. He took Natalia from her mother. It was a terrible thing he did. And he used others to help him."

She tried to let what he said sink in. How could Natalia belong to him? "But my brother, Bobby, is Natalia's father," she whimpered. "Carmela was her mommy. She died in an accident."

His face turned dark while his hands clenched. "Is that what they told you? Carmela died in an accident?"

"Yes, a long time ago when Natalia was a baby. She lives with Bobby now in New York." Her eyes locked on his, the madness within them causing a shudder through her body.

He cupped her chin, his fingers digging into her flesh. "You know nothing about where Natalia belongs," his voice lashed at her. "They have fed you lies."

Her chin aching, she tried to push his hands away. "You can talk to my daddy about all of this when he comes."

"I told you before, he is not coming. Not yet, anyway." He released his grip, his eyes fixed on hers.

"Then, when? When is he coming?"

"That is for me to decide. You must stay here until things are settled between your father and me." He went and paused at the door. "Later, I will have some food brought to you." He pointed to a bucket in the corner. "Use it if you need to go to the bathroom. For now, you are to keep quiet, or I will have to teach you a lesson. Do you understand?"

"Y… yes," she replied, trying to stop her voice from shaking. He disappeared through the doorway. She cringed at the sound of locks snapping shut on the other side.

Her mind spun. How could Natalia belong to him? Could they have lied to her? It was strange this man knew so much about her family.

She rolled onto her stomach, burying her face into the pillow to muffle her crying. She was certain her daddy wouldn't hurt anyone.

Exhausted from the whole ordeal, she stopped crying and fell asleep. Dreams invaded her mind, and she was riding her Bella again with the wind in her hair, the feel of the horse's soft mane beneath her fingers.

She galloped along the trail on Uncle Dalton's ranch, deep woods on either side. Suddenly, Bella reared up, and she fought to keep from tumbling off. She looked ahead. A dark man stood in the middle of the trail. A jagged scar ran down his cheek. Her breath caught as he reached for Bella's reins …

CHAPTER 51

CARRIE

Pulling up to Dalton's house, Carrie found it odd that the truck wasn't parked in front as usual. She hurried up the steps. Jack appeared in the doorway, a bottle of beer in his hands and a lopsided grin on his face.

"I thought I heard somebody drive up."

"Yes, hello, Jack. Is Joann here?"

"No. She went into town earlier to run some errands."

"I know. She stopped by the restaurant and offered to pick Izzy up from school." Carrie glanced at the sun dipping below the horizon. Muscles tightened in her stomach. "They should be here by now."

Jack swiped his cell from his back pocket. "Come in, Carrie. I'll give her a ring and see where she's at."

They walked into the living room together while Jack called. A frown crossed his face. "Funny, it went to voicemail."

Carrie took out her phone and tried calling. She left Joann a quick message then called Izzy's phone. After eight rings, her tiny voice rang out. 'This is Izzy. I'm busy, so please leave a message.'

Carrie's heart flip-flopped. "I'm worried, Jack. It's going to be dark soon, and we can't reach either one of them."

Jack set his beer down. "You didn't spot the truck anywhere on your way here?"

"No. But I wasn't looking."

"I'm sure they're okay. Let's give it another twenty minutes. If they're not here by then, we can take your car and backtrack just in case."

Her legs trembled, and she eased into a chair. Jack sat across from her on the sofa while a thousand thoughts ran through her mind. Maybe they stopped somewhere. Izzy was good at talking people into things. Or they had an accident and need help. Or... She jumped up. "I can't sit here another minute. Let's go, Jack. We have to find them."

Carrie raced down the front steps. Rick came toward them from the barn. "Carrie is something wrong?" he called out.

"Yes...I mean, I think so. Joann picked Izzy up from school. They should have been here by now, and I can't reach either of them. I want to check the road and make sure they didn't have an accident."

"I'll go with you." He looked at Jack. "You stay here in case they show up."

Jack shrugged. "Makes sense, I guess."

Carrie jumped into the Range Rover. With Rick behind the wheel, they tore down the main drive and away from the ranch. They cruised along. She kept her eyes peeled for any sign of the truck while Rick did the same. About half a mile down the private road, he slowed, then stopped.

"What is it?" Carrie asked.

"Tire tracks. Over there."

"Yes. I see them." She jumped out of the Range Rover with Rick at her heels. They followed the tracks for several yards.

Carrie's breath caught. "They're leading off the road, Rick."

They hurried over to the edge of a ravine. She peered over the side. "Look, there. It's the truck."

Before Rick could stop her, she headed toward the vehicle, almost losing her footing several times while making her way down. The rear passenger door hung open, and the front airbag had deployed. There were traces of blood splattered on it. Rick came up behind her. He walked around the entire truck, checking inside and then bending to peer underneath.

Frantic, Carrie looked around. "Why aren't they here!" She backed away and rushed toward the woods calling Izzy and Joann's names. Stopping at the edge, she turned to Rick. "Izzy might be okay," she said. "Her backpack is missing. She must have taken it with her."

"Now, stop and think a minute Carrie," Rick said. "None of this is making any sense. Joann's purse is in the car. Her cell phone is inside, yet no one heard from her. Does Izzy have a phone?"

"Yes."

He held up a cell phone with a pink sparkled case.

A sick feeling welled up inside her. "That's Izzy's phone."

"I found it underneath the rear seat." He frowned, lifted his cowboy hat and set it back down on his head. "Carrie, I hate to say this, but from the looks of those tracks, and a second set of others, it seems they were forced off the road."

"Forced off the road?" Her eyes searched his. "You don't think this was an accident?"

"I have my doubts," Rick said. "Look, it's getting dark. I need to round up some of the men for a proper search. Let's go back to the house. You can wait there in case one of them shows up."

"No. Absolutely not, Rick. I'm staying right here while you go for help. That's my little girl and my best friend out there. I want to search with you."

"Okay, but please stay here until I get back."

He hurried up the ravine. The sound of the car pulling away against the silence of the woods made her panic grow. Where could they be? She went over to the truck again, bloodstains on the airbag fueling her fears.

The sun dipped below the pines while she shouted for Izzy and Joann again. Her cell phone vibrated, and she whipped it out of her coat pocket. It was Nick.

"Oh, thank God," she cried. "Nick, there's been an accident. Joann went off the road. She had Izzy with her, and now we can't find either one of them."

Met by silence on the other end, she said, "Nick, did you hear me? Izzy and Joann are missing."

"Carrie, listen carefully."

Gooseflesh crawled up her arms at his odd tone. "Nick, Izzy is missing and I—"

"I know."

Blood rushed to her head. Her hand shook so hard she almost dropped the phone. "What do you mean? How could you …?"

"I received a phone call. Dalton and I are on our way back. We'll be landing shortly."

"A … phone call. From who?"

"I know who has Izzy."

"What are you saying? Someone… has her?"

"I promise you I will get her back."

Her legs gave way, and she fell to her knees. Chills crept through her body. Her throat ached, and she struggled to swallow while her stomach clenched so tight, she felt it might burst. Not again. This couldn't be happening. After Carmela died, he said they didn't have anything to worry about anymore.

Somebody had taken their daughter all because of him. Everything always led back to his past, but the possibility of losing Izzy and Joann was too high a price to pay.

"I'm calling the police, Nick."

"No, Carrie. You mustn't do that. You'll be putting Izzy in jeopardy."

"Her life is already in jeopardy! Our daughter is gone. I don't know where she is or if she's hurt. Joann is missing too, and you expect me to do nothing."

"Please. You need to trust me."

"Trust you? How dare you even ask for my trust. You lied to me again, and you're lying put our daughter in danger." She eased up on shaky legs and gripped the side of the truck to steady herself.

"You have to give me a chance, Carrie. Believe me, I didn't think anything like this would happen. I will find Izzy. I promise. I'll be there soon."

Carrie ended the call as tears flooded her eyes. She didn't want to hear anymore. Dark shadows spread out across the ravine. Night had descended on the woods. Her fear grew, spiraling out of control with the possibility of losing Izzy forever clawing its way inside her mind. The person who took her daughter was someone connected to Nick. A person so determined that they forced the truck off the road. And what of Joann? Was she still alive?

The sound of automobiles from above the ravine made her look up. Rick, holding a large flashlight, was followed by a dozen other men.

"I don't think we're going to find anything," she said.

He placed his hand on her shoulder. "So, you heard?"

Carrie peered up at him. "Yes. Nick called."

"I spoke to Dalton a bit ago," he said. "But I still want to look. Make sure no one is out there hurt."

"I'm going with you. I can't stay here and do nothing."

Rick went over to the truck. He dug inside the glove box and pulled out a flashlight, handing it to Carrie. "Okay, let's go."

CHAPTER 52

NICK

After an agonizing plane ride, Nick arrived home to a silent house. Michael sat with Valentina in the great room. Upon seeing Nick, he jumped up and ran toward him. He lifted his son up and held him close. Michael wrapped his arms around his neck, and he inhaled the scent of his little boy's skin, lips brushing his cheek.

"Daddy, you're home."

"Yes, I'm here now." He nodded at Valentina. "Where's Carrie?"

Her eyes moist, she said, "Upstairs in Izzy's room." She went over to Nick. "I will stay with Michael. Carrie needs you."

"Thanks." He set Michael down on the sofa. Bright blue eyes looked up at him.

"Where is Izzy?" he asked.

The pit of Nick's stomach tightened. "She'll be home soon."

Nick climbed the stairs, his feet leaden, each step an effort. He paused in the doorway to Izzy's room. Carrie lay on the bed in a fetal position facing away from him, clutching a pillow to her chest. Ace, sprawled at the foot, rose, tail between his legs, and whimpered. Nick went and rubbed his head. "I know, boy."

Nick eased onto the bed. Brushing back a wave of Carrie's hair, he said, "I'm sorry, I—"

She slapped his hand away and pushed herself up against the headboard. "Don't, Nick." Her eyes were red from crying, her lids puffy and raw, the look of betrayal on her face shattering him inside.

"So, what now? Now that our daughter's gone. I'm sure you have some kind of plan to get her back," she snapped. "I trusted you, Nick. I trusted you once again, and now look where it's gotten us."

"Carrie, if I thought something like this could happen, I would have done things differently. We had no idea he came back across the border from Mexico."

"We? What do you mean, we?"

"Dalton and I have contacts. They assured us he wasn't in the states."

"You keep saying he." She clutched the pillow tighter. "Who has my daughter? You tell me right *now!*"

He pictured Miguel Medina. A sick feeling welled up inside him. Forcing the words out, he told her about Miguel and Tahoe. "We didn't have time to chase him if we had any chance of taking Carmela's body with us."

Carrie gasped. "You... cut his face?"

"It was self-defense, and even then, Miguel still managed to shoot off a round."

"Causing the bullet wound on your shoulder?" she asked.

"Yes."

A chill marched up her spine. Her eyes bore into his.

"What?"

"Then he's been here a while. Izzy might have spoken to him."

"What are you talking about?" He began to pace. "When?"

"The day I spent with Izzy in Rapid City. We stopped for ice cream. She pointed him out, said she felt sorry for him because of the scar on his face."

He clenched his fists. Miguel had been near all this time, watching, and waiting.

Carrie set the pillow aside and eased off the bed. "Don't you see, Nick? If only you had told me. I might have known who the man was. Izzy would be here, now, safe at home with us."

He reached for her. "I'm sorry. I didn't think…"

She stepped back. "That's just it. You didn't think. Because of you, Izzy is gone! I keep imagining all these horrible things being done to her. We don't even know if she's alive. And what about Joann?"

He hung his head and took a breath. "Miguel called me. Izzy is alive."

"How can you be so sure?"

"Because he wants something in return. She's his bargaining chip. I'll hear from him again, then I'll know what to do." He paused. "But I'm not sure about Joann."

She rubbed her temples. "Let me get this straight. You're saying he wants something. Like what? Ransom money?"

"No, Miguel has more than enough money. He used to be Carmela's ghost." He took another step toward her. "I'll get Izzy back. I won't let anything happen to her."

Before he could react, she flung herself at him, fists beating against his chest. Tears poured down her cheeks. "Something has already happened to her! I will never forgive you for this. I won't survive losing her."

His hands encircled her wrists as he attempted to calm her. "Listen to me. I promise you, I *will* bring Izzy home."

Her eyes filled with fury. "Pray that you do, Nick."

He broke eye contact and stared past her. "Carrie, you know I'm not a praying man."

"Then you had better start. Because if anything happens to Izzy, we are done, Nick. Do you hear me? We are done!" She pulled away from him and ran out of the room.

He collapsed onto the bed, his eyes drawn to a picture of Izzy and Bella in a silver frame sitting atop her dresser. A tear trailed down his face. All this was his fault. He made the wrong call thinking Miguel would try to get even by confronting him, never envisioning any harm coming to his family.

Carrie's last words rang in his ears. She never pulled any punches. If he didn't rescue Izzy, their life together would end— his life would end if anything happened to his little girl.

He recalled his conversation with Dalton, certain now what he had said about bad people, rang true and Miguel Medina was at the top of the list. Anger at what he might do to Izzy and may have already done to Joann ignited inside him. He stood and wiped at his eyes. Staying strong for Izzy became a must. Sitting and waiting would not bring his daughter home. He needed to find the trail leading to Miguel so he could end things once and for all.

His cell phone buzzed. It was Dalton. "Any word?"

There was a pause at the other end. "We found Joann."

Nick's stomach sank at the tremor in his friend's voice.

CHAPTER 53

BIANCA

Bianca set the tray on the small nightstand next to the bed. Shadows clung to the corners of the walls. The portable heater hummed. Her breath caught as she studied the sleeping girl, covers pulled up to her chin. She tapped her shoulder. Izzy stirred and came awake.

She flung the covers aside and sat up. "Bianca, I'm so glad you're here. Will you take me home now? Take me to my mommy and daddy?"

Izzy's arms went around her neck, and Bianca hugged her tight. "*Lo siento mucho,* Izzy. I cannot."

"But why?" Tears pooled in her eyes. "I want to go home. I'm afraid of that awful man."

"You must be calm." She clutched Bianca tighter, her small body trembling. Gently, she removed Izzy's arms from around her neck. "I have brought you something to eat."

Izzy drew back and scowled at her. "I don't want anything to eat! Please, call my daddy. Call him and tell him where I am so he can come and get me."

"No, I cannot. You must listen to me. Do whatever he tells you. Do not upset him. Otherwise, he will hurt you."

"What do you mean?" Izzy wiped at her tears.

"He will let you go after he settles things with your father."

Izzy studied her for a moment. "He told me Natalia belongs to him." Her face lit with confusion. "But that can't be right. Bobby's her father."

"That is not for you to worry about."

"But how can he say Natalia should be with him?"

Bianca's heart thudded inside her chest. "Izzy listen to me. You must never question him." She grabbed Izzy's arms. "Promise me. Promise me you will not anger him."

"Okay…" Izzy pushed her away. "You're hurting me."

"I am sorry. I did not mean to, but it is important to try and keep him calm."

"Did he ever hurt you?" Izzy asked, rubbing her arms.

Bianca met her frightened eyes. Dare she explain what Miguel was capable of? How her every waking moment filled with trepidation. This poor child was totally unaware of how high the stakes really were.

"No," she lied. "So long as you obey him, everything will be fine." She retrieved the tray and set it in front of Izzy. "Now, come, please, you must eat, even if it is only a little."

Izzy hesitated before dipping the spoon into the bowl of soup. She swallowed several mouthfuls, then pushed the tray away. "Is my Aunt Joann okay?"

"I am sure she is fine." Bianca twisted the cap off a bottle of water and handed it to her. "You must drink also."

Izzy swallowed a few sips, then looked at her. "But I saw her. I know she needed help."

"Yes, and he called for help after he took you with him. I am sure she is fine."

Doubt in her eyes, she said, "He did?"

"Yes. Now, I need to go."

Izzy reached for her hand. "Please stay with me. I don't want to be here alone. What if he comes back?"

She smoothed the dark tangle of bangs sweeping across Izzy's brow. "I told you what to do. He is downstairs. Listen, and you will be okay." She dipped her hand into the shirt pocket of her work blouse and took out Sarah's necklace.

Opening the clasp, she said, "Here, let me put this on you." She secured it around her neck.

Izzy fingered the four-leaf clover. "This means good luck."

"*Sí.* When you feel frightened, hold onto the clover, and you will stay safe. Tuck it beneath your sweater. Do not let him see it."

Izzy stuffed the necklace down. Bianca prepared to go, and she grabbed at her. "Don't leave me."

"Do not worry, I will come back." She went to the pile of books in the corner and shuffled through them. Finding one with a picture of a princess on the cover, she handed it to Izzy.

"Try to keep your mind busy and eat a bit more. This will all be over soon." Bianca hurried out the door, locking it behind her.

Downstairs, Miguel sat on the end of the bed, arms folded across his bare chest while she finished doing her hair.

"What did the girl have to say?" he asked. "Was she surprised to see you?"

"*Sí,* of course." She slipped into her coat. "She is frightened and only wants to go home." As she walked past, he grabbed her arm.

"And what did you tell her?"

Bianca hesitated, knowing better than to pull away. "She could not until things were settled between you and her father."

The darkness in Miguel's eyes intensified. "Regardless of what happens between us, she will never go home."

The word never took on a life of its own cementing itself inside her brain. "She mentioned her aunt."

"And?"

"I said not to worry… that you sent for help."

"Good. It is better she does not know the truth."

"I must go, or I will be late for work." She bent and kissed his lips.

Miguel released his grip. "Remember to act surprised if anything is said about Izzy or Dalton's wife."

*   *   *   *

Hands clamped to the wheel, she drove to *Buena Comida*. Not a hint of the turmoil inside must show on her face.

At the start of her shift, everything seemed normal. None of the staff mentioned the accident or Izzy missing. The only telltale sign something might be wrong was evident in Rosie's demeanor. Usually sharp, she appeared distracted. Several times, Bianca observed her check her cell phone, a frown on her face.

For her part, Bianca acted like it was just another day bartending. She laughed and joked with some of the regular customers. When it came time for her break, she saw Rosie go outside and decided to follow her. Miguel would be pleased if she gained any new information.

Stepping into the frigid November air, she pulled her jacket tight against her body. Rosie's hair was done up in neat rows of evenly spaced braids. The collar of her long wool navy coat lay hidden underneath a multi-colored wool scarf. Her face appeared stoic. She stared off into the distance.

Turning her head when Bianca came up beside her, she said, "Girl, what are you doing out here?"

Bianca put on her best smile. "I wanted some fresh air."

"This is more than fresh. It's almost freezing." She shoved her bare hands into the deep pockets of her coat. "By the looks of the sky, I have a feeling we're in for an early winter storm."

"Is everything alright?"

Rosie avoided her eyes. "Sure. Why do you ask?"

"You did not joke with the staff today like you sometimes do."

"Meaning what?" Rosie snapped.

Her tone took Bianca by surprise. "Never mind, I thought—"

Rosie, at once apologetic, said, "Sorry, I don't mean to sound harsh. I'm worried about someone, and I guess it's starting to show."

"Can I be of help?"

Rosie's features softened. "That's so kind of you, Bianca, but I'd rather not discuss it. It's a private matter."

Bianca nodded. "*Sí,* I understand."

"Let's head back inside. Carlos made his *Sancocho* soup. It's perfect on a day like this. I'll have him prepare some for us."

Despite everything, the vision of the traditional hearty soup made with potatoes, yuca, corn plantains, and meat made Bianca's mouth water. "Thank you, Rosie. I would like that."

For the next twenty minutes, Bianca forgot about Izzy locked in the attic. She inhaled the aroma of the *Sancocho*, relishing a break from all the emotions swirling inside her.

Later, her shift finished, she left the restaurant, ugly thoughts creeping in. Was there any possibility Nick would refuse to hand over Natalia? If so, what then? Either way, Izzy's life hung in the balance. She meant nothing to this man who had killed others for so many years.

It was dark by the time Bianca turned onto the driveway. The house loomed ahead. She cut the engine and stared at the dim attic light seeping through the cracks in the clapboards above.

Remembering the night of the party and how she vowed to help Miguel cause misery for the D'Angelo's made her feel ashamed. They had been nothing but kind toward her.

What transpired between Miguel and Nick had nothing to do with the poor innocent girl locked away upstairs. Clearly, women always suffer for the sins of the man.

What could she do to stop this madness? Guilt-ridden over Sarah's death and her part in it, now she might face another murder since Miguel had chosen not to let Izzy live.

Pain gripped her middle. Her hands cinched her waist. She willed herself not to cry out. How different things would be if Alejandro hadn't betrayed her.

She got out and trudged toward the house. This had become her life now, here with Miguel. A life she never bargained for but one she was destined to live.

CHAPTER 54

DALTON

Dalton sat on the edge of the bed. He pressed a cold cloth to Joann's forehead. The bruise had turned an ugly purple, but at least the cut on her lower lip from the airbag no longer oozed blood. Deep scratches lined the side of her neck where branches had scraped her tender skin. Tormented by the possibility of losing her, he blinked back the water standing in his eyes.

One of his men found her alone, hiding in the woods. Following a trip to the emergency room to make sure there were no internal injuries and to obtain a sedative, it was late the next day by the time he brought her home.

Beside herself at not having saved Izzy, and short of her continual weeping, she had said little about the accident thus far. With Nick and Carrie on their way to the ranch, he needed every single detail without pushing her too hard.

She blinked and opened her eyes. Reaching for him, she asked, "Did you find Izzy?"

"Not yet. But we will, Red."

Pushing herself up against the pillows, she squeezed his hand, tears building again. "Have you spoken with the authorities?"

"No."

Her face paled. "I don't understand. What are you waiting for? You told me earlier at the hospital you would call. Some horrible man took Izzy, and you haven't called them!"

The moment he prayed would never come had arrived. Knowing her, she'd accept nothing short of the truth. "Please, Red. Try to stay calm. I will explain everything, but first, you need to tell me what happened. All I know so far is someone ran you off the road and took Izzy."

Her tongue passed over her bruised lip. "We were almost home when I noticed a car following behind us. I didn't recognize it. I thought someone was lost, but then, they drove right up to the bumper, forcing me off the road."

"What kind of car was it?"

"A Cadillac. I think. A black Cadillac SUV."

"What happened next?"

"I lost control. The truck nose-dived down into a ravine, and we crashed into a tree. I remember the airbag going off. I must have blacked out for a moment. When I came to, a man was leading Izzy back up to the road."

"Can you describe him?"

"I didn't get a real close look. He was tall, with tan skin and dark hair. I heard Izzy scream. I knew something must be wrong."

"Was he alone?"

"I didn't see anyone else."

"Go on," Dalton said.

"I unbuckled my seatbelt and kicked the door open. That's when I saw..." She covered her face and wept. "Oh, Dalton, I was so frightened."

"I know this is hard, but you need to tell me the rest."

Drawing in a deep breath, she continued. "He headed back down into the ravine carrying a gun in his hand, and I knew he was going to kill me. I took off into the woods, hoping he would chase me so Izzy might have a chance at getting away. I just kept running. By the time I realized he hadn't followed me, I had gotten so turned around, I wasn't sure where I was."

"It's okay, Red. The ranch is a pretty big place. It's easy to get lost, especially in the woods. You did the right thing." His eyes locked on hers. "He didn't follow you because it was Izzy he wanted. He couldn't waste time trying to find you without the possibility of getting caught."

"What do you mean it was Izzy he wanted?"

Before he could answer, the doorbell rang. "That must be Nick and Carrie. You rest a bit."

Dalton hurried and opened the front door. The look on Carrie's face said everything. "I'm so sorry, sweetheart. We'll find her. I promise you." He looked over at Nick. "Come inside. Red just finished telling me what happened."

"How is she?" Carrie asked.

"Other than a few bumps and bruises, she's okay, but she's blaming herself."

They went into the living room, where Dalton repeated what Joann told him.

Carrie eyed Nick, then Dalton. "We know she's not to blame. How much have you told her, Dalton?"

He avoided her eyes. "Well, I..."

"Just what I thought. You and Nick keeping secrets brought us to this. You know how much I care for you, but if anything happens to Izzy, I'll never be able to forget your part in the whole thing. You know how dangerous this man is."

His heart dipped inside his chest. "Carrie, believe me, if we were aware Miguel had crossed the border, we would have made sure everyone stayed safe. My sources are usually pretty good."

She took a step back and folded her arms. "Oh, really. Well, you'd better rethink trusting your sources because he's been here a while. Izzy and I saw him in Rapid City. Since you both kept this from me, I had no idea who he was."

His body tensed, and he eyed Nick. "He's been here in South Dakota?"

"Apparently. Carrie's right. But like I told her, his kidnapping Izzy never crossed my mind. I'm the one who planted that scar on his face. His beef should be with me and only me. A ghost doesn't do what he did."

Carrie whirled around. She pointed her finger at him. "But you did exactly that! You snatched Natalia from Carmela, and now he's taken Izzy."

Anger flashed in his eyes. "Carrie, you know full well, all of Carmela's drug running and dirty dealings put Natalia in jeopardy."

"That may be true, but Natalia was her daughter, whether we liked it or not, and it got her killed."

"So, what are you saying? We should have left her with Carmela. Try telling that to Bobby. He came to me for help, and as I recall, *you* had no problem with it."

"Okay, you two, enough," Dalton interrupted. "Arguing over what we can't change isn't going to fix anything."

Nick and Carrie fell silent. A hollow feeling hit Dalton's gut. Things could turn ugly if they didn't find Izzy soon. It would tear the two of them apart forever. There would be no forgiving on Carrie's end, and Nick wouldn't survive losing Izzy. Blaming himself for Carmela was one thing, but this…this was so much more.

"Let's stay on point," Dalton said. "Carrie, please talk to Joann. She needs you. Nick and I will put everything into locating Miguel Medina. He's left a trail somewhere, and we'll find it."

She cut her eyes at Dalton and placed her hands on her hips. "And what am I supposed to tell Joann since you haven't acknowledged your past?"

Dalton paused. "I trust you to tell her the truth. I'm ready to deal with the consequences, whatever they may be."

"Oh, I see," Carrie quipped. "You want me to do your dirty work."

His cheeks heated. Carrie was right. Only he couldn't look Red in the eye and tell her himself, see the hurt and disgust on her face. For the first time in his life, the word coward flashed before him. "I'm sorry. I will probably lose her over this. It rips me apart inside." He looked away, his shoulders sagging.

"Look," Carrie said. "I'll do this for you, but only because I want you and Nick to concentrate on finding Izzy. I don't know how all this will end. Either way, we are all going to pay the price."

Carrie went down the hall and Dalton led Nick into his study and shut the door. He poured each of them a drink. They downed the shots, and he refilled their glasses. He motioned for Nick to sit, the agony on his face almost unbearable to look at.

"Who else have you told about Izzy? Have you called Bobby?"

"No. I need to make him aware. I had to tell Valentina Izzy was missing and that I'm handling things. She's with Michael. Ace is there, and she knows the dog's commands. Rosie knows, too. We can trust her. I appreciate you sending Rick over to the house."

"No problem." Dalton sipped his drink. "Well, on my side, Rick knows, of course. Jack's been pestering me, but I haven't said anything to him about Izzy. Have you heard from Miguel?"

"No, nothing. It's what scares me the most." His eyes brimmed. "What if she's…"

Dalton held up his hand. "Don't do this to yourself. I doubt he's harmed her. My intuition is telling me he wants more than you and Izzy. I can feel it."

Nick shifted uncomfortably, then hung his head and stared at the floor. "Right now, I'd give anything to have my daughter back. She must be scared out of her mind. We both know what Miguel is capable of."

"But Izzy's tough, like you, and she knows you'll be coming for her. Now, first things first. I think he's still in South Dakota. Carrie saw him, so it's a given he's been holed up somewhere nearby. I have a real estate friend I can contact, see what's been bought or leased in the last six months."

"At least it's a start," Nick said. "I'll drive into Rapid City and ask around. With that scar on his face, someone in one of the stores might have seen him. I'm friendly with most of the owners. Some are regulars at the restaurant."

Dalton nodded, then grew silent, a faraway look in his eyes.

Nick finished the rest of his drink. "What?"

"Remember when I told you about my cows being slaughtered?"

"Of course."

"You said it wasn't something somebody connected would do."

"Yeah, it seemed odd to me at the time, and Frank did deny it."

"Those bullets came from a high-powered rifle."

Nick raised an eyebrow. "Miguel's handiwork more than likely."

"Probably so. Which means he's not only gunning for you. He had every intention of murdering Red. With Izzy in his car, I figure he couldn't take the time to chase her and increase his chances of being seen."

Nick took out his cell phone. "Means anyone involved with Tahoe is at risk. Bobby needs to bring Natalia here. Miguel may have others working with him, and we can't be in two places at once."

About to punch in Bobby's number, his cell buzzed. Unknown number flashed on the screen. Nick put it on speaker. "Hello."

"How is your beautiful wife holding up? Is she missing her daughter?"

Nick shot up from the chair. "Listen to me, you son of a bitch. Nothing better happen to Izzy."

"Calm down, *amigo*. Izzy is fine. A little frightened, maybe. But she is a fighter like you."

"I'm not your *amigo*, Miguel. Tell me what you want, so we can end this thing. My daughter has nothing to do with you and me."

"Now this is where you are wrong," Miguel said, his voice laden with contempt. "You murdered Carmela and seized her daughter. Natalia does not belong to you. I want her back. Until then, Izzy remains with me. Be a good ghost, Nick, and don't do anything foolish, or your daughter will suffer."

Nick's heart beat like a fist against his chest. "If you hurt her, Miguel, I swear I'll —"

The line went dead. Dalton's eyes locked with Nick's. "Call Bobby, now. I'm sending the jet."

CHAPTER 55

CARRIE

Carrie paused outside the bedroom door. Here she was having to break the news to Joann about Dalton being a hitman for hire while her daughter was in the hands of a despicable man who might or might not kill her. Her heart ached to hold Izzy in her arms. How could she and Nick stay together if anything happened to her? Lied to and betrayed by him, her resentment toward him took hold, gripping her like a vise, refusing to let go despite his promise to bring Izzy home safe.

She opened the door and eased down onto the bed. She surveyed Joann's face, blotchy and red from crying. The angry purple bruise on her forehead and swollen lip, a testament to what she had been through. "I'm sorry, Joann. If I had known..."

Joann reached for her hand. "I'm the one who's sorry." Her eyes watered. "I wanted to help her, but I couldn't."

"Trust me, if you tried to stop him, we wouldn't be sitting here talking. He was determined to kidnap Izzy."

Joann pulled her hand away. "You know who he is?"

Carrie steeled herself. Seething inside. This was Dalton's responsibility. "Yes. He's a man Nick, Dalton, and Bobby had some dealings with."

"What do you mean dealings?" She inched herself farther up against the pillows. "Has *everyone* been keeping things from me? First, Dalton wouldn't call the authorities, and now, you're sitting here telling me you know who took Izzy." Her chest heaved in and out.

Carrie stared down at the patchwork comforter. Joann meant the world to her. From the first time they met in Laurel and down through the years, she cherished the bond between them. Now, their friendship teetered on edge. How could she tell Joann the man she loves is a killer for hire?

"Carrie don't look away. Be honest with me."

She swallowed hard. "It's time I told you everything, beginning with how Nick and I met."

"You said he helped you get away from Travis."

"Yes, but I never told you the whole story, and I'll understand if you hate me after I do."

"I could never hate you, Carrie." Her eyes filled again.

"Listen before you commit to that." She took a deep breath and began, "Nick and Dalton are what's known as ghosts. Hired killers at the top of their profession."

Over the next thirty minutes, while her friend's face filled with horror, she revealed everything. "They never talk about the killing. But I know for sure, Nick murdered Travis, and as to what happened to Carmela in Tahoe, I've been told very little."

Joann's face paled. "And Bobby…is he?"

"No, no. They helped Bobby get Natalia, that's all."

Joann reared up. "You knew all of this, and you let me marry Dalton!"

"It wasn't my place to tell you." Carrie rose and backed away.

"Wasn't your place!" Joann declared. "You're my best friend, Carrie. How could it not be your place to warn me and let me make my own decision?"

The hurt tone in Joann's voice broke her heart. "You're …
right. But when I saw how much the two of you loved each other,
I didn't want to ruin things." She sat on the edge of the bed again.

"Joann, listen to me. Nick and Dalton are good people. The
men they've killed were criminals, heads of major cartels."

"Is that supposed to make me feel better? You're
disgusting, Carrie. Because of what they've done, your daughter
is missing, and you're sitting here defending them." Her eyes
narrowed to pinpricks while she scowled. "I'll put this to bed for
now but only for Izzy's sake. She's innocent in all of this."

"Thank you, but I want you to know Nick kept things from
me. He never told me about this man. I believed we were safe.
I'm not sure my marriage will hold up after this."

Joann glared at her. "I can't understand how it's lasted this
long. Marrying a killer and raising a family with him. How have
you been able to live with yourself?"

Carrie walked to the door, turning to her one last time. "It's
really no mystery, Joann. In spite of everything, I fell in love
with him." She stepped out and closed the door.

As she came up the hallway, Carrie caught sight of Dalton
and Nick leaving the study. They stopped and stared at her. "It
didn't go well, Dalton. You need to talk to her."

Dalton turned and headed to the bedroom. Carrie, her
nerves frayed from her conversation with Joann, asked, "Have
you heard anything?"

Nick reached for her hand. "Come, I'll explain in the car."

Refusing his hand, she brushed past him. They rode in
silence for a few moments until Carrie, about to burst, said, "Are
you going to just sit there or start talking?"

Eyes on the road, his face a stony mask, Nick said, "Dalton
is reaching out to see if we can locate where Miguel is holed up.
I need to drive into Rapid City and make some inquiries." He

sped up the ramp and onto the freeway. "Bobby is flying in with Natalia tonight."

"You told him about Izzy?"

"No. I think it's better we do it in person. You know how close they are."

"Of course." Carrie crossed her arms. "Is that all?"

"Miguel called."

Her heartbeat accelerated. Hands gripping the leather seat, she asked, "Is Izzy okay?"

"Yes. I think so."

"What the hell do you mean, you think so!"

Nick cut the wheel. The car jerked to the right, and he came to a stop on the side of the freeway. He turned toward her, his face full of fury. "Look, I understand you're scared out of your mind. The two of us butting heads isn't going to help bring Izzy home." He looked away and grew silent.

Feeling suffocated, Carrie opened the door and got out. She shut out the sound of the traffic whizzing by and leaned against the fender. Nick's love for Izzy equaled her own. Whatever had befallen them before this, he'd always been in control. This time, Miguel Medina had outsmarted him. The helplessness must be killing him inside.

Nick stood in front of her, a lost look in his eyes. "I failed you all those years ago in Lugano. I promised myself it would never happen again, and I was wrong. I know all this is unbearable, but I need you on my side, at least for now."

"I am on your side." Tears pooled beneath her lids. "Only I can't shake this dreadful feeling in the pit of my stomach. I'm imagining all sorts of things." Her eyes pleaded with his. "Tell me, what does Miguel want?"

He brushed at the tear running down her cheek. "Natalia. He wants Natalia."

She tried to absorb his words. Bobby's face flashed across her mind. "That can't happen. We would never trade one for the other."

"No. But if I have to, I'll make Miguel believe we will."

Her fears growing at the possibility of losing either child, she said. "We need proof. Before you attempt anything with Miguel." She paused, then forced the rest of the words out. "We need proof Izzy is alive."

"Miguel's not stupid, Carrie. Right now, Izzy is his bargaining chip. He's going to want to negotiate, and when he does, I'll make sure she's okay."

He pulled her close, and she rested her head against his chest. "You have to save our daughter, Nick."

"I will. You can count on it. Miguel Medina will regret the day he took her from us."

They barely spoke on the rest of the ride home with Nick refusing to let go of her hand until they pulled up to the house. As he drove away, she focused on the taillights.

The hard task of telling Bobby mere hours away, she needed a few minutes to herself before seeing Michael. Collapsing onto the front porch steps, memories of Izzy swirled in her head. She recalled the first time she held her in Lugano. Her sweet little girl with the flecks of gold in her green eyes, just like her father. The mother-daughter moments between them and the day they gave Bella to Izzy.

Her hands wrapped around her middle, the possibility of losing Izzy tearing her apart inside. She almost couldn't stand to think anymore. She hung her head and wept. Her love for Nick had always outweighed his past and all the danger it brought with it, but if Izzy were gone for good, their love for each other wouldn't survive.

Joann's angry face reared up, cutting through her like a knife. She had lost her best friend forever. Who could she look to for comfort now?

Wiping her tears away, she pulled her cell phone from her pocket and dialed.

"Aunt May, it's Carrie. I need you."

CHAPTER 56

BOBBY

It was late in the evening when Bobby set the suitcases on the porch. He glanced at the black pick-up truck with Hidden Creek Ranch painted on the side, parked a distance away, then up at the dark cloud-filled sky. Snow was due to arrive for sure. He breathed in the crisp air so distinctly opposite from New York City. Retrieving a sleepy Natalia from the rear of the rental car, he kissed her forehead. "Come, Natty. We're here."

Natalia fisted her tiny hands, then rubbed her eyes while he carried her up the steps. Nick's urgent call demanding he fly here with Natalia on Dalton's jet couldn't mean he was about to hear good news. The front door opened. Bobby took one look at his mother's face, and the dread building within him on the flight to South Dakota took hold.

"Mom?"

Without a word, her eyes puffy and red, she reached for Natalia. "Grandma's so glad to see you." She wrapped her arms around her and went up the hallway while Bobby deposited their suitcases inside and followed.

Ace galloped toward him, and he bent and rubbed his head. "How are you, boy?"

In the great room, Carrie set Natalia on the sofa and removed her coat before seating herself beside her. Adding logs to an already blazing fire, Nick turned when he saw him. "Glad you're here, Bobby." Ace settled himself a few feet away, paws crossed in front.

Rick sat opposite the sofa, cowboy hat perched on the arm of the chair, his jacket hanging across the back. He nodded in Bobby's direction but didn't speak.

Bobby glanced around the room. "Where's Izzy and Michael?"

Carrie brushed back a lock of Natalia's hair. "Michael's upstairs with Valentina."

Natalia's eyes lit up. "Izzy, too?"

"Just Michael," Carrie said. "You go ahead, sweetheart, and I'll be up later."

With Natalia out of earshot, Bobby caught Nick's eye. "What's going on? Where is Izzy?"

Nick pointed to the sofa. "Please sit. We have something to tell you?"

His stomach knotting at the tone in Nick's voice, he sat next to his mother.

"We need you to stay calm, Bobby," Nick began. "Izzy's been kidnapped by Miguel Medina."

Bobby jumped up. At first, his mind refused to absorb Nick's words. "What do you mean? Miguel's not even in the country."

Nick leaned against the mantle and folded his arms. "I'm afraid he is. Dalton's sources failed. I guess he paid enough people off to cross the border undetected."

"I don't understand. How was he able to get a hold of Izzy?"

While Bobby paced back and forth, shaking his head, Nick related the details of the kidnapping. When he finished, Bobby stopped and looked him in the eye. His gut twisting, he asked, "Is Joann okay?"

"Thankfully, yes," Nick said.

"And Izzy?"

"I believe so."

"You believe so? My little sister is in the hands of a killer, and you don't know for sure!"

Carrie looked up at him. "Nick thinks she is because Miguel called and told him what he wants in order for us to get Izzy back."

"It all relates to Tahoe, doesn't it?"

"Yes," Nick said.

"Well, it's pretty clear after you cut him so bad, he'd want revenge."

Carrie's chin dropped. "Which makes things even worse. Leaving him with that awful scar serves as a reminder of you every time he looks in a mirror or… looks at Izzy."

"I know," Nick said. He turned away, his eyes focused on the fire.

They fell silent until Bobby, his frustration growing, said, "So, what's the plan?" He motioned toward Nick. "How do we get her back?"

Carrie reached for his hand. "Bobby, please come and sit down."

"Don't try to placate me. Just tell me what our next move is."

"It's not that simple," Nick said. "He wants Natalia."

Bobby's heart jerked. He couldn't have heard Nick right. He pictured Natalia, then his little sister. "But—"

"Bobby, listen to me," Nick said. "I'm not going to let that happen. I'll get Izzy back without giving up Natalia."

Bobby dropped down onto the sofa next to Carrie. He draped his arm around her and squeezed her shoulder, feeling her body tremble. "Mom, I don't know what to say."

She gave him a weak smile. "We have to put our faith in Nick and Dalton."

For the first time, Rick spoke. "We're in the process of trying to locate Miguel. Once we know where he is holed up, we can figure out what to do next." He picked up his hat and prepared to leave. "Personally, I believe he had help in planning all this."

"I agree," Nick said. "He either brought someone with him or recruited somebody here. The only question now is who."

Rick set his hat on his head and retrieved his coat. "I'm going back to the ranch. I'll talk to the fellas in the bunkhouse. They ride into the city off and on for supplies and such. One of them might have seen someone or something unusual."

Nick extended his hand. "Thanks, Rick. Let me know if anything pops up."

"Sure thing." He turned to Carrie. "Stay strong. We'll get your daughter back." He strode toward the hallway. "I'll let myself out."

Bobby sucked in a breath, rage building inside him. Poor Izzy, in the hands of that monster. He might have hurt her already.

"I called May," Carrie said. "She'll be here tomorrow."

"What did you tell her?" Nick asked.

The instant Bobby spotted Nick's angry look, it became clear things between them were not good.

Carrie stood up. "That I needed her to come. And when she gets here, I'll tell her everything."

Nick frowned. "Careful, Carrie."

"I'm *not* going to lie for you anymore, Nick."

"I only meant—"

"I know exactly what you meant." She cut her eyes at him. "I should have realized when I questioned you at the cabin that night. For a split second, your expression changed. You lied to me."

"That's not true. I had no idea Miguel had entered the country."

"But you *knew* it was a possibility."

Bobby had never seen them go at each other this way, and it scared him. "Please, stop arguing. All we have to do is get Izzy back."

Carrie spun toward him. "Don't interfere, Bobby. Not when you're keeping secrets too. I asked you about Tahoe. You could have told me about Miguel Medina, but like Nick, you kept it from me."

Hurt written all over her face, all he could muster was, "I'm sorry."

She turned back to Nick. "Understand this, when May gets here, this time, I *will* tell her everything. She can make up her own mind. Maybe, I'll lose her, too, like I lost Joann."

Bobby's heart skipped. "What about Joann? Nick, you said she was okay."

"Oh, she's fine, alright," Carrie snapped. "Since I, not Dalton, had to tell her she's married to a killer!"

Bobby's head swam. "Dalton never told her?"

"No, he left that job to me. Seems he couldn't face telling her himself."

Nick's eyes blazed. "Carrie, *enough*."

"I'll drop it for now, but you better find out where Miguel Medina is holding our daughter. Only this time, you're not leaving me behind. When you know where Izzy is, I'm coming with you." She brushed past Bobby and ran from the room.

Nick sat and stared into the fire while Bobby eased down across from him. "This is bad. Real bad," Bobby said. "We have to find Izzy and get rid of Miguel. God, she must be terrified."

"Bobby, I'd never say this in front of your mother but Miguel is unpredictable. He's not your ordinary killer for hire. Miguel's known for not following the rules."

Despite the warmth of the fire, gooseflesh crawled up Bobby's arms. "That bad, huh?"

"He was Carmela's hitman. Word was at the time, he did some horrible things to people before he killed them."

"Like?"

"Torture, among other things. You don't want to know the details, and I won't tell you, anyway."

"Were they Carmela's orders?"

"Probably not. But details of a kill would have been reported back to her."

Pain gripped Bobby's heart. "Meaning, she never put a stop to it."

"Correct. Look, I don't want to dwell on the past. Carmela is gone, Natalia's with you, and that's as it should be." He paused a moment. "Bobby, I'd be lying if I said I wasn't scared for Izzy.

I choose to believe Miguel wouldn't hurt a child, but deep down inside, I know it's a real possibility."

"So, what are our options?"

"The main thing is to stall him until we know more." Nick stood and tossed another log onto the fire. He glanced at his watch. "No way I'm going to sleep tonight. I'll wait up. Dalton is bound to call."

"I hope things are okay between him and Joann."

Nick gave him a half-smile. "Truth is, we both had it coming, Bobby. Me from your mother and Dalton from Joann. You go on and head upstairs. I'll wake you if I hear anything."

"Sure." Bobby left and made his way up. Stopping outside his mother's bedroom door, he leaned against it, listening to her weep, his heart breaking. Nothing could comfort her until they brought Izzy home. She had suffered for so many years when she lost him. The possibility of them not being able to rescue his sister was unbearable.

He trudged up the hallway, his tears building. What would the future hold for all of them if they couldn't save Izzy?

His cell buzzed. It was Ronnie. "Hello."

"Bobby, I'm still here at the Rehabilitation Center. Mom called and said she was in a car accident. Should I leave here and catch a flight?"

He hesitated. "What did she say?"

"Other than a few bruises, she's fine."

The last thing he wanted was for Ronnie to cut her rehab short. "Listen, I'm here in South Dakota with Natty for a visit. I'm told she's fine. I'll check on her and let you know if you need to fly in."

"Promise?"

"Of course. Is everything okay with you…I mean, how is rehab going?"

"A little rough in the beginning, but I'm coming along."

"I'm proud of you, Ronnie."

"Thanks, Bobby. I'll wait until I hear from you."

He settled Natalia down for the night, then went to lie in one of the guest bedrooms. Hands laced behind his head, he stared at the ceiling. Tears formed in his eyes as fear gripped him.

A terrified Izzy was out there somewhere. From what Nick said, Miguel's unpredictable behavior didn't bode well for her.

He pictured his little sister's face, the heaviness in his chest mounting. Pushing up against the pillows, he tried to catch his breath and quiet his pounding heart.

They would never have peace until all the ugliness from the past stopped intruding into their lives. He prayed Miguel Medina was the last of that ugliness.

"Hold on, Izzy," he whispered. "We'll bring you back home."

CHAPTER 57

DALTON

White flakes drifted from dark clouds. Dalton turned from the window and went up the hallway. He tapped on the bedroom door and twisted the knob. Joann, resting against the pillows, looked away when he entered.

He approached the wingback chair next to the bed and sat. "We need to talk, Red."

"I think I've heard enough from Carrie." Her bottom lip trembled. She looked down at the comforter, her fingers twisting the edge.

"No, you haven't. I know you're hurt and angry. I deceived you, and it's something I've never done to the people I care about. All I'm asking is to let me tell you how I came to be the man I am."

"And then what, Dalton? Do you think I'm just going to say okay, and we go on with our lives as if nothing has happened?"

"No, I wouldn't expect you to. But you deserve the truth."

She reared up, her cheeks flamed red, making the purplish bruise on her forehead more prominent. "How can I even trust you to tell me the truth?"

He looked down at the floor for a moment. "And I don't blame you."

"You, Nick, and Carrie made a fool out of me by leaving me in the dark."

"Sweetheart, please give me a chance."

"Don't you sweetheart me, Dalton Burgess! You're a liar, plain and simple."

Her words pierced his heart. "I…I didn't tell you because I knew if I did, you probably wouldn't have married me."

"Well now, it's a bit late, isn't it?" Joann pulled the comforter up and rested her hands on top, her deep brown eyes boring into his.

Being too afraid to expose himself had cost him her love. His mouth went dry, and he paused before saying, "Look, Red, at this point, I don't care whether or not you want to hear me out, but I'm going to tell my story anyway."

He cleared his throat and began, starting with his father remarrying, followed by the night of the fire, then his determination to hold onto the ranch. He ended with his meeting a stranger in a bar who showed him how he could do it.

"More than anything, I wanted to keep the promise I made to my father. This land has been in my family for generations, and I wasn't about to give it up without a fight."

"Cattle ranching is a tough business, Red. You can't control the price of beef. You're tied to Federal, State, and County regulations besides dealing with blizzards and droughts." Dalton paused a moment, letting what he said sink in. Hoping it made sense to her. He went on to tell her about his and Nick's killing the heads of cartels, Carmela's deception, and the night she died in Tahoe.

"No matter what your opinion is of Nick, the man saved my life… twice. I wouldn't have survived without him, so if there is any chance you think I will turn away from him *or*

Carrie, you're wrong. As much as I love you, I could never do that, Red."

"I've never shied away from who I am... that is until I met you. I didn't want to taint what we have. And since I'm coming clean, there is something you need to understand. I have no regrets over those I've killed. They were bad men... every single one of them."

Her eyes filled, and he reached for her hand. She pushed it away, her stony silence drilling into him.

"Please say something, Red. Anything."

Eyes glittering with rage, she said. "If you don't find Izzy, I wonder if you'll have any regrets then."

"We're doing everything we possibly can. We'll find her, and the man who took her will die."

"You're so smug. So sure of yourself."

His body tensed. "Because, like it or not, I know how good Nick and I are at our craft. I owe that man, and I'll do whatever it takes to help him get his daughter back."

Joann touched the bruise on her forehead and winced. "My only concern right now is for Izzy."

Dalton eased up. He paused in the doorway. "I love you, Red. I understand if you can't forgive me, but Carrie needs you. Don't blame her for Nick's and my shortcomings."

Before she could answer, he left, closing the door behind him. She would either accept him or not. It was out of his control. His priority right now became finding Izzy. Inside his study, he poured a shot and downed it, then collapsed into the chair behind his desk.

He pictured Carrie and her anger toward him for not being honest with Joann. A prickle of shame went through him. It had been his job to come clean and not send another person to do his bidding. When all this was over, he'd find a way to make things right between them.

He massaged his temples, attempting to ease the pounding in his head. So much had happened over the past few days. He'd made Jack aware the people in Vegas wouldn't bother him anymore. Of course, he couldn't tell him the real reason why, just that he had settled the debt with Frank DeLuca. He'd probably hear about the murders. Dalton didn't care what conclusions he drew because he still wanted Jack far away from the ranch. He intended to inform him soon enough.

The doorbell rang, and he glanced at the clock on his desk. It was almost midnight. He hurried down the hall and peered out the window. Rick and Alejandro were outside.

Dalton pulled the door open. The two men stood before him, their hats and jackets covered in a light dusting of snow. He beckoned them inside. "What's up, Rick?"

Rick tapped Alejandro's shoulder. "Tell him what you told me."

Alejandro dipped his head and removed his hat. "*Señor,* Rick asked me if anything unusual happened on my last trip to Rapid City."

"And?" Dalton prompted, impatient.

"There was a man in a black Cadillac parked on the main street. He put the window down when I went by." Alejandro looked at Rick.

"Go on." Rick stared at him.

"He stared at me, and I tell you, *Señor* Dalton, I will not forget his face. He had a long scar down the side of his cheek. I know it sounds strange, but it was almost as if his dark eyes went right through me."

"Probably, Miguel Medina, alright." Dalton smoothed his mustache. "Was he alone?"

Alejandro hesitated. He looked from Rick to Dalton. "*Sí.* I did not notice anyone with him."

Disappointed, Dalton asked, "Anything else?"

"I had extra time before returning to the ranch. I stopped at *Buena Comida,* and I think he followed me there."

"Any chance he tailed you back to the ranch?"

Alejandro shrugged. "I did not see him again."

Dalton sighed. "No, you probably wouldn't." He stared at the floor.

"What are you thinking, Boss?" Rick asked.

"I believe he's the one responsible for shooting my cattle, but that's minor compared to what he's done now."

Alejandro's brows drew together. "If I may ask, what has this man done?"

"Kidnapped a little girl."

Alejandro's eyes went wide. "You know this for sure?"

"Yes," Dalton said. "I appreciate you telling me all this. It confirms he's been here a while. I just wish we knew more."

Dalton called Nick and brought him up to date. So far, they were still back at square one.

His instincts always served him well, and his gut kept telling him Miguel wasn't far away. He had no claim to Natalia. With Bobby being her father, they were within their rights to help him get her away from Carmela. Not let her grow up with a drug queen.

But what Miguel did went against every code a decent ghost upheld.

He wandered to the living room window, his eyes fixed on the thick flakes spilling from the sky.

Izzy was out there somewhere, her kidnapping like solving a puzzle. One bit of information linking to another, allowing them to put all the pieces together to find her and eliminate Miguel. Their only enemy, time. Was there enough of it to save her.

CHAPTER 58

MIGUEL

Miguel finished his morning coffee and set the mug on the counter. Still mad at himself for not being able to kill Dalton's wife, he cursed under his breath. Chasing her could have resulted in being discovered. But this was no time for distractions. He must remain focused on his primary goal.

The longer he stayed in South Dakota, the more Nick's chances were of finding him. His demand for Natalia was the bait. Control of the situation must be in his hands. Once all this business was finished, he'd rid himself of Bianca. Her cowboy no longer mattered. He would not waste what little time he had pursuing him. He picked up the second burner phone, dialed, and waited.

"Hello."

His body tensed at hearing the voice on the other end. "So, ghost," he said. "You know what I want."

"This is between you and me, Miguel." Nick's voice beat like a drum against his ear. "Why involve the children?"

"It is not just between us. Because of you, Carmela is dead!"

"Carmela is dead because of Diego Silva. She ran out of the house calling for Bobby, and Diego shot her."

Miguel paused. Did this man think he was an idiot? Carmela would never do such a thing not when less than an hour before he had held her in his arms. His hand curled into a fist. "Diego lay dead with the others. I saw him with my own eyes."

"Yes, after *Bobby* killed him."

"You are lying!" he hissed. "I knew Carmela well. Much more than you and that son of yours. I cannot bring her back, but I can raise her daughter. The girl does not belong with your family. Give Natalia to me, and all of this will end."

"It's not that simple, Miguel," Nick said. "Bobby has her with him in New York."

"No, no, *amigo*. We do not live in the dark ages. He can fly here within hours."

"And I'll make those arrangements once you give me proof my daughter is alive."

"Izzy is very much alive…right now."

"Proof, Miguel. You give me proof of life!"

"If you insist." He ended the call, turned off the burner phone, and crushed it beneath his shoe. Storming into the bedroom, he retrieved another one and headed up the attic stairs. The fury inside him rising, he unlocked the door.

Izzy sat on the edge of the bed. When she saw him, she inched away, fingers digging into the comforter. Miguel crossed the room and stood staring into Izzy's eyes, the words Nick had spoken regarding Carmela haunting him. Did she intend to return to Bobby and make things right with Nick and his family, leaving him to languish without her love? No, he refused to believe she would do such a thing.

He held up the cell phone. "Now, listen very carefully, Izzy. I am going to call your father. When he answers, you must tell him you are okay."

Izzy blinked back tears. "I'm not okay. I hate it here."

"You will do as I say." He studied her frightened face. The apprehension her father and mother were feeling right now would never measure up to his loss. They needed to experience losing someone they loved for good. Someone *they* could *never* get back.

Miguel fingered the handle of the knife at his waist. Whether they gave Natalia up or not, Izzy would die. A lasting reminder to them of what they had cost him. Until then, he must make every attempt to have them bring Natalia to him.

Izzy pulled her knees up to her chest and wrapped her arms around them. "When can I go home?"

"When your father gives me what I want."

"You mean Natalia?"

"Clever girl, you remembered."

"But…but what if he won't give her to you?" she asked, her voice shaking. "I don't think he would give Natalia to a bad man like you."

"Enough! No more questions." He dialed Nick's number. "Here is your proof," he barked into the phone. "Listen to your daughter." He motioned and held the cell to Izzy's ear.

She shook her head no.

Miguel hovered over her. "Talk to your father. Tell him you are okay."

She pursed her lips and turned away.

"Tell him!" he demanded. His patience gone, he clutched a handful of her hair. Izzy kicked and screamed while her fingernails dug into his hand. He dragged her backward off the bed and flung her onto the floor.

She scrambled up, lunging for the phone. "Daddy, please come and get me," she screamed. "He's keeping me here in the attic—"

Miguel clamped his hand around her mouth, then shouted into the phone. "There, you see, your daughter is alive. Now, you have forty-eight hours to bring me Natalia. I will let you know the details."

Miguel ended the call. He grunted as her teeth clamped onto the soft flesh of his palm. On instinct, he pulled his hand away. *"Hijo de puta!"*

Izzy wrangled herself free. She scrambled to the door, her footsteps echoing on the stairs.

Cursing, Miguel shut off the cell phone, crushing it beneath his foot. He took off down the stairs. If Izzy managed to escape, his leverage would be gone. Nick was sure to ask for proof again after hearing his daughter's screams, but it wouldn't stop him from making her regret her disobedience.

Miguel flew through the living room. The front door stood wide open. Snowflakes, carried by the rushing wind, blew in and settled across the wood floor. He caught a glimpse of Izzy disappearing into the woods. Pulling out his knife, he took off after her.

CHAPTER 59

BIANCA

Dragging a cloth along the length of the mahogany bar, Bianca caught her reflection in the polished wood. The image of Izzy locked in the attic kept running through her mind. If the D'Angelos did not agree to give up Natalia, then what? Miguel had made things clear regarding how little Izzy meant.

The dread inside her heart grew, recalling how easily he'd done away with Sarah. The same fate awaited her if she dared to cross him.

Alice approached, smiling from ear to ear. "Bianca, that cute guy is out back again. He wants to talk to you."

She tossed the rag aside. "Who? What are you talking about?"

"You know who. The married guy from the party, the one working at the Dalton ranch."

Trying not to act surprised, she waved her hand. "Oh, my friend from Mexico. He said he might stop by to say hello. Can you tell Rosie I am taking a break? I won't be long."

"Sure. But Bianca, remember he's married."

"I told you before. He is just a friend. Nothing more," she said, pushing open the swinging door to the kitchen.

The aroma of spices simmering in pots on the huge stove hung in the air as she hurried past Carlos and the other cooks. She removed her coat from one of the many hooks by the back entrance and threw it on.

Outside, a light dusting of snow blanketed the blacktop. She glanced around, drawing her collar up and shoving her hands deep inside her pockets.

Alejandro stood nearby, his brow furrowed, his face filled with anguish. "Bianca, we must talk."

"I do not think you should have come here again. We have nothing to talk about."

He gave her a disapproving look. "I think we do. It is regarding your so-called friend, the man in the Cadillac."

Her fingers curled and grasped at the wool lining. "What about him?"

"I believe he has done something terrible. *Señor* Dalton is looking for him. There was mention of a kidnapping."

"What has all of this to do with me?"

"If you know where he is, you must tell me, Bianca."

Refusing to give anything away, she said, "No. I have not seen him for a while."

Alejandro moved closer. "I believe you are lying."

His words seeping into her chilled body, she shouted, "I am telling you the truth!"

He gripped her shoulders. "A little girl's life is at stake."

She shook herself loose and stepped back. "What do you take me for? Do you think I would put a child in danger?"

He locked eyes with her. "There is something different about you, Bianca. I felt it the last time we spoke."

The deep wound in her heart threatening to explode, she said, "It is because of *you* I am different. You have destroyed our love. You betrayed me. Do you think I would remain the same?"

Tears building, she looked away. "Please do not come here again, Alejandro. Go back to your wife. I have nothing left to say to you."

She turned and ran inside, hurrying past the kitchen staff and into the restroom before they could see her cry. Locking the door behind her, she leaned over the sink, her tears raining against the white porcelain.

Her body heaved. She raised her head and stared into the mirror. There was much truth in what Alejandro said. Accepting the awful things Miguel had done turned her into a shell of her former self. The Bianca Flores who fled Mexico to find the man she loved no longer existed.

How different things might have been if Alejandro's love for her had not died. Her dependence on it had brought her across the border with a killer. She belonged to Miguel now and all that he stood for had become hers too.

Wiping her eyes, she turned away from the mirror. With her hand on the door, reality hit her full force, making her pause. Could she bear the burden of Izzy's murder? Or was it the one thing she *wasn't* willing to do for Miguel?

CHAPTER 60

JACK

Learning next to nothing about his brother's trip to Vegas, Jack, determined to uncover the details, dialed Mel's number.

"Well, Jackie boy, after what happened, I wasn't expecting to hear from you," Mel's voice boomed through the line.

His ears perked up. "Maybe you can enlighten me."

"Then you haven't heard?"

"Heard what?"

His tone dropped a notch. "Frank De Luca was rubbed out, along with Duke and Tony."

"Taken out? You mean...?"

"Their bodies were found in the desert. Looks like a mob hit. Guess you're off the hook, you lucky son of a bitch."

"Who do they think ordered the hit?"

"No one is sure. Everyone is scrambling. This whole thing might turn into an all-out war for Frank's territory."

Jack paused and bit his lower lip. "Jeez. Where do you stand in all of this, Mel?"

A snicker came through the line. "Me? When the dust settles, I'll figure out whose side I'm on. Until then, I'm not stepping foot in Vegas or anywhere near mob territory."

"Sounds like a good idea. Look, I gotta go. Thanks for the update." Jack ended the call and headed straight for Dalton's study. Few words had passed between them since his return from Vegas, but Mel's news caused a rumble deep within telling him Dalton and Nick were involved in Frank's death. He tapped on the study door.

"Come in," Dalton called out.

Jack eased into the chair across from the desk. Ever since Joann's accident, everyone appeared to be tiptoeing around. He could tell his brother's focus wasn't on the day-to-day operations of the ranch.

"Sorry to bother you."

Dalton eyed him. Clasping his hands behind his head, he leaned back and stared at Jack.

"Well?"

Jack squirmed, searching for the right words to escape his brother's unpredictable anger. "I...I was wondering about Vegas. You haven't said too much."

A muscle in Dalton's jaw twitched. "You only need to know a couple of things concerning Vegas. Number one, it's been taken care of, and number two, you better make certain it never happens again. Because if it does, you won't get any help from me."

Jack's body went stiff at his words. It was a sure bet Dalton wouldn't divulge anything else, leading him to believe his suspicions were correct. His brother and Nick handled his problem by eliminating Frank.

"It won't happen again," Jack said. "I promise, from here on out, no more gambling for me. I've come to realize it hasn't served me well in life."

"I wish I could believe you." Dalton fell silent, a faraway look in his eyes.

"On another note," Jack began. "Something is going on around here. I'll understand if you don't want to tell me, but I'd like to help."

"You, help?" Dalton muttered. "I doubt there is anything you can do. Nick's daughter, Izzy, has been kidnapped."

For the first time, Jack detected the fear in his brother's eyes. "Seen her riding here a few times. Seemed like a sweet little girl. Why would somebody nab her?"

Dalton moved to the edge of his chair, his palms planted flat on the desk. "You don't need to know why. Apparently, this person has been here in South Dakota for a while. Alejandro got a good look at him, but at the time, he didn't think to say anything."

"That figures," Jack said.

Dalton eyed him. "What do you mean?"

"If you ask me, Alejandro's been keeping secrets. I happened to overhear him talking to one of the gals that works at the restaurant the night of the party."

"So, what of it?"

Jack rubbed his chin and leaned back in the chair. "Wasn't an amicable conversation. These two had a history. This woman became real upset. Mentioned how she thought of nothing but him since he left Mexico. Seemed like she assumed they would be together, then he questioned her about how she came across the border."

"What did she say?"

"That she paid money to cross. He didn't seem to believe her. Then, this cute blonde appeared and called him her husband."

"Yes, he married a local girl," Dalton said. "They have a baby on the way."

"True, but it didn't sit well with the first gal. A real firecracker, that one…a jilted woman. She was quite upset, even threw her wine glass onto the pavement."

"What did she look like?"

"Pretty, long, dark curly hair, an accent, of course. I think he called her Bianca."

Dalton sat up straight. "You're sure?"

"Positive," Jack said. "Alejandro called her Bianca." He paused, trying to read Dalton's face. "I don't know if any of this helps—"

"It just might," Dalton broke in. "I need to make a few calls. Saddle Rio and ride to the south pasture. Give Rick and the men a hand setting up feed alongside the windbreaks for the cattle. They're predicting a winter storm."

Disappointed at being dismissed, he said, "I'd rather stay here. I mean… in case you need me."

"Look, I appreciate the information. I'm not sure what it all means, but right now, Rick could use you in the south pasture."

Jack got to his feet. "Whatever you say."

*   *   *   *

Bundled up in a heavy winter jacket, Jack saddled Rio and slipped on his work gloves. Riding beneath overcast skies, spitting flurries, he headed for the south pasture. Memories of the long South Dakota winters flooded back once again and the importance of protecting the cattle from the coming storms. How he had hated setting up breaks.

Reaching the pasture, he observed Rick, Alejandro, and several other men breaking up bales of hay dumped near the tractor. They set them inside the windbreaks made up of 8-foot-long boards nailed vertically to two or three 16-foot-long ones and held in place by, 2x6- inch horizontal stringers nailed to posts. Rick's horse munched hay beside the break.

Jack got down off Rio and strutted over to Rick, his boots crunching on the frozen grass. Frigid wind sliced the air making his eyes water.

"Dalton sent me to help out."

Without looking up, Rick hooked a bale and dragged it toward the break. "We're almost done." He turned to the men. "Take the truck and the tractor to the north pasture. I'll finish up here."

He turned to Jack. "We'll scatter the last of these bales for bedding and spread it out along the break."

About to drag a bale, Jack stopped. "You don't care for me much, do you?" he asked.

Rick gave him a sullen look. "Let's not play games. I believe the feeling is mutual." He folded his arms across his chest, his eyes locked on Jack's. "From the minute you set foot on this ranch, I got a bad feeling. I don't trust you, and I'm rarely wrong about these kinds of things."

Jack paused, trying to keep his rising temper from exploding. He spit and frowned at Rick. "Do you get any bad feelings regarding my brother?"

"Don't catch your meaning."

"Oh, I think you've been working around here long enough to catch it. I'm guessing my brother is into more than just ranching. Can't prove it, but I know I'm right."

Rick's eyebrow raised. "Is that so?" He dropped his arms and grabbed a bale hook hanging on the break and dug it into the hay. Ignoring Jack, he removed a wire cutter from his back pocket. He released the hay and began spreading it out.

The muscles in Jack's neck tightened. How he despised this man. He hitched up his pants and stomped over to Rick. Pointing a finger within inches of his face, he said, "I think you know more than you're telling."

In one swift movement, Rick brushed his finger away and landed a punch square on his jaw. A jolt of pain shot through him. Jack lost his balance, falling backward onto the ground. A tooth wobbled inside his mouth and came loose.

Before Jack could stand up, Rick planted his foot square on his chest. His eyes ablaze, he looked down at him. "Don't you ever come up on me again." His boot pressed harder. Jack moan and pushed at Rick's foot. "If you're so sure you know something, then ask your brother but don't go questioning me." He eased his foot off and stepped away.

"Get the hell out of here, Jack. I don't want or need your help. Take Rio and head back to the house."

Jack struggled to his feet, fists clenched at his side. He spat out the tooth, blood trailing along his chin. "I promise you'll regret putting your hands on me." His jaw aching, he brushed off the front of his jacket and stalked over to Rio. He refused to take any more of this cowboy's crap. Let's see what he does when I come back here with my .45.

Mounting Rio, he rode away, taking the horse into a gallop. The snowfall grew heavier. Halfway down the trail to the house, Rio reared up on his hind legs. Caught unprepared, the reins slipping from his hands, Jack fell off, landing hard on his back. Rio whinnied and bolted into the woods.

"What the hell is the matter with him?" Jack muttered, struggling to his feet. He rubbed the bottom of his back and swore. About to set off down the trail, a low growl made the back of his neck tingle. He swung around, peering through the swirling snow.

A few yards away, a mountain lion perched on a large rock, its tawny fur dotted white. Yellow eyes locked on him. Pointed canines flashed beneath its curled lip. It rapped its front paws against the rock's surface, its gaze held steadfast on Jack. A low growl, then a hiss broke the silence of the surrounding woods.

Jack searched the ground, now covered in white, for something to defend himself with. Failing, he began backing away. Fear spiraled through him, his mind searching for an escape.

The mountain lion snarled, drew back on its haunches, and leaped, knocking him to the ground. He flailed and screamed, feeling the force of the animal's weight on his chest. His fists beat against the thick fur to no avail. Sharp claws dug into his face.

The animal sunk its teeth into the soft flesh on his neck. Something warm and wet flooded his hands, streaking the white snow red. He shrieked, his fists continuing to pound on the mountain lion. Warmth left his body. Darkness overtook him, and he lay still.

CHAPTER 61

CARRIE

Carrie cinched the tie on her bathrobe. Her hand shook as she lifted the mug of coffee and tried to avoid May's eyes. She'd spent the early morning hour confessing everything to her regarding Nick, including what happened to Travis. May remained silent until she finished. Now, as they sat across from one another at the kitchen island, she braced herself for her aunt's response.

"I always had the feeling something wasn't quite right," May said, her usually soft voice taut while worry lines planted themselves on her forehead. "From the moment you arrived in Laurel and up until the day you suddenly left, I could sense it."

"Then, when I came to Lugano, you told me some of it, but I always suspected there was more. Only this... this isn't what I expected. Not in a million years. And poor Bobby, all the hurt he's gone through."

Carrie wiped at the tears perched beneath her lids. "I'm sorry. I should have confessed everything sooner and let you decide whether or not you want anything to do with us."

Pain evident on her face, May said, "After all this time, haven't you learned anything about me?"

"What do you mean?"

"Carrie, when it comes to family, you, Nick, and the children are all I have. In some ways, I wish you hadn't told me, but in others, I'm glad you did."

"So, now what?"

May stood up and cupped Carrie's chin, gently raising her head. "Now, you need to focus on Izzy. Do you believe Nick will find her and bring her home?"

She took May's hand and squeezed it. "I want to…but he kept so much from me. Izzy would be here with us if only he'd been honest about everything."

"But you don't know that for sure, Carrie. If the man who kidnapped Izzy is as determined as you say, he would have stopped at nothing to get to her."

Carrie let go of her hand. "Maybe, but I'm still angry."

"Where is Nick right now?"

"Dalton called last night, and he left with Bobby early this morning. They might have a lead."

"I hope so," May said. "I know Nick will do whatever is necessary to find Izzy. This is so hard, but we need to stay positive."

She looked into May's eyes. "If anything happens to her, I don't know what I'll do. This sitting and waiting is driving me crazy. We will never give this man Natalia. Nick has to find Izzy before…" She collapsed into May's arms and sobbed.

May stroked her hair and patted her back. "You have to be strong, Carrie. You've been through so much, and I know you'll get through this too. Let's go into the great room and sit by the fire."

When they were settled, Carrie said. "There is one last thing I want to tell you."

May inhaled, her eyes searched Carrie's face. "What is it?"

"I went to see my father."

"You mean Alex?"

"Yes." She related all of it to May including his visit to South Dakota.

Her aunt gave her a dazed look. "So, your mother didn't tell me the truth. At least he did try to find you and Bobby."

Carrie scowled at her. "He only waited fifteen years."

"You can't keep holding a grudge, Carrie. It sounds like he's trying." She stared into the fire a moment. "Does he know about Izzy?"

"No, I haven't told him."

"That isn't fair. No matter how you feel, he deserves to know. She is his grandchild, after all."

Carrie got up and wrung her hands. She paced, then stopped. "I guess I should call him."

May nodded. "It's only right. You probably need him more than you think you do."

Carrie picked up her cell phone from the end table. She finished speaking just as Michael flew into the room with Natalia and Valentina trailing behind. He flung his arms around Carrie's waist, and she brushed back his dark curls."

"Is Izzy coming home today?" he asked.

"Maybe. I'm not sure, Michael." She crouched and met him eye to eye. "But your grandpa is coming."

A puzzled expression on his face, he said. "You mean Grandpa Alex, who visited us?"

She looked up at May. "Yes, he's catching a flight before the storm hits."

CHAPTER 62

IZZY

Heart exploding inside her chest, Izzy flew out the front door. Frozen leaves crunched on top of the snow as her feet beat a path toward the woods. Flakes fell from an overcast sky while the trees spawned long, dark shadows beneath their bare branches. Oblivious to the numbing cold, she huffed rapid breaths and kept going.

Her sweater snagged on the tips of a Highbush Cranberry. She tugged at it until she broke free, a thick thread unraveling and trailing down her arm.

Burrs clung to her socks, pinching the tender skin on her ankles forcing her to cry out. A stitch in her side made her gasp, and she slowed a bit. His voice, carried by the harsh wind, called her name. Her panic elevated to new heights, her eyes searched for an escape.

"Izzy, you must come back!" He shouted. "I will not hurt you. You will freeze to death out here."

Teardrops left icy trails along her cheeks. She picked up her pace, fighting to see beyond the blur. Frigid air seared her lungs, causing her breath to catch. Which way should she go?

Surrounded now by towering pines, everything looked the same. Without a clear trail, she dashed to the left, hoping to gain distance.

The sound of his voice grew nearer. She searched for somewhere to hide. Spotting the trunk of a tall wide oak, she ducked behind it. Pressing her back against the rugged ridges in the bark, she tried to catch her breath.

Leaves and twigs snapped on the low hanging branches farther back, each one louder than the next, proof he grew closer. Her body shook. She reached beneath her sweater. Fingering the four-leaf clover, she prayed he wouldn't find her.

"Come now, Izzy," he called. "I know you are here. Let us return to the house where it is nice and warm."

Heavy breathing came from a few feet away. He was on the other side of the tree. She could feel it, visualize him there. The hair on the back of her neck tingled. Frigid air wrapped itself around her body while her eyes combed the woods. She spotted light forming up ahead through the trees.

Pushing away from the trunk with the palms of her hands, she dashed toward it. Pumping her legs faster, all the while hearing his footsteps behind her. She arrived at the edge of the woods. Her heart sank. A large meadow covered in a light blanket of snow loomed before her, with more woods on the other side.

Determined, she charged ahead. The wind howled across the open space. Blinding streams of snowflakes rained down. Her foot caught in a rut. She stumbled, her left ankle twisting to the side. She cried out and fell to the ground.

Within moments, her cries turned into a screech as his hands pulled her to her feet, and he dragged her back toward the woods.

"You little *perra!* I will teach you not to run from me. One hand went around her neck, fingers pressing in, the other brandished the knife. His eyes bulged. The scar on his face changed fiery red. "I should squeeze the life from you, then cut you into tiny pieces and leave your dead body here for your father to find."

He stared at her a moment longer, then released her neck. Snatching the back of her collar, he started for the house, the knife still in his hand.

Izzy gasped for air. Pain shot up her leg. "Please, Mister, my ankle hurts. I can't walk."

He stopped and looked down at her. "That is not my fault. You should not have run away."

"I want to go home!" she cried. "Call my daddy again. I want to talk to him."

"Too late. When I asked you to speak, you refused." He hoisted her up under his arm. Her head dangled forward, her teardrops falling onto the snow below.

Izzy kicked and pounded her fist on his thigh to no avail. What would he do to her now? Take his knife and slice her open? Her father always told her he would never let anything bad happen to her no matter what. Surely, he was looking for her at this very moment.

They reached the house, and he carried her up to the attic. Shoving the door with the heel of his shoe, it banged shut, the sound piercing the room. In two strides, he was at the bed. He tossed her face down onto the mattress. His hand pressed against the small of her back.

"I will get some rope and tie you to the bed," he snapped. "How would you like that?"

Her stomach lurched. She strained her neck and lifted her face up off the comforter. "Please no. I won't run away again."

In less than a second, he flipped her over onto her back, the knife now inches from her chest. He held up his injured palm where her teeth marks were stamped into his flesh. "First my cheek, now this! How am I to trust you?"

Her eyes riveted to the knife, she blurted out, "I'll behave, I promise. Please, I'll be good."

His brows knit, and he paused.

Remembering Bianca's warning, she tried to placate him. "I'm sorry I scratched your face, and I'm sorry for hurting your hand."

"No," he said, moving the knife closer. "I am certain you are not sorry." He studied her for a moment. "I am sure your father has never mentioned me. A good ghost would not."

"A ghost?"

He returned the knife to the sheath and continued staring down at her. His breath slowed.

"You have your father's eyes. I remember them well from the hospital."

"The hospital?"

"Yes, he and I had a conversation when Natalia was born, and I went to see Carmela. He threatened me." His finger trailed along the scar on his face. "And he made good on his threat. But he also made the mistake of letting me live. He should have killed me, then you might not be here now."

Izzy fell silent, the look on his face warning her any response could anger him further. He sat on the edge of the bed. Inching away, she leaned back against the pillows.

"You see," he continued, "As I told you before, your father is just like me. A killer for hire. A man who gets paid to murder people."

She tried not to react. It was lies. All of it lies, intending to scare her. Her daddy would never hurt anyone.

Thunder loomed behind his dark eyes. "You do not believe me, do you?"

Arms gripping her middle, her voice a whisper, she said, "My father is good."

"I guess there is no convincing you," he spat. "Your father loves you, of course, and it is all you have come to know regarding him." He strode to the door. "Bianca will empty the pail and bring you something to eat. You are lucky I need you right now. Otherwise," he patted the sheath, "I would have used my knife on you." He shut the door. The sound of locks snapped on the other side.

Izzy waited for his footsteps to recede before removing her shoes. Raising the hem of her pant leg, she rubbed her swollen ankle. Wind howled around the eaves. Her eyes drifted to the boarded-up window.

Easing from the bed, she hobbled over to it and inspected the screws. Her fingers reached and yanked at one corner to no avail. She made her way to the bed and sat. Her eyes burning from too much crying, she held back new tears. The swelling in her ankle grew, the throbbing now worse than before. She longed for the safety and security of her home. To be with her mommy and daddy, who loved her.

The heater droned on. Her eyelids grew heavy. Exhausted from her attempted escape, she curled up underneath the covers. Images of the knife flashed before her. She sat up, trying to still her racing heart. Clasping her hands together, she whispered, "Please, Daddy, come and find me before he kills me."

CHAPTER 63

BIANCA

Bianca stepped out of the shower. Izzy's cries mixed with Miguel's heavy footsteps on the attic stairs. Her head jerked at the sound of the attic door slamming. She grabbed her robe and ran to the foot of the stairs. The muffled sounds of Miguel's voice could be heard through the closed door, his tone making her insides shudder.

Her eyes followed the wet footprints across the living room floor. Had Izzy tried to escape? If so, Miguel's anger would be unimaginable. She hurried back to the bedroom and put on her uniform. Her mind racing, she took her purse and started for the front door.

"Bianca!"

Miguel descended the stairs. Stopping, she steeled herself, and forced a smile. "What is it? I am leaving for work."

He pointed to a chair in the living room. "Not so fast. Sit."

Legs weakening beneath her, she eased into the chair. She let her purse drop to the floor while he sat opposite her. His eyes raked over her body, the thunder behind them more intense than ever before.

"I have just come from chasing Izzy through the woods."

Feigning horror, she put a hand to her lips. "What happened? How did she escape?"

"Never mind. I will ask the questions." Hands in his lap, he leaned back into the chair.

Her skin prickled at the sight of his fists clenching.

"Do not mistake me for a fool, Bianca. You would be wise to tell the truth, something I have found you are not capable of doing."

Her body filled with crippling fear. She grasped her middle. "*Mi amor*, please, I do not know what you are talking about."

Rising slowly to his feet, he towered over her. "*Mi amor?* You say those words to me as if they have meaning."

He squeezed her shoulders, pulling her up. A whimper escaped her lips. His face inches from hers, hands encircling her wrists, he said, "How easily you tell your lies. Did you think I would not find out about him, this cowboy of yours?"

She tried not to move, not to breathe. His fingers curled around the hair at the nape of her neck, yanking her head back. Her scalp burned from the pressure. Not wanting to see the ugly twisted scowl on his face any longer, she squeezed her eyes shut. "There is nothing between us. I gave him up a long time ago."

"Open your eyes, Bianca, and look at me. Then why did you keep his letters?"

An icy chill ran through her. Her lids fluttered. She opened her eyes and pleaded, "Please, Miguel, you must believe me. I love only you."

"What do you know of love? You used me to cross the border. I do not like being used, Bianca."

She dissolved into tears. "I will not lie any longer," she sobbed. "At first, I only wanted to be with Alejandro, but I realized how much my feelings have grown for you. I belong to you, Miguel, and no one else. Let me show you."

He released her and stepped back. Bianca retrieved her purse from the floor and opened it wide, revealing the empty lining. "I destroyed his letters a long time ago."

His eyes narrowed. "I would like to believe what you say is true about loving me. But doubts still lay heavy in my mind."

"I have done everything you have asked of me. Does it not prove anything to you?" She tossed her purse onto the chair. "I have not betrayed you regarding Sarah or Izzy when I could have easily done so." She swept shaky fingers along the scratches Izzy had raked across his cheek. "We must finish this together, take Natalia and go far away from here. It is all I want, Miguel."

His face softened a bit, and he stepped away. "I am having a hard time believing you."

"Please, Miguel. My loyalty to you has not changed. What can I do to convince you?"

His eyes locked on hers. "Kill the girl."

She froze at his words. Her heartbeat thrummed in her ears. Scrambling, she said, "But you need Izzy in order to get Natalia."

"There are other ways of accomplishing that." He pulled his knife from the sheath and pointed to the stairs. "Come and show me just how loyal you are."

Bianca climbed up in front of him, each step filled with dread, every muscle in her body squeezed tight. Unlocking the door, she stepped into the attic. Izzy lay beneath the covers asleep. Miguel tapped Bianca's shoulder, and she turned.

He held out his knife. "Go on," he said, his voice a low growl. "Do it."

She reached, her hand trembling inches from the blade. Miguel flipped the handle toward her, and she gripped the knife. Dare she lunge at him, thrust the blade deep into his chest? No, she wasn't strong enough to go up against him. She hesitated, and he pushed her forward.

Bianca studied the sleeping girl, then, holding the knife with both hands, she raised her arms above her head, inhaled deep, and brought the knife down. Her body jerked, the tip stopping inches from Izzy's chest, her arm burning as Miguel pulled it back. He grabbed the knife away from her.

His eyes bore into hers. "Bianca, do not ever betray me again."

Her knees weak, but her mind relieved, she said, "You have my word."

"Prepare something for the girl to eat. Then, go to work so they do not become suspicious. Time is passing quickly."

Trying hard not to react further, she went downstairs, fixed a bowl of soup, and filled a glass with milk all the while still feeling the handle of the knife between her hands. Upstairs in the attic, she set the tray on the bedside table. Izzy woke, and Bianca filled with anguish at the sight of her tear-stained face and when she drew the covers back, her swollen ankle. She sat on the edge of the mattress and held out her arms.

"Izzy, I am sorry."

Izzy pushed her away. "Don't touch me! I hate you, and I hate him. I want to go home. I know you could help me, but you won't."

She lifted the tray and placed it on Izzy's lap. "You must understand. I do not like what he is doing. I am afraid, too. Please, eat so you can stay strong. Your father will come for you. I am sure of it."

Without a word, Izzy picked up the spoon and began to eat. Her eyes drifted to her swollen ankle. "It hurts a lot."

"I will get some ice." Bianca hurried downstairs, locking the attic door behind her. Miguel eyed her as she put ice in a plastic bag and wrapped a kitchen towel around it. Returning to Izzy, she laid it on top of her bruised ankle.

"Here, this will help. I must leave now. Finish eating and try to get some rest."

"I…I don't want you to go."

Bianca's hand swept her bangs. "I wish I could stay with you, but… "

Izzy eyed her uniform. "You're going to the restaurant, aren't you?"

She rose and went to the door. "Eat and rest, Izzy. This will end soon."

On the drive to work, her insides wound tight at the memory of the knife stopping inches from Izzy's chest. Unable to focus, she pulled to the side of the road. What if Miguel had not stopped her? Would she have done what he asked and plunged the knife into Izzy?

If Miguel went through with his intention to kill Izzy, would he make her watch? Or worse, force her to do it? A burning fear gripped her. She could run but running away meant only one thing—looking over her shoulder for the rest of her life, never knowing when or if Miguel would find her. Then there was the matter of money. She didn't have much of her own, not enough to last anyway.

Could living with a murderer turn *her* into one? Taking several deep breaths, she pulled back onto the road. There had to be a way out for her… and for Izzy.

CHAPTER 64

NICK

On the drive to Dalton's, Nick couldn't get Izzy's terrified screams out of his mind. He had never felt so helpless in his whole life. Rage boiled inside, growing stronger by the minute. Miguel Medina would come to regret ever having laid a hand on his daughter.

Bobby remained silent, his eyes locked on the swirling snowflakes blanketing the road ahead. Nick hadn't mentioned hearing Izzy to Bobby or Carrie. They were all in enough turmoil, and he hoped the call from Dalton would bring them closer to finding Miguel.

When they arrived, Dalton led them to his study. Nick was surprised to see Alejandro, already seated, hands gripping the brim of the cowboy hat in his lap.

Dalton motioned for them to sit. He poured three shots of whiskey. Handing one to Nick, then Bobby who declined. He took the remaining two and sat across from them behind his desk.

Nick noticed Dalton hadn't offered one to Alejandro. It wasn't like him. He swallowed his drink and set his glass aside. Anxious, he asked, "You have some news?"

Dalton glared at Alejandro. "Go on, tell them what you told me."

Alejandro cleared his throat, his eyes darting briefly to each man. "I saw the man I think you are looking for in Rapid City some time ago." He hesitated and cleared his throat. "He was not alone."

Nick leaned forward. "Who was he with?"

"A woman who works at your restaurant. Bianca Flores."

Bobby shot up from his chair. "Are you sure?"

"*Sí.* She got out of his car. A black Cadillac. The man had a long scar on his left cheek."

"The thing is," Dalton said. "Alejandro failed to tell me all of this when I first asked him if Miguel was alone."

Nick cut his eyes at Alejandro. "Why did you keep this information to yourself? That man has my little girl."

"Please understand. I went to see Bianca when I learned about the kidnapping. She denied any involvement. She told me she had not seen this man for a long while."

"How do you know Bianca?" Bobby asked.

Alejandro glanced at Dalton, who pounded his fist on the desk. "Tell them the rest. Now!"

"We were engaged to be married back in Mexico. But I had to leave because I killed a man. It was an accident, but he came from a prominent family. I did not think I would see Bianca again."

Nick's mind spun. "How did she end up here?"

"I believe this man helped her cross the border. I am not sure what their relationship is. I only know what she has denied."

Dalton stood. His voice thundered across the room. "After all I've done for you, Alejandro. When Rick brought you here earlier, you lied to me knowing a girl's life is at stake."

"*Señor* Dalton," Alejandro pleaded. "I am very sorry. Please forgive me."

"If it wasn't for your wife expecting a child, I would let you go. I'm more than disappointed in you. Don't ever lie to me again. Get back to the north pasture and finish working on the break for the cattle."

Hat in his hand, his head hung low, he rose and went to the door. He looked back at Nick. "I am sorry. I hope you find your little girl."

When he was gone, Bobby thrust an impatient hand through his hair and paced. "I can't believe this. Bianca?"

"It makes sense," Nick said. "Miguel is smarter than I thought. He inserted a mole into our restaurant. Someone who would feed him the information he couldn't get himself."

Bobby stopped pacing. "What are you saying?"

"He had to find out where Izzy went to school, what her routine was. Bianca was probably the one who gave him those details. The only slip-up was Joann being behind the wheel. It should have been Valentina."

Dalton sat and finished off one whiskey. He smoothed his mustache, then rested his elbows on the desk. "You're right, but if he knew Izzy's routine and the make of Valentina's car, how did he end up following Joann?"

"Good question," Bobby said.

"Carrie could have mentioned something," Nick suggested. "When this whole thing happened, she was here at the ranch expecting to find Izzy and Joann. She must have come from the restaurant."

"How do you want to handle this?" Dalton asked.

Bobby's face flushed. "I say we go to *Buena Comida* and confront her."

"That's all well and good," Nick said. "But we need to get her on our side so she can't warn Miguel. We don't know if he forced her into all this or if she had a choice."

"So," Bobby said, "Now what?"

"We let Carrie and Rosie handle this part," Nick replied. "Between the two of them, I think they should be the ones confronting her. Better doing it woman to woman."

"I agree," Dalton said.

Nick got up. "How is Joann?"

"Still digesting things. At this point, I'm not sure where I stand. She's been holed up in the bedroom ever since Carrie talked to her."

"I'd like to see her," Bobby said.

"You can try. Master's at the end of the hall."

"Don't be too long. We need to get back to the house," Nick said. "Miguel is not a patient man. The clock's running down."

Nick stepped out onto the front porch. Dalton grabbed his jacket and joined him waiting for Bobby. A light dusting covered the front walk. Heavy, somber, steel grey clouds dipped lower in the sky, discharging a burst of thick snowflakes.

"I think this is good news," Dalton said. "We will get Izzy back. I can feel it."

Nick turned to Dalton. "There's a bad storm heading this way."

"Yeah, my men have been setting up breaks for the cattle all day. But it might work in our favor."

"Listen," Nick said, "I didn't want to say anything in front of Bobby, and Carrie doesn't know either. When Miguel called the last time, I asked him for proof of life. I guess Izzy refused to get on the phone, and…" Nick stopped, swallowing hard at the lump building in the back of his throat.

"Go on. What happened?"

"He tried to force her. She called out for me… said she was being held in an attic." Nick's eyes filled. "The last thing I heard was her terrified screams. I don't even want to imagine what he might have done to her. Miguel is evil through and through. I know he wouldn't hesitate to hurt or even kill her."

Nick looked into his friend's eyes. "I want to believe she's okay, but…"

Dalton draped his arm around Nick's shoulder. "I know this is tough. But Izzy is a fighter. She'll give Miguel a run for his money. The main thing we need to do now, is concentrate on Carrie getting to Bianca and finding out where he's holding her. Then we can start making plans to rescue Izzy."

"You have to hold on. We will find her. Next time we see Izzy, she'll be safe, and Miguel will be dead."

CHAPTER 65

DALTON

Nick drove away with Bobby as Rick pulled in and approached, the somber expression on his face telling Dalton something was wrong.

"Breaks go okay?" Dalton asked.

Rick nodded. "The breaks went fine, but I'm afraid I have some bad news about Jack."

Dalton's head throbbed. Why couldn't his idiot brother stay out of trouble? "What did he do now?"

Rick removed his hat. "I think we had better go inside, Boss."

"Sounds serious." Dalton closed the door behind them. "Well?"

"Jack's dead."

His jaw went slack, his breath quickening. This was the last thing he expected to hear. Despite all the heartache Jack caused, he never wanted him dead. Not even after the fire. "How?" he asked.

"It ain't pretty, Boss. Looks like a mountain lion attacked him. A couple of the men said they might have seen one poking around last week. We spotted some tracks and did a search, but we never found anything."

Dalton grabbed his Stetson off the hall tree. "Take me to him."

"Before we go, I need to tell you something. Jack and I exchanged words out by the south pasture." Rick paused and broke eye contact. "He got a little too close, and I threw a punch. Jack climbed onto Rio and tore off. A while later, the horse came back to the barn without him. I figured something was wrong, so I went looking."

Dalton studied him, gauged the guilt in his eyes. "Look, we've known each other a long time, and I can say with certainty, if you threw a punch at Jack, he probably deserved it."

"But—"

"Never mind," Dalton snapped. "We won't speak of it again. Now, take me to Jack."

"There is one other thing," Rick said. "With the kidnapping going on, I didn't bring it up." He proceeded to tell him about Joann almost bitten by the snake. "I have a feeling if I hadn't come along, things might have turned out different."

Dalton paused, letting what Rick told him sink in. He could understand Jack wanting to harm him, but Joann? Certainly, there was more to the whole thing. He clapped Rick on the back.

"I'm glad you were there. There's no telling what Jack might have had in mind."

The two men climbed into the truck and rode out to the woods. Rick led him to the body. Shocked at first, Dalton knelt for a closer look. An expression of horror masked Jack's face. His eyes were wide open, staring up at the sky. Deep gashes lined the torn flesh on his neck. Defensive wounds marked his hands where the leather had been torn from his gloves. Dark blood pooled around his body, crystalizing on the frozen ground.

Something gripped Dalton deep inside. All the hatred he carried for so long regarding Jack receded. He stood and turned to Rick. "I'll call the authorities and report this, then make arrangements for the body. A mountain lion sighting is rare in this area. There's a vicious animal somewhere out there. Livestock needs to be protected as well."

*   *   *   *

Several hours later, with Jack's body having been removed and the local authorities gone, Rick dropped Dalton at the house. He went upstairs to Jack's bedroom. Removing his Stetson and jacket, he sat on the edge of the bed. Nothing felt right. Jack was dead, Izzy was in the hands of a monster, and Joann was barely speaking to him.

For the first time since the death of his parents, he hung his head and wept. His breath heaved. A tightness filled his chest while he tried, but failed, to hold back his feelings. A hand touched his shoulder, and he looked up.

"What is it?" Joann asked.

He quickly wiped at his face. "Jack's dead."

"Dead? What happened?"

"Attacked by a mountain lion. It's rare. Guess he happened to be in the wrong place."

She cinched the sash on her blue bathrobe and sat next to him. The bruise on her forehead, though still visible, had begun to fade.

Her hand found his. "I'm so sorry. I want you to know even though I'm grappling with everything you told me, I still care for you a great deal."

"Thanks, Red. That means a lot to me."

"I haven't made any final decisions. But for now, tell me what I can do to help you get through this."

"Though it pains me to do so, I'm going to lay him to rest next to my parents. Because no matter what, they would have wanted me to bury him there. The funeral home will pick up the body from the Coroner."

Joann withdrew her hand and rose. "Is there any word on Izzy?"

"We have a good lead. If it pans out, Nick and I will bring her home."

Her brown eyes blinked. "I don't want to know any details regarding your actions. I hope you understand."

"I do." He got up, his palms cradled her face, and his eyes locked on hers. "There is one thing you can do for me if you're feeling up to it."

"Anything, Dalton. What is it?"

"Go and see Carrie."

"But I don't want to leave you here alone at a time like this."

"I'll be fine. You asked me what you can do." His hands slipped away. "That's it."

She nodded. "I'll call her right now, then shower and dress."

"When you're ready, Rick will drive you over."

With Joann gone, Dalton went to the closet and surveyed Jack's clothes. "Guess I'll be buying a suit," he muttered. He removed everything and placed it on the bed. Sighing, he opened the dresser drawer. Reaching for the pile of shirts, he felt something underneath them. His hand familiar with the feel of a .45, he removed it and set it on top of the dresser.

He shook his head. "What the hell were you going to do with a gun, Jack?" Lifting the shirts, he spotted a large brown envelope.

With dusk about to settle in, he switched on the bedside lamp, sat, and opened it. His eyes scanned the document, and he jumped up.

"That son of a bitch." He stared again at the amount—two million dollars in life insurance taken out on him by his brother. The one good thing he did by telling him about Bianca was diminished. Nothing need be explained now, Jack's intentions were clear.

How disappointed Jack must have been when he returned from Vegas unharmed. If he were dead, only Joann stood in his way. Rick had been correct about the snake. What other devious plan was he formulating?

A tremor shot through his body like a thunderbolt. Jack hadn't changed one bit. His intentions were evil as always.

Grabbing Jack's suitcase, he shoved all his belongings minus the .45 inside. Ripping the insurance policy apart, he chucked it in too.

He pulled out his cell phone and dialed the number for the funeral home. "Yeah, there's been a change. I want my brother cremated. Yes, you heard me right." He paused, listening.

"Ashes? No, I won't be picking them up. Yes, I know it's highly unusual. My brother was highly unusual, too, so I don't give a damn what you do with them."

CHAPTER 66

CARRIE

Carrie sat at the dining room table with Aunt May and Alex. Soft overhead lighting illuminated the space while heavy clouds continued to gather outside the tall windows. The three of them sipped coffee, waiting for Nick and Bobby's return.

Carrie met her father's eyes. "It means a lot to me, your being here."

Alex ran a hand through his silver hair. "I'm glad you called. I only wish it were under different circumstances. I want to be there for you, whether things are good or bad. I didn't do it before, but I can now. Izzy is my granddaughter. I fell in love with her the first moment we met."

"She sure can do that to you," May said, lifting her cup.

At the mention of Izzy's name, tears pooled in Carrie's eyes. The thought of her daughter out there somewhere, suffering, was almost too much to bear.

The three of them jumped at the sound of the front door opening. "In here," Carrie called out. The sight of Nick and Bobby coming through the doorway made her heart pump faster. "What did you find out?"

Bobby glanced at Nick. "I'm going to check on Natty."

Nick let out a breath. "Bianca's involved in this."

Carrie stood up. "What do you mean?"

Nick repeated to them the information they had learned from Alejandro. Her head swam at the news. All this time, she had felt sorry for Bianca. Recalling several conversations, her hand flew to her chest.

"What is it?" May asked.

"I'm the one who talked to her about Izzy and her school. She got most of the information she needed from me."

Nick's arms came around her. "You had no idea what she was up to. None of us did."

Her eyes held his for a moment. "What about Sarah? Do you think she's involved in her disappearance?"

"The thought crossed my mind. Looking back, it was all too convenient, Sarah disappearing and Bianca getting hired."

Carrie wiggled free. "If all of this is true, I'm going to rip that woman apart!"

"Hold on, Carrie," Nick said. "I feel the same way, but we need her on our side. If Miguel forced her into this, she'll probably want out. Having done things against your will, you more than anyone know what she's feeling. I want you to check the schedule and see if Bianca is working today, then call and alert Rosie. Make sure Bianca doesn't leave before you get there."

Carrie ran into the den. She opened her iPad and pulled up the schedule bringing the tablet with her to the dining room. "Bianca is scheduled for a late shift. I'll call Rosie on my way over."

"Carrie, please be careful," May said.

"Don't worry." She glanced at Nick. "I've handled worse." Her cell buzzed. Joann's number popped up, and she declined the call. Her priority right now was getting to the restaurant to talk to Bianca. Joann could wait.

As she pulled on her coat, Alex went to her. His eyes watered. "Whatever you need, remember I'm here for you."

Surprising herself, she hugged him, then hurried out the door.

* * * *

Carrie arrived at *Buena Comida* and went straight to Rosie's office. Her arms came around Carrie.

"What can I do to help?"

Carrie hugged her back then flopped onto a chair across from the desk while Rosie sat behind it. Telling Rosie about Izzy's kidnapping had been hard but necessary for her. Without Joann's support, she needed someone else besides Nick to lean on.

Rosie clasped her hands together and leaned forward. "I have to ask you something?"

"Anything," Carrie said, knowing what was coming.

"You said the police are not involved. At this point, don't you think they should be?"

Carrie studied her face for a moment, the sincerity in her dark eyes putting her at ease. "I've never told you much about my past, and I don't want you to take this the wrong way. I treasure you as a dear friend." She hesitated. "But there is only so much I'm willing to tell you. It would sadden me if anything were to ruin things between us."

"It's okay. You tell me only what you need to. None of us, no matter how close we are, reveal all our secrets."

"This man," Carrie began. "The one who took Izzy did it out of revenge. I can't speak about the circumstances leading up to this, but he and Nick had some dealings a while ago, and he blames Nick for things…going wrong."

"Will he hurt Izzy?"

Carrie's heart thudded, the constant burning in the pit of her stomach swelled. "That's what we're trying to avoid."

"What does he want? Money?"

"No, he wants Bobby's daughter in exchange for Izzy."

An audible gasp escaped Rosie's lips. She drew back into her chair, holding up her hand. "Okay, enough said. You're probably right in not wanting to tell me the details." Releasing a breath, she asked, "Can Nick get Izzy away from this man?"

Carrie's eyes watered. "I have to believe he can." She proceeded to tell Rosie about Bianca and their suspicion she played a part in the whole thing.

Rosie's face lit with fury. She slapped her palms on the desk and shot up, sending the chair out from under her. It slammed up against the metal filing cabinet behind her.

Pacing back and forth, she spewed, "That bitch." She stopped and turned to Carrie. "Do you think she's involved with Sarah's disappearance too?"

"She could be." In all the time she'd known Rosie, Carrie had never seen her this angry.

Rosie checked the clock on the far wall. "She should be arriving for her shift any minute." Folding her arms, she leaned against the edge of the desk. "Don't worry. When she gets here, we will find out what her involvement is in this whole thing." Her brow arched. "And then we'll decide exactly how to handle Bianca Flores."

CHAPTER 67

BIANCA

On the drive to *Buena Comida*, Bianca slid the window down, letting a blast of icy air rush in. Snowflakes drifted from the sky, then thawed on the hood of the car, leaving shimmering droplets of water behind. Taking several deep breaths before closing the window, she tried to erase the image of Miguel's angry face.

How long ago did he find the letters? She counted herself lucky to be alive. So far, it seemed convincing him of her loyalty had worked. But what if he changed his mind?

She parked in the lot and went inside the restaurant, signing in on the computer. Removing her heavy winter coat, she hung it on one of the hooks at the back entrance. Greeting the kitchen staff, she moved through the swinging doors into the dining room. She shouted a quick hello to Alice, then stepped behind the bar.

Surprised to see Carrie walking toward her, she tried to keep her face neutral while straightening the various liquor bottles.

"Hello," Bianca said, without turning around.

"Bianca, Rosie needs to see you for a moment in her office. She might need you to work a double tomorrow."

She swung around. "Sure." Taking note of the dark shadows under Carrie's eyes made her stomach dip. Why was she here today and not at home worrying about Izzy?

"Are you okay, Mrs. D'Angelo? You do not look well."

"Just tired. You go on. I'll cover the bar until you get back."

A low rumbling deep within accompanied her on the walk to Rosie's office. Something did not feel right. Taking a breath, she knocked on the door.

"Come," Rosie called out.

Bianca stepped inside. Rosie sat behind the desk, her fingers moving over the keyboard. Without glancing up, she said, "Sit, please. I'll be with you in a minute."

Bianca eased into the chair. The office door opened, and Carrie came in. She turned the lock and leaned against it.

Every muscle in Bianca's body went taught. Fingertips digging into her thighs, she asked, "Am I in trouble?"

Rosie turned away from the computer screen. "You tell us, Bianca."

"I...I do not know what you mean."

In two strides, Carrie towered over her. She bent and gripped the arms of the chair. Bianca drew back. "You better start talking. Where is my daughter? What has Miguel Medina done with her?"

Bianca stared into the eyes she once found so beautiful, now filled with hate and fear. She lowered her head. Rosie stood. She tapped Carrie's shoulder, and she moved away.

Folding her arms, Rosie leaned on the desk. "Girl, you have no idea how much trouble you're in. Where I come from, we handle things two ways. Easy or hard. Now, you choose which one."

Bianca fell silent. Salty tears stung her lips. A few moments went by before she said, "He forced me to help him. You must believe me."

Carrie dove past Rosie. She lunged at Bianca, pulling her up from the chair by the front of her blouse. Buttons popped, several came loose and scattered across the floor. She shoved Bianca against the far wall.

"You tell me right now. Is Izzy alive?"

Almost numb inside, Bianca nodded. *"Sí,* your daughter is alive."

"Where is she? Tell me, or I swear I'll break every bone in your body!"

Bianca shielded her face. "Okay, okay."

Carrie let go. Her knees giving way, Bianca slid down onto the floor. She looked up at a raging Carrie. "I will tell you everything, but you must protect me from him. Miguel will kill me."

"Maybe you deserve to die," Rosie spat.

"No, please. I can give you the address where he is holding her."

Carrie shook her head. "I'm afraid that's not enough, Bianca."

Bianca pushed up against the wall and slowly rose to her feet. "I will do whatever you ask. Miguel is a bad man. If he does not get what he wants, he *will* kill Izzy." She hung her head. "And I am sure he has plans to kill me too."

The horror-stricken look on Carrie's face fueled her own fear even more. "I promise to help you get your daughter back, Mrs. D'Angelo."

"And what about Sarah?" Rosie asked, her ebony eyes fixed on hers.

"Sarah? I do not know anything about Sarah. She was a good friend to me."

"So," Carrie said. "You didn't have anything to do with her disappearance?"

"No, of course not. I swear to you."

"What about Miguel?" Carrie asked. "You better tell me if he was involved in any way."

Bianca hesitated, trying to gather her thoughts. If she told them how she lured Sarah to the house and what Miguel had done, they would never protect her from him. "No, Miguel has done nothing to Sarah."

Carrie pointed her finger inches from Bianca's face. "It seems strange Sarah going missing led us to hire you. It doesn't sit well with me."

Tears flooded Bianca's eyes again. "I am telling you the truth. A terrible coincidence Miguel took advantage of. He demanded I make friends here to get information for him about Izzy's school, and when Sarah went missing, he made me apply for this job to make it easier."

Carrie stepped back and leered at her. "God help you, Bianca, if we find out you're lying about Sarah or anything else." She picked up Bianca's purse and emptied the contents onto the floor.

"What are you doing!" Bianca cried.

"Checking for a weapon."

"A weapon? I do not have a weapon."

"With what you've gotten yourself involved in, we can't trust you," Carrie snapped at her.

"I understand, but you must try now."

Carrie eyed her. "What other choice do I have?"

"I will help you to save Izzy from Miguel. Please, Mrs. D'Angelo, I do not want anything to happen to her."

"Something already has," Rosie said. "So, you better make things right."

"Okay, let's go. You're coming to the house," Carrie said. "If you want us to try and protect you from him, you need to prove yourself by helping us rescue Izzy."

Bianca gathered the contents of her purse. She went outside with Carrie, following her in her car. This could be her way out. If she helped them get Izzy back, she could gain her own freedom. Miguel no longer trusted her. Whether or not he got Natalia, he would kill Izzy for sure, and then, she would be next.

CHAPTER 68
NICK

By the time Carrie returned to the house with Bianca, blankets of heavy snow covered the Ponderosa Pines. She removed her coat and boots and had Bianca do the same. Nick appeared in the hallway. "I called Dalton. He's here with Rick."

He glanced at Bianca. "Go on inside and sit down." She slinked past him and disappeared into the great room.

Carrie's hands fisted. "How can you act so calm. Do you realize what she's done?"

Nick lowered his voice. "I think you know me better than that, Carrie. If we want her help, we need her on our side. Otherwise, things may turn against us. Did you check her purse?"

"Yes, Rosie and I did before I left. No weapon inside."

"Did you ask her about Sarah?"

"Yes, she said neither she nor Miguel had anything to do with Sarah going missing."

"Do you believe her?"

"Maybe. At this point, the only thing I'm worried about is Izzy."

"Listen, I have something else to tell you."

Her face filled with fright. "About Izzy?"

"No. Dalton's brother Jack is dead. Killed by a mountain lion."

"How horrible," Carrie said. "Is Dalton okay?"

"Long story, but he's fine. Turns out Jack wasn't such a good guy. I'd appreciate you not mentioning anything about it right now."

"Sure, if you think that's best." They started up the hallway.

"Joann is here."

She stopped, her eyes wide, she looked up at him. "I thought I lost her friendship for good. Are things between her and Dalton alright?"

"I don't know, and I didn't ask. I'm leaving that one alone." They continued into the great room together.

Bianca sat looking terrified on the sofa while Dalton, Rick, Bobby, and Alex remained standing. Nick had asked Aunt May to stay upstairs with Valentina and the children. He didn't want either one involved in any of this.

Joann rose from a chair by the fire and rushed over to Carrie. Pulling her to the side, she said, "Oh hon, can you ever forgive me? I'm sorry I haven't been there for you."

Carrie squeezed her hand. "You're here now, and it's all that matters."

Joann gave her a hug, then stepped back. "But as I told Dalton. I don't want to know the details. I'll wait upstairs with Valentina and the children. I hope you understand."

"Of course. Do what is right for you. I'm comforted knowing you're only steps away."

"Okay," Nick said, "Everybody, let's listen to Bianca."

Over the next twenty minutes, Bianca told them about the house, its location, the layout, where Izzy was being held, and what she knew regarding the surrounding property. "He is alone there with Izzy."

"Has he hurt my daughter?" Nick asked.

"No, but Izzy has fought him. He has marks to prove it. She is a strong little girl."

Nick eyed her a moment. They needed Bianca, but he didn't want her in the room while they discussed a plan.

He nodded at Alex. "Would you take Bianca into the den?"

Alex frowned at her. "Come with me, young lady."

With Bianca out of earshot, Nick brought up the internet on the large flat screen and went to Google Earth. He put in the address Bianca gave him. "A Drone isn't practical in this weather, and even if it were clear, Miguel might spot it. Google Earth isn't updated regularly, so I'm hoping we get a good look at the place without snow covering."

Nick zoomed in on the property, and all four men studied the screen. The picture, taken in clearer weather showed a modest house surrounded by acres of woods and a meadow.

"Shouldn't be too hard," Dalton said. "Especially with the heavy snow that's forecast. It will hamper visibility."

"Yeah, but it's the approach I'm worried about," Nick said. "Snow is gonna be pretty deep across the meadow, never mind the woods. Plus, if we use snowmobiles, Miguel will hear us coming."

Dalton grinned and smoothed his mustache. "I think I have just the thing we need. It must be fate. It arrived about a week ago. I ordered it for use on the ranch."

Rick grinned back at him. "I agree, Boss. It will drive through anything."

"What the heck are you talking about?" Bobby piped in.

"My Shaman. It's an all-terrain vehicle capable of moving over any surface on land or water. Snow is no match for this monster. Enough room inside for us and our weapons. If we move slowly across the meadow, it will be hard to discern any engine noise, especially with the wind picking up."

Nick clapped him on the back. "What would we do without you and your toys?"

"So, now what?" Carrie asked.

Dalton raised an eyebrow. "Well, the men and I—"

"Oh, no, you don't," Carrie said. "I already told Nick I'm going with you."

Bobby placed an arm around her shoulder. "Mom, I don't think that's a good idea. It's too dangerous."

She eyed all the men. "You're not going to talk me out of it."

Silence enveloped the room. The four men glanced at each other. Finally, Nick spoke.

"Carrie can hold her own. She's coming." His cell phone buzzed.

"Unknown number," he said, putting a finger to his lips and placing it on speaker. "I'm here, Miguel. Bobby flew in with Natalia right before the storm hit. How do you want to do this thing?"

"I think it best to do the exchange out in the open. That way, there is no, as you Americans like to say, funny business."

"I agree," Nick said. "Is this the end of things between us?"

"*Sí*, all I want is to raise Natalia. Carmela would have wished it. I will not bother you again."

"Since I'm agreeing to your terms, I need to know my daughter is okay. I heard the screams, Miguel."

"I will call you in a few minutes."

Carrie got to her feet and rushed over to Nick. "Screams? What are you talking about?"

"When I asked him for proof of life, Izzy yelled into the phone. I heard her scream, then the line went dead."

Carrie swayed, about to collapse. Nick eased her onto the sofa. "Why didn't you tell me?" she cried.

Bobby glared at him. "You should have said something. We have a right to know what's going on."

Before he could answer, his phone rang again. He placed it on speaker once more. "I'm here. Let me talk to Izzy."

"Daddy," Izzy's voice squeaked.

Miguel came back on. "There, ghost. Now you know your daughter is alive.

Nick's gut twisted. He wanted to tear Miguel apart. "Not so fast, Miguel. You could have recorded that. Put her on again."

There was a moment's silence before they heard Izzy again.

"Daddy?"

"I'm here, baby. I need you to answer a question for me. It's very important, so I know you're okay. What is your favorite thing to do, Izzy?"

"R...ride, Bella."

"Okay, baby. You stay strong for me."

"Izzy!" Carrie cut in, jumping up. "Are you okay, honey?"

"Mommy, I want to go home. Please come and get me."

Miguel's voice broke through. "I will call tomorrow with a meeting place."

The phone went dead. Nick pulled Carrie close. "We are going to get her back."

Her bottom lip trembled. "We have to."

Dalton cleared his throat, but his eyes were moist. "Now, before we run out of time, we need to decide how we move forward."

His muscles wound tight, Nick rubbed the back of his neck, then checked his watch.

"First, we send Bianca home. She's our eyes and ears on the inside. We need her on the road now, before the storm hits full force. She can tell Miguel the restaurant closed early. I'll alert Rosie."

"You know for sure we can trust her?" Rick asked. "Cause if she breaks, everything goes to hell."

Carrie nodded. "I think we can. Bianca's terrified of Miguel. She's desperate to get away from him."

Nick brought Bianca back into the great room. She looked at all of them. Fright in her eyes, she said, "I am sorry. Truly, I am."

"I bet," Bobby snapped.

Nick locked eyes with her. "We need you to drive home. Tell Miguel the restaurant closed early. Whatever you do, you must act as if everything is okay. Keep your cell phone close, in your pocket, and on vibrate. I'll text you when we approach the house. Text me back, then keep Miguel distracted. Can you do that?"

Bianca nodded. She gave Nick her cell number.

"Bianca, your part in this is important," Carrie said. "Miguel forced you to help him do a terrible thing. Now it's your turn to make things right for Izzy."

"I know. I will not fail you, Mrs. D'Angelo."

When she was gone, Dalton said, "I'll take Joann home, then Rick and I will get things ready. Let me know when you're on the way."

Nick walked them to the door, his heart heavy after hearing Izzy's voice, but thankful she was alive. He didn't trust Miguel. The scar he left on his face, a constant reminder of their hate for one another. If they didn't make a move to rescue her soon, Izzy might not live much longer.

CHAPTER 69

CARRIE

A white tempest continued to fall from the darkening sky, growing heavier with each passing hour. Numb inside, Carrie remained silent while Nick navigated the Range Rover across the snow-packed surface of the roadway. All three wore heavy parkas, woolen hats, ski pants, and boots.

Bobby sat in the rear, plying Nick with what-ifs. "What if Bianca turns on us?" he asked.

"That's a possibility," Nick said. "But I get the feeling she's had enough of living in fear with a man like Miguel. We're her ticket out."

"What if Miguel makes us before we reach the house?"

No longer able to stand his questioning, Carrie swiveled around and glared at Bobby.

"Enough already. We all know there are a million things that could go wrong, but your bringing them up isn't helping any."

His face red, he sank into the seat. "Sorry."

Nick reached over and patted her hand, quickly pulling his arm away as the car swerved on the slick surface, sliding to the left. He steered it back onto the almost deserted road.

With visibility deteriorating, they arrived at Dalton's without further mishap. Nick stopped next to a massive, grey, eight-wheeled SUV parked in front.

"Wow!" Bobby said, climbing out of the car. "Uncle Dalton wasn't kidding."

Carrie and Nick stood next to him, trying to take stock of the monster vehicle in the swirling snow. An ominous wind howled around them. "This is exactly what we need," Nick said. "One less worry about getting stuck or tipped in the storm."

They hurried inside. Joann greeted them in the hallway. "Dalton and Rick are waiting in the dining room." She went over to Carrie, busy dusting the snow from her dark green parka with her gloves and slipping her boots off. Nick and Bobby did the same before continuing down the hall.

"Listen, hon, Dalton told me you're going with the men. I know you're worried sick about Izzy, but do you think that's wise?"

Carrie took in the genuine concern in her friend's eyes. "Whether it is or not, I need to do this. I'll go mad if I have to sit and wait at home for the outcome."

"Just be careful, Carrie."

"Don't worry, I will."

Once gathered in the dining room, Joann took her leave. Dalton motioned for them to follow him into his study. Every muscle in Carrie's body tightened at the sight of the weapons laid out on a table in the corner of the room. There were several rifles and handguns, plus night vision gear and goggles.

Dalton picked up one of the 9mm guns. "I've used the army's cleaner lubricant preservative on all the weapons. It will hold up at -35 below. We should have no worries about the freezing point."

Dalton pointed to the barrel. "We have shoot-off muzzle covers on all of these weapons. With the driving snow and wind, we need the barrel protected."

Bobby fingered the tip of one of the weapons. "I've never seen anything like this before."

"Don't know how much the night vision will help since visibility is poor," Dalton continued, "but then again, I still think the weather works in our favor. At least until we make it up to the house."

"I agree," Nick said. "The weather's looking pretty bad right now. According to the forecast, we're due for a small break. It might give us enough time to reach the property before the next wave starts, so we better get moving. We'll work out the rest of the details on the way." He handed Carrie one of the smaller handguns.

"Here, this is an FN Five-seven. It's a good sidearm, has super low recoil, but the bullets can pierce body armor. It holds 20 rounds. It will be easy for you to handle."

Carrie didn't reply. Memories of shooting Travis surfaced. A wave of nausea threatened her gut. Knowing her daughter's life hung in the balance, she pushed back her feelings.

Grabbing the rest of the equipment and donning their boots again, they followed Dalton. Outside, Nick tugged at Carrie's arm, holding her back from the others.

"Look, it's been a long time since you fired a gun. I hope you won't need to, but I want to know how you're feeling about it."

Carrie locked eyes with him. "If there is any way I get to Miguel before you, rest assured, I will empty this weapon into that animal." She continued down the steps and over to the vehicle.

They climbed into the Shaman. Amazed at the enormous interior, Carrie surveyed the four rows of seating and massive cargo room in the rear, where Rick had stored the rest of the weapons.

"This is awesome," Bobby said, pointing to what resembled a cockpit. A steering wheel and single driver's seat sat in the middle surrounded by controls. Glass wrapped around the front and sides for optimal visibility. Dalton climbed into the driver's seat

"What are the specs on this monster?" Nick asked.

"Eight wheels powered with individual steering," Dalton said. "Plus, suspension systems. They can work totally independent from one another if need be." He let out a chuckle. "Comes with a crab mode so you can turn the wheels in the same direction and crab walk."

Nick raised an eyebrow. "No shit?"

"Only has a top speed of 45mph, but this sucker can move over anything you put in front of it other than a brick wall."

Carrie leaned forward, peering over Dalton's shoulder. He started the engine and entered their coordinates into the navigation system.

"We need to stay on back roads. She's not legal on public ones," Dalton said.

They settled into their seats with Nick and Carrie behind Dalton and Bobby and Rick in the rear.

Nick leaned forward. "From what we saw on Google Earth, the best approach is from the left side of the meadow. It's pretty much wide open. When we reach the edge of the woods, we leave the vehicle and fan out, making our way toward the house. We'll stop a few yards away, and I'll text Bianca. When she gives the okay, we advance."

"Rick and I will cover the rear of the house," Dalton said.

Nick nodded. "Sounds good."

"What do you want me and Mom to do?" Bobby asked.

He looked at Carrie. "You're not going to like this, but I need you and Bobby to hang back a bit in case…"

"In case what?" Carrie glared at him and tugged on her gloves.

Nick glanced from Dalton to Rick. "In case things go south, Izzy needs another chance. That second chance is going to be you and Bobby."

He paused, a strained look on his face. "I don't know what weapons Miguel may have, and if he happens to spot us or Bianca folds, even though he's outnumbered, there is always the chance of us being… eliminated."

At his words, a shudder passed through her body. Nick, Dalton, Rick, and even Bobby had more experience with this kind of thing than she. But no matter what happened, she wasn't leaving there without Izzy.

"Okay," she said to appease him. "I'll stay with Bobby."

Nick's weather observation was correct. Though much lighter than before, snow still streamed from a dark sky and a blistering wind whipped around the vehicle.

The journey across snow-packed trails proved to be no problem for the Shaman. They lumbered along, and by the time they reached the meadow, Carrie's mind had conjured up several scenarios. She glanced at Nick, wondering how many times he'd dealt with similar dangerous situations.

His demons were proof enough of his many kills. Only this time was different. Izzy belonged to them, and his stony silence for the rest of the trip revealed how painful all this was.

They reached the meadow, its vast surface buried underneath deep pockets of snow. The wind picked up. Dalton cut their speed, reducing the engine noise. The storm reasserted itself once again. Heavy flakes battered the windshield. Dalton maneuvered across the meadow and along the edge of the woods surrounding the property. He cut the engine.

Rick passed a 9mm to each of the men. "I don't think the night vision is an option. Rifles?" he asked.

Carrie observed Nick reflect for a moment. Visibility outside the windows was almost non-existent.

"Gaging distance is going to be an effort," he said. "I'm comfortable with the handguns. Pass around the extra clips."

Each of them well armed, snow goggles over their eyes, they exited the vehicle into the howling wind. Carrie's breath caught. She pulled her hood up over her woolen hat and forged ahead with Bobby behind the men. Barely able to see the figures in front of her, she swiped at the barrage of icy snowflakes stinging her cheeks in the biting wind. Reaching inside her parka, she pulled her turtleneck collar up and over her mouth.

Navigating the high snowdrifts became increasingly difficult. Wind cut through the tall pines, their stiff branches bending under the weight of the snow. Carrie struggled to remain upright. She pictured Izzy's face, the driving force keeping her moving.

Carrie was thankful when the snowfall grew lighter, and the wind died a bit. Able to see clearer now, a dim light glowed in the distance. Her heartbeat ramped up. A flutter swept her chest. Izzy was inside that house with the man who held her prisoner.

She came up behind the men. Nick signaled and pointed ahead. They were almost to the house. He braced himself against a tree trunk, his back to the dying wind, and pulled out his cell. She prayed Bianca would not betray them.

Although she tried to hold onto the belief, they would be successful, doubt clawed at the corners of her mind—doubt about not only the outcome but after. Still wounded by Nick's failure to tell her about Miguel Medina, the rift between them hadn't healed.

She had always accepted his past and lived with the consequences, but Izzy's kidnapping overwhelmed her. Would they ever really be safe?

The snow picked up again, along with the wind. She tried to control her shaking limbs. With the light emanating from the house no longer visible, her fear grew. All she wanted was to see Izzy again.

Nick motioned them forward, which meant he must have received a text from Bianca. They moved slower now, taking refuge behind wide tree trunks. The house came into view before disappearing again behind a heavy squall.

Approximately 50 feet from the house, she stopped and waited with Bobby while Nick, Dalton, and Rick forged ahead. Her breath caught as Nick took one last look behind him, then vanished from view in the wind-driven snow.

CHAPTER 70

BIANCA

Fighting her way through the heavy drifts, Bianca hurried up the steps and across the porch. During her white-knuckle ride from Carrie's house, her mind flew in fifty different directions. Her instincts told her to flee, to keep driving, and never look back, but the deep-seated guilt stamped inside her made it impossible for her to betray the D'Angelos.

The knowledge of how much of an accomplice she had been in Sarah's death and the kidnapping of Izzy became increasingly challenging to live with. At this point, she no longer trusted Miguel, certain he planned to kill her. Miguel was not a forgiving man.

Taking a deep breath, she put her key into the lock and stepped inside, pushing the door shut against a sharp blast of wind.

"Bianca?"

She recoiled at the sound of his voice. "S*í*, Miguel." Removing her coat and boots, she went into the kitchen, where she found him, arms crossed, leaning against the counter.

"You are home early."

"They are closing the restaurant because of the storm."

He rubbed the stubble on his chin. "I am hoping the weather will not hamper my meeting with Nick tomorrow."

"How will you do the exchange?"

Miguel wet his lips. "Exchange? There is to be no exchange. I do not believe Nick is going to hand over Natalia. I have *never* believed it."

"What do you mean?"

"I am certain when we meet, he intends to kill me, but right now, I have the advantage. I have made him think I will hand over his daughter alive." A look of pleasure ignited his face while he continued. "Instead, he will watch as I slit her throat."

His words hit her like a barrage of tiny needles pricking her skin. He intended to kill Izzy from the very beginning. Everything he told her back in Sedona and up to now were lies. It became clear to her his sole objective had been Nick all along. This whole ordeal had nothing to do with Natalia.

"But what do you stand to gain, Miguel?"

"You still have no idea what this man has taken from me." His fists clenched. The shadows behind his eyes enlarged. "There are no secrets between you and me when it comes to my feelings over the loss of Carmela. I do all of this in her memory. Having Nick's daughter is the thing driving him mad right now, and for him to witness her death, just as Carmela witnessed her father's, is enough to put her soul to rest."

"Once we are face to face and Izzy is dead, I will finish him off. When I am done with Nick, Dalton and Bobby are next."

Afraid to ask, she said, "How is Izzy?"

"The girl is fine," he snapped. "Fix her something to eat… her last meal."

Willing her hands to stop shaking, she prepared a sandwich and a glass of milk. Her stomach clenched, and she forced herself to focus on arranging the tray.

"Do what you must, Miguel. I want to be far away from here with you. I have had enough of South Dakota," she said, to reassure him of her loyalty.

Without waiting for an answer, she went up to the attic. Izzy was perched on the edge of the bed, her eyes red from crying.

"I have brought you something to eat." She set the tray down and sat beside her.

Izzy looked up. "I talked to my daddy and mommy today."

Bianca took her hand. She lowered her voice. "We must speak quietly. I do not want Miguel to hear us."

"Why?"

"I spoke to them, too."

"You did!"

"Hush, Izzy. I need you to listen carefully."

She squeezed Bianca's hand. "I knew you would help me."

"Your father is on the way here. There is a terrible snowstorm outside which will keep Miguel from seeing or hearing him."

Izzy scrambled off the bed. "What do I have to do?"

Bianca caught the light and love in Izzy's eyes. Her heart twisted inside her, remembering her family back in Mexico, how they were unaware of the person she had become living with Miguel and how ashamed they would be of her.

Confident of what she needed to do to get Izzy free and ignoring the jolt of her pulse and the terror spiraling inside, she continued, "I am going to leave the door unlocked. Put your coat and sneakers on. I will draw Miguel's attention. When you hear me call, you must run as fast as you can down the steps and out the front door."

Izzy's eyes filled. "But I tried once before, and he caught me. He said he'll cut me up with his knife if I try to run again."

Bianca pulled her close. "No, no, Izzy. Your parents are nearby. They are waiting outside, and I will make sure Miguel does not come after you. Run straight into the woods and do not stop." She cupped her chin. "Understand? *Do not stop!*"

Izzy nodded and slipped on her coat and sneakers.

Bianca kissed her forehead. "I am sorry for everything." She rose and walked to the door. Her cell buzzed. With one last glance back at Izzy, she went down the attic steps. Before she reached the bottom, she responded to Nick.

Taking a deep breath and mouthing a silent prayer, she went into the kitchen. Miguel stood looking at his phone. Searching for a weapon, she eyed the knives in a holder on the counter, but they were too far out of reach.

"Tomorrow is an important day, Bianca. You must be ready to leave. I suggest we start packing later tonight. The storm is passing. The major roads will be cleared."

"*Sí.*" She moved past him to the coffee pot. Her jaw clenched while she poured some into a mug. Her back to him, she concentrated on the rising steam. Lifting the mug with both hands, she swung around and aimed for his eyes, throwing the hot liquid into his face.

Miguel yelled and reared back. He rubbed his eyes as she grabbed a knife from the block on the counter.

Gripping it with every ounce of her strength, she threw herself at him while she screamed, "Run, Izzy! Run now."

"You bitch! I will kill you!" he yelled, seizing her wrist and twisting it.

Izzy sped by the doorway. The knife dropped from Bianca's hand. She raised her foot, kicking Miguel hard between his legs. He doubled over, and she wrenched herself free.

Chest heaving, she ran out the open front door, her eyes catching sight of Izzy disappearing into the swirling snow. No matter what, the little girl must make it to safety. If Miguel caught up to her, she would face his rage and give Izzy a chance to get farther away.

At the bottom of the porch steps, a burning gripped her back. Stumbling, she fell face forward, collapsing into a deep pile of snow. She sucked in air, each breath agonizing. Cold seeped through her body. Forcing herself to crawl, she inched forward, willing her mind to ignore the burning between her shoulder blades.

Bianca's eyes searched through the steady stream of huge flakes forming a curtain around her. She managed to look up. A figure hovered over her, and she stretched out her hand before fading into unconsciousness.

CHAPTER 71

NICK

Nick moved forward into the barrage of white, the house barely in view. About to pull out his 9mm, his eyes were drawn to the tiny figure running straight at him. In an instant, his whole world opened up.

He bolted toward the edge of the woods. "Izzy!" he cried above the howling wind. "Over here."

"Daddy!"

He lifted her up into his arms, his heart battering against his chest. Her legs wrapped around him. Tears stung the corners of his eyes. He pressed her closer, the heaviness in his chest releasing. Turning away from the house, he cursed the heavy snow, and retreated into the woods.

The wind whipped, sending an onslaught of white flakes cutting off his visibility. Finally, they parted. Carrie stood ahead, braced against a tree, her arms held out. "Give her to me!" she shouted. Bobby appeared behind her.

"Take her to the Shaman," Nick said.

Carrie held her tight, kissing her cheek before handing her over to Bobby. "Get her out of the cold." She looked at Nick. "I'm going with you."

Knowing it was useless to argue, Nick nodded. They watched Bobby disappear into the woods with Izzy.

Turning toward the house, they arrived in time to find Dalton and Rick carrying Bianca. A thin line of blood trailed behind them in the snow.

"She's still alive," Dalton said. "Rick will take her back to the vehicle."

The wind picked up once again while the snow fell harder and faster. They helped Rick get Bianca up and over his shoulder, and he took off.

Nick pulled out his 9mm. Carrie followed behind with Dalton. There was a lull in the wind. The snowfall grew lighter while the house came into full view. A figure in a dark hooded sweatshirt stood several yards away near the far side, grinning at them.

"So, Ghost, you have come to see me!" Miguel shouted. Dalton raised his gun. Nick pushed his arm down. "No, this is between him and me. I need to finish it."

Miguel fired a round. A bullet whizzed by the top of Nick's head. Carrie and Dalton ducked behind the tree trunks. Nick waited, then inched around the trunk and peered out, his 9mm at the ready. Miguel had disappeared.

He nodded at Dalton, then turned to Carrie. "Stay with Dalton."

"But…"

"Miguel is mine."

Carrie was visibly trembling. "Be careful."

He removed his goggles, crouched, and took off, continuing past the porch railing and along the side of the house. A long line of thick bushes flanked his left. Too late, he spotted tracks, realizing his mistake.

Miguel charged at him from between the bushes, knocking him to the ground. Nick's gun flew from his hand, lost in the snow. He struggled to his feet in the huge drifts.

Grinning, Miguel tossed his gun aside. "We are even now, Ghost. Let us finish this!"

Miguel lunged again. Nick drew back his arm, landing his fist squarely below Miguel's jaw on his windpipe. He gasped and fell backward. Nick leaped on top of him. They grappled in the heavy snow—pain shot through Nick's ribcage. Pushing away, he fought the pain and got to his feet. He stared at the handle of Miguel's knife protruding from the side of his parka.

Nick stepped back. Gritting his teeth, he quickly pulled the knife out. The tip dripped with his blood. Ignoring the burning agony, he tackled Miguel again, now on his feet. The two men tumbled into the snow. Nick reared up, raising the knife.

He looked into the man's eyes—the man who had taken his daughter and almost destroyed his family. His adrenaline surged. This kill would be neither clean nor quick.

He plunged the knife into Miguel's stomach, twisting the handle.

Miguel screamed. Nick twisted the handle, yanked it out, and stabbed him again. He got up and backed away. Heat flushing through his body mixing with the bitter cold, he watched Miguel crawl on all fours toward the rear of the house, blood pouring from his wounds, leaving trails of deep red in the white snow. Holding his side, Nick followed, the bloody knife still in his hands.

Carrie ran up beside him. Her eyes drawn to the blood running down the side of his parka, she tugged at his arm, but he yanked it away.

"I need to finish this."

They reached the rear of the property in time to see Miguel struggling to stand. He grabbed at a low hanging branch by the edge of the ravine. Pulling himself up, he swayed, his dark eyes drilling into Nick. His breath came in spurts, the front of his sweatshirt now soaked with his blood.

"You think you have won?"

"There is no winner. This is a reckoning, Miguel. We're both accountable for all we've done. Now, I just have to learn to live with it."

Miguel fell to his knees. His hands wrapped around his middle. His blood continued to pour onto the snow. Nick hovered over him.

He pinned Nick with his eyes. His mouth gaped open for a moment while his chest heaved. "You will see me in your nightmares, Ghost."

Nick raised his leg and kicked Miguel in the chest. His arms went up, and he fell backward into the ravine, his dying screams echoing from the darkness below.

CHAPTER 72

CARRIE

Carrie checked the temperature of the water, then poured in a generous amount of bubble bath. "Get undressed, Izzy, while I fetch some fresh towels."

When she returned, Izzy sat up to her chin in bubbles. "This feels good, Mommy."

Carrie knelt beside the tub. Her hand swept across Izzy's bangs, and she kissed her forehead. "I'm so glad you're home." She visualized her daughter being held prisoner by Miguel. A sick feeling crawled through her.

"Izzy, did that man do anything bad to you? I mean… did he touch you someplace he shouldn't have?"

She peered up at her. "He yelled at me a lot. I tried to run away once. That's when I hurt my ankle, and he threatened to cut me up with his knife."

Carrie's breath caught. If Miguel were alive and standing here today, she would tear him to pieces.

Izzy looked down at the bubbles. "He said bad things about Daddy. He said Daddy was just like him… that he killed people." She glanced up at Carrie. A tear escaped her eye. "He called him a ghost. Mommy, what did he mean?"

Carrie's stomach clenched. "No, no, Izzy. None of it is true. He wanted to upset you. Your father is *nothing* like him." She picked up a washcloth and gently passed it over her face before moving on to her neck. "You need to try and forget about those awful things he said. He's gone now, and he will never hurt you or anybody else ever again."

Something shimmered beneath the bubbles catching Carrie's eye. She pushed them away with the cloth and fingered the gold chain. "What's this?"

Izzy reached down. The four-leaf clover between her fingertips, she said, "Bianca gave it to me. She told me it was good luck and it would keep me safe."

A hard thud hit Carrie's chest. Blood rushed to her head. "Are you certain Bianca gave you this?"

Izzy nodded. "Maybe it's why you were able to rescue me." She fingered the necklace again. "Do you think it's magic, Mommy?"

"I don't know, sweetheart." Her composure slipping, Carrie helped her finish bathing. Tears stung her eyes when she spotted Izzy's swollen ankle. Grabbing a heated towel from the rack, she helped her out of the tub, and wrapped it around her. Hugging her tight, she breathed in her daughter's scent.

"I love you so much, Izzy."

"I love you, too, Mommy."

She finished drying her off, then waited while Izzy put her pajamas on. "Can I have the necklace?"

Izzy frowned. "Why? I wanted to sleep with it."

"That's not a good idea. The chain is thin. You don't want it to break, do you?"

"No. I guess you're right."

Carrie undid the clasp. "I'll give it back to you tomorrow."

"Where's Daddy? Is he okay? Why didn't he come home with us?"

Carrie recalled the blood seeping through Nick's parka when he returned to the Shaman. His wound, thank God, had not been deep enough to do much damage. She and Bobby had left him and Bianca at Dalton's where a doctor friend would stitch him up and take care of Bianca.

"Uncle Dalton will make sure he's okay, then he'll come home later tonight. Now, let's get you into bed."

"Can I sleep in your room tonight?"

"Of course. I'll even leave the light on for you and stay until you fall asleep."

*   *   *   *

The following day with Nick home and everyone in the house still sleeping, Carrie went downstairs to the study. Her injury turning out minor, Bianca was recuperating at Dalton's ranch, and she had volunteered to pick her up. Due to the poor visibility in the snowstorm, the bullet wound she sustained had not been life-threatening. On a clear day, Miguel's shot would have landed with deadly accuracy.

Twisting the knob on the safe, she opened it and removed the FN Five-Seven revolver. Inserting a clip, she tucked it underneath her heavy wool sweater.

The roads had been cleared overnight, and by the time she pulled up to Dalton's, Bianca was waiting outside. She climbed in as Carrie forced a smile. "Feeling better?"

"*Sí.* Thank you for offering to take me to the house to get my things. It is so kind of you."

"No problem. I'm happy to do it."

Carrie gripped the wheel, making small talk, sick inside over the discovery of the necklace. Sarah had worn it to work at *Buena Comida* almost every day. She had remarked on it, with Sarah telling her it had been a gift from her parents.

They drove up the driveway, and Carrie parked. Bianca got out of the car. She sucked in her bottom lip. "I am a bit sore."

"I'll help you pack." Carrie followed her inside. Her eyes drifted to the attic stairs. She quickly turned away, not wanting to imagine her daughter locked in that awful place.

In the bedroom, Bianca threw her things into a suitcase. Carrie wandered over to the dresser and collected a bottle of perfume and some earrings. She handed them to Bianca.

"What about Miguel's things?" Bianca asked.

"Nick will take care of them later."

Bianca zipped the suitcase and glanced around. "I guess that is everything."

"Not quite everything."

"What do you mean?"

"Come outside, and I'll explain."

Bianca wheeled the suitcase with Carrie walking behind her. When they reached the car, she stopped and stared at Carrie.

Pulling Sarah's necklace from her pocket, Carrie dangled it before her. "Izzy told me you gave her this."

Bianca stepped back, color draining from her face. "Please, let me explain."

Carrie drew out the revolver and released the safety. "Go on, start talking."

Eyes filling with tears, her arms cinched her middle. "Miguel made me do it."

"So, *you* killed Sarah?"

"No! I only brought her here. I lied and said there was a party. Miguel killed her."

Carrie let loose the rage building inside her. "It's all the same thing, Bianca," she snapped. "If it weren't for you, she would still be alive. You're as much responsible for her death as Miguel."

"But I—"

"You lied your way into gaining Sarah's trust. Then you lied to get a job at *Buena Comida,* knowing Sarah was dead. You pumped me for information about Izzy's school so Miguel could kidnap her." She looked with disgust at the woman standing before her. Blood rushed to her head. "What did Miguel do with Sarah's body?"

Bianca sobbed and buried her face in her hands.

Carrie waved the gun at her. "Look at me, Bianca! I said, where is Sarah's body!"

Her head came up, and she met Carrie's eyes. "A... a place called Crystal Lake," she stammered. "In the trunk of her car, beneath the water."

Carrie's stomach knotted at her answer. She took in the frightened face before her. "I am curious about one thing. If we hadn't found you out, would you have helped Izzy escape?"

"I would have never let Miguel hurt Izzy!" She wailed.

Carrie raised the gun. "That's not what I asked you."

"Please, Mrs. D'Angelo," she pleaded. "You must understand how scared I became of Miguel. He was a terrible person who forced me to do awful things."

"Maybe so, but I found out the hard way many years ago we always have a choice, Bianca. No matter how scared we are of someone. I promised myself I would never kill anyone ever again but standing here right now, in front of you, I don't think I can keep my promise."

Bianca's lip twitched. "But surely you have never killed anyone. People like you have everything. You have never suffered the way I have."

Carrie almost laughed. "You know very little about me, Bianca, or what I am capable of." She pictured Izzy locked away in the attic and what might have happened to her. Then she pictured Sarah. How terrified she must have been before she died.

She cocked the revolver. "I'm sorry, Bianca."

Arms stretched out before her, Bianca pleaded, "I beg you, please do not kill me. I will do anything you ask. I will even go to the police and tell them I am the one who brought Sarah here."

Carrie raised the gun and took aim. She shook her head. "It's too late for that."

A gunshot ripped through the air. A bullet hit Bianca dead center in her forehead. Carrie jumped back. Bianca's body jerked. Eyes wide, she collapsed to the ground and lay still.

Carrie stared at the unfired weapon in her hand. Whirling around, she came face to face with the shooter.

CHAPTER 73

DALTON

A bitter wind whipped across the front porch, almost taking Dalton's Stetson with it. He hurried inside, going directly to his study. Removing his hat and coat, he laid them aside and put fresh logs on the fire, then poured a shot of whiskey.

Sinking into the leather chair, he studied the orange flames licking the wood. The past few months had brought so much turmoil into all their lives—first Jack, then Ronnie, and ending with Miguel.

A smile crossed his lips knowing Izzy was safe at home with the people who loved her. He shuddered to think where things would stand now if they hadn't rescued her.

He never doubted Miguel Medina would have put an end to her. The man was pure evil through and through. Men like him didn't deserve a place in this world. Something he had tried to impress on Nick.

Wicked people continued to walk this earth. But the time had come for him to stop killing. He'd done enough, and in his heart, he believed it was all on the side of good.

He sighed and swallowed his drink, wanting to savor the taste and the comfort of the fire. His brother's death was fast becoming a distant memory. It no longer affected him once he uncovered Jack's true intentions. Some people can't change no matter what.

His musings were interrupted by a light tap on the door. "Come in," he called out.

Dressed in jeans and a maroon cable knit sweater, Joann sat down across from him. She pointed to his glass. "Got any for me?"

"Sure thing, Red." He rose and poured her a drink, surprised when he gave it to her, and her hand briefly wrapped around his fingers. Things between them were strained ever since Carrie revealed the truth about him.

Dalton eased into his chair again and waited. This was a conversation she needed to start. He would have to live with whatever decision she made. He studied her beautiful face in the firelight and the gold highlights weaving through her red hair.

Her brown eyes caught his. "I guess it's time I tell you how I feel."

"If you're ready." His body tensed, and he worried he might lose her."

"When Carrie first told me…everything, I was shocked and hurt. I felt deceived by all of you." She leaned forward and stared into her glass for a moment.

"I'm sorry," Dalton muttered. "I never meant for you to feel any kind of way about all of it. I thought it would be best to keep it from you. I've always prided myself on being an honest man, and for the first time in my life, I was dishonest with the person I care for more than anyone else in this world."

"Still," she said. "You should have told me everything and given me the chance to decide for myself. You never even mentioned Jack until you received his letter. Makes me wonder if he hadn't shown up here, would you have told me about him at all. Dalton, when two people love each other, trust plays a big part in that love. If we don't have trust between us, then we don't have much at all."

Ashamed, her words hit him like a slap in the face. "What now?" he asked.

Joann sipped her drink. "Is there anything else you've kept from me?"

Dalton pictured Ronnie. "Yes, one other thing." Exposing Ronnie's addiction and Derek's death would shock her again, but like Nick and Carrie, he'd found out, keeping secrets could destroy so much. Telling her about Ronnie proved difficult watching her face change to one of deep hurt. He left out the part about Rick injecting the heroin. There was no need to drag him into the middle of things. Instead, he told her he eliminated Derek with a quick bullet.

He finished, then drained his whiskey, letting what he said sink in.

Joann put her drink down and stood up. She looked away and paced. Minutes ticked by, her silence deafening. She stopped and turned to him. "I wish she had come to me."

"I understand, Red. But there was Derek and those videos to deal with. I'm hoping you won't mention any of this to Ronnie. From what Bobby said, she's doing great and will be finished with rehab soon. She's too ashamed to tell you how she got mixed up in all of this, and she doesn't know my part in it, either."

She studied him another moment before walking over and sitting on his lap. Her arms came around his neck, and she kissed his lips. Her brown eyes looking deep into his, she whispered, "Thank you for saving our daughter."

The word *our* repeated in his head, filling him with warmth. "Red, I know I need to earn your trust." His voice was low and tender. "I'm hoping you'll forgive me and give me a chance to make you happy again."

"Of course, I forgive you, but I need to make something perfectly clear." She stroked his cheek, the softness returning to her face. "I can't help myself. I love you, Dalton Burgess, and I always will."

She melted into him, and he kissed her long and deep.

CHAPTER 74

BOBBY

Bobby lowered his Glock and tucked it underneath his jacket. Several moments passed before he walked toward Carrie. His steps sure and steady, his mother's shouts ringing in his ears.

"Bobby! Bobby! No, no, no!" Carrie knelt beside Bianca. Dead eyes looked up at her. "This was not for you to do."

"I couldn't let *you* kill Bianca."

She rose and faced him. "How did you…?"

"Izzy," he said, his voice barely audible. "She told me you took the necklace from her, and she described it to me. I saw Sarah wearing that necklace at least a dozen times. After you drove away from the house, I knew what you intended to do."

Her eyes filled. "But now it's my fault you have to live with this."

"I'm okay with what I did. Sarah was a good person. She didn't deserve to die, and Bianca helping Miguel kidnap Izzy sealed it for me."

Carrie engaged the safety on the gun. "I didn't want this for you, Bobby." She looked down at Bianca. "I'll call the authorities… give them an anonymous tip on where to find Sarah's body. At least her family will have closure of some sort."

"I see you're all done," a male voice said.

They both jumped. Rick stood a few feet away.

"What are you doing here?" Carrie asked.

"Bobby called me. No worries. I need to get rid of Miguel's body anyway. One more is not a problem. You go on home and let us take care of things."

Bobby motioned at Carrie. "I'm staying to help Rick."

"But—"

"I need to do this." He handed her his Glock. "Put this thing away and don't let Nick see you do it. He'll ask too many questions."

Rick tipped his black cowboy hat back on his forehead. "Nick knows I'm collecting Miguel. It's all he knows. So, you decide if you want to keep it that way."

His mother left, and Bobby helped Rick with the bodies. They labored through the deep snow and deposited them inside the Shaman.

"Thanks for staying, Bobby. I do appreciate it."

"No problem."

"I know from Tahoe this wasn't your first time," Rick said. "Are you sure you're going to be okay?"

Bobby pictured Sarah. Her bubbly demeanor and smiling face. He marveled at the calm inside him. Tahoe had caused sleepless nights, but he was confident killing Bianca wouldn't do the same thing. "She got what she deserved," Bobby said. "I can live with it."

* * * *

Later, Bobby pulled up in front of the house, surprised to see his mother waiting outside.

"Bobby, listen, what Rick said about telling Nick.?"

"What about it?"

"I can't keep this from him. Not when I was so angry at him for not telling me about Miguel. If I expect honesty from him, I need to be honest, too."

"You really want to put this on him? He's not going to like the fact we did something behind his back."

"But it's the right thing to do."

Bobby pointed toward the front door. "Well, then, lead the way."

In the kitchen, Carrie put on a pot of coffee. Nick's voice and the children's laughter sounded from the great room.

"I put the guns in the safe," Carrie said. They sat at the island, hot steaming mugs in their hands. Ace trotted into the kitchen and nudged Bobby's leg.

He rubbed the dog's head. "I know what you want."

"So, where did you two run off to this morning?" Nick leaned against the doorway, a lazy smile on his lips. "I woke up, and both of you were gone."

Bobby looked at Carrie. "Go on. This is your idea."

Nick winced and fingered his bandaged wound as he slid onto a stool next to Carrie. "Sounds serious."

She set her mug down. "It is. I need to tell you something, but before I do, I want you to remain calm. This is all my fault. Bobby shouldn't have gotten involved."

Nick looked from her to Bobby. "What is she talking about?"

Bobby glanced over his shoulder.

"Don't worry, the kids are watching a movie," Nick said. "Tell me what happened."

Bobby's heart thumped, but he forged ahead. "I shot Bianca."

Nick jumped up. "You did what!"

"I asked you to remain calm," Carrie said. "Please sit down and listen."

Bobby related the story of the necklace and how he followed his mother to Miguel's place. "I couldn't let my mother shoot Bianca." He locked eyes with Nick. "Besides, none of this would have happened if we had come clean about Miguel in the first place."

Nick's eyes flashed. "Don't try to justify your actions, Bobby. Both of you were wrong. Killing someone stays with you for the rest of your life. Did you ever stop to think there might have been another way to settle things? Shooting a woman is something even I've never done."

Bobby squinted at him. "Are you being serious right now? As much as I loved her, look at what letting Carmela live all those years ago did to this family. I thank God every day that in the end, at least I have Natalia. Poor Sarah had her life taken away, and we're partly to blame. What Bianca did was unconscionable. To lure Sarah to her death and go on as if nothing happened, then help Miguel kidnap Izzy. You ought to be—"

"Stop it, Bobby!" Carrie slapped her palm on top of the island. Enough about what everyone should have done. The fact is, we can't change any of it." She rose and placed her mug in the sink. "I'm going to check on Izzy and Michael while you two finish up here." Halfway around the island, she stopped in front of Bobby. Her hand brushed back the hair falling over his right eye. "I'm not happy you have to carry this, but I understand you did it for me."

When she was gone, they grew silent for a few moments until Nick spoke. "Look, Bobby, you're like a son to me. I'm concerned killing Bianca will haunt you. I don't want you to suffer because of it."

Bobby let out a breath. "And you're the father I never had, and I appreciate everything you've done for me. But you need to let this one go. I'm not sorry for what I did. Trust me, this won't keep me up at night."

* * * *

Six weeks had gone by since Izzy's kidnapping, and Bobby looked forward to celebrating the Christmas holiday in South Dakota. Nick had promised no more ghosts were waiting to threaten their family. Sarah's body was recovered to the relief of her grief-stricken parents. Bobby wished they could have returned her necklace to them, but it would lead to too many unanswered questions.

He cherished his free time with Natalia. The wine business was doing well, and the restaurants were turning a profit. His art clientele increased to a size where he found himself needing to hire an assistant. With Lucy, whom he'd known from one of the galleries on board, he became unstoppable.

Ronnie, released from rehab a month before, returned to her old self. Dinner dates between them became the norm, although she insisted on staying away from the clubs for now.

Today, with Christmas approaching fast, Bobby hurried in and out of the stores on Manhattan's Fifth Avenue. The city buzzed with life. Santa-clad bell ringers anchored each corner. Store windows festooned with garlands of red and green framed moving figurines depicting holiday scenes. The nutty scent of roasted chestnuts from street vendors filled the air.

His arms laden with packages, Bobby arrived at his last stop. Tiffany & Co. would have something special for Izzy. Her disappointment when Carrie did not give Sarah's necklace back, instead telling her it was lost, would ease if he replaced it.

He set his bundles aside while he perused the counter. A tag pendant with a red heart in 18k gold caught his eye. Having them engrave Izzy's initials on it added the finishing touch. Gathering up his packages, he left the store and headed for his apartment. He needed to pack his and Natalia's things for their flight later tonight.

Rounding the corner, icy wind blasted his face, making his eyes water for a moment. He blinked and lowered his head against the wind. Failing to see ahead, he crashed directly into someone. His bundles flew out of his hands and landed on the sidewalk. Bending to retrieve them, he heard a female voice.

"I'm so sorry," she said.

Without looking up, Bobby gathered everything together. "No worries. It's okay." He rose, and his breath caught. Familiar green eyes looked at him. Eyes he would know anywhere. The same ones that had stared back at him across a lab table in high school.

"Darcy?" he asked. "Darcy Grant?"

CHAPTER 75

CARRIE

Carrie settled onto one of the chaise lounges by the pool, delighting in the scene around her. Most of the people she loved were here today. Dalton and Joann sat on the opposite side, sipping drinks. The rift between them gone, they appeared more in love than ever before. Ronnie and Justin were due to fly in later in the evening and would stay at the ranch for the next week.

Alex perched on the edge of the pool steps, his eyes locked on his grandchildren. Kate had passed away four months ago, and the sorrow on his face slowly faded with each visit to South Dakota.

Having accepted her father's shortcomings, she'd grown to appreciate he took ownership of his past mistakes just as she had. Forgiveness led to freedom, and she embraced it with a whole heart for him and herself too. Her past no longer weighed her down as it had done for so many years. It had taken a little longer for Bobby, but in the end, their love of art bonded the two men.

Aunt May came across the patio, a cold drink in her hands, and sat near Alex. After much debate, she had agreed to come and live with them. She was getting on in years, and the house in Laurel needed too much attention. She and Alex made peace with each other regarding Helen and were developing an easy friendship.

Carrie smiled at Bobby and Darcy lying side by side in the grass on large striped beach towels taking in the sun while Ace dozed beside them. Who would have imagined an old high school crush would be what he needed to heal? This past week, he revealed his plan to ask Darcy to marry him. Carrie was thrilled when he asked her to help him pick out a ring.

Natalia, seated nearby, played with a doll. She grew to look more and more like Carmela each day. Carrie liked to believe she would be happy with the way Bobby was raising her daughter. He loved her more than life itself, and now he'd found someone else to love him too.

There was no more mention of Bianca and what Bobby had done. The bond between him and Nick remained stable, with Bobby voicing his choice of Nick for future best man.

A sense of calm came over her watching Izzy, Michael, and Valentina splash in the water, their laughter almost bringing a mist to her eyes. Following months of night terrors and the fear of sleeping alone, her daughter was finally herself again. She had returned to her own bed and appeared to sleep peacefully through the night.

"What are you smiling about?" Nick stood looking down at her.

"Happy, I guess." She patted her stomach. "And full of your superb grilling."

"Glad you enjoyed it. Come with me. It's time for something else."

Carrie rose and slipped her hand in his. "We have company, you know."

Nick smirked. "My, my, where is your mind, Mrs. D'Angelo?" He pulled her toward the house. "We need to get dressed."

"Dressed? But I thought…"

Inside the doorway, Nick wrapped his arms around her. He bent and kissed the nape of her neck. "I know what you're thinking. That can wait a while."

Upstairs in the bedroom, they took off their bathing suits and threw on clothes. Nick led her outside to the garage. "Remember you made me promise to give you a ride."

Her eyes lit up, and she felt herself blush. "The Lamborghini?"

"Yup. We're going out to the runaway so I can show you what this baby can do."

*   *   *   *

An hour later, Carrie braced herself as Nick put the car in gear, and they raced down the runway together. Heart pushing against her chest, the exhilaration almost too much., she gripped the seat, trying to control her delight in the speeding car and the love she felt for the man sitting beside her.

Nick grinned at her while they headed back toward the house. "So, what did you think?"

She placed her hand on his thigh and squeezed. "I loved it. Actually, I wouldn't mind doing it again sometime."

"It's a date. Just let me know when."

He pulled into the garage and cut the engine. They climbed out of the car, and Nick led her into the house and up the stairs.

He closed the bedroom door and turned the lock. "Now, what was that something else you had in mind earlier?"

"I think it's better if I show you."

She harbored no regrets over how their lives had played out because she knew they were meant to find each other. Life had been a series of highs and lows, threatening at times to tear them apart.

Only theirs was no ordinary love. It tested limits, crossed boundaries, and defined who they really were, but it always brought them back together again.

Carrie lifted her head and focused on his green eyes. Her arms settled around his neck. She kissed his lips, her body coming alive once again inside the arms of the man who had saved her.

EPILOGUE

BOBBY

MANY, MANY, YEARS LATER

They called her crazy, but Bobby knew better. The explanation was clear. She simply couldn't live without him any longer.

Bobby swiped at the lock of grey hair falling over his right eye while sitting at the long dining room table in South Dakota. He studied the faces seated around him, chairs now filled with a new generation.

Darcy sat to his left, the soft, loving, glow on her face apparent while she talked to Natalia seated across the table beside her husband, Jake. Next to the day she was born, walking her down the aisle had been one of the most emotional days of Bobby's life. A vision in a white lace wedding gown with a long train, the spitting image of her mother, he'd held back a fountain of tears.

She'd graduated from Harvard with a business degree where she met Jake, who recently set up his own law practice in Napa. They resided in the house willed to her by her mother and raised their two children, Steven and Elena, while Natalia continued to run the winery with great success. Carmela's love of riding had also left its mark on their daughter. The first time Bobby watched her ride, he couldn't help but recall the memory of riding with Carmela all those years ago, her arms gripping his waist, the wind sailing past as they galloped ahead.

Nicholas sat on Natalia's other side. The son he and Darcy had raised and named in honor of Nick made them proud when he enlisted in the Marines, climbing up the ranks over the years to First Lieutenant. He and his wife Deborah currently resided in Washington, D.C., with their daughter, Amy.

Michael emitted a deep chuckle, catching Bobby's attention and making him smile. Out of all of them, Michael had moved the farthest away. A marine biologist, he resided in Hawaii with his wife, Clare, and their two sons, Mark and Jason.

Veronica and Justin were also married with children of their own, making Joann and Dalton happy grandparents well into their old age.

His thoughts turned to those who were missing. Aunt May passed away years ago and Alex not too long after. The memories they left behind made him smile. He still missed discussing art with his grandfather.

Bobby's eyes drifted to Izzy, seated at the opposite end with her husband, Dylan. Her love of horses had led her to Veterinary School. While tending to several sick racehorses, she met Dylan, a trainer, and as she had told Bobby, 'fell madly in love.'

He smiled at the memory of Nick meeting Dylan for the first time. It was more of an interrogation than anything else, but Nick grew close to his son-in-law when he saw how much he adored Izzy. They had two boys of their own, Cameron and Brandon. Bobby was delighted when they bought Dalton's guest house, moved from Kentucky, with Dylan setting up a stable to train racehorses while Izzy set up her own practice here in South Dakota.

He recalled the day Izzy had asked him the question lingering inside her. The question he was certain he would have to answer one day. Was her father a hired killer, as Miguel Medina had told her?

Steeling himself, he had looked into her eyes, and with all the conviction he could muster, he simply said, 'No. Don't ever doubt your father was a good man who loved this family more than anything else in the world.'

Bobby rose from the table. He wandered to the tall windows in the great room, the valley below once again blanketed in snow. He'd long since retired from the art world and moving here with Darcy where there were so many fond memories made sense.

Bobby struggled at times when he thought about his mother and Nick. His mother was grateful Nick had gotten to walk his daughter down the aisle and meet his grandchildren, but later, his loss was too great, and she was never the same. But Bobby understood.

For a man who lived such a violent life, Nick had died a peaceful death. His mother found him in his favorite chair by the fire, head dipped to his chest, his eyes closed. Still, all those years later, he had never managed to forgive himself for Carmela witnessing Ricardo's death. It haunted him up until the end of his life.

After Nick died, the light in her violet-blue eyes dimmed, only shining for fleeting moments when she looked at her children and grandchildren. The fine lines pressed into her delicate skin did little to alter her beauty even as her raven hair quietly turned to silver.

Bobby had come for a visit alone on the day she disappeared. Waking from an afternoon nap, he searched the house for his mother in vain. Hanging onto the slim hope she had gone to Dalton's, he called them. Not finding her there, he ventured out into a winter storm to look for her, the blinding snow and wind signaling a warning of what he might find.

The next morning, he found her at the cemetery, lying across Nick's grave, the place she had insisted on visiting at least every other day since his death. Hypothermia had set in. His mother was gone. When the news broke, those familiar with her said she had lost her mind. But they could never understand what she and Nick felt for each other transcended everything. Like a thread, it wrapped around their core, binding them together. The type of love he'd been lucky enough to have found with Darcy. A safe and solid love, not one built on uncertainty, like his and Carmela's had been.

As for his part in killing Diego and then, years later Bianca, he never harbored any sleepless nights. He believed as his Uncle Dalton did. Evil people did not deserve a place in this world.

Standing by the window now, watching the snowfall, filled Bobby with an odd sense of comfort, knowing his mother and Nick were together again, their souls resting in each other's arms.

His body relaxed when Darcy came and stood next to him. He draped his arm around her shoulders while they focused on the white flakes cascading from the sky.

"Beautiful, isn't it," Darcy whispered.

Bobby bent and kissed her lips. "Like you.".

The snow grew heavier, cutting off the view to the valley. The wind roared across the eaves of the house, then formed a parting veil in the distance.

Bobby breathed deep. He pressed his face up against the glass, and, for a brief moment, he swore he caught sight of them walking hand in hand. His mother took one last glance back, a smile on her face, then she disappeared with Nick into the swirling snow.

After trying her hand at several different careers, Stephanie decided to pursue her dream of writing a novel. Growing up in the Brooklyn neighborhood of Gerritsen Beach, her love of writing began with Saturday trips with her mother to the small local library where children would gather to hear a story read by the local Librarian. After the story ended, Stephanie would pick out a book to take home and read. Throughout her teen and young adult years, Stephanie's desire to someday pen a novel of her own always simmered in the background. But it was not until years later after a career in Patient Accounting and a stint as a Licensed Realtor that her dreams of becoming a writer flourished with a move to the Pocono Mountains in Pennsylvania. It was there that the first novel, in her trilogy, *Redemption* was conceived followed by *Retribution* and *Reckoning*. Drawn to thriller and suspense novels, Stephanie is dedicated to giving her reader's fast-paced, high stakes, page-turning stories that keep you on the edge of your seat and are full of surprising twists. She resides at her lake home in Villa Rica, Georgia with her husband and two cats. When not found pounding her keyboard into all hours of the night, Stephanie enjoys swimming, travel, and games of Mexican Train with her besties in her community and fellowship with the Carrollton Writer's Guild of which she is a member. Stephanie is currently at work on a new novel which is slated for release in 2022. You can find her online at **www.stephaniebaldi2com.** Or follow her on Facebook and Twitter at **sbauthor7.**

The Sicario Files

Redemption

Retribution

Reckoning